ALTAF FATIMA was born ...
moved there around 1857 fro...
education in Lahore, after pa...
degrees from the Punjab University. She taught Urdu literature at
Islamia College for Women in Lahore for several years. She has now
moved to APWA Girls' College, also in Lahore, as a professor in the
Urdu department.

She has published three novels, *Nishaan-i-Mehfil, Dastak Naa Do (The
One Who Did Not Ask)* and *Chulta Musafir*, as well as three collections of
short stories, *Woh jisay chaha gaya, Jub diwaaren girya kurti hain*, and most
recently *Taar-i-unkaboot*, which was published in 1990. She has also
translated from English into Urdu, Harper Lee's novel *To Kill a Mocking
Bird*, and a collection of political essays by eminent personalities, *Barrey
aadmi, aur unke nazariyat*.

Out of all Fatima's work, *The One Who Did Not Ask* has enjoyed the
most sustained success in Pakistan. An adaptation was presented on
Pakistan television a few years ago and an abridged translation was
serialised by the prestigious Karachi monthly, *Herald*.

RUKHSANA AHMAD taught English Literature at the University of
Karachi before moving to Britain in 1973. She has freelanced as a writer,
journalist, translator and playwright since 1986.

Her last play *Song for a Sanctuary* toured London and the regions in
spring and autumn 1991 and was broadcast by BBC Radio 4 in
February 1993.

She has also compiled, edited and translated a collection of feminist
Urdu poetry from Pakistan entitled *We Sinful Women* (The Women's
Press, 1991).

ALTAF FATIMA

THE ONE WHO DID NOT ASK

(DASTAK NAA DO)

Translated from the Urdu by
Rukhsana Ahmad

HEINEMANN

Translator's acknowlegments

I am grateful to the author for giving us permission to translate this work, to all my colleagues, friends and my family who were supportive during the long and arduous labour involved in the process, to the Arts Council and Heinemann for making this project possible, to Ranjana Ash, Ronald Warwick and Lakshmi Holmström for their steadfast support, and more specially to Rashida Alvi and Begum Sabiha Hussain for guiding me throughout.

Heinemann Educational
A Division of Heinemann Publishers (Oxford) Ltd
Halley Court, Jordan Hill, Oxford OX2 8EJ

Heinemann: A Division of Reed Publishing (USA) Inc.
361 Hanover Street, Portsmouth, NH 03801–3912, USA

Heinemann Educational Books (Nigeria) Ltd
PMB 5205, Ibadan
Heinemann Educational Boleswa
PO Box 10103, Village Post Office, Gaborone, Botswana

FLORENCE   PRAGUE   PARIS   MADRID
ATHENS   MELBOURNE   JOHANNESBURG
AUCKLAND   SINGAPORE   TOKYO
CHICAGO   SAO PAULO

This translation © Rukhsana Ahmad 1993
First published by Heinemann Educational in 1993

Series Editor: Ranjana Sidhanta Ash

British Library Cataloguing in Publication Data
A catalogue record for this book is available from the British Library.

Cover design by Touchpaper
Cover illustration by Paul Jackman

ISBN 0435 95084 3

Phototypeset by Cambridge Composing (UK) Ltd, Cambridge
Printed and bound in Great Britain
by Cox & Wyman Ltd, Reading, Berkshire

93 94 10 9 8 7 6 5 4 3 2 1

To my mother,
who was the fountain-head of all my writings,
and all my passions

and still is

Introduction to the Asian Writers Series

Heinemann's new Asian Writers Series, aided by the Arts Council of Great Britain, intends to introduce English language readers to some of the interesting fiction written in languages that most will neither know nor study.

For too long popular acclaim for Asian writing in the West has been confined to the handful of authors who choose to write in English rather than in the language of their own cultures. Heinemann's entry into the field should dispel this narrow perspective and place modern Asian writing within the broad spectrum of contemporary world literature.

The first six works selected for the series are translations of novels from five languages: Bengali, Hindi, Malayalam, Tamil and Urdu. The six novels span seventy-five years of change in the subcontinent. *Quartet*, one of Rabindranath Tagore's most skilfully constructed and lively classics, was first published in 1916, whereas the most recent work chosen, *The Fire Sacrifice*, was written by the up-and-coming Hindi novelist Susham Bedi and first published in 1989.

These first six titles face the normal problems affecting literature in translation, not least the difficulty of establishing an exact parallel of the thought or verbal utterance of the original in the target language. When the source text is in a non-European language and embodies a culture and literary style quite alien to English language readers, the translator's task is made even more difficult.

Susan Bassnett in her invaluable work on translation studies describes the typical colonial attitude to the literature of the colonised as a 'master and servant' relationship, with the European translator attempting to 'improve' and 'civilise' the source text. At the other end of the scale she describes a kind of 'cannibalism' in which the translator almost 'devours' the text to disgorge a totally new product. Fortunately, the translators of this series fall into neither category but manage to retain a balanced view of their craft.

While it is very important to produce a translation that uses a style both readable and engaging to an English language readership, it must not obscure the particularities of literary devices, figures of speech, and aesthetic detail that the author uses to convey his or her sensibility, imagination and verbal artistry. Should such faithfulness to the original produce in the English version a greater degree of sentiment or charged imagery than the reader might expect, one hopes that he or she will be ready to accept the novelty of writing from an unfamiliar source.

In publishing the Asian Writers Series, Heinemann is taking a bold step into an area which has been neglected for too long. It is our hope that readers will respond with interest and enthusiasm as they discover the outstanding quality of these novels.

RANJANA SIDHANTA ASH, SERIES EDITOR, 1993

Introduction to *The One Who Did Not Ask*

Unlike some of Altaf Fatima's later short stories, which are infused with a conscious literary quality and are almost too elaborate in their construction, *The One Who Did Not Ask* appears to be an artless, almost ingenuous narrative, powered by the sheer energy of its story. In fact, this simplicity of style and technique conceals a sophisticated mastery of the medium.

Fatima's characterisation is painstaking and precise, and her structure manages to hold together a vast array of characters and several complex themes, sometimes even inherently anomalous and contradictory positions. The narrative moves forward with the surge of a river against the backdrop of two vast civilisations which inhabit either bank, doomed to separate existences simply because of the nature of things. Gaythi and Safdar Liu Chu live out the drama of this separation in a microcosm which replicates the reality of the Asian continent. The brutal, stony divide of the Himalayas which partitioned two ancient cultures as they developed along parallel lines, remains insurmountable for people in that world.

The novel proposes that there is something germane to these cultures which militates against confluence, insists upon the 'otherness' of foreigners and refuses to acknowledge that what they have in common, the human dimension, could have brought them closer. That 'something' is an imperative linked to class and privilege as much as it is an aspect of language, religion or manners; and it is inextricably bound to gender. It forces people, especially women, to conform. When challenged it springs back and reasserts itself with unashamed violence and redoubled force – as in the scene where the otherwise graceful and dignified Ammah Begum attacks Gaythi with her slipper in a public area of the house and has to be literally pulled away by Arjumand.

Even Safdar respects the sexist norms common to both cultures and guides Gaythi towards 'ideal behaviour'. The fact that he is a Muslim helps to underline her mother's obsessive class prejudice. In spite of their common religion, the Indian characters around him cannot view him except as an alien and their reluctance to interact with him at any other level but as an embodiment of the racial 'other' raises the novel from the stature of an ordinary love story to a serious and challenging examination of the nature of prejudice. It is this intuitive perception at the heart of the novel which attracted me to it and made the labour of translation worthwhile.

The other Partition, that which divided the Indian sub-continent itself, is a further strand which criss-crosses the first and forms a bulkhead dividing the story. Like other momentous events and traumas of history, the Partition has generated a tremendous outpouring of literature, much of it mourning the pain of separation, or the horrors of the blood-letting which accompanied it. Unlike Manto's short stories, '*Thanda gosht*', '*Khol do*', or the profoundly surreal, '*Toba Tek Singh*', which portray the violence of the predominantly male outside world with a disturbingly graphic conciseness, this novel distances us from it. The fear and danger are captured accurately enough even if the horrors are counter-balanced by acts of real human kindness, like Mali's touching loyalty. Fatima's strategy is one adopted by other eminent women writers in the sub-continent. In Khadija Mastoor's *Aangan*, (literally, *The Inner Courtyard*) for example, the focus remains primarily on the interior world of women, as it does here, indirectly but realistically reflecting their distance from the political process. In both novels as the story progresses the action expands to include women soaking up their resourcefulness and transforming their lives.

The One Who Did Not Ask commands a favourable position in the impressive body of Urdu fiction by women, echoing contemporary themes, style and strategies, but Fatima has some unique strengths as a writer. Foremost amongst these is her skill as a narrator. If E. M. Forster's claim that 'the story is a lifeline which the novelist throws to the reader', is valid then her readers can safely bank on survival. The story moves pacily, with an almost impatient energy, punctuated by, 'Then', and 'then' and 'And then', in the manner of the oral tradition of story-telling.

Her other great accomplishment is her ability to empathise equally with a wide range of characters, notwithstanding their heroism, or their failures. The plot of the novel is constructed almost entirely from a collage of points of view. Each section of the story establishes a particular perspective, and even minor characters like Margaret, Mali or Bakhtiar add to the depth by supplying 'real' insights and comments which buttress or bridge it quite seamlessly. Saulat's transformation from a vulnerable figure of pathos to a bitter and tyrannical antagonist is as convincingly realised and portrayed as Gaythi's, accurately highlighting the power which marriage bestows on women in that world where to be single is to be deeply vulnerable. Safdar's lonely and alienated existence symbolises the central theme of alienation. He finds in Gaythi a kindred spirit, equally out of harmony with her surroundings. Both fight back in their own characteristic ways, Gaythi with vociferous aggression, and Safdar with a quiet, seemingly passive diligence, each aware of the other's pain but unable to help, except in a fitful and fractured manner, doomed to failure within the system.

In this battle of the individual versus society the central contradiction is inherent at the heart of the thesis. Whilst Fatima plumbs the depths of the individual's frustration and pain in a world where tradition, family and faith reign supreme, and identifies and exposes the mechanics of each tyranny, the ideal she flags is a glorious past. Here, somehow – incredibly – collectivism, in the sense of community, overcomes the pain. Gaythi's lengthy stay at her grandmother's house spawns thoughts to that effect:

> 'There was a sense of a collective in the lifestyle of this home. The selfish god of individualism had not yet crossed its threshold . . . Maybe it was the informality and egalitarianism of this household which had endeared it to her so much.'

Elsewhere, Safdar regards the cruelty meted out to him quite matter-of-factly as an adjunct of urbanisation and materialism. Wealth is associated with evil, and traditional values – even the worst of the feudal kind – assume elegance and graciousness, softened by a rosy glow, as, for instance, embodied in Gaythi's father. This is not hard-headed political analysis but a romantic idealisation of the past.

Nostalgia is a mood favoured by Urdu writers. It is integral to the Muslim consciousness. Writers have often delved into the past and bemoaned the loss of an ideal age, free of the vicious evils of the present. This is accompanied by a deep instinctive desire for change, but within the old framework of references. It is illustrative perhaps of the phenomenon identified so accurately by Graham Swift's history teacher, Tom Crick, in *Waterland*:

> '. . . though the popular notion of revolution is that of categorical change, transformation – a progressive leap into the future – yet almost every revolution contains within it an opposite if less obvious tendency: the idea of a return.'

Gaythi herself shows awareness of the revisionist elements in the revolution which uproots them. Her dislike of Chacha ji's son, Noor-ul-Huda, exemplifies this. He is presented as someone almost fanatical and rigid in contrast with his own tolerant father, who respects other people's space and, sadly, dies defending a Hindu friend. Huda represents an aspect of the Muslim League which irritates Gaythi. There is also a pained awareness of the increasing monoculturalism of the new country, as Lahore is denuded of its Hindu and Sikh residents after the Partition.

It is significant that Gaythi's struggle for emancipation is lost even as the larger political struggle is successful and gives way to a new world. This disarming of a powerful rebel is accompanied by a loss of energy and pace in the narrative, of the kind you might envisage in a river approaching the sea. There is a sense of surrender, resignation, and loss, but also of gain.

Gaythi herself, transformed from a daughter into a mother, behaves curiously. As her own power in relation to her mother increases, her desire to rebel declines proportionately, supplanted instead by a wish to cherish and protect her ageing parent. This stranglehold of love which families exercise, weakens the clarity of her own perception of injustice and chokes off the larger, instinctive humanist aspirations of her youth. She succumbs to the meaner gratifications of personal relationships in a world which offers her security and protection, where maturity means a willingness to compromise.

RUKHSANA AHMAD, 1993

Translator's note

Families are of central importance in the majority of South Asian cultures and kinship titles are, therefore, very precise in detail. Since narrative points of view are so focal to the structure of this novel some characters are conceived and presented only in terms of their relationship with the heroine, Gaythi. Her mother, for example, remains virtually nameless throughout, and is referred to instead as Ammah Begum. That title is substituted by a third person pronoun in Urdu *woh* (unmarked for gender) when we enter her thoughts or the story is being told from her point of view. Occasionally, to make this easier for the reader, we have used 'Gaythi's mother' or 'her mother', instead of 'she'. Likewise, Chachi jaan is not a name but a relationship term.

I felt it might enhance understanding of some of the underlying tensions in the extended family if the reader understands the relationships as exactly as they are described by their titles in Urdu, which is why I have retained them in the translation. For instance, mothers are frequently closer to their own blood relations than they are to the in-laws (paternal aunts and uncles to their children).

Though it is not absolutely essential for the reader to understand them precisely, a list of these titles is supplied below to help achieve this. In addition, Urdu words italicised in the text can be found in the Glossary on p. 334.

Kinship titles

Abba father

Ammah mother

Baji older sister

Barrey Bhaiyya older brother: i.e. Sheharyaar

Begum literally lady; makes the address more formal and appended to mother
  only in quite posh and self-regarding families; more usual to add *jaan* or *ji*

Bhaiyya brother (affectionate)

Chachi jaan aunt: father's younger brother's wife. Her late husband would have
  been Gaythi's *Chacha jaan*; also used to denote intimate non-family relationship

Chote Bhaiyya younger brother: i.e. Bakhtiar

Dadi Ammah grandmother: father's mother

jaan literally life; meaning darling

Mamoon jaan uncle: mother's brother

Mian literally gentleman/sir; formal and pompous as *Begum* above

Mumani jaan aunt: mother's brother's wife

naani maternal grandmother

Phupho aunt: father's sister (could be real or a cousin, like Hashmi Begum)

Tai jaan aunt: his wife

Taya jaan uncle: father's older brother; in some families also referred to
  affectionately as *Barrey Abba* – older dad

'The dervish lives in this world in peace and tranquillity
For him, all the people on this earth belong to one nation
That is, they all belong to the territory of the heart
And for him, they are all his own children.'

LAO TZU

1

That afternoon, the foggiest that January, felt more like an evening. Earlier Mali had hoed the flower-beds, expecting a shower. Pink, yellow, white and azure sweetpeas, in their prime, leaned against the golden bamboo sticks. A gentle fragrance hung in the cold mist. Orange and blue flowers brooded glumly in their heart-shaped beds as smoke curled out of the chimneys against a deep, penetrating silence.

A bicycle flashed by the gate, someone jumped off and entered the compound, dragging it along on the red gravel, looking round as he traversed a few yards.

'Crunch, crunch,' said the gravel and he called out, 'China Man, China Man.'

A thin voice chanted behind him, 'Chin, chin, China Man.'

He swung round to see another bicycle behind him. A uniformed bearer pedalled home two little girls, dressed in blue tunics and white bloomers, one sat in front of him and the other at the back. One of them had large, wide open eyes, a delicate nose and two thick, golden plaits. The other girl's eyes were small and triangular, her nose was flat and her hair was trimmed very short as well.

The girl with the small eyes and flat nose jumped off the moving bicycle, tossed her heavy bag across one shoulder, slung her coat over it and said again, 'Chin, chin, China man.'

'O, Baby, wear your coat!' he rejoined. 'The cold's too much. You'll be dead.'

'Baby' stuck her tongue out in reply and China Man waved a fist at her.

As the servant came to a stop the girl with the large eyes and thick plaits slid off the bicycle, gently lifted her satchel to her shoulder and walked sweetly towards the porch.

'Hey, you, Cheena! Is that you again? The Begums are resting. What are you doing here at this time?' The bearer waved China Man out as he herded the flat-nosed girl into the house preventing her from heading off in some other direction.

China Man secured his heavy bundle to the carrier, clipped his trouser legs carefully and whistled as he swished away on his bicycle. But soon his happy melody dissolved into sad notes. He heaved a sigh and became silent, leaving the unfinished tune to drift in the air.

As he rode away, for some unknown reason, he remembered his home. 'Who knows, Peking may be as miserably cold as this too!' he thought, staring into the distant fog-smudged horizon. 'I wonder what my mother is doing right now. Mother, with her wide beautiful mouth, her thin body and lotus hands which have fought with hard work to stay soft, and my two sisters. I wonder if they go to school or not.'

Thoughts run along interminable lines. Memories of his family gave way to memories of prawn soup, green chillies and vinegar relish and fish cooked with skeins of grated carrots. If all those things had remained affordable he might not have had to leave school so early to wander the streets, feeling homeless, in a foreign land.

He was still very young, just turned seventeen last December, and that very day he had received a letter from his mother. He had kept it since, in the pocket close to his heart. Usually only men use a brush so skilfully. When his mother was a girl it was still rare for women to be educated but she was the daughter of an instructor from a religious school who was famous for his brush strokes.

Every now and then, he would take out the letter very affectionately, look at the words written in vertical lines, kiss them, then fold it and replace it carefully. It was unusual in China for a boy's mother to produce such faultless characters. His eyes felt moist, his neck stiffened with pride. He jerked his head. His straight, black hair slipped down his forehead and he pushed it back with a second jerk. A girl on a bicycle, dressed in a red coat, overtook him. He scrutinised her dark skin, arched eyebrows, almond eyes, shapely nose and sighed again.

'Ugh, I am sick of these fine noses and sharp features; utterly fed up.' A shiver of hatred seized him briefly, and then he remembered again, 'That was an interesting house I stumbled into today, very like a rest house, set in the wilds, far away from towns and settlements, or, like a rest house on a hill station. And those two little girls returning from school!'

The thought of the smaller, slender girl sent another shiver of distaste through him. That fine nose, those wide-open innocent eyes. And, how rude that other fatso was! Elephant. Ha, ha! He laughed aloud. His receding childhood returned sometimes.

2

2

She chanted from her perch:

> 'Berries to eat, ripe and raw
> I ate a peacock friend of mine
> It's *you* my belly's screaming for,
> Only you can fill this belly of mine.
> Hee, hee, haw, haw.'

All the children below burst out laughing. She jumped off with a thud, pockets bulging with half-ripe berries, red and yellow, sweet and sour. They sprawled like a carpet below the tree. Bundoo, Shabrati, Madhoo and the sweeper's boy, Chunna, were busy picking them, eating and filling their pockets simultaneously.

Arjumand sat on the stump of a peepal tree a short distance away. Her thick golden plaits hung in front of her shoulders, broad red ribbons shone through them. Her red polka-dotted dress was fastidiously clean and becoming. Her eyes as wide open as saucers, she watched Gaythi very sadly picking and munching berries with that horde of professional disciples.

'What a scruffy creature she is,' she thought, noticing the stains that spattered her creased green frock.

Gaythi's short hair was tousled, her crushed green ribbon had lost its bow and hung below her ears. Her shoes lay far away on the lawn.

'What if Ammah Begum sees her in this state.' The thought grieved Arjumand even more.

'*Bibi*, this is really dishonest. You can't eat our share of the berries any more!' Chunna raised a voice of protest.

'Why? Why ever not? I *will* eat them. I'm the one who's shaken all of them off the tree.' Her triangular eyes danced with mischief.

'*Waah*! These berries are our share. We'll take them, they're ours.' Shabrati tugged hard at the hem of her dress.

Arjumand's heart missed a beat, she shivered and closed her eyes. But Gaythi, plump and podgy, hit out at Chunna and Shabrati as she tucked into the berries again with relish.

At that very instant Ammah Begum peeked through her window and called out , 'Arjumand, Gaythi!'

Panic-stricken, Arjumand opened her eyes and saw Ammah Begum's beautiful, angry eyes staring at them through the window.

3

Arjumand rose, lifting her dress delicately in answer to that first call. Walking fast, but with measured strides, towards the house, she called out to Gaythi, 'Come on, Gaythi, Ammah Begum is calling us.'

'Hum. Go on, I'm coming,' she smacked her lips on the sweet and sour berries dipped in salt and chillies.

'Well? Where is she now?' Ammah Begum stared at Arjumand again.

She was forced to answer, 'She . . . she's there.'

'Where is she? Can't you say it?'

'She . . . she's picking the berries.'

'Is she picking them, or stuffing her face?' Ammah Begum gritted her teeth.

'*Jee*, Ammah Begum, she isn't stuffing her face, she's eating them!' A scream escaped Arjumand's lips as she tried to suppress her sobs.

'Not stuffing her face, but eating them!' Ammah Begum repeated, a smile softening her voice which was still angry. 'Sharif, Sharif,' she called, looking towards the door, 'just call that witch here.'

The witch pouted as she looked down at the hem of her skirt, ripped by Shabrati's tug. Quietly, she entered the bathroom through the back door, changed her dress at top speed and went into the dressing room, feeling mildly repentant at the state of her hair and the crushed ribbon as she glanced in the mirror. She pulled the ribbon out with great difficulty, drew a jagged middle-parting, looked at her flat Mongolian features from every angle and came out completely satisfied that she was fit to be presented to Ammah Begum.

On the verandah Sharif grabbed her arm, 'Come on, Begum Sahib wants you.'

'Begum Sahib wants you,' she mimicked, pulling a face, 'you think you've brought me in, don't you? Well, you haven't. I've come by myself.'

Unabashed, she went and stood before Ammah Begum, who was busy tweaking Shabrati's ear.

'Well? Will you make a fool of Bibi again?'

'Let go of his ear, Ammah. He didn't make a fool of me!'

She turned on her. 'So you're here, your highness! Now get lost, you! Don't you dare fool around with the girls ever again.'

Gaythi looked at Shabrati's tears with remorse and said, in an offended tone, 'Don't shout at him. I asked for it myself.'

'Be quiet. You interfere in everything.'

'But you're beating the poor fellow for no reason at all,' she muttered almost to herself.

'You're muttering like a servant, again.' A resounding slap caught her cheek, but instead of turning red, her face turned white as paper. She licked her parched lips but stood dry-eyed.

Then suddenly she spoke, 'Yes, I'll keep on muttering like this.'

'Just try it. I'll smash your face in.' Another two slaps landed on her face. Arjumand ran between the two of them crying.

'Someone is here to see you, Begum Sahib,' Sharif announced and Ammah Begum went to the dressing room to tidy her hair.

'Arjumand, why did you have to jump in? I wanted to defy her. Just to see how badly she would beat me,' she said contemptuously as she left the room without shedding a single tear.

Shabrati, who had gone out earlier, peeked round the door and Arjumand died of shame. To think that Shabrati, the cook's son, should have seen Gaythi, her own sister, being smacked.

As she gazed calmly out of the window of her own room, Gaythi noticed China Man standing by the gate and stuck her tongue out at him. He laughed to himself, 'She's strange, this fat girl!'

3

'What is the name of this town, and its significance?' he wondered as he roamed some of its wider streets. He had little to do with the town itself. Its name did not really matter to him. Neither that town nor any other like it could be his. Everything about it was unfamiliar and strange. He was surrounded by so many unfamiliar things that he could not even count them.

However he knew well that on God's vast earth there were huge cities. Cities like Calcutta, Bombay and Madras, and even Karachi, where he had first landed. He had felt calmer when he found his Chinese compatriots with their broad faces, triangular eyes, flattish noses. Short, stocky women, dressed in traditional clothes, clip-clopping with a firm, quiet dignity, and those wonderful cooking smells which rose from their congested kitchens in the flats – fish, prawns and garlic bread. You could get everything there. There was even a huge Chinese restaurant with a menu listing many more dishes than he had heard of even in China.

'Anyway, ordinary people could never afford to eat that well in China.' He tried to be content. 'It's only in this vast country people can. But despite that, most of them look half dead.' Jealously contemptuous, he would grimace.

5

Nevertheless, Karachi was quite a nice town. But that wretched Sang did not let him stay on. Within six months he had snatched him away. True, he had given him employment, but why could he not have chosen a larger city? A big city, like Karachi, where there was a Chinese community, so it didn't feel that alien. But, somehow, Sang had liked this small town, where there was not a single Chinese resident other than themselves.

At night-time he worked on Sang's machine for making shoes. Four days a week he worked as a salesman in his shoe store and two days a week he pedalled his bicycle selling the finest examples of Chinese handicrafts round Civil Lines and the houses of the more affluent locals.

'China Man, China Man.' He would enter the compounds of the bungalows and the villas, intoning in a comical voice, pitching it high and low. For hours he would stand leaning against their porches, or the steps to verandahs, adjusting the white celluloid clips which held his trouser legs, and if he saw a Begum Sahib peeking he would become alert and repeat respectfully, 'China Man, China Man.'

At the slightest hint he would slam down his heavy bundle on the shining verandah floor and sit himself down, leaning against his wares. When the Begums came, delicately turning up their noses, and sat on the cane stools laid out on the verandah, he would open his bundle and scatter his invaluable samples of Chinese handicrafts at their feet . . . bedcovers, silk night-suits and dressing gowns, table-cloths, tea-cosies . . . a veritable exhibition of fine arts. Though inwardly impressed by this display of industry and craft, they would say, 'Ugh, take that bedcover away, it's useless. Huh, this set isn't that nice. How come you want ten rupees for that?'

They would ask him to drop his price and he would keep blinking his tiny slanting eyes as he fought for each paisa. He fought but his eyes and lips would keep smiling, as he dealt pleasantly with each criticism.

'Come on. Three rupees for this tea-cosy! Never! I am not going to pay that much. What's so special about it?'

'Don't, then. Don't pay even one rupee.' He would narrow his eyes. 'But this takes long, long time. Our women have to . . . er, er, . . . to make it,' he would forget the Urdu word for 'hard work' and wave his hands like a comic.

'What hard work does this take? Nothing. It's a two-minute job.'

'Yes, Begum Sahib, this work looks like a two-minute job to you?' He would start wrapping and folding things to threaten them. But if he still did not find them interested, he would ask, 'Will you have it for so much?'

6

quickly reducing the price by one or half a rupee. It was a headache but he always sold to the bungalows.

When he loaded his bundle on his bicycle again he would chafe inwardly at the thought that those Begum Sahibs always condemned his wares. They could not have guessed how precious and dear these things were to him. They were the handiwork of the most deprived women of his country who did not earn enough to eat in spite of the extreme hard work and eye strain. They could not have known how much he loved those blossoms in silk thread, the bridges, the rivers, boats and temples. When he sat with all his goods scattered round him he felt as if he were surrounded by the environs, history and culture of the ancient civilisation of China, and within it, he saw himself representing the sanctity of a Buddha.

This happened one very cold day too. Sang had been irritable with him since early that morning. But he sat quietly at the back of the shop, working on the machine for cutting leather, listening to his ignominious comments. Sang's anger was understandable. In the past two weeks he, commonly known as Safdar Yaaseen, had not earned him a single paisa from his vending.

'What's the meaning of this idleness?' Sang asked him, sitting cross-legged on a low stool in the manner of Gautam Buddha. A black robe concealed his short, stout frame. The embroidery on the right panel of his robe depicted the ancient love story of Ng Tai bidding farewell to her school fellow Shan Po, under a weeping willow. Sang's fat and reddish rolls of flesh shook. His stomach jutted forth, like a prominent crag, from the centre of the flab dangling from his chest. His straight black moustache dipped helplessly on both sides of his chin like the whiskers of a crab.

The essence of Sang's diatribe was that he was idle and good for nothing. That he must be afraid of visiting the bungalows, or else why should he fail to sell his goods? That he was always too busy wasting his time.

The real reason behind Sang's grousing was that Safdar would take up his paint brush at the first opportunity. He would use pieces of silk or bamboo screens, and if he found nothing else, he would knead coloured rice flour to make and unmake pictures, 'wasting his time' – even though these activities never began until late at night.

'After this month, I'll settle your account and then you can do what you please.' He threatened him like this towards the middle of almost every month although it would be furthest from his intentions to do so. Safdar was a hard-working fatherless boy who kept his own counsel and was without subterfuge. You could say anything to him and he would not answer back. His greatest quality was that he would sort out Sang's accounts in no time at all, a skill which Sang did not have; and, he would do all these jobs so happily for such a small wage that Sang had taken on the responsibility for his meals.

Every afternoon Sang's quiet, childless wife served Safdar a bowl of rice with prawn sauce, or fish and bamboo shoots, which she placed before him on a low table. She watched him attentively, as he ate his rice with the glossy white chopsticks, and refilled his bowl even before it was empty, avoiding Sang's attention.

He felt as if she were his own mother watching him eat. That was the only thing which helped him ignore Sang's grumbling. He would sit like a child enjoying his meal.

Sang's wife was taller than most Chinese women, and plump. Darker patches peeked through the pallor of her skin. Dark smoky circles surrounded her almond-shaped eyes. Just below the bone of her right jaw hung two hairs. Her hair was streaked with lightning shots of grey. Her face was sad and silent but her gait was wonderful, as if she were afloat on water, as if each step played dance music, like the tinkle of ankle bells.

'She isn't Sang's wife, really, she is his mistress,' Li Yang, a distant nephew of Sang's, whispered to Safdar. 'She was a famous dancer in her time. Moved like lightning, she did. Sang has left behind his wife and numerous mistresses in a huge mansion with four courtyards. Its back garden is full of lion-headed fountains and elegant pillars delicately carved with flaming dragons. Those mistresses and his extremely fat wife keep themselves busy with pointless distractions.'

For Li Yang this was the most important piece of news and for Safdar this information was highly irrelevant.

Today, while Sang grumbled at Safdar, Li Yang, who appeared to be busy on the machine for stitching shoes, was actually waiting for the latter to retire to his flat at the rear so he could gossip about his mistresses again. But Safdar did not give him the chance. He left the machine and rose, picked up his bundle from the store and tied it to his bicycle. He wrapped his woollen chocolate brown trousers round his legs, clipped them and pushed his bicycle hard, speeding along the relatively quiet tarred road. Quiet, because it was a Sunday, and it was very cold. Safdar's eyes were moist with tears. He felt discontented and melancholy.

4

Sad and lonely, he nearly passed by the gate of the house which looked like a rest house on a hill station, without even glancing at it, when he heard Mali calling him, craning over the low garden wall. 'O, Cheena, will you come here?'

Cheena stopped, came near the wall and spoke without dismounting, 'What for? I've been so many times. That damn fool bearer always says, "Cheena, don't make a racket, the Begums are sleeping." I ask him, "Do your Begums sleep all the time?"'

Mali laughed. The plait knotted on top of his head laughed too.

'Not this time, Cheena. Go in. She told me to look out for you.' Then he stuck his neck forward confidentially, '*Bibi* is getting married, you see, so they've been waiting for you.'

'Why should they wait for me if she's getting married? I am not a bridegroom,' Safdar blinked his eyes innocently.

'Get away, you clown. Go and sell your stuff. Bibi's going to a posh home and she'll take a huge dowry.'

He jumped off the heavy bicycle, dragged it along and shouted loudly, near the bathroom window, 'China Man, China Man.'

Everywhere was still as usual. Disappointed, he turned round after the third call. But a mature, dignified, queenly face appeared at the window and addressed him in an extremely gentle but authoritative voice, 'A-ay, go and wait on the verandah. We're just coming.'

Having got permission, he headed quickly towards the verandah, hurled his bundle on the floor and sat down. Maalan walked past him wearing a long red and black skirt, a short tight-sleeved blouse and a blue scarf. Safdar longed for a fine white bamboo screen and a brush so he could steal all the suffering and music of this hard-working middle-aged woman's person and capture it in bamboo sticks. But unfortunately his lot was to deal with those arrogant and bad-tempered women.

The door to the passage opened. A broad, flushed face peeped out, almond-shaped slanting eyes, aglow with fever, flashed to the sound of, 'Chin, chin, China Man!'

'Come here, little one.'

The flat-faced but attractive girl hid behind the door. He ignored her until she crept out softly, then he shouted, 'Haa-ooo!' close to her face.

'Ruffian!' she said at once, with dignity, 'let me see your things.'

'Run along, fatso! Elephant! What's your name?'

She sat down on the coir stool, offended. He was interested in her, as if she were family. 'Tell me your name?' he asked.

Gaythi turned her face away.

'Annoyed? OK, I'm sorry. Tell me what you want?'

An inadvertent smile trembled round her lips and eyes but she struggled very seriously to restrain herself.

'Aren't you our little one then? Tell us your name, and I'll give you some chocolate.'

'I've already got some chocolate,' she bragged.

'Then say your name.'

'My name is Gaythi Ara Begum.'

The young foreigner burst into a loud laugh without meaning to.

'Ruffian. You, cheat, you . . . donkey, you!'

Once again there was a rustle in the passage. The Begum with the beautiful, angry eyes emerged, wearing a white broderie anglaise sari and a voile blouse. She addressed Gaythi, looking deeply displeased, 'Once again you're out here. Go and lie down.'

Unaccountably, China Man cowered too. 'Salaam Begum Sahib!' he said, in a muted tone, as he opened his bundle.

She turned towards the girl again, 'Didn't you hear me? Go in. Tell Chachi jaan to come and see the stuff.'

'I'll see it too,' she said in a deep rebellious tone.

'Certainly not. You won't stay for another minute. Do you want a spanking while you've got this fever? I've said it now. Go inside.'

'Go inside!' the plump, insolent girl repeated her mother's words with defiant hatred as she went in, her head bowed. She looked even more Chinese in her blue checked silk pyjamas. Inexplicably, Safdar felt nostalgic and heavy-hearted again.

Begum sat on a stool rummaging through the things without any expression of appreciation. If there had been a pile of vegetables or grain before her she would have treated it likewise, her eyebrows arched, unyielding.

'With an appreciative eye you can revel even in the beauty of vegetables,' Safdar thought to himself in his purest Chinese.

A grating sound drew his attention to the door again. It was Chachi jaan, slim, fine-featured and morose. Dark and silent eyed, she came and sat a little behind her sister-in-law, a terribly oppressive helplessness coloured the whiteness of her clothes. Begum kept seeking her opinion about everything, but she had no personal opinions. Safdar's quick mind grasped the situation in moments.

A civilised, muted horn sounded in the porch, a car door opened and was shut very carefully. A girl dressed in a white sari with a red border and a soft cotton blouse, notebooks and inks in her hands, descended and turned towards the verandah. Her face was as calm and luminous as the full moon. Her crisp golden hair hung in a thick plait which dangled just above her waist.

'There's Saulat herself. We were just waiting for you,' the sad widowed aunt smiled brightly.

Saulat looked even more interesting as her long black lashes dropped.

'Ah, so it's this *Bibi* whose marriage Begum Sahib wants to make?'

'Allah! So this wretch knows it already.' Chachi looked with interest at the intelligent boy who seemed quite different from ordinary Chinese people. His colouring did not remind her of the yellow belly of a toad. The bridge of his nose also seemed quite prominent and his hair had the slightest hint of a wave.

Begum addressed the girl, ignoring his comment. 'You're very late today?'

'*Jee*, I just went to drop someone.'

'Who?' eyes blazing.

'Surraiyya.'

'Why? Since when has Surraiyya been that used to cars. Where was her bike? I don't like this. It doesn't make sense that you should keep the car for hours on end. Here, try this night-suit on.'

The girl looked at her mother with surprise and distaste.

'What's happened to your brain? Why are you staring at my face? Go and put it on in the dressing room.'

She came out after almost twenty minutes wearing baggy pyjamas in white cotton, a broderie anglaise shirt and a pleated pink scarf. She came and stood by her aunt, shy and annoyed, holding the night-suit.

'It's fine,' and she dropped the night-suit on the heap of clothes.

'Can't be! You don't know anything. You should have let me see it!'

'Ammah, it's all right. I couldn't have come out here in it.'

Begum picked up the almond silk night-suit extremely angrily and said, 'Come and try it on for me.'

As they entered the passage she nagged, 'You look fed up with everything. Nothing seems good enough.'

Safdar had sharp ears and he was very clever. He spoke confidentially to Chachi, 'Who is your girl marrying?'

'An important officer, in the army. A very big man.'

'Huh! How big? Big as an elephant? If he's an officer, tell me his rank?'

'What's the point. You're only a peasant.'

11

'I haven't dropped from the skies. I know everything.' He realised that this Begum did not merit deference.

'He's a lieutenant colonel, and a landowner.'

'Oh! An old man then?'

'Why old? How much is this bed-cover?' She tried to change the subject.

'Well, a kid wouldn't become a lieutenant!'

'Well, isn't that clever! You can't be selling much. I'm asking you the price of the bedcover and you're talking nonsense.'

'Together the bedcover and pillowcase are twenty foal lupees. Want them?' He tossed them rudely at her just as the big Begum returned with the same night-suit.

'We don't really like the fit. Can't you give us one of this size?' She perched on the stool as she handed him a piece of paper.

Saulat stepped on to the verandah quietly. Her eyes were red and moist, wispy hair scattered untidily on her brilliant forehead. She came and sat down on a stool. Her mother glared a warning at her bored and indifferent face and she steadied herself.

That day Safdar Yaaseen sold a lot of things and got orders for several more, tied his bundle, loaded his bicycle and left, whistling. The girl with the large innocent eyes and thick brown plaits stood near the gate sneakily eating sour tangerines. At the sight of him she hid them and looked up at him innocently but he did not notice her as he passed, his eyes were on the sky above.

5

The garden was utterly still. Mali had gone to his hovel. Gaythi looked around, jumped on to the wall and sat astride it. She was sucking a long bar of chocolate with relish, her plump legs swung on either side of the wall. Her black almond-shaped eyes seemed estranged from her surroundings but her face seemed content.

She spotted China Man from a distance and mimicked, 'China Man, China Man.'

He came near her.

'What are you up to, Baby?'

'Nothing to do with you.'

'You are vely nawty.'

'China Man, why do you lisp?'

'What's a lisp?'

She laughed aloud and said in English, 'You can't say words! Say: "very naughty".'

But he laughed.

'Won't you go in?'

'Why not. I've a beautiful kimono for your sister today.'

'Go on, then.'

'Maybe your Mummy's asleep? She might spank me.'

'Are you afraid of Mummy too?' She was talking in English now.

'Yes, very,' he replied.

'Does your Mummy beat you as well?'

'Oh no! Cuckoo. My Mum is lovely, she adores me.'

'Really? Where is your Mummy? Bring her over.'

'She lives very far away, in China. I'll let you meet her if you come with me.'

'That far? Never! Does she really live that far, she must be strange,' she looked at him enviously. How lucky! His mother is too far away to tell him off all the time, she thought.

'That means you can eat lots of sour things, and you don't have to sleep in the afternoons. Do you miss her?'

'Terribly. I haven't seen her for two years. You're lucky to stay with your mother.'

'Really,' she dismissed that carelessly. 'Want some peanuts?'

'Give them here, Cuckoo.'

'Why do you call me Cuckoo. My name's Gaythi.'

'Your name's Cuckoo.' He brought his face close to hers.

As she pulled out the peanuts from her pockets, he asked her, 'When is your sister getting married?'

'Don't know. Sometime. Quite soon.'

'Will you miss your sister, Cuckoo?'

'Not at all. She shouts at me a lot. She's always telling me what to do and what not to do. She is a real *Lord Sahib*. I pray that she should go.'

He laughed aloud, 'You know I've seen your brother-in-law. Why don't *you* get married to him?'

'Get lost, nut-case,' she protested in Urdu.

'He looks just like you really, and he's plump.'

'He looks like you. In fact, he looks worse than you. Chachi jaan said to me he looks Chinese.'

'You do too.'

'So when did you see him?'

13

'I got a kimono for your sister and he came when she was trying it on. He looked just like Chiang Kai Shek in his uniform. He got up and tried to assist her. I don't think your sister likes him, Cuckoo.'

'How do you know?'

'When he was tying the sash for her she just stood there frowning, displeased. Even when he went in she stood with her back towards him. When I looked at her face there were tears in her eyes. I went closer and asked her, "Is the kimono all right, Miss?" and she said, "No," softly. Then I asked, "Is this your fiancé?" but she said nothing. She just stood there, turning the ring on her finger. You know what I said to her?'

'What?' Gaythi asked him eagerly.

'I said to her, "Why are you marrying this Chiang Kai Shek? Take my advice and let your sister with the Chinese face marry him".'

'Ruffian!' Gaythi waved a fist at him. 'Don't come round here.'

'OK,' He pushed the pedals.

'Listen, wait.'

'What is it?' He turned.

'What did Saulat Apa say to that?'

'What could she say? She dropped the kimono on the chair and said, as she was leaving, that it was too big, she needed a smaller one and she would write the size down for me. When she returned her eyes were red, she was biting her lip. Cuckoo, your sister is very beautiful and very arrogant. But I have to say, those kind of faces don't please me.'

'Who's asked you to be pleased?' She felt irritated. 'Miserable wretch, sticks his nose everywhere,' she muttered in Urdu.

'All right, Cuckoo. You are probably cursing me now. I am going then, to give your sister her kimono.'

'My name's not Cuckoo. Call me Gaythi.'

'Can't say that.'

When he returned, after delivering the kimono, that plump and interesting girl whose conversation he enjoyed, was gone. She had jumped off the wall and dashed off somewhere.

6

'Whatever is ordained for me.
I must endure, anyhow.
Even the heart broken by malice and enmity

> finds respite from all its griefs, eventually.
> Death, difficulties and their solution,
> all come in their own time.'

Lovely and refined, Saulat Jehangir picked up the piece of ordinary white paper and looked at it carefully, once again. The poem had been inscribed on it in beautiful Chinese letters with a red pencil. In the middle, set slightly apart from it, was an English translation of the poem in an unformed handwriting. This was the last stanza of the poem. She threw the paper on the table, then picked it up again, and started reading it once more.

> 'How shall I teach the children of emperors
> the principles of Li (of virtuous and upright conduct)
> And how can I make them learn the qualities of Cin Zi (decency)
> It is only the power of Qing (respecting the feelings of others)
> that makes me hold my tongue.'

'Yes, it is only the power of Qing that makes me hold my tongue.' Saulat Jehangir looked at the photograph on her writing table. A quiet face made beautiful only by its meekness and willingness to please.

'Isn't that true?' She examined the face which seemed silent and indifferent. Then she moved away from there, annoyed.

Darkness was everywhere, and indifference. Even in that well-lit room with its beautiful French windows, its transluscent white walls, and its curtains steeped in the bluish-green hue of deep seas which rustled against the doors. A room furnished tastefully with simple but exquisite furniture. It wasn't just that room but every single wall, the threshold, even the green paths in the garden and the trees seemed indifferent. All of them, knowing her innermost desires, had declined to meet her eyes. No one had tried, even to talk to her, except that cheeky but extremely perceptive Chinese boy – with whom her only link was some items for her trousseau that had been bought from him.

'But how impulsive and uninhibited he is! He starts talking without a prelude. That day he said to me, "Why are you marrying that Chiang Kai Shek?"

'Yesterday, when he came again to deliver the kimono, and saw me alone on the verandah, he came up to me. He asked me, with the greatest humility and gentleness, to try on the kimono and then stood aside himself, waiting patiently.

'I put the kimono back on the table after trying it on, and told him, "This is absolutely fine." He then folded it aesthetically and placed it

15

before me again, saying, "May God bless it for you, and may you use it with happiness." Then, I don't know why, but my eyes filled with tears.'

It is true that he had said those words with such sincerity and simplicity that Saulat's comely eyes had brimmed with tears.

'What's this? In China, where I come from, the bride's weeping is not approved of!' He smiled mischievously.

She had sat looking at the exquisite handwork on the kimono in silence. 'Miss, have you chosen this kimono, then?' he had said to distract her.

She nodded her head slowly instead of saying anything. And then he spoke, without any preamble.

'You seem sad today, and you looked miserable the other day in front of your fiancé too. You are unhappy over this marriage of yours, aren't you?'

If it had been another time, and someone else instead of him, she would have kicked the table in front of her, walked across to the other end of the verandah and shouted with all her strength, 'Get out of my sight this minute!' But this was different. The man who uttered these words was a different kind of man. His intentions were not false. He was not saying it to ridicule her or to relish her helplessness. His voice was sincere and his manner was unaffected.

That is why Saulat Jehangir, whose heart wanted to cry out and shout at the top of her voice that she was unhappy about this wedding, quietly nodded an affirmative in reply.

He sat down near her on his bundle, without her permsision.

'So, can you not declare your opinion on this matter, Miss?' he spoke English reasonably well.

'You could say that.'

'Then you don't need to grieve.'

'Why not?'

'Do you know that whatever does not issue from our wishes and our opinions is called destiny.'

'What do you mean by that?'

'Nothing. Shall I recite a Chinese poem to you?'

She laughed sadly. He talks nonsense, this boy, 'Go on.'

A melodious stream of Chinese words poured out of him in very moving and attractive tones.

'What's this *chin, chu, chu*? I don't understand a thing! If you can translate it into English, then tell me.'

'I can't do it out loud, but I can write it down for you. I'll write it, if you'll allow me?'

'Write it. Take this piece of paper.'

16

He took a red pencil from his pocket and started drawing Chinese letters.

'Write it in English, naa?'

'You are really impatient. Beauty should be dignified and indifferent.' He upbraided her like an elder, and in a little while began writing the English translation, and recited the words of the last stanza as he wrote them.

> 'Whatever is ordained for me,
> I must endure, anyhow.'

And then he wrote the last words:

> 'Death, difficulties, and their solution,
> all come in their own time.'

After a moment he wrote another line, and then raised his head to ask, 'Shall I write the translation for this line too?'

'Translate everything that you've written down.'

The red pencil moved again, slowly, hesitantly.

'Good looking and comfort loving girls forget their past and make a compromise with the present. And you will do the same.' . . . Safdar Yaaseen.

'Safdar Yaaseen! Who is he?'

'That's me,' he placed a finger on his chest very innocently.

'Oh! But you're Chinese.'

'The Chinese can be Muslims too, Miss.'

'So you're not a Buddhist?'

'What difference does it make if someone is, or isn't a Buddhist?'

'That's right. It makes no difference.' Saulat Jehangir rose quickly, in a panic. She became a little apprehensive about this clever young man from mysterious China, who had managed to reduce her to a level beneath hers, with just one hint, in only a few words. It did not befit the dignity and status of someone like her that she should sit and discuss the philosophy of life with an insignificant boy like him, who was obliged to go round peddling goods from door to door .

'OK. You should come by, some time, to pick up the money for the kimono from Mummy.'

'Not to worry, Miss.' He got up at once and, picking up his bundle, smiled a meaningless smile, as if to say, 'You were right to make me feel that I am a mere pedlar.'

Saulat Jehangir went inside, read the translation of the Chinese poem over and over again, and then kept it in her notebook.

17

It was remarkably strange that a circumspect and cautious girl like her should have found solace through the words of a common salesman. Since that day she gave up thinking about Zubair, the owner of that humble, eager-to-please, intelligent face, in the photograph on her table. He was just a journalist, who could only attempt to look well-dressed in home-spun kurtas and white pyjamas because he could not afford fine, expensive suits. Someone who was so well-educated and rich in spirits that the huge gaps in his material life did not worry him at all.

But 'just education and high-mindedness would not be enough to sustain a lifestyle,' she had been told. 'And then, of course, what is the need for educated and idealistic people to form relationships with those who have been raised in the lap of luxury, and whose standard of living is far beyond the estimation of ordinary people?'

Saulat Jehangir had been told things like, 'You are not used to discomforts. Within a few days every ideal and preference dies, and only one thing remains, and that is need. The need for money. Wealth is the greatest power on earth. You can buy all manner of prestige, every convenience and every comfort with it.'

She would sit quietly listening to everything with displeasure but with concentration. Even though she never argued back she was still subjected to every argument based on logic and reality.

'Look, only wealth gives you status in the eyes of others. If you have no money you lose your worth within days.'

She would sit quietly staring into space, unable to see anything around her, even Ammah Bi, seated right in front of her. Only her voice and her measured words would continue to pour into her ears.

'It is nonsense to say that he's too old. Look here, all these young boys are extremely irresponsible. For them the only kind of girls who are suitable are the ones who have been raised in ordinary families and are used to difficulties. For girls like you the best husbands are men who are imposing and serious. Do you not see that we have raised you in the most luxurious circumstances? You are not used to hardships. And comfort is life's greatest need.'

Not used to hardships! Not used to hardships! Am I not going through enough hardships now? she would think rebelliously, but with the greatest cowardice, pulling a meek face, she would murmur, 'Ammah Begum, it's time for the Zohar prayers. You have to say your prayers.'

Then, no one knows how, Zubair came to know that Ammah Begum was of the opinion that boys, born and bred in the middle class, with middle-class fortunes, were extremely repressed and he took offence. He stopped communicating even with Saulat, of all people.

18

'A curse on all of you who were raised in affluent homes. I don't care if I am related to you, I shall never see your face again,' he thought to himself, and with a splendid lack of concern, immersed himself in his own routine. 'It's all nonsense, there's no such thing as love,' he bluffed himself into believing; and sat down to write an even more powerful editorial for the following day. He did not even deign to tell Saulat Jehangir that he was annoyed with her, that he was breaking off relations with them because he had not been raised in a bungalow or a mansion but in a modest and ancient home.

When she ran into him one day and started talking to him he just said, 'I am sorry but I am in a hurry right now. I have to meet the manager of the newspaper. You know I am only an employee. And conversations! What do they matter? There is a whole lifetime for those.' His voice sounded unconcerned and resolute but as he started to climb on his bicycle again, she noticed that his expression was more subdued than usual and he was even more obliging than normal.

Everyone thinks that Saulat is happy and content except that Chinese boy with a face like Guatam Buddh. 'Safdar Yaseen, whether or not you are a Buddhist by conviction, you are a Buddhist all right. Your mind and your heart are enlightened. How quickly you read the state of my heart!'

She picked up Zubair's photograph and looked at that face which was made eternally beautiful by its silence and humility. 'All right, then, Zubair Khan. If you know how to be arrogant then remember that I am a descendent of the Great Mughal, too.'

That evening she heard Ammah Begum telling Abba Mian, 'Saulat is fine now. Yesterday she went to the cinema with Asif Jah quite happily and how pretty she looked sitting next to him.'

'Hum. Huh.' Abba Mian sat with his beautiful hookah by his side, its tip, soaked in rose water, in his mouth. He gurgled on it constantly, as if he were reluctant to believe what he was told.

When they had returned that evening Asif Jah had bought her a huge box of chocolates and masses of roses. Yes, she was extremely happy yesterday. And Asif had said, 'Ammah Begum, she is still a little girl.' Saulat, who was standing behind the pillar on the verandah, listening to their conversation, found herself far away. Instead of Ammah Begum's voice she could hear the young, genteel and musical voice of Safdar Yaaseen in her ears.

'How shall I teach the children of emperors
the principles of Li (of virtuous and upright conduct)

And how can I make them learn the qualities of Cin Zi (decency)
It is only the power of Qing (respecting the feelings of others)
that makes me hold my tongue.'

'Yes, Ammah Begum, it is only the power of Qing that makes me hold my tongue! Or, it is my lack of strength?' she thought quietly to herself, and tiptoed away from there.

7

That afternoon too, Begum Jehangir had ordered one of her twin daughters, Gaythi, to lie down in bed. She believed that this grounding, achieved through forced bed-rest, was a more civilised and well-bred punishment compared to others, and that it was more effective. Gaythi, bless her, received this punishment virtually every day, whilst Arjumand would rarely ever get it. Her twin daughters differed from each other enormously in both looks and temperament. Arjumand, with her pure Mughal features, was healthy but delicately built. Gaythi was stoutly built and had Mongolian features; and whilst Arjumand was extremely reasonable and obedient, Gaythi was self-willed and uncontrollable.

Being subjected to hours of bed-rest like a hospital patient was the punishment she hated the most. It had a strange effect on her. Lying in bed the whole day, as if she were sick, she would become aware of anger and rebellion simmering inside her, raising strange spectres in her head.

Sometimes she would imagine herself taking off with her bed and her suitcase to Mali's hovel, and sometimes to Dadi Ammah's house. Occasionally, she would imagine that Abba Mian had been persuaded through her stubborn insistence to send Ammah Begum off on a ship to some unknown destination, and had married the *Paan walli*, who would make *paans* for her packed with peppermint and spices, and fill her coat pockets with peanuts in the winter. What fun it would be if that really happened! She would laugh aloud to herself as she lay in bed.

'Why are you laughing like a lunatic?' Ammah Begum would scold.

Gaythi used to tease Arjumand so much over her innocence and her politeness that gradually she was developing a sense of inferiority. In reality, Ammah Begum, who constantly scolded and punished Gaythi, was thoroughly fed up with her. For some reason, she was slowly developing a real aversion to the girl. A strange hatred would stir in her heart against her which would soften towards her only on the day she had meted out a truly harsh punishment. She experienced an almost indefinable pleasure and happiness whilst spanking her. She would throttle her quite uncontrollaby at the slightest provocation. She could not understand these feelings in herself, because Gaythi's illness or pain would cause her the same screaming anguish which she felt for her other children. In fact, seeing her helpless and vulnerable when she was ill gave her a strange sort of satisfaction, too. She would tend to her with the utmost care and consideration, amazed at the change in herself.

Then something happened one afternoon whilst they all sat on the verandah at the back of the house, busy sewing clothes. The comforter for Saulat's trousseau was under discussion. Chachi Jaan thought that the best choice would be a very pale sea-green shaded scarf to cover the bright green Benarsi material they had used for the interlining. And Ammah Begum was of the opinion that the fine patchwork border would look best if it ran along the bias. Saulat sat at a slight distance from them on a cane stool, with her back towards them, stitching a tea-cosy.

The sky was slightly overcast and Ammah Begum had turned off the ceiling fan since there seemed to be sufficient breeze after a very long hot spell. Both the girls had been put to bed in their room as usual and now it was nearly time for them to wake up.

But rousing Gaythi from her sleep that day was not a problem. The cool and pleasant breeze had driven away the few stray chances of sleep which might have wandered in her direction. She stood in the window, listening very attentively to the nightingale cooing in the back garden. The damson tree swayed with a gust of wind just once and its branches, loaded with the fruit, almost touched the ground. When she saw those black damsons Gaythi's heart could no longer hold out.

She shook Arjumand's shoulder, 'Arjumand, Arjumand, come, let's go to pick some damsons.' Even Arjumand could not sleep in that enticing weather, but she lay faking sleep. Her eyelids, screwed tight in pretence, were flickering. At every sound she would stop breathing and force her eyes to be still with great difficulty.

'Shh. . .' she said softly, 'what if someone sees us?'

'So what? The worst that could happen would be a beating.' Gaythi tossed out carelessly and went out.

Chunna sat under the Neem tree counting his marbles.

'Come on, Chunna. Let's pick some damsons.'

'Not me. You'll have to pick them yourself. I can't take a beating with you.'

Chunna hid the marbles quickly, because he had several of hers in his collection.

'Don't come then, you wretch. Who's going to beat you?'

'Who's going to beat me? Eh? That day you got Shabrati into trouble.'

'All right, then. Don't bother. Who wants you, anyway.' she said as she climbed up the tree.

In spite of his refusal, Chunna came as well and stood under the tree.

'Shall I come up too?' He peeped at her from down below.

'Don't you dare come up now. If you do, I'll push you off the tree.'

Chunna had no choice but to look for and pick up the fruit off the ground. 'I hope to God she falls off,' he cursed her inwardly.

She sat comfortably on a cushion, eating them with great relish. She had pulled out a packet of salt from the pocket of her dress and taunted Chunna: 'I've even got some salt here. I am eating mine with salt.'

'I hope she breaks her hands,' Chunna cursed silently.

They heard the tinkle of a bell. It was Safdar Yaaseen's bicycle. He entered the house now without calling out loud.

Chunna tried to frighten Gaythi from below the tree. 'Begum Sahib is standing at the bathroom door, looking this way. You're going to get a beating today. Save me! I'd better run.'

Gaythi lost her cool. Her foot slipped as she tried to climb down in a panic and, by some strange mischance, she landed on the ground with the cushion. As she took the tumble, the only thought that remained in her head was that she had missed all the fattest and the blackest damsons on the tree.

As soon as she had fallen she heard the sound of a tinkle and a bang as if someone had let a bicycle drop on purpose. When she tried to raise herself a moan escaped from her lips. She turned her head round to look up helplessly. China Man stood close to her, just by her head, bent over her, a look of concern on his face.

'Cuckoo! I hope you are not hurt?' he asked.

She gave him a look of utter defencelessness and shut her eyes instead of answering him.

Safdar Yaaseen bent over her again. A wave of pain and impotence flashed in her eyes like the surge of agony in the eyes of a wounded lion. And then she lay there with her eyes closed as if she were lying on her bed. Her fine pink dress was spotted heavily with purple stains of mushy damsons, her lips were purple and there were no shoes on her feet. Her straight black hair straggled on to her forehead. A sharp pebble had pierced it on the left side and opened a cut which was oozing fresh blood.

As she lay there in that state she could have passed for a Chinese girl. He bent down and called her gently, 'Cuckoo!'

Chunna gauged the seriousness of the situation and sprinted away straight back to his quarters. Safdar took a handkerchief from his pocket and placed it on her wound to soak up the blood slowly. 'Cuckoo,' he called out again but since she did not reply he placed a hand on her forehead to try and rouse her. It felt absolutely cold.

'She is unconscious!' he then realised for the first time. He lifted her as gently as possible in his arms and walked quickly towards the verandah over the crunching gravel.

Both his hands were full so he could not press the bell. Instead, he called out as loudly as he could, 'China Man, China Man.'

'Hush. Why are you making such a racket?' Saulat opened the door on her balcony with some irritation but she stopped short when she saw him.

'Oh! What's happened to her?'

'I saw her fall just as I was entering the gate, and I threw down my bike at once, but she fell before I could reach her.'

'Oh,' Saulat's face turned as white as paper.

'Hurry up. Tell me where I should put her. She is very heavy; my arms are tired.'

'Oh!' Saulat went inside.

'How crazy she is!' Safdar thought. 'Am I going to stand here for the rest of my life, carrying this heavy sister of hers ?' He bent his head to look at her face and smiled to himself. 'Who says that she is her sister? She looks like a very special girl from my own country.'

All pandemonium broke loose in the gallery. Several footsteps drew close.

'Come on, bring her in,' Chachi jaan called to him in a very perturbed voice.

He went into the room which was her mother's bedroom. She herself sat on a wooden divan, her head between her hands. He stood near the headboard even after he had laid the girl down on the bed.

Saulat came, sat beside her and began to feel her pulse.

'Is her pulse all right, child?' Ammah Begum asked with a tremor in her voice.

'It is absolutely fine. Now please don't worry so much.' But when Saulat tried to straighten the twisted foot Gaythi's whole body convulsed.

'It looks as though she may have fractured it.'

'Ah! So the blessed girl's gone and broken a bone now?' Her mother was close to tears.

'We should try to bring her round,' Safdar felt bound to say to Saulat.

23

'Oh, yes.' Saulat dashed into Ammah Begum's dressing room to fetch a bottle of eau-de-Cologne.

Gaythi opened her eyes slowly in response to the splashes of cold water and the smell of the eau-de-Cologne. When she saw the whole family gathered round her she felt a sense of triumph and satisfaction permeate her being.

'Fetch some hot milk.' Chachi jaan shook her hands in a panic and Saulat hurried away to fetch her a cup of hot milk.

The room was decorated in extremely good taste and everyone who was standing around, or sitting there, was good looking and attractive. However Safdar Yaaseen was completely unaware of this at the time.

When they saw that she could not drink the milk lying flat on her back, a feeding cup was found in the medicine cupboard and the milk was poured into it. But Gaythi pushed away every hand that held it for her.

Then Safdar Yaaseen knelt down beside her. He took the cup from Saulat's hands without saying anything and held it to her lips. 'Drink it, Cuckoo,' he urged and Cuckoo drank the milk without pause as she looked at him with eyes which smiled in spite of the pain brimming up in them.

Then she said to him in a whisper, 'Chin, chin, China Man, you've come into the house. We'll lock you up in that big cupboard today. Now you won't be allowed to go home.'

'Never mind. You are not in pain now?'

'I am in great pain. I've broken my bones.' She smiled pathetically.

'You are very brave,' he pushed her hair, which was blacker than the blackest clouds, off her forehead.

Suddenly a look of displeasure descended on Ammah Begum's face — as if something improper had occurred. She turned round towards Saulat and said to her, 'Tell him to go outside now.'

Saulat just looked at her and then, with some embarrassment, said to him in English, 'Thank you very much for your sympathy. You can go now. We are going to take her to the hospital.'

'Let your father know,' her mother commanded.

'I have phoned him. He is going to send the car now.'

'Why? Didn't you tell him that she has a fracture.'

'He would have been worried for nothing. Maybe she hasn't. I may be wrong. She seems to be chatty enough now.' She looked at Safdar as she spoke, as if to tell him to leave.

He got up gently and went out without wishing anyone goodbye.

'Ah, Abba Mian, I've got a really bad pain,' Gaythi sobbed for her father who was not there, instead of her mother; nevertheless the reply came from her.

'See what happens when you disobey? Serves you right for trying to pick *jamuns*. Just this morning you were ordered to stay in bed, and in the afternoon you go off again to kick up the dust.'

Gaythi responded to her criticisms by clenching her teeth and holding back the next painful moan which rose to her lips. She turned her head round and saw that Arjumand stood near the door terrified.

8

When they took her on a stretcher to the car they saw that the Chinese salesman was still sitting on the steps, his back against his bundle. His bicycle lay at his feet as he attentively watched the eagles hovering against the sky.

'Ay! You can go away. We're all preoccupied right now. We won't be buying anything. Come another time when things are more peaceful,' Begum Sahib called out in a tone of displeasure.

He stood up quietly, picked up his bicycle, fixed the bundle on to the carrier and said to himself, 'Begum Sahib, whether you thank me or suspect that I am still waiting here in the hope of a sale, I'll never be able to tell you that I am here for her sake. When I see her, or when I speak to her, I feel as if I were at home.'

When Gaythi was wheeled into the X-ray room for screening, Saulat became quietly aware that there was a strange face amongst the members of the family waiting for the result. It was the face of that boy, Safdar Yaaseen. The screening report indicated that she had broken the bones in her thigh and in her left wrist . But the X-ray report was still awaited. She was taken into a side room on a stretcher and left there whilst they waited. Chachi jaan was sent back home. Saulat was following the doctor around and Ammah Begum sat on a chair by the bed. Safdar Yaaseen peeped through the net curtains on the window. She seemed calmer than before. She was reading a thin book which she held in her right hand with great difficulty.

'What a lot of endurance Cuckoo has!' he thought with pride. Without any reason his eyes became moist and he moved away from the net curtains. It was nearly four o'clock in the afternoon. The doctor came and put a temporary bandage on her and she was taken to a room which had been vacated for her.

They had taken her away, pushing her stretcher somewhere deep inside the building and he could not find out which room she had been taken to. He waited for quite a long time but since no one came out that way he stepped off the verandah and went towards his bicycle. He saw that the bundle was fixed on the carrier as usual. It sent a shiver down his spine. 'Oh, God! What a fool I've been. What if someone had walked off with it?' The very thought made his head spin with fear. 'That would have been splendid compassion!' He laughed at his own folly. 'God has been merciful.' He saw their car when he reached the gate. Stopping near it, he asked the driver, 'What's the number of Baby's room?'

The driver, who was resting with his forehead against both hands crossed on the steering wheel, started. He looked very tired. 'I don't know anything. They'll be here soon; and they should be able to tell you.'

Saulat came down the staircase at the back which was the nearest, and turned towards them. She was accompanied by a tall and extremely handsome man. A few steps behind them was her mother, walking slowly on weary feet. They all seemed calmer than before. They got into the car chatting. As the driver started the engine, he addressed the gentleman, pointing towards Safdar. 'Sahib, this Cheena Man wants to know Baby's room number.'

'Why? What's the matter?' Sahib exclaimed with some surprise and Saulat whispered something to him. Turning his large, hooded eyes towards him, he came out of the car and spoke to him with great courtesy, 'I am very grateful to you for your sympathy. The child is in room number ten, on the second floor. I am sorry you have had to wait so long for her.'

'It doesn't matter.' Safdar bowed slightly before him. 'I'll go now.'

Sahib returned to the car once again and it sped out of the gates with a swoosh. But Safdar's eyes were still riveted to that dignified and distinguished person, dressed in a white *sherwani* and *churidar* pyjamas. Even his large, twisted moustache expressed his goodness, his decency.

Safdar was not at all aware of the fact that features like that man's were typically Mughal. However, he kept thinking to himself that this man must be a descendant of the ancient kings of this country.

9

'Now Ammah Begum and Saulat Apa will gloat, seeing me out of action like this,' Gaythi thought, looking at her incapacitated self, her leg strapped in bandages.

Now they won't complain about me making a racket all the time. But ... but Shareef will fill the hovel with hay and I will not be able to bounce on it. And Mali and his children will pull all the leaves off the *Charpatta* and I won't be able to knead them into bread. Her eyes filled with tears at the thought of so many deprivations. 'I don't know whether or not I'll ever be able to get up and run around like before.'

She wanted to talk to Chachi jaan to escape her worrying thoughts. So she called out to her. 'Chachi jaan, where are you for goodness' sake?' She moaned as if she were in severe pain.

Her aunt, who was in the bathroom washing out the feeding cup for her, came out in a panic.

'What's the matter? Has your foot become painful again? You are so naughty and restless. No wonder your mother's always cross with you.'

She smiled. 'I'm feeling restless. Please come and sit with me.'

'It's so difficult to look after someone else's child.'

'But you do it all the time. And you never stay with Ismat Apa and Talat Apa. They're always alone, poor things.'

'Why? They're not alone. Your grandmother is with them.'

'So what? They must miss you. Dadi Ammah is not their mother. Right! I've guessed it now. They must be very naughty too. That's why you get cross and leave them.'

'No, child. They are not naughty.' She looked away, a little sadly.

These were not things to be talked of aloud. It had been at her own discretion. Only after the death of her husband had she realised for the first time how important it was to have at least someone to call your own from your maternal home. Otherwise in-laws become strangers too, despite the relationship. Not having the support of her own family and not being the mother of a son had given her a strange sense of inferiority.

'These daughters of mine will marry outsiders and then my relationship with this family will become just nominal. What links would then be left between my girls and this family which used to be the most respected in the clan? The only way I could strengthen my connection with it would be through marriages within the family. Their eldest uncle never enquires about their welfare, nor mine. Nor does their aunt – their father's sister –

who only visits after several years, and then declares repeatedly that it is "her mother's breath which draws her to that house". If anyone cares about me and my daughters it is Gaythi's father!'

And so she had decided to cling to him for support. For some time now, her suspicion that Sheharyaar had a soft spot for Ismat had turned to certainty; and since then she had been willing to serve her sister-in-law in every possible way. And she spent a lot of time with them.

'*Bhai*, you don't talk at all. Hunh, hunh.' Gaythi was preparing herself for a weep.

'What can I talk to you about, tell me? If you like, I'll tell you a story.'

'A story?' she said after thinking about it for a few moments, 'No, I don't want to listen to a story. Tell me something funny.'

'Something funny? Well, only your Cheena can tell you that when he comes. He talks just like a copycat clown. I can't talk like that. Now, listen, have some grapes.'

She shook her head sulkily.

'Shall I give you a tangerine?'

Gaythi closed her eyes.

10

Every second or third afternoon he would slink away quietly to the hospital, disregarding Sang's whinging. Very quietly he would climb up the stairs to the second floor and knock at the door to room number ten. She would call out, 'Come in,' looking at the door with enthusiastic eyes. He would come up to her bed and bow to her, an extremely comical expression on his face.

'How is the girl who loves *jamuns*?'

Sometimes he would say, 'How is the Blue Fatty?'

'I've got so skinny and you still call me Fatty,' she would laugh.

Chachi jaan, too, felt relieved when he was around. She would go off to visit the patients in the other rooms and sit and chat with their attendants. He would bring sour *chooran*, lemon drops or some other small, inexpensive gift for her which she devoured with great pleasure.

Safdar Yaaseen's visits became even more special for Gaythi since he always came at a time when no one else was at all likely to come, and she was fed up of lying in bed. He would tell her jokes and do impersonations making her laugh to her heart's content. Occasionally, she would be crying with pain or restlessness, but as soon as she saw him enter the room her tearful eyes would brighten up. Amused at his chat, his silly questions and his interesting little tricks, she would forget that she had been lying strapped to a hospital bed for the past fifteen days, and was desperate just to be able to sit up.

Gaythi felt delighted and diverted by his visits but nevertheless his status was no more than that of a flighty bird which decides to stop in mid-flight just to come and settle on a window-sill. Or that of an insignificant wild flower which has chosen to bloom in an unexpectedly absurd spot, drawing someone's attention to itself for a brief moment, only to be dismissed almost immediately. This was the reason why his casual visits were not mentioned to anyone else. Possibly, Gaythi would also not have said anything about them because she was accustomed to keeping secret those things which interested her profoundly.

But he would sit for hours with this sick, loud-mouthed girl, trying to entertain her. And when his bicycle left the hospital gates he would feel a certain gratification, almost as if he had spent that time in his own home.

Saulat discovered these secret visits one evening when she noticed two little red and yellow glass ducks and a little dog on Gaythi's bedside table.

'Where did you get these?' she asked, brushing Gaythi's hair with utmost gentleness.

Instead of giving her an answer, Gaythi concentrated on looking at the pictures in her new storybook.

'Oh, it was that China Man ... you know who I mean? He often comes round to see her,' Chachi jaan informed Saulat, as she offered her some chopped beetle nuts and cardamom from her bag.

'Really! Does he often come to see her then?' Saulat asked with a mixture of wonder and eagerness. He was indeed a strange boy.

'Of course. She forgets her pain when he is around.'

Gaythi could see out of the corner of her eye that this information had not pleased her mother.

'But you should have returned these things. This was not at all necessary,' she reproached her sister-in-law.

'What could I do? I don't even know when he left these on her table and took off.' Chachi jaan had left her own part of the story completely out of the discussion. On several occasions she herself had asked him to fetch her *paans*, cardamoms or ice.

She would phrase her requests quite artfully: '*Bhai*, you really seem to be an angel of mercy – arriving just at this moment! I've been missing

29

my *paans* all morning. Could you fetch me some, maybe a couple of annas' worth?' And he would dash off to get them.

Or, if the ice in the thermos was finished, she would hold up the flask saying, 'They needed ice in the room next door and they just came to ask for it, so our thermos is now empty. When this Baby of yours wants a drink of water, what am I going to do?'

He would offer to fetch it without her having to say any more. 'Really! I'll get it just now for our Baby. Ice for our Baby.'

'*Bhai*, at least take some money for it then,' she would make a half-hearted offer.

He would leave the room saying, 'O *Baai*, what's the rush! I'll take the money some other time.'

'Well, you should have thought of it. Anyway, give this to him now,' Ammah Begum placed a tenner on her palm. 'And, look, you should just tell him that Baby is better now. In another two or three days we'll be taking her home, as soon as her plaster is done. There is no need for him to come any more.'

'What's the harm, Ammah Begum? He keeps her entertained.'

'No. She can't be that crazy! She has so many books, so many things and then your Chachi jaan is here all the time. We all come every morning and every evening.' Ammah Begum looked quite annoyed so Gaythi did not consider it wise to meet her gaze.

'How is my child, now?' Suddenly, her tall and handsome father kissed her forehead.

'Abba Mian,' she put her arm round his neck and started crying without any reason.

'What's this? You're my brave son. Brave sons don't cry now, do they? What happened?'

'Abba Mian!'

'Yes, child.'

'When will I be able to get up?'

'You still have to stay in bed for a few days.'

'But for how long?' Huge tears slid from her eyes and rolled steadily down her cheeks.

'Ouf! That is a truly difficult question to answer. And you already know how bad I am at arithmetic. I'll tell you some other time.'

His beautiful hooded eyes filled with a mixture of pain and pity. He dried her tears with a towel that lay beside her and then went and sat next to his wife.

'She is in such a state already; and she still has the plaster to endure.'

30

'Yes. Well, she is paying the price for being so naughty. Look how pale she's become in the last few days.'

He looked at her sadly.

'Bring her some toys when you come to see her tomorrow.'

'Certainly.'

Gaythi turned her head to look at her handsome father and beautiful mother, admiring her father's big, upwardly curved moustaches with affection. Chachi jaan who had covered her head and retreated into a corner at the arrival of her older brother-in-law, spoke quietly to Saulat. 'We've completely run out of soap.'

'I'll send some tomorrow with Ghafoor.'

'Don't forget to bring some talcum powder when you come tomorrow.'

'Very well,' Saulat also spoke softly.

When they were all ready to leave and Ammah Begum bent to say goodbye, Gaythi asked, 'What is Arjumand doing?'

'She is reading the *Qura'n* with Maulvi Sahib.'

'Please do bring her tomorrow.'

'All right. You should have your milk; you look so pale. Don't be difficult about it,' she warned.

'Don't even mention milk to her. It just produces floods of tears,' Chachi jaan told her softly.

Ammah Begum glared at her, 'That's her all right! You should tell her off.' Gaythi shut her eyes.

However when he saw his wife dab her eyes after she had got into the car, Jehangir Mirza became concerned. 'What's this! Why should you be crying?'

'Well, I can't help worrying about it. What if the bone doesn't set properly? She is only a girl.'

'You shouldn't start worrying about it in advance. There is no reason why it shouldn't set properly.'

11

'Hello, Cuckoo.' He came and sat beside her on a stool.

She woke up from her half-hearted dozing, looked up at him and spoke sadly.

'Chin, chin, China Man.'

'Yes, Cuckoo?'

'Don't you feel hot? You come out in the heat of the sun.'

'I do.'

'Then why do you come out when the sun is blazing.'

'Because I want to.'

'O – ho! You *are* a real lord. Because I want to.' She really envied this man. She wished she could answer Ammah Begum and Saulat Apa in the same vein when they scolded her for running around in the sun.

'I'll go out in the sun – because I want to.'

Chachi jaan came out of the bathroom drying her hair and he gazed at her long black wavy locks with great interest. After she had dried her hair she took a comb and began to unravel it gently. She sat on a chair near the door at the opposite end of the room with a large tufted towel on her lap. She took only a few strands to comb out at a time. Her soft round fingers and tapering wrists moved gently in her hair. Each graceful movement of those shapely fingers held not only all the refinement and sophistication of an accomplished and thoroughly domesticated house-wife, but also the decorum of an ancient code of culture and long years of good breeding. Her manner and style demonstrated that the history of generations through the centuries is concealed in every curve and twist of the human body, and in all its movements.

She sat combing her hair, unaware of his presence and indifferent to it. Then she gathered her hair together, pushed it under her scarf and proceeded to clean the comb slowly and carefully, winding all the loose hairs into a ring on her index finger and spitting on it carefully, before going back to the bathroom to dispose of it. She came and stood near him when she had finished.

'So you've come?' she asked gently.

He stood up when he saw her standing by him.

'Would you leave a little early today?'

'If you tell me to go, I will, sure.'

'Well, yes! She hasn't slept at all today, and if she goes to sleep when it's time for her mother's visit, her mother will be cross with me for not giving her a rest this afternoon.'

'Yes. That's all right,' he said good-naturedly, picking up his cap. Then he spoke to Gaythi, looking at her with affection, 'Cuckoo, go to sleep now, goodbye.'

Gaythi looked at him with sadness in her eyes as she shut them, but she pricked up her ears to hear what Chachi jaan was saying to him.

'And, just a moment.'

'What is your command?' He turned round.

'These toys . . . that you . . . er . . . er.' Knowing his sincerity, she was nervous of saying what she had to say to him.

'What did you say?'

'Nothing. We wanted to say . . . why did you bring these toys for the girl?'

He did not understand what she meant and just stood there with his mouth open.

'*Arrey bhai*, the thing is, her mother has given me these rupees. Take the money for the toys.'

'The money for the toys?' He got offended.

'Yes, I'm afraid so. And listen, she also said to tell you that we will be taking her home shortly, in the next two or three days. You don't need to trouble yourself any more.'

He was looking at her attentively.

'Don't you understand what we mean? You see, we . . .'

'Yes . . . yes! I understand. It's a good thing. It's OK, it's OK,' he spoke in a wounded voice and walked out of the door.

She just lay there the whole afternoon pretending to sleep. When they all arrived in the evening her face looked worn out. That evening Abba Mian brought her a hush-a-bye doll and a wind-up cat. She glanced at the toys and kept them on the table. Then she took a small box from under her pillow and drew out from it the yellow glass duck and placed it before her eyes which had filled with large tears.

They had all snatched away from her a living, walking, talking toy. How good he was at imitating monkeys and what funny faces he could pull!

Her heart overflowed with a sullen grief.

12

It was the first wedding in their family. Despite that, it had been a quiet affair. But why? Who could have guessed the real reason? Most people had constructed different hypotheses, based on what they knew.

Chachi jaan figured that her sister-in-law did not want her relatives and the family to witness this ill-matched marriage which she had arranged, since she feared they might put the bride off with their whispering.

Contrary to this, her mother-in-law felt that from the very first day her older daughter-in-law had always insisted on flouting every rule and law which mattered to the family. Her eldest son, Gaythi's uncle, had given his daughter in marriage to someone within their family, and now Jehangir Mirza's daughter should also have married within the family. But, instead, she was slowly breaking loose from every constraint which the family or the tribe could impose.

'*Bhai*, the truth is' the mother-in-law commented 'that we are not happy with this mis-match. If the boy had been one of the family, we could have overlooked this flaw. Anyhow, who are we to say anything?'

'The thing is, her own family is so small. One brother and one sister,' Chachi jaan also whispered.

'Well, you can cut the family right down to as few as you want. That depends on you. God forgive us! And save us from backbiting.' She quickly turned to say her Zohar prayers.

'Then, one has to admit, my own son is to blame as well. He is so busy with his shooting and hunting that he is going round as if he were a guest at his own daughter's wedding.' She resumed the conversation in the middle of the prayer again when she paused to say her salaams.

'Yes. That's right. Bhai Sahib does behave like a guest. He never interferes in anything. Bhabi jaan is really lucky,' Chachi jaan said, tacking a glittery edging on to a scarf.

'*Arrey*, nor did the one who died. He never interfered in anything. Life betrayed him. All our boys have been free of that habit. Your father-in-law never interfered in anything either, God rest his soul.'

Chachi jaan kept her head lowered as she stitched the edging on to the turquoise scarf. She had probably been reminded of her own brief but comforting relationship.

'Come to think of it, Hashmi is not far away from here. Doesn't even take an hour to get to her. But I've been thinking for a few days now of asking Jehangir to bring her over at least.'

'Well, you don't have to ponder over it that much. You only have to mention it to Bhai Sahib. After all, she is the granddaughter of your father's real brother.'

'Yes! Let me see . . . I'll raise it today. Sheharyaar is also arriving on the train which comes in about now. If the worst comes to the worst we can send him to fetch them.'

Biting off the thread with her teeth, she said, 'Bhai Sahib is staying in Sheharyaar's room and Bhabi's brother and sister-in-law are in the room upstairs. Where is Sheharyaar going to stay?'

'Just listen to that! It is his own house. Boys don't need rooms of their own. But, yes, if Hashmi decides to come, you can put her up in your room.'

'Yes. I shall say to Ismat and Talat, "You can sleep with your Dadi Ammah".'

'Now, listen, Dulhan. I think you should come back with me as soon as the wedding is over.'

'I'm also thinking along those lines,' she said in a lifeless tone.

When Sheharyaar arrived he went to Dadi Ammah's room as soon as he had met Ammah Begum.

'By the grace of God, you look as tall as your father now,' she said, stroking his head.

'And Chachi jaan is as high as my waist now,' he bent low to greet her.

Ever slim and petite, Chachi jaan greeted him fondly, 'God protect him, but he does look just like his uncle used to.'

'Is that so, Chachi jaan? Do I really look that much like him?' Sheharyaar asked.

'Exactly. May there be seven Qurans between you and him, but you do have the same hands and feet, the same features.'

Dadi Ammah looked at him with a mixture of grief and eagerness.

'Then I am his son, aren't I?' He embraced his aunt again. 'See! That's why I want you to accept me as your son.'

'*Arrey*! You are my son, already. How can I make you that?' She kissed his forehead and looked at him with extremely proprietorial eyes.

'Well, that's enough showing off! Come and talk to me now. There are so many jobs waiting for you.'

Both of them swung round together to look. Ammah Begum stood behind them, frowning visibly, her face flushed.

'Did you see that Bhabi? Isn't he mischievous?' Chachi jaan tried to hide her embarrassment.

'He isn't really mischievous! But he does show off rather a lot. Come,' she said regally.

Sheharyaar bowed his head and followed her out.

'Stop this constant flitting about all over the place. You aren't as much of a workaholic, Ismat, as you make out. You must try to sit still occasionally, at least for a bit.' Sheharyaar placed his hands on Ismat's shoulders, pushed her into a chair and sat down in front of her.

'But, Barrey Bhaiya, I have lots of things to do.'

'Don't keep calling me Barrey Bhaiya every few minutes as if you were a little girl.'

'Then how should I address you?'

'I'll tell you some time.'

'And what do I call you until then?'

'Shall I tell you?' Gaythi crept out of her hiding place behind the chair.

'O you Mongolian Chinese! So you've been hiding here, eavesdropping!' Sheharyaar pinched her chubby cheeks, 'So tell us what Ismat should call me.'

'She should call you Mr Sheharyaar Sahib.'

'That sounds just splendid! You little donkey!'

Ismat laughed at that too.

'Ismat, whatever anyone asks you to do remains undone. It would be better if you simply refused point blank in the first place. I asked you to get the sugar weighed.'

'Just coming, Barri Ammah.' She rose to go.

'I wish I hadn't made the mistake of asking you in the first place,' Ammah Begum continued, deeply angry, 'you can leave it now. I'll do it myself,' and she moved on. 'Sheharyaar, of course, has nothing to do with any of the work.' They heard her voice recede in the distance.

'Barri Ammah gets annoyed very quickly. It's the first time I've sat down since this morning,' she said, taking offence.

'Look, Ismat, you've got to learn to do things the way Ammah Begum likes them.'

'Why?'

'Because I am saying so. That's why.'

'You're a fine one to say that,' Ismat sulked.

'Be quiet, Ismat. Don't talk nonsense all the time.' Ismat looked in surprise at her mother, who had just rebuked her with those words, but was looking at Sheharyaar with great affection. 'You shouldn't even bother to speak to her. She is such a loudmouth!'

'Yes. We'll have to get her mouth stitched up.'

'Sheharyaar Mian believes in pampering only his paternal relatives,' his maternal aunt came to sit by him and complain.

'Well said, Mumani jaan. In fact, I was just getting up now to go and look after my maternal relatives.'

'Away with you, lad! There's not much I don't know about you! She slapped him affectionately on his back.

'What do you know then?' Sheharyaar's head fell before her sharp gaze.

'Shall I say it to Apa jaan? Put in a word for you?'

'No thank you. I am my own recommendation.' He laughed aloud and Ismat rose in bewilderment.

36

Her mother took her aside and told her off. 'If I hear you answering back Sheharyaar I shall smash your face in.'

Ismat, who had just noticed Barri Ammah walk past her with an abstracted look, her head lowered, left to go and sit in her grandmother's room.

'Hashmi Apa's son is indeed a strange boy,' Gaythi reflected. No one had told her what her relationship was with the mother of this boy, Masood, nor did she ask anyone. But she was so delicate and beautiful that she started addressing her as Hashmi Apa.

Gaythi had been very surprised to discover that the boy did not have a father. She wondered how he managed to live without a father.

He was slim, taller than his years and dark skinned. His thoughtful eyes made him look very interesting. He was different from all of them in many ways. She and her other cousins spoke English fluently and had servants to help them dress. They all took hours to get ready. But Masood, Hashmi Apa's son, was different. He did not have a very impressive wardrobe nor an ayah or bearer to accompany him. You could count all his outfits, which were very ordinary, on the fingers of one hand. In fact, his shoes were quite old. He would polish them every morning and evening to give them a shine. He would go into any one of the bathrooms, at some time during the day, and bathe and dress himself. On several occasions her maternal cousins had laughed at his clothes and his shoes but it did not seem to ruffle him at all.

'Just look at your shoes, Masood Khan,' Gaythi's maternal cousin, Salman, ridiculed him.

'I have seen them,' he replied seriously.

'You should change your shoes now, 'Arjumand advised him sympathetically. 'Salman is laughing at you.'

'They're my shoes, not his. What has he got to do with my shoes?'

'The point is, these shoes and the striped shirt make you look as if you were the son of a cook,' Salman commented, bringing his own face very close to Masood's. Masood looked at him for an instant and then slapped him full on his fair face.

Salman growled, 'I'll deal with you, Masood Khan.'

'What will you do? Do it now, if you want to show us all.' Gaythi came forward. 'You are talking such pointless nonsense.'

Arjumand took Salman by the hand and drew him away.

But this did not mean that Gaythi herself did not argue with Masood. He pinched her for some reason and she smashed her fist on his back. 'You're such an ass!'

37

'Flat-faced Cheeni, Madam Chiang Kai Shek!'

'*Arrey*! Does that rude man come to your house too?'

'Which rude man?' Masood pouted his lips at her contemptuously.

'The one who calls me Cuckoo. He's really bad.'

Suddenly she remembered that he was not at all bad. When she was ill, and fed up of lying alone in hospital, he used to walk in wearing a comical expression on his face, just when she was getting restless. He would try to amuse her and make her laugh. And now she had not seen him for several days, or even thought of him.

Safdar had spent that whole afternoon painting a scene on a piece of silk with a very fine paint brush as he sat in a corner of Sang's shop, and Sang had spent all that time scolding him for having done it. Safdar had not remembered at all that the beautiful and arrogant girl who did not like her fiancé was getting married around that time. Nor had he thought of the little girl who looked so very Chinese, for whose pleasure he used to make trips to the hospital, in the blazing afternoon sun. It was not something to dwell upon.

Jehangir Mirza called Sheharyaar and said to him, '*Bhai*, would you take Arjumand and Gaythi to buy them new shoes? Your mother's been after me. I can't really take them now, can I?'

He saw Masood heading towards them. The heels of his shoes were completely worn, and in spite of his attempts at polishing it, the leather had lost its colour in various places. He looked at his shoes closely and realised that Gaythi was right.

The night before when Ammah Begum had asked Abba Mian to take Gaythi and Arjumand to buy them new shoes, he had seemed startled.

'Who? I have to go and buy their shoes? You mean, for these girls?'

'Who else? Do you think I meant all the girls in the neighbourhood?'

'No. What I meant to ask was, did you really mean that *I* should take them to buy new shoes?'

'No. I was only joking!' Ammah Begum grumbled in sheer vexation. 'It is the limit, really! What an attitude! Bhai jaan always gets his children's new shoes himself. And here, I mention it for the first time in my life, and he seems to be going up the wall.'

'Well, Begum, the thing is . . . it is partly because you haven't let me get into the habit of doing these things. You are so alert and smart yourself that you have turned me into quite a useless creature.'

'Have I done that? You've always been like that – like the idle rich. I had no choice but to take on all those jobs. My sister-in-law's so lucky even her clothes are chosen by Bhai jaan! Not at all like you; we could be dressed in rags for all you care.'

'Don't talk like this, Begum. Er, I . . . ' He lost his composure. He was thinking to himself, 'What can one say about the men in your family? They're clever business people. We're the useless kind.'

He kept quiet for a little while then he asked in a depressed voice, 'So, is it not possible for the bride to take them shopping for their shoes?'

'As if she will have the time tomorrow!'

'Then ask Ghafoor, maybe he can do it.'

'Never mind the advice. I'll manage somehow.' She felt aggravated.

He turned to go to his room, thankfully emerging from the terror he felt at the very thought of going shopping for children's shoes.

Gaythi, who was lying on her mother's bed, raised her head and thought, 'If Ammah Begum takes us for our new shoes Masood will not be able to get a new pair. But if you ask Abba Mian for anything a couple of times you can get it.' She followed him on quiet feet and peeped into his room from behind the curtains.

Abba Mian, dressed in a beautifully embroidered muslin shirt and white pyjamas, stood on the emerald green carpet in his room looking quite lovable. His twisted moustaches and the black Saleem Shahi slippers on his gentle feet were all familiar and benign expressions of him. He walked, wearing down the ancient carpet beneath his measured gait, 'What a comical sight it would make . . . to be sitting with the girls ordering pair upon pair of shoes for them to try on and then to have to strike a bargain with the shop owner, and to have to debate the merits of various types of shoes!' A smile touched his lips.

'Abba Mian,' she addressed him as she came near him.

'Yes, my child,' he bent low towards her. She looked tiny next to him.

'Abba Mian, please take us yourself to buy the shoes tomorrow.'

'But why, my child?'

'Because I want you to.'

'Splendid! You're wonderful. The trouble is your father is an absolute nincompoop in the matter of buying new shoes.'

'So now what's going to happen?' She became concerned.

'Why, my child? What is the problem?' He looked at her with mocking eyes.

'The problem is, Abba Mian,' she decided to come clean about it, 'I'm asking you because if I ask Ammah Begum she'll get cross with me.'

'What do you need to ask Ammah Begum then?'

'Er . . . Abba Mian! Masood's shoes are so rotten. Really rubbish. All the kids laugh at him.'

'Which Masood?'

'Hashmi Apa's son.'

'Apa? She's not a sister to you, she is your aunt.'

'Doesn't matter. I'm talking about Masood. Salman said to him yesterday, "You look like the son of a cook!" And Masood hit him really hard. Then I said to Masood, "*Bhai*, you should get some new shoes." But he said that he has only one pair of shoes and he got annoyed with me. Now if you come, you can get him a new pair of shoes as well.'

He stopped in the middle of his walk and sat down on a chair.

'Gaythi, come here. Come near me.'

She came near to him looking serious. He took both her small, plump hands in his own large ones and looked into her eyes, thinking, What a generous and sensitive heart she has, this daughter of mine who looks so Chinese! He considered her simple, almost plain features. How beautiful they were, how peaceful and content! Then he kissed both her hands and touched them with his eyes, saying, 'Gaythi, shall I tell you something?'

'Tell me,' she said with interest.

'You are the most beautiful of all my children.'

'Are you laughing at me?' she burst into laughter herself.

'I am telling the truth.'

'OK, Abba Mian! Now about the shoes?'

'I'll tell you in the morning. Now you'd better go to sleep, or else . . .' He looked at her with a smile.

'Or else Ammah Begum will beat me.' Her eyes glittered and she ran out of the room.

Gaythi was right, he thought again, and then said to Sheharyaar, 'When you go, take Masood with you as well.'

'What for?'

'He also needs new shoes. Hashmi Begum gave me some money last night for a new pair for him. Here it is. It's the price of a pair of shoes and a pair of slippers.' Then he turned to the newspaper again.

Sheharyaar stood near his chair. 'Abba jaan.'

'Yes,' he glanced up from his newspaper. 'Did you want to say something to me?'

'Er . . . Abba Mian,' and then he spoke quickly, 'I also want to order a pair of shoes.'

'OK then, do it, and speak to your mother about the money for the girls' shoes and yours.' He turned his attention to the paper again.

'The thing is Abba Mian, that Ammah Begum will say, "Why are you ordering shoes now?" She has just sent me a pair she ordered last month.'

'Then you really don't need them, do you?'

'I would like a new pair for shooting.'

'OK then, you order them. Put them on my account.'

Father and son looked at each other, their eyes shone with a conspiratorial glow. When Sheharyaar had left the room the thought struck him, quite unprompted, 'Why is it that my children and I plot against Begum all the time?'

Sheharyaar made a sign to call Masood and told him to go and sit quietly in the car, so none of the other children would know.

'Why, where do we have to go?'

'Just go and sit there. I'll call Arjumand and Cheeni.'

'Are you coming, Fatty Khan?' He wrung Gaythi's neck playfully.

'Where to, Barrey Bhaiya?'

'To eat shoes?'

'Hum . . . Go away!'

'Do you want an ice cream or don't you want that either?'

'Yes, of course I do.'

'Then come.'

'Shall I call Masood?' Gaythi suggested.

'What does he want to go for?' Sheharyaar said with a dry look.

When she got into the car she saw that Masood was already sitting there and she muzzled his hair with delight.

'You witch,' he gritted his teeth and pulled her hair.

'Oh, God! You've crushed my hand,' Arjumand was bewildered at their fighting.

'*Yaar*, Masood. What's all this fuss? You're older, you should let her off.' Sheharyaar laughed.

When they stopped in front of the Chinese shop, Arjumand commented innocently, 'Bhaiya, this is a shoe shop.'

'So what? Why don't you eat shoes instead of an ice cream?'

He took the three of them into the shop. Sang was in the shoe room alone. Someone was working on the machine inside.

Sheharyaar ordered shoes for Masood and both the girls. Masood was startled, 'Who? For me? I'm not buying new shoes.'

'Then don't. Your mother gave the money to Abba Mian and asked him to get you new shoes. I'll return it to her.'

'When?' Masood asked incredulously.

'Last night.'

Masood agreed to buy new shoes and chose a pair and so did Arjumand, who quickly fell for a pair of brown ones, but Gaythi could not make up her mind. She flitted from brown to black, with one eye on

41

the pair which was multi-coloured. A part of her wanted the red pair. Sang got quite tired of fetching and carrying. Finally only those shoes which were in the workshop remained to be seen.

He called out to someone, 'Liu Chu,' and then he said something in Chinese.

After a brief episode of rattling, Liu Chu emerged carrying before him a tower of a dozen or so boxes of shoes.

'*Arrey*! So he works here as well? Are you a shoe wallah too?' Gaythi began talking nonsense.

'Yes, Cuckoo. I am a shoe wallah too,' Liu Chu, who seemed a bit taller than the majority of his compatriots, sat down on his haunches on the straw mat near her to slip a shoe on her foot. 'I could hear you in there, you were being really difficult,' he said.

'You are Liu Chu. Do you eat mice?'

'Don't be silly,' Sheharyaar felt obliged to scold her.

'Let her go on. That's how she talks.'

'It seems you two know each other.'

'I bring Chinese handicrafts to your house.'

Sheharyaar thought this boy spoke clearer and more fluent English than most ordinary Chinese shopkeepers.

'Barrey Bhaiya, when I was in hospital he used to come every day and make me laugh. He is a real monkey, an apish monkey.' Gaythi stuck her tongue out at Liu Chu.

'Stop talking nonsense and pick your shoes.'

She started fussing again.

'That's quite enough. This one's fine. Now don't take it off. After all we can't get you Cinderella's shoes.' Gaythi bowed her head and accepted Liu Chu's advice.

Sang had taken his seat by the counter and was behaving like a typical Chinese salesman, quoting inflated prices. Sheharyaar, who knew the game too, started arguing with him. He did not usually bargain with shopkeepers but he enjoyed haggling with Chinese salesmen, relishing their irritated and argumentative broken English. Exactly the same thing happened that day too.

Sang went off to sit in the workshop, grumbling and annoyed, declaring that he would not reduce the price by a single paisa, that Sheharyaar should leave the shoes. Sheharyaar followed him, smiling, and started the debate again. He pulled out his cigarette case, took one and offered one to Sang. As soon as Sang had accepted the cigarette he dropped the price by four rupees, but the negotiations continued. Suddenly Sheharyaar's gaze fell on the easel which stood in a corner, hung with an incomplete painting and he asked Sang, 'Do you make silk paintings here too?'

Sang, annoyed that his own problem remained unresolved, pointed towards Liu Chu and said, 'That is his folly.'

'May I have a look at it?' Sheharyaar said in a warm tone.

Masood and Arjumand stood outside but Gaythi had followed him in.

When Sang returned to the counter to write out the receipt, Liu Chu placed his painting before Sheharyaar who was gazing at it with silent, appreciative eyes. 'Do you sell them?'

'No. It's just a hobby.'

'Have you painted other things too?'

'Just a few. I don't really get time to indulge my enthusiasms,' Liu Chu's voice echoed the pain of unfulfilled desires.

'Mr Liu Chu, if I want to buy this incomplete painting from you when it is finished, what kind of price would you like to be paid for it?'

Liu Chu fell into deep thought. Sheharyaar felt that he was not prepared for such an offer and therefore looked quite shocked. He tried to speak, but there was a stutter in his voice and he could not decide what price to name.

Sheharyaar smiled, 'I am a student, name a price that I can pay.'

'It is still incomplete,' he evaded the question.

'So what? Finish it in a couple of days and let me have it. I'll come and get it whenever you say.'

Safdar did not want Sang to know about this so he spoke quickly, 'Give me your address and I will bring it round myself.'

'My address? Er . . . if you know her,' he pointed towards Gaythi, 'well, I am her brother.'

Both of them turned round towards her. She was busy examining something that stood on a table in the corner.

She looked at them and spoke, 'Barrey Bhaiya, please buy me this.'

'What is it?' Sheharyaar looked at the object which appeared to be a rubber toy.

'Look, how beautiful it is.' She was about to touch it.

'O, Baby, don't touch it. It is still all wet,' the Chinese man jumped tensely.

'Wet?' Sheharyaar asked in surprise.

'Yes. This is a dancer of the Chu period, and she's been made out of rice flour, kneaded into a dough.'

'Who's made it?'

'I have.'

Now Sheharyaar looked at it closely. Her hair was styled in the manner typical of Chinese dancers. She held an umbrella in one hand and a fan in the other. There were flowers in her hair. All the delicacy and refinement of each feature was real enough, but beyond that, her face carried the living and vibrant quality not only of her class but also of the period.

Sheharyaar's mind went blank, void of appropriate words of praise and admiration, as he thought to himself without uttering a single word, 'These ancient inheritors of the history of culture are still wonderful.'

'Won't you sell us this either?'

'That belongs to Sang. I have made it to his order. It is meant for an important European officer.'

But Gaythi continued to gaze at the doll with avaricious and tempted eyes.

'Don't worry, Cuckoo, I'll make you another one.'

'When?'

'Soon.'

'Will you really keep to your word?' Sheharyaar asked.

'The Chinese don't take their word lightly. Believe me, whatever happens, you will get both these things by the day after tomorrow. There is one thing, however; don't start looking out for me before eight o' clock in the evening. I work at this shop.'

When Sheharyaar left Sang's shop and went to sit in the car he was thinking about the Chinese race: 'Are these short people with their flat faces and slanting eyes giants in intellectual terms?' Then he thought, 'Why is it that as soon as we start thinking of China we also start thinking of opium? Who knows what they might have attained, if sucking pellets of opium or smoking it had not become their favourite pastime.'

Meanwhile Liu Chu, that is, Safdar Yaaseen, stood beside his incomplete painting. In his imagination he could see a woman with sad eyes, soft, rounded fingers and tapering wrists, handing him a paltry, lifeless ten rupee note, saying, 'Take this, the money for the toys. And listen, she also said to tell you that we will be taking her home shortly in the next two or three days. You don't need to trouble yourself any more.'

'You don't need to trouble yourself any more,' he smiled with contempt.

'I was wrong to promise this brother of Cuckoo's. I don't need to go to these arrogant people.'

Then a voice rang in his ears, 'The Chinese don't take their word lightly.'

'That's right, the Chinese don't take their word lightly!' He smiled and turned towards his machine for cutting leather.

*

44

It was the thirteenth night of the moon, damp and interesting. Sleep had already set up camp in the neighbouring bungalows. In that house, too, the older people had either dropped off to sleep or were busy finishing essential tasks. On the front lawn you could see a few beds laid out in the moonlight. The bedlinen shone brilliant white. At a slight distance from the beds a lot of young girls and boys sat on a squarish, large, low wooden divan. It was draped with a white sheet and a pale yellow carpet and yellow satin bolsters, against which leaned Saulat, dressed from head to foot in yellow. She wore a tawdry bracelet of silvery tinsel on her left wrist. She did not seem at all shy at that moment. There was a helpless, defeated smile on her face and a deep inner sadness in her eyes.

The girls were busy thumping the *dholak* tunelessly; they would start singing a line or two from a song and then dissolve into giggles. Sheharyaar reclined between Saulat and Ismat. His arm was around Saulat's waist but his eyes were absorbed in their worship of Ismat's fine featured and extremely rebellious face. He was teasing the girls and laughingly trying to persuade them to finish at least one song from beginning to end. But they were in the mood for giggling rather than singing. His oldest uncle's daughter who was called Mah Jabeen pulled the *dholak* towards herself and raised a few notes in a lovely voice.

> 'Blessed bridegroom, don't come to my house,
> There sits . . . er . . . who shall I say . . . ?'

Confusion ensued. 'Tell me whose name shall I take? Tell me who sits there?' No one remembered. So Mah Jabeen began again.

> 'There sits the guard, my love. . . !'

Sheharyaar slapped Mariam, his maternal aunt's daughter, on the back.

'You sound as if you are singing an English tune. Sitting there winding up the notes like a Mem Sahib.'

'Huh! For God's sake,' Mariam grumbled.

Ismat glanced at Sheharyaar. He had her uncle's physique, and the same handsome, swanky face. The top buttons on his milk white shirt, with its embroidered neckline, were undone and he looked really wonderful. He was gazing at her too.

'Barrey Bhaiya, do up all your buttons,' Ismat turned on him in her confusion.

'They'll get done up. You get on with your business,' Sheharyaar rebuked her. 'I say, what is the matter with your throats? Have you caught the damp air of the monsoons?'

'Come on, let's start,' Mah Jabeen displayed her readiness again.

45

'Blessed bridegroom, don't come to my gardens . . .'

'There's only one good buffo here,' Sheharyaar applauded Mah Jabeen.

'Waah! Are you in your right mind?' said Mah Jabeen, feeling offended. 'We're going to sing to our heart's content now. But we'll keep our lips sealed at your wedding. Will you sing at his wedding, Ismat?'

Sheharyaar spoke before Ismat could answer, 'You will sing. Ismat daren't sing. Let her try it. I'll cut her throat out and throw it away.'

'Where will you throw it?'

'Somewhere around here. OK, that's enough. Stop talking rubbish and start now.'

'Blessed bridegroom, don't come to my gardens . . .' the girls picked up the refrain again.

They heard a bicycle bell ring several times. 'It must be the telegram wallah,' the girls and Sheharyaar decided.

No one heard his heavy footsteps either. He advanced silently. Once he even thought about going back but Sheharyaar had already said something about the Chinese not keeping their promises. Anyhow, he was determined to deliver those things. He had seen Sheharyaar from a distance and proceeded without thinking.

'China Man, China Man,' he stopped short and called out in a quiet voice.

All the girls fell over Sheharyaar exclaiming, 'Oh!', 'Oh God!' or, 'Death!' with the exception of Saulat who had always been serious and poised. The other girls were mumbling in a panic, 'Who is he?' 'Is he a genie?' 'Oh God, what's going to happen now?'

All of a sudden, Sheharyaar remembered. He pushed all of them aside and got up. 'Someone comes, there is a rustle and all of you just die. It must be that Chinese boy.'

He went up to him. Liu Chu held the painting, which was wrapped round a fine wooden stick, and a delicate box in his hands.

'Well done! You kept your word. I was not really expecting it.'

Sheharyaar unwound the silk quickly. Those dim and sad lines painted with a very fine brush were not clearly visible in the moonlight.

'Have you decided on a price for this?' Sheharyaar was impressed inwardly but his face remained indifferent.

'Price?' Obsessed with keeping his word, he had, in fact, still not thought about it. Before he could think of a price, he remembered that there was to be a wedding in the house. That girl who was not happy with her marriage was going to be wed, the girl for whom he had written out a few verses as a homily. He started and said, 'There's no price for this.'

46

'Why not? Then I shall not accept it.'

'It is not for you. It is a wedding present for the bride. If you'll allow me I will write a few congratulatory words.'

'Certainly. Will you write them in your own language?'

'I'll write the translation too,' he said searching his pockets. Then he placed a piece of paper on the box and lit the torch and kept it before him. His pencil moved fast and expertly, forming the words in Chinese and then he wrote the brief text of the translation in English.

'Beautiful and young bride, these words from Lao Tzu's poem are also dedicated to you:

> "To know others is wise
> But to know the truth about yourself is the sign of an enlightened
>   conscience
> He who conquers human beings becomes the victor
> But he who conquers his material instincts
> Is the one who deserves to be called powerful and strong."'

He pinned the paper to the silk and offered the box to Sheharyaar. 'And this is Baby's dancer.'

'Oh!' Sheharyaar was fascinated by this young expatriate. He seemed quite different from the ordinary Chinese pedlars and shopkeepers.

'Come and give this present to the bride yourself, then. She is sitting here as well. The girls are singing wedding songs for her.'

He hesitated about going in front of that large group of strange, retiring girls, but in spite of that he advanced towards them.

'Go on, take it, Saulat. It is your first and perhaps the best wedding gift ,' Sheharyaar drew Saulat's attention to Safdar Yaaseen.

Saulat looked at him with a sad if somewhat imperious look in her eyes. A few months ago he had told her quite rudely, 'I would advise you to get your sister Gaythi married off to this Chiang Kai Shek.'

'What a rude man he is,' Saulat thought to herself. At that very moment his calm voice echoed in her ears.

> 'Whatever is ordained for me,
> I must endure, anyhow.'

That humble and young representative of Far Eastern civilisation knelt down to bow before the bride holding up the gift in both his hands. Ismat jumped up to switch on the light in the porch to see the painting.

The young artist looked at this bride dressed in pale yellow and thought, 'It seems as if someone has plucked the stars from the firmament and kneaded them into dough made with milk and rice flour to mould this bride.'

Without hearing a word of thanks he left in a flurry. The light was switched off and the *dholak* boomed again with a loud thud.

'I am a skein of silk, I am a gold star.'

This time the words were being sung seriously. The voices sounded melodious. No one knew why. It is possible that that melancholy and sorrowful painting had woken the spirit of the song in them.

Sheharyaar accompanied him to his bicycle. He stopped and asked hesitatingly, 'Can I ask you the meaning of these words. They sound very sweet.'

Sheharyaar repeated them gently, affectionately, in English, 'I am a skein of silk, I am a gold star.' And then, a little cross with himself, he said, 'You just cannot translate these words, they *are* very sweet indeed.'

The stars twinkling in the sky really did seem as if they had been folded into rice flour and milk, as if that rather bland Chinese boy had taken away with him the essence and the spirit of those sweet words.

'Your name is Liu Chu, isn't it?' Sheharyaar asked.

'My name is Safdar Yaaseen. Chinese Muslims have names which have two components; one is Chinese, and the other is Muslim.'

'I see. You must come again some time.'

'I'll try.'

What possible interest could Sheharyaar have had in his coming again or not? He went and sat amongst the bevy of girls once again.

'What song shall we sing now? What shall we sing?' the girls were asking each other.

'Ask Saulat,' Sheharyaar suggested.

'Tell us, go on tell us, Saulat Apa,' Ismat pestered her.

Saulat surveyed the scene. After finishing all her chores, Ammah Begum had come to lie down on a bed which lay at quite a distance from where they sat. She bent down to whisper into Ismat's ear, 'OK then, why don't you sing that song again which you often sing, the one about the old man?'

Ismat took over the *dholak* quickly and began to sing in her tuneless voice,

> 'I was doomed to marry an old man, oh, dear me
> All the others went shopping but he came along with me
> All the others bought cucumbers,
> But he bought a stick, oh, dear me. . .'

The girls and Sheharyaar fell about giggling. Ismat continued,

48

'All the others went hunting but he came along with me
All the others shot partridges,
But he shot a crow, oh, dear me.'

Sheharyaar laughed aloud.

'Have you gone mad? Where did you pick him up then?' Then he put on an awe-inspiring voice, 'I can hear all your nonsense.'

Ismat looked up from the *dholak* and her smiling eyes met his. Saulat glanced surreptitiously at her athletic young brother who was laughing. He sat very close to her with an arm around her waist and so did Ismat. She was looking at her brother, smiling, with very possessive and proprietorial eyes. Without reason Saulat began to suspect that she had intended to spite her and a bitter hatred for Ismat rose in her heart.

With a soft and gentle voice, Saulat's young and petite maternal cousin asked Ismat in English, 'Sing it once again, I've never heard songs like that before.'

Ismat started again without hesitation, 'I was doomed to marry an old man, oh, dear me.'

Ammah Begum, who had been lying on her bed, suddenly became restless. Saulat's head was bent low now. Drip, drip, two warm tears fell on Sheharyaar's hand. 'What's this, eh? Saulat Ara,' he embraced her lovingly.

Saulat sobbed silently, and Sheharyaar placed his other hand over Ismat's mouth, 'That's enough, stop it now.'

Ammah Begum glared at him instantly, 'Do you know what time it is? It is past eleven o'clock. And you are causing all this racket. You aren't still so young as to not know that there is only one more day to go. Stay up all night and you're sure to sleep all day. Your father and uncle will be busy hunting, of course.' She had omitted to mention her own brother and brother-in-law. 'Where's Bakhtiar?'

'Bakhtiar has a temperature. He's sleeping round the other side,' Ismat spoke up.

'What can I do, if he has a temperature?' Anmah Begum rounded upon her, 'You people won't reduce this noise. You can't even remember to ask your grandmother how she is, or offer to help with the work,' she said, notwithstanding the fact that Ismat had spent the whole day helping to iron, fold and tack for presentation all the clothes for the bride's trousseau. The other girls flitted away suddenly like a flock of birds. Only Saulat, Ismat and Sheharyaar remained. Ammah Begum stared at Saulat and then spoke gently, 'Why are you looking like this? Now don't you go exhausting yourself that much.'

Quiet and absolutely calm, she rose slowly. As she slipped her foot into the soft, velvety shoe, she thought, 'I was right to make her hear the words of that song. But why did she mind it so much?'

Ismat had gone. Sheharyaar followed Ammah Begum, his head hanging low.

Saulat laughed to herself. 'What will Chiang Kai Shek look like, sitting next to Ammah Begum, I wonder?'

When she put her other foot down on the ground someone grabbed it. Any other girl in that situation would have screamed. She was absolutely alone. But she remained calm and bent down to see who it was. Gaythi lay on the grass, under the low wooden stool, holding her foot.

'What is it?' She stooped to drag her out.

'Give me my doll.'

'What doll?'

'The one China Man gave you.'

'Where were you?'

'I was here.'

'Why?'

'Listening to the singing.'

If she had done this at bedtime on any other occasion she would have twisted her ears and dragged her before Ammah Begum. But something new occurred to her now.

'That's all right. This is how girls should be. If they don't break the rules and codes when they're children they end up having to marry Chiang Kai Sheks.'

She went to her room and opened the piece of paper clasped in her fist. 'So what's the advice Confucius has to offer today?' she thought sarcastically. For some reason bitterness and contempt were fighting for dominance in her personality. She read quickly:

'"To know others is wise
But to know the truth about yourself is the sign of an enlightened
    conscience
He who conquers human beings becomes the victor
But he who conquers his material instincts
Is the one who deserves to be called powerful and strong."'

She repeated the words to herself.

'You are mad, Safdar Yaaseen,' she smiled with contempt.

And that night, as he lay in his bed, Safdar felt something akin to loneliness. After a very long time he had seen the members of a household

50

and a family laughing and enjoying themselves. His heart was also longing to be reunited with his own family, with all the members of his own household.

When she was leaving her father's house she felt as if that day she were leaving her old self behind with that house. Now, Begum Saulat Asif Jah's link with that quiet, reserved, sensible and extremely sensitive girl, who was known to the world as Saulat Jehangir, was finally broken.

'And now ... O wild heart, the manner of your life shall be this...' she thought, as she climbed into the car decorated with jasmine and sat calmly by the side of her Chiang Kai Shek. She was perfectly at peace. She had tidied and arranged her hair and put on some light make-up by herself.

She looked like a houri in her pearly silk sari. Before leaving her room she had locked her wardrobes with her own hands and had removed the sadly smiling photograph from the frame which stood on the table and placed it on the bottom shelf of her wardrobe along with some of her old shoes.

As soon as the car crawled out of the gates she swung round to look back. In the dead centre of the beautiful garden of her house she saw flames leap up to consume her innocence and her girlhood. She could see countless spectres of relationships, memories and dreams as they crowded into heaps offering themselves to those flames in silent funeral pyres. In the heart of those leaping tongues of flames she could see the steady person of Zubair, smiling sadly too. At the rear of that caravan, the last image she could see was of that Chinese boy, Safdar Yaaseen. He was descending from the heights slowly, in a posture of surrender, his face happy and his eyes peaceful, both his hands holding out a piece of paper which said, 'But to know the truth about yourself is the sign of an enlightened conscience.'

She calmly watched the beautiful and stupid world of her maidenhood burning in those flames and then looked away. It was a pleasant evening; the streets which had been freshly sprinkled with water emanated a gentle fragrance. Chiang Kai Shek heaved a sigh of relief and lit a *Three Castles* cigarette. He always smoked those. Saulat found the smell intoxicating and hypnotic. Of her own volition she leaned her lovely forehead against his broad and strong shoulder. Ammah Begum's insistence or instructions had nothing at all to do with this action of hers.

At that exact moment in time as he sat in his office, Zubair raised his head with a start. He lifted his left wrist and looked at the time and then

51

bent over his incomplete editorial once again. These days he was working a double shift, which made him extremely tired.

13

After Saulat's departure the house began to empty of guests too. The first to leave were Ammah Begum's sister, brother, and sister-in-law. Next it was Mr Shehzad's family. Hashmi Begum had been eager to leave since the day after the bride had been sent off. Every time the car was being loaded she would insist that all she needed was a lift to the station, she could board the train herself. After all Anand Pur was not very far. But Jehangir Mirza would reassure her each time, 'Why do you worry? Just stay for today, tomorrow morning I will have the car drop you off.'

His mother too could only rest in her own space and was eager to leave for that reason. They also felt that Ismat was missing her college. This time, however, Ismat insisted on taking her mother with her when it was time to leave.

'All right. I shall come too,' said Chachi jaan, gathering together her scattered belongings with a huffed look. Then she sat down near her mother-in-law on the wooden stool and said, 'Should I wrap your *paans* in a napkin? Look, Ammah Jaan, you are my witness. I have not retaliated against anything. But I did not expect this of my sister-in-law, Bhabi.'

'Since you have taken it all so well so far, you may as well keep quiet for a little while longer. Bibi, I was never for it, but I held my tongue because I thought you might think I am opposed to it. My dear, as far as I am concerned, there's nothing to choose between the two of them.'

The moment she had heard from her mother that they were leaving, Ismat had started packing furiously. Neither Ismat nor Sheharyaar knew about the little skirmish which had occurred in the room at the centre of the house the day after Saulat had left. But Ismat was certainly aware that on this visit her aunt, Barri Ammah, had seemed annoyed with her without any reason. She kept criticising everything she did and feeling irritated with her on the slightest provocation. She had tried very sincerely to help with the wedding arrangements but instead of praise she only heard the complaint, 'Just look at that, Ismat couldn't even manage this little thing . . .'

52

Besides, she kept scolding Sheharyaar, 'Why should you worry about anything? You're too busy fooling around.'

When he sprayed dyes on to the clothes of his maternal cousins Azra and Mah Jabeen during the ritual game with colours, she did not utter a word of complaint. But as soon as he sprayed Ismat with the colours, she became irate, 'Come on, stop it now, Sheharyaar. I don't like this monkeying around. Go now, go outside and get the chairs arranged on the lawn.'

That was all she knew. She did not know that her mother had had a lecture from Barri Ammah's mother before the latter had departed from the house: 'Bibi, what are you planning to do? You should be worrying about Ismat now as well. Even the girls who have fathers, God protect them, can't be left waiting around for too long. And there you are, letting your daughter become a lawyer, or a barrister.'

She thought that this was perhaps the prologue to Sheharyaar's proposal for Ismat's hand and said, laughingly, 'I am worried but I don't have any sons. She can at least graduate.'

'Enough, I say, there isn't the time for that.' Bhabi's sister-in-law's expression clearly said something else. 'The moment you see a boy who's reasonable and suited to your status you should finalise things immediately.'

'Yes, that is a point,' she said absently with a sinking heart, 'if only I could find someone like that.'

'There are plenty of boys,' Sheharyaar's maternal aunt elaborated in a conciliatory and innocent manner. Then, because she sat very close to her she started whispering into her ear, singing praises about the virtues and brilliance of a young man who worked in her husband's firm. 'At the moment he earns two hundred rupees. He intends to do his BA. When he qualifies his grade will improve. And I think that the greatest thing is that he is all alone.' She emphasised his aloneness. 'He'll do whatever we ask him to do. Your brother is really fond of him.'

Then she said in a loud voice, 'You think about it. If you give me an answer by this evening I can get it all fixed up as soon as I get back. These days no one passes up a good match.'

'Arrey bhai, that's why we said "yes" to the offer we got,' Barri Ammah said with her eyebrows arched, 'the thing is, what is so special about our girl that should have made us hesitate (although Saulat was much prettier than Ismat)? And then, we didn't have only one daughter to think of, we have to think of all of them. This year we have to send Sheharyaar to England too. If God sees us through the next five years then we'll have his marriage to arrange.'

'May God fulfil your hopes with His blessings. But I will say this, don't get the boy engaged to anyone until he returns,' her mother intervened, 'a boy who is earning can find a match of a totally different calibre.'

Ismat's mother felt as if her sister-in-law's mother's mouth were the tip of a volcano pouring forth boiling lava and brimstone, which hissed and whistled round her ears raining a deadly fire on the green fields of her most cherished hopes and wishes. But when lava comes to the boil, it really does boil. She grasped her hand and continued, 'To tell you the honest truth, my daughter, I don't really approve of marriages between first cousins. You should also understand this. Times have changed now.'

'You don't need to tell me these things, I understand everything myself,' she had retorted, as she left the room.

'Did you ever hear anything like this before now? I was surrounded by the enemy, like Imam Hussain himself.' She narrated the whole episode secretly to her mother-in-law, her lips dry and parched.

Bhabi's sister-in-law had noticed her reddened eyes and said, 'Why are you grieving, there's no dearth of good boys for nice girls. Why don't you consult your mother-in-law and I will speak to that boy as soon as I get back.'

'No Bibi. There's no need for any advice. She is just being silly. It will happen when and wherever fate intends. She is not short of boys. There's no shortage of boys within the family,' her mother-in-law spoke up for her, somewhat astringently.

'People in the family all go for status. They undervalue girls for no good reason,' Sheharyaar's maternal aunt rubbed it in.

'We *ourselves* don't care for the ones who do. You shouldn't worry; Ismat isn't short of proposals. Whoever told you that . . . ?' she laughed to underline her point.

Whilst this battle was being fought inside, Sheharyaar was on the verandah outside, shaking Ismat by the shoulders, 'Do you see the final destiny of girls, Ismat Ara? You should also watch where you're headed. You can finish your studies now, and start learning housework. No more college for you.'

'Who are you to say that? Why should I stop going to college? I want to do my BA.'

'There's no need, I don't care for very highly educated, highly mannered girls.'

'Who cares for what you like?' she laughed.

'Just look at me and say that again.'

And she ran indoors laughing.

14

The clock struck five somewhere in the distance. It was a damp and quiet evening in the middle of November. She opened the bathroom door gently, looked around and slipped out quietly to come and sit on the bathroom steps. The vegetable beds and the broad bean vines wrapped round a bamboo trellis were right in front of her. To the left of the steps was the basin where the dirty water drained. It brimmed with the unclean water crowned with algae, on the surface of which foamed a fine layer of soap, like cream frothing on top of the milk, a greenish-white creased skin.

She wished she could slowly scoop up that layer of cream in an earthenware bowl, so she could sell it . . . but . . . in a flash her attention was diverted by the cawing of the crows heading for their nests. Black crows, which hovered round the peaks of the trees, mossy green against the blue of the sky.

'I wish I had been a crow, I would have had fun. I suppose the question never even arose of my becoming an eagle.'

She deeply admired the flight of an eagle. She would lie on the rooftop for hours watching with longing the eagles soar to great heights. They appeared to be almost swimming in the air rather than flying, as if they were floating along with the current.

'What a shame that one is not destined even to be a crow,' she thought miserably, and immediately another thought stirred in her head, 'God only knows where Ammah Begum picks all those oddball patterns for knitting sweaters. If only she would listen to me, I would design one. It would be blue all over with a green border and would have row upon row of tiny black crows all over the front. But who would dare ask her for anything? She'd start getting cross, or pretend she'd never heard it. Huh! She'll never listen to anything at all.'

The memory of the dirty water crowned with a fine layer of soap, like cream frothing on top of the milk, popped up in her head unbidden. 'It could be sold as cream scooped up in earthenware bowls. But who would buy it? If I were even to mention to Arjumand the idea of selling the stuff she would be petrified, as if one were expecting her to eat it as cream. And Masood is gone now too. That wretched Hashmi Apa wouldn't leave without him. How Abba Mian and Ammah Begum begged them to stay, but she left after just two months. Two months is hardly any time at all. So many plans and schemes were left unfinished.'

Around the back of the house, in a corner of the vegetable garden, they had started digging up a tiny well together. The fortress they were building along the wall of the kitchen had also been left incomplete. The play about Hatim Tai which they had planned to stage could not be performed either because they could only rehearse it the one time. She was to be the old woman in it, Masood was the old woodcutter and Chunna was to play Hatim Tai. And Arjumand Begum had refused to accept a role of a status lower than that of a king, even in a play.

'Bhai, Masood's departure has left life a little incomplete. But there is one thing, Masood used to fight ever such a lot. Well, never mind. Yes, well, the crows. They've got to be put on to something. Never mind. I'll ask Liu Chu to make me a kimono which is green and blue and which has black crows all the way down the front. The trouble is that that wretched Liu Chu won't listen to me either. He laughs at everything. He'll never call me Gaythi. Goes on with his refrain of, "Cuckoo, Cuckoo," and sometimes, he may even call me a cat. He says I eat mice. When did I ever do that?' she reflected, and then looked at the dirty water in the basin again. 'What if someone sees me sitting by this filthy basin? I shall be in big trouble.'

'Come away! Playing with dirty water?'

'Why shouldn't I play? I am going to play with it!' She retaliated aloud against the imagined rebuke and picked up a stick that was lying near her, stuck it in the water and began to churn it around as if it were milk.

The filthy soap-ridden water splashed out all around the basin and a pleasant whiff of damp earth reached her nostrils. That smell always overpowered her. Involuntarily, she prostrated herself on the moist ground, and began to sniff the soil.

Mali, who was watering the beds of sweetpeas, thought to himself, 'This Bibi really loves the earth.'

It was supposed to be Gaythi and Arjumand's study hour. Thump, a great big fist landed on her back, 'You wretch!'

She turned round stung. Ammah Begum was staring at her with murderous eyes. Her punishment was to stay in bed for that whole evening. It was good that that wretched Masood had already gone. He always teased her when she got that punishment.

Masood's mother, Hashmi Begum, had to come to visit her in-laws in Anand Pur on several occasions. She had to stay there for months on end because of the court appearances necessitated by an ancient litigation battle over some property.

After having visited them at Saulat's wedding she made a point of coming to see them each time as well, and would stay for at least a month when she did. Masood would also come with her. No matter how long it was between visits he and Gaythi always felt as if he had never been away. As soon as he came they would take up their unfinished games again. And now Masood's interests had changed. For example, he had taken up an air gun and a sling shot, so Gaythi took these up too. She would even go with him for a swim in the little pond at the back.

Masood would catch butterflies for her butterfly collection. She would collect foreign stamps from letters for his stamp album and would try to impress him and rub it in for hours when she gave them to him.

'Sir, it's only I who can collect all these stamps for you. (As if collecting stamps were a life-threatening business!) Sir, I took this stamp off Barrey Bhaiya's letter.' She told him the history of the stamps which came from France. 'And this came from a letter which Mamoo sent from Singapore. And these ones were brought by Liu Chu from Hong Kong and Peking for me, respected Sir!' She would stress the 'respected'.

'Really! So does your Liu Chu still come regularly?' Masood would ask, casually gathering up the stock of stamps.

'So what else should he do, stop coming? He is such a wretch! I can't tell you how hard it is, Sir, to get those stamps out of him!'

'Huh, what nonsense you talk. Sir, indeed!'

'Why? So you should be grateful.'

'Grateful? Never!'

'Why? That doesn't make sense.'

'All right. Just hold your butterflies.' He would hand her a bag full of multicoloured butterflies.

'Oh! Sweet!' She would jump up at the sight of those colourful butterflies packed in the bag, 'Oh, Masood! So many butterflies! It must be very hard to catch so many of them,' she would say in English.

Masood was probably aware that his English was quite bad in comparison with Gaythi's so he never tried to speak it in front of her. He used to reply in Urdu, 'How I catch them has got nothing to do with you.' And he would turn his attention to something else.

16

It is always the same with children. Their families are always moaning that they do not pay any attention to their studies. At least if they grew up quickly they would be rid of their mischief and pointless tantrums. But this is how it goes: they may be quite different today from what they were yesterday. Before you know it they have changed quite dramatically.

That is what happened with Gaythi and Arjumand. Those three years that whizzed past could have been six. You could barely recognise them.

Arjumand had reached her Cambridge University O-levels, but Gaythi had lost interest and had failed the examination. She was not at all upset about having failed.

If someone taunted her with the failure she would retort rudely, 'Whether one fails or passes has nothing to do with anyone else. No one has the right to criticise someone for that. We study for ourselves, not for others who only know how to pick holes in things.'

Who could deal with a girl who was as ill-mannered and brazen as that? Arjumand was working extremely diligently, as if she owed someone a debt. Her conversation had acquired even more gentleness, and the element of innocence and amazement in her personality had redoubled by several degrees.

Gaythi would tease her. 'Arjumand, all you need is a pair of wings. It seems they clipped your wings before they sent you down from heaven.'

Although many things had changed in their lives, the routine and environment of the household was the same. As if no time had elapsed at all.

Mali was going round with a little trowel turning over the flowerbeds and pruning the trees just as he used to. Maalan, his wife, with her mahogany complexion and her tinkling ankle bells still went round with her veil stretched across her face and one of her little babies in her arms.

As always, the cook would still be standing next to the stove rapidly rolling out chappatis and arguing with Gaythi who used to creep into the kitchen at the first opportunity and ruin the dough and the flour in her unsuccessful attempts at rolling them out.

Even China Man still came occasionally, with his bulky bundle tied on his bicycle, calling out, 'China Man, China Man.' But these visits became rarer. Sang had put on a lot of weight. His ankles and heels appeared to be frilled with the flesh that overhung from his calves and his paunch protruded even more shiny and globular than before. Most of the time Safdar had to stay in the shop because of Sang's poor health. But Sang, concerned that Safdar Yaaseen might forget his place if he were allowed to manage the shop all the time, from time to time would send him on his sales round on Sundays.

Whenever he went out on a round he would go to their house without any real reason. He still found that girl with the Chinese features interesting. Most of the time he would find her, absorbed in reading, perched on the same garden wall at the back, her feet dangling. As he passed by the house during winter afternoons, or summer evenings, his bicycle would come to a stop near that wall.

It was strange. He went from house to house, but this was the only house to which he came without volition, almost unable to restrain himself. As soon as he reached those streets his heart would long desperately to go there as if it were yearning to return to his own home. What connection could there be between this house and his own? This was a large, well-off household which had never known even a hint of poverty or deprivation. The lady of the house was dignified and fortunate. The children of the house were happy and self-absorbed.

Whereas his home was in one of the darkest and narrowest alleyways in Peking. It had a small backyard and tiny rooms. There were no luxuries in that house. The slim teacher who belonged to an ancient religious order could not dream of luxuries. Abundance and wealth had never visited that household. In spite of this huge class difference, as soon as he saw the gates of Gaythi's house, Safdar Liu Chu felt he was close to his own home and could not possibly return without visiting it.

There could only be one reason for that, he decided. The only reason for this sense of belonging was the presence of a very familiar and dear Chinese face; the face of someone whose nature smelt of poverty rather than power, who, contrary to the traditions of the rich, was given to a friendly informality and was in the habit of giving her attention to all and sundry. Perhaps it was because of this strong and powerful feeling that his bicycle would crawl up to that back wall and come to a halt near it. He would jump off it, and say, 'Hello, Cuckoo.'

And Cuckoo would shut her book and smile immediately, with a mixture of indifference and affection.

'Hello! What've you got?' She would remain seated astride the wall and Liu Chu would sit at its base, leaning against it, his feet spread out before him, talking nonsense.

'What are you doing, Cuckoo?' he would ask.

'Are you really a Chinese doll ? I suppose those are buttons and not eyes? Can't you see what I'm doing?'

'Cuckoo, is there a mirror in your house?'

'Why? What a crazy question!'

'Have you ever looked in a mirror?'

'What have you eaten today, a frog or a mouse?'

'You eat mice.'

'Why should I? Ugh! God save us . . .'

'Ugh!' he would imitate her, 'God save us. Why should I eat them? Am I not a Muslim?'

'Who do you think you are?' She would always deny him that.

'I swear by God. I am the son of a renowned teacher. I have Arab blood in my veins.'

'Go away, you liar! Arab blood.' She would pull a face.

'I'm telling you the truth. My sister doesn't look Chinese at all. She's not flat-nosed and beady-eyed like you. She is taller than you, her complexion is golden and her nose is quite high.'

'Maybe it is. Say the *kalima*, then.' He would recite the first prayer of the Muslim faith in a perfect accent.

'All right! We'll believe you if you can recite the Chapter entitled Rehman.'

He would intone the prayer very melodiously and then feel overcome with the power of his own recitation.

'You are so cunning! Where did you learn all that?'

'There are schools and colleges for Muslims in Peking where pupils learn to recite the Quran.'

'You couldn't have been to college?'

'Why not? Why ever not? If my father had not died do you think I would have come to this country of yours to wander the roads?' His yellowish-gold skin would be darkened by a shadow, and noticing the sadness on his face she would change the subject.

'Would you like some peanuts, Liu Chu?' she would rummage in her coat pockets.

'Yes, Cuckoo. Will you have some chocolate?'

'Someone your size going round eating chocolates! Aren't you ashamed of yourself?'

'A girl your size sitting on a wall? Aren't you ashamed of yourself?'

For the past three years they had talked in this manner. Often a few months would pass when they did not see each other but neither of them used to miss the exchanges.

17

He sat in the shop working on the accounts. Chi, the little golden-haired poodle, lay curled at his feet. Startled by the sound of familiar, heavy footsteps, he put his pen down and looked up. Gaythi stood by the showcase looking at the shoes.

He rose like an attentive salesman and came to stand beside her.

She turned round and said, 'Hello,' carelessly.

'Oh, you're by yourself today. So you've grown up a bit, perhaps.'

'I came on my bike today. I badly needed a new pair of shoes. Look, this old pair is completely worn out now. But I couldn't ask anyone at home to come along.' Then she said to him confidentially, 'Maybe you don't know. I failed my exam you see. So everyone is annoyed with me.'

'That was inevitable. What else did you expect, reading all those stories and tales during your exams? But why did you come out alone? You could have come another day.'

'No, I couldn't. Arjumand and I are leaving for my father's family home on tomorrow night's train.'

'Where's that?'

'What does it matter to you? You always say that you're not interested in the names of our cities. They're all just cities to you, big ones, small ones and even smaller ones. So tell me. What's the name of this city?' She started poking fun at him, as always.

'Forget it. How do I know? All I know is that all big cities are the same, whether they are in China, in Italy or in India,' he said with great self-assurance. 'I'm telling you the truth: you get the same toffee-nosed and arrogant Begums, the same hen-pecked husbands, the same half-dead clerks, the same wicked, paunchy shopkeepers, the same starved, semi-naked labourers, swarming beggars, stray dogs and children, and you get the same patients writhing restlessly in hospitals and evil blood-thirsty doctors ready to suck their last drop of blood.' Talking in that vein, he sounded more like a mad philosopher than a shoe salesman.

'Stop it, and be quiet now, Confucius! Show me some shoes.' She changed into a formal, respectable client, sat down in the chair with a thud and very crisply demanded to see shoes of various designs.

61

She was dressed in a light blue, short-sleeved shirt with a tennis collar, and a white silk shalwar. A white scarf was slung carelessly round her shoulders.

'It is strange, how I have never observed the lines and curves of this girl's body until today,' he thought. 'What I notice about her is her face, which dominates her entire person. Absolutely plain, with a flat nose and almond-shaped eyes. Smiling lips which are full, rounded and glow red like cherries with her golden young blood. Friendly and eloquent eyes which do not let the beholder's eye stray in any other direction.'

As was her wont, she criticised heavily, and negotiated intensely before she bought a pair of shoes and left the shop.

'She is really mean,' he thought putting away the money in the cash box.

The next evening Gaythi and Arjumand left for their grandmother's house to spend their holidays with her in a city which she did not name to Safdar, nor did he want to know its name. Truly, what's in a name?

18

This time she found her paternal family home very interesting: courtyard upon courtyard, alcoves along the sides of the courtyards, arched doorways and octagonal pillars and the so-called 'royal' raised platform seat outside the main window of the house. A large inner courtyard was surrounded by tastefully arranged varieties of jasmine and kaani. A sizeable square in the southern corner of the courtyard had been planted with moulsari, queen of the night and weeping nyctanthes – all these features were fascinating and absorbing for her – as if they composed a Middle Eastern dream, in which she had lost herself.

They seldom visited this family home and never stayed more than a few days. On earlier occasions she had been too young and at a stage in her life when she was completely unaware, unable to reflect on things and form opinions about them.. But, this time, she observed this house and its traditions very carefully and with great enthusiasm, as if she were visiting for the first time. There was a sense of a collective in the lifestyle of this home. The selfish god of individualism had not yet crossed its threshold. In a manner of speaking, Dadi Ammah was the ruler and owner of the house. She would come and occupy her 'royal' platform seat outside the window after she had finished her morning prayers, and sitting out there she would say all the rest of her prayers and tell all her rosaries, running the entire household in between.

Both her sons had settled in far flung places and her daughter was married to someone who lived quite far away too. Her widowed daughter-in-law also spent most of her time elsewhere, even though both her daughters stayed permanently with their grandmother.

The rest of the house was occupied by distant maternal aunts, aunts by marriage and grandmothers. Various alcoves and courtyards were occupied variously, by the 'grandmother from the village', by 'the aunt from the area of the red coloured well'. The kinships with these occupants were so complex and so distant that some real experts found them hard to work out let alone Gaythi. Perhaps that was the reason why it was considered objectionable in that household to try to trace a relationship to its last and finest detail.

If she thought that someone was being too inquisitive and was asking too many questions about how people were related to her, Dadi Ammah would respond in a very authoritative manner, saying, 'Well, as I said, *Bibi*, she is a relation. When someone is related to you, there are no "whats" and "whys" about it. You can't compare the bonds which even a drop of blood makes to what might be tons of friendship.'

The truth is, in that house, the maintenance of appearances and old obligations mattered even more than kinships and blood relationships. At the far end of the courtyard there was a long verandah with a series of small alcoves opening on to it, which were full of women and children, who Dadi Ammah said were the families of their age-old servants and should be greeted each morning, just like all the other grandmothers and aunts who were kin.

One of those alcoves housed an almost crazy old lady who became suspicious and lost her temper with any or everyone at the slightest provocation. For instance, one day she decided that the young ladies of the family had rummaged through her bundle and had stolen and destroyed all her good luck charms. Then again, another day she alleged that someone had stolen the carefully preserved hair from her son's first shave which she had always kept in a tiny box in her trunk. She wept the whole day over the mere suspicion, claiming that she had accepted her son's death, he belonged to God and was only in her charge for a short while after all, but why should someone steal his hair which he had left in her charge?

Dadi Ammah insisted that she ought to be greeted every morning. She was the youngest daughter-in-law of their grandfather's nanny. Second in the pecking order was the wife of Amami. Her husband was their grandfather's favourite attendant. She was not really crazy but she was a firebrand. She was constantly on the look-out for little complaints against the girls or anyone else. She would tell Dadi Ammah tales about any trifle she considered worthy of reporting. Then there was Gaythi's grandfather's ayah's middle daughter, Sarwari, with her three children. Now that she was a widow, she had become Dadi Ammah's responsibility.

It seemed as if the house had been overrun by older women. The younger contingent were negligible in numerical terms. The only children in the house were Gaythi's young cousins, Talat and Ismat and Choti Nani's orphaned granddaughter, Kaamni, besides Sarwari's three children. This was perhaps why the house was peaceful, otherwise there would have been unending clashes between the older and the younger generations. Ismat and Talat were so devoted to their grandmother that it never occurred to them to do anything which might go against her wishes.

This house had an atmosphere of its own. Someone would be nursing her hip, and someone else would be complaining about a hiatus of flatulence. The politics of the household was not dissimilar. If the cream on Chachi Barri Begum's milk did not seem thick enough she would moan to everyone, 'Did you hear this, sister? Mehangoo's daughter-in-law is diluting the milk. There was the skimpiest membrane of cream on the milk today.'

The 'Grandmother from the village' would whine endlessly about Naseeban's inability to chop betel nuts properly. 'God save us, they feel like rocks rolling round in your mouth.' Whereas, poor Naseeban genuinely believed that she had cut them as fine as grains of millet. That absurd assertion would turn her face red with anger. And, Choti Nani would spend her entire day fuming about the fact that there were more people in the world whose work demonstrated a greater lack of correct manners than anything else.

This house, and everything about it, was new and interesting for Gaythi. Maybe it was the informality and egalitarianism of this household which had endeared it to her so much. Arjumand was not very happy there. To her the house felt strangely boxed-in and close. But, in spite of that, she had been kept amused because of Talat, Ismat and Chachi jaan. She had stayed mostly in their rooms. But Gaythi wandered all over the house with such familiarity as if she had lived there all her life. Each brick and every stone of the house had a legend attached to it. Countless stories, connected with her father, her uncle, her aunt and her grandfather were scattered in every corner of the house.

She took as much interest in the female relations who were guests and

64

their numerous children who came to visit her grandmother as Dadi Ammah herself. She would meet them with great warmth and enthusiasm, sit beside them, carefully memorise the exact nature of their relationship and then treat even their children with gracious hospitality.

And so, the days were slipping by, one by one, in this interesting house. It was early one morning, as Gaythi lay under the shade of the dense moulsari, on a small charpoy, reading a newspaper, when someone knocked on the door and said, 'May I come in?'

She laughed to herself, 'This is a nice way of doing it. People who come here call out to announce themselves, and people who come to our house ring the bell.'

The voice sounded sweet, sensible and familiar.

'Yes, Master, come in,' Naseeban, who sat amongst the roots of the weeping nyctanthes tree, sang out cheerfully.

Gaythi did not move but just lay there, facing the other way. Then she saw a tall and dark-skinned boy, who held a few notebooks in his hand, going towards Dadi Ammah. 'He looks so smart!' she thought to herself, admiring his back.

'Barri Begum wants you,' Shagoofa came and told her. She put down the newspaper and walked towards them trying to cover up her short hair under her skimpy little scarf.

19

'So that was you, Masood Mian,' she reflected, later that afternoon, sitting by the tatty. 'I had forgotten about you.

'But do you remember, you came to Anand Pur for several years, and you used to come to visit us? What good friends you and I were in those days. According to Ammah Begum you had completely ruined me; I'd become worthless.

'And you would beat me up for little things. And just now, first you refused to recognise me and then you looked at me closely and laughed, saying, "She is not the Mongolian, is she?"

'Well. Yes, that is as it should be. Actually, you are not to blame for this, Masood Khan. Your amber eyes are beautiful, your swarthy face is attractive and serious, but I! As you said, I am just a plain Mongolian with Chinese features. Damn Safdar Liu Chu.' She cursed Safdar Yaaseen without any reason, as if somehow he were to blame for her looks. 'He's given me an inferiority complex. I'm not at all surprised that you failed to recognise me!' Her dejected heart was unaccountably caving in to a sense of worthlessness, and in this depressed state she dropped off to sleep. When she woke up that evening, later than usual, she saw that Ismat, Talat and Kaamni were whispering to each other, and a great conspiracy was afoot. They were always conspiring on that scale. For instance, they would hatch a plot to prepare a spicy, sweet hash made with tamarind pulp, or plan to feast upon unripe green mangoes with salt and chillies.

'What is it? Tell me, for God's sake,' Gaythi asked inquisitively.

'Nothing. Hope you won't let the cat out of the bag,' Talat said.

'Waah! If she asks Dadi Ammah, we might get permission easily,' Ismat expressed her opinion as she whispered into her ear the news that Masood had got some passes to a poetry session at his college for his own mother, for Ismat, Talat, their mother, Kaamni and the others.

Gaythi did not know exactly what happens at a poetry session but she said at once, 'I'll come too.'

'We'll have to get Dadi Ammah's permission,' Talat rolled her eyes round craftily.

Gaythi's Chachi jaan arranged to have tea at Masood's house, and they planned to go to the poetry session straight from there. They needed permission for Gaythi and Arjumand to go with them. Arjumand had declined of her own accord, saying, 'Bhai, I won't go. And, what is this poetry evening anyway?'

But Gaythi was ready to go before anyone else. In that group, Kaamni was the only one who observed purdah. They travelled through narrow streets and alleyways on a *tonga* which eventually brought them to Masood's house, coming to a halt beside the narrow passageway.

Masood's spirits were dampened at the sight of Gaythi, and he wondered, 'Why have they brought her along? What is she going to say when she sees this tiny little house of ours? And then what, when she sees my rotten little state subsidised college? Her mother can't stand relatives like us. I remember how she behaved on the odd occasion when she was forced to visit us; she would sit with a cloth over her nose, as if she were sitting in the midst of a stench, and she has never allowed her girls to visit homes like ours. What a bore that Ismat and Talat should have dragged this wild girl along.' He felt put out with them.

It was, indeed, the first time that Gaythi had visited this tiny hen coop of a house. A miniscule courtyard, surrounded by steep walls of small bricks and a little verandah, with arches like lunettes and delicate octagonal pillars. There was an alcove along its side, which led, finally, into the single, wide but deeply buried room.

Dadi Ammah's house was old fashioned too, but it was extremely spacious and pleasant. For a while she kept wondering which portion of the house they were in, but then she realised that that was the entire house.

There were neither sofas nor chairs in that house, nor carpets. Its doors were without pleasantly coloured and styled curtains, but, in spite of that, there was something about that house. Something strange, mysterious and somnolent. The courtyard had been sprinkled with water and tidied. There were flowerbeds along the walls. In the corner at the northern end stood a small, low, wooden stool draped with a clean, printed cloth. Next to that was a wooden stand for the water pots, made of fragrant unfired clay, filled with water and covered with copper plates, highly polished and engraved. One end of the wooden divan was draped with a prayer mat and at the other end was a container for *paans* and all their required ingredients, as well as a plate for serving them, which held fresh jasmine buds and the *paans* wrapped in a neat piece of damp red cotton.

At a slight distance from this stool stood two bare charpoys and on these lay some square, colourful, and heavily patterned fans woven out of bamboo. They had all started chatting and laughing as soon as they entered the house, except Gaythi and Masood.

Masood was silent, piqued at the thought that Gaythi would be horrified and secretly shocked at their tiny home. And Gaythi was silent, almost as if she were stunned. For she felt as if she were a spectator to lost glories and magnificence which still appeared to be wandering, bereft, in this tiny home. Masood's mother Hashmi Begum was in the kitchen preparing tea for them since she knew of their visit. She called out to Gaythi's Chachi jaan from there, 'So you're here, sister-in-law? Your skirts must be heavy . . . it took you all this time to come out?'

'What can I do? These girls take ages to dress up. There's no end to their toiletries!'

Instead of replying to that she called out to Masood, 'Could you go out to pay the fare for the *tonga*, son. There's money in the *paan daan*.'

'What's this? You should give up this formality of paying the fare,' Chachi jaan said, entering the kitchen.

'Why should we give it up? You people are fashionable, but we follow the old rules, *bhai*.'

The girls would have followed Chachi jaan into the kitchen but Masood held them back because of Gaythi. 'Huh. They don't think of anything! Now they're dragging her into the kitchen.'

He was not the kind of boy who was ashamed of his own status, but, because of his regular visits to Gaythi's home, he knew very well her family's attitude towards people who were old fashioned and of limited means. And this realisation still remained with him, in spite of the time which had elapsed since.

All the girls sat down on the beds out there, dangling their feet. Masood teased Gaythi to escape his own panic and boredom.

'So, Gaythi! One can understand all of this lot going to this poetry session, but what are you going for?'

'Whatever they're all going for!' Gaythi had beaten him as far as she was concerned.

'They're all going to listen to the poetry.'

'So will I!'

'Do you know what a poetry session is? They'll be reading very difficult and abstruse verses. You won't be able to understand them. Tell me, can you read and write some Urdu?'

For the first time in her life Gaythi felt impoverished at her lack of Urdu, and though she spoke fluent English with great ease, she was even more discomfited and embarrassed than before. She retorted crossly, 'I didn't know that you didn't want me to come to your poetry event. But never mind. You people can drop me at home on your way out.'

Masood had not intended to hurt this innocent girl. He laughed, '*Arrey*! Since when did you start taking offence over jokes?'

Hashmi Begum came out of the kitchen bearing a teapot. The girls stood up when they saw her and greeted her. She blessed them and returned to her kitchen alcove and started bringing out the crockery and snacks from the meat-safe.

Kaamni followed her quickly, 'Let me take the crockery for you,' and she sat down to arrange everything on the tray. Gaythi saw her from a distance, a girl of delicate build, with a darkish complexion and pretty eyes which she kept lowered, who was arranging things for their tea like a hostess. Masood took the tray from her, brought it outside and placed it on the wooden stool.

She observed Masood for the second time that day. Dressed in a white lawn *kurta* and grubby pyjamas, his hair in a tangle, he was talking to the three girls intimately, about all those occasions and days which they had spent together and in which Gaythi did not feature, even remotely.

She felt out of place and estranged, even from Ismat and Talat. They all had similar complexions, they all seemed to blend well together, informal and relaxed. Whilst she, even though she was quite closely related to them, seemed a stranger – different from them in every way.

'*Arrey*, Kaamni, are you going to finish the savouries all by yourself?'

Masood grabbed the plate of guava savouries from her hand and Kaamni dropped her eyes a shade lower.

Gaythi felt overpowered. 'Why ever did I come here? He hadn't invited me and he didn't even recognise me this morning. After all, he is the owner of this small, scrubbed, polished and extremely civilised home. I had no right to come here without his permission. He is right to ignore me.'

Hashmi Begum had started talking to Chachi jaan after having inquired from Gaythi about the health of everyone in her family. Gaythi just sat there, feeling suffocated.

Masood went to fetch the *tongas* and when they were all getting into them he seated Gaythi in the one he was going to ride in himself. The wide roads and the damp evening breeze had ended that painful feeling and now he was merrily talking to Gaythi as well. He remembered too all those pranks they had played together.

'Oh, yes, Gaythi, whatever became of Safdar Liu Chu? He was so entertaining; and how good he was at mimicking animal noises!'

'Yes, he was! He still comes, sometimes.'

'Oh, hasn't he gone back yet?'

'No. He still calls me Cuckoo and he teases me just like he used to. And Ammah Begum scolds me sometimes that I am too free with him.'

She got carried away and started talking in English. Masood's accent was very good now and you could not tell that he had not been to an English middle school. She began to feel more comfortable. Before they knew it they had reached the marquee where the poetry session was to take place. No one was in purdah except for Kaamni and Masood's mother.

Masood teased Kaamni, 'Where does this pot of kohl come from? Come on, Kaamni, take off your cloak and give it to me.'

'Come on, stop it now. Don't be crazy,' Hashmi Begum levelled the veil on her cloak and scolded Masood as she moved closer to them.

Once again Gaythi felt intensely aware that Kaamni was very close to these people. The scorpion characteristic, concealed in her temperament, began to stir. The desire to grab someone and to possess them, which is typical of those who are born under the sign of the Scorpion.

20

Those narrow, winding alleyways seemed sad and dusty. But they were ancient and very mysterious. Poverty and decency resided there. They appeared to be the veins running through the very body of humanity. Veins bearing blood which was old, sluggish, and intoxicating. So somnolent that every one of them, totally absorbed in the present, lost in the maze of memories and indifferent to the future, was mesmerised into a crawl along an unknown and endless road, like a tortoise. Who knows where this road begins, and where it may lead to? This nameless journey of theirs continues from one generation to the next.

'Can life be so oppressed and petrified!' Gaythi marvelled, as she looked out through the bars in the window of Masood's room.

'This muezzin from the mosque, with his white beard and tired eyes, whose shoulders are bent and whose pyjamas do not reach below his ankles, as prescribed by the Shariah. And this water-carrier, who carries his heavy leather water-bag between his shoulder blades and his bent back; these women, shuffling around in large "shuttle-cock-style cloaks", and all the inhabitants who live behind these yellowish decaying walls, what sins could they have committed to have this retribution visit them?' Warm tears lapped in her tiny, slanting eyes, attempting to alleviate her pain.

Unbidden, a strange rebellious smile appeared on her pleasant face. 'And if Ammah Begum were to find out that I am here, she would raise hell. She would certainly be rude to Dadi Ammah too and would say to her, "What right did you have, old woman, to allow my daughter, raised in the lap of luxury, to endure this awful environment? To allow her to observe this life which I had never allowed her even to imagine".'

Just the thought of Ammah Begum's anger made her feel that every inch of her body was trapped in invisible chains; the powerful, golden chains of class and status. Every pore in her body cried out in pain. But never mind that now! She had been staying at Hashmi Phupho's house for the past two days, and was enjoying herself, as if she had lived there since the beginning of time.

She would lie down in the afternoons and pull the string of the manual fan suspended from the ceiling, tied to her big toe, with such expertise, as if she had never slept beneath an electric fan. In the afternoon, she would rise before Hashmi Phupho had woken up, to go and light the coals in the stove and boil the water for the tea. And then, quite early in the evening, she would lay a tablecloth on the clean, wooden stool and enjoy eating the hot and delicious dishes spiced with green chillies.

After staying in that house for two days she had forgotten the painful feeling that she did not belong with her relatives, her compatriots – the majority of human kind. The hurtful feeling of alienation and loneliness, the shameful sense of belonging to the tiny minority of the privileged had almost been erased.

These feelings, with which the land of her forefathers, with its narrow houses and alleyways, had rewarded her, were all new and unique for her.

Gaythi was intensely aware of the novelty of these thoughts and imaginings, as if she had been burdened with a very sacred trust. Her sense of her own importance had grown during those days in the same manner in which a woman who becomes a mother begins to feel more important and begins to value herself.

Why was this house and this environment so dear to her? She was willing to swear that Masood's person had nothing to do with it at all. Masood's personality was endearing, he was slightly arrogant and was independent almost to a painful degree. Certainly, all these things were enough to make him likeable, and indeed, lovable.

But Gaythi's attachment to this world and her fondness for it had nothing to do with Masood. She could have hated all that and still loved him. So far, she had been unable to decide whether she should form a meaningful relationship with this boy who studies at college all day, gives tuition during the evenings and, then, late at night, sits in his sad, comfortless room struggling with his books.

Actually, since the very first day, Gaythi had fallen for the silent atmosphere, the traditional ways, style and observances of the household. She visited the house several times after the poetry evening and then Hashmi Phupho invited her to a prayer meeting.

Gaythi's grandmother and Chachi jaan stayed there long after the other female guests had gone. They were all chatting when Hashmi Begum commented, 'These girls must think that their Phupho lives in a hen coop of a house!'

'Waah, that's not fair, Phupho! I do like your house. I'd really love to stay here for a few days,' Gaythi interjected.

'You are welcome to. It would be my pleasure, do stay. My house is not worthy of it, otherwise there's no way I would not have asked you to stay. If your Dadi Ammah would allow you to, you can both stay today.'

If anyone else had sought permission for them to stay, Dadi Ammah would not have allowed it under any circumstances. But she did not

71

object for fear of hurting Hashmi. Arjumand panicked at the very thought of staying in that tiny cramped house and when Dadi Ammah climbed into the *tonga* she got in quickly with her.

Later that evening Ramzani delivered clothes for Gaythi to wear for the night and for the next two days.

'Heavens, what a wretch Gaythi is! The way she just stayed on there. How annoyed her mother is going to be when she hears about it!' Dadi Ammah thought to herself. She was quite afraid of her daughter-in-law's quietly insolent manner.

Masood had always found something startling and exceptional in Gaythi's disposition. But he did not expect that she would be able to adjust to his modest lifestyle and blend into the household as if she had always lived there.

'She is a strangely impulsive and unconventional kind of girl!' Whenever he thought of Gaythi, he found her deeply interesting. But to find someone interesting is neither so exceptional nor so unusual as to make anyone in their right mind brood over it seriously. However, it did succeed in driving away the initial feelings he had had about his home and his status in Gaythi's presence. Watching her stay in his house without fuss or ceremony he forgot that there was a powerful class barrier between him and the girl. He completely lost sight of the fact that in spite of the same blood running in their veins, their paths were quite separate.

He would ask her casually, 'Gaythi, could you fetch me some water, please?'

'You're so lazy. Go and fetch it yourself.' She would refuse, conforming to old habits, and then hand him a cup of water almost immediately after that. When she sat by his mother chopping ginger, green chillies and coriander leaves for the curry, he would creep in beside her and say, 'Heaven forgive us, what a clumsy girl! Just see how crudely she's chopped all the spices!'

'So what? It's only got to go into the curry.' Gaythi would try to excuse her slovenliness as a housewife.

'Silly! You have to chop spices finely and delicately for the curry! Aren't these thick things going to float in the gravy like worms?'

'You are such a fusspot,' she would laugh.

'This is not fussing. It's princely taste.' Then he would say in the manner of older people, 'O you slovenly woman! You'd better learn all these things or you'll lose face before your in-laws.'

Embarrassed at the mention of in-laws she would drop the knife and say,

'Do you see what Masood is up to, Phupho?'

'He is silly. Go on now, you shouldn't be sitting here in the smoke.' She would suddenly remember that it was indeed a little unfair to make her sit in that heat.

She could probably have stayed a week without getting bored but Dadi Ammah sent for her on the third day. When she left, the house felt empty to Masood. In the past, when Kaamni and the other girls used to visit the house, the place would liven up for a while, and when they left it would feel quiet, but after Gaythi's departure he felt as if a permanent resident of the house had defected. Without her the house did not seem merely quiet, it actually became unendurable. He flung down his books in his room and stood brooding purposelessly in the alleyway for a very long time. There was a muddiness in the blue of the sky and the eagles were circling to a melancholy rhythm. The alley seemed quiet and stricken too.

When Gaythi returned to the crowded house with the platform seats it felt like a desolate wilderness to her. There was a deep sincerity and truth in every feeling of hers and this made her aware that the lantern dangling from the arch in Hashmi Phupho's house was more interesting than the bright electric lights here. There was an inexplicable restlessness within her. Sometimes she would sit down to help Bufatan Bua in her rummage through her bundles and at other times she would go and sit by the Village Grandmother, in her alcove, to listen to ancient stories. Occasionally, she would go over to Chachi jaan's part of the house to sleep there.

Alternatively, she would drag a small bed under the moulsari tree and lie down on it with a book.

'*Bhai*, I've had enough of a holiday now,' she decided after twenty days, feeling fed up. She lost interest in Ismat and Talat's company as well. Poor Kaamni seldom got away from her grandmother in the first place and then, she was quiet and preoccupied anyway.

'Dadi Ammah, please send us home now!' One morning she managed to utter what she had wanted to say.

'My dear, you came to stay for two months, and it is only a month since you arrived. Your father is due to come soon, why don't you go back with him? I am not going to keep you against your will,' Dadi Ammah replied, turning the key in her suitcase.

21

'This year it's hotter than usual everywhere,' he dropped the newspaper in his hands and spread out his feet on the low table before him. He was dressed only in a vest and khaki trousers. His broad chest seemed much lighter-skinned than his face which had burnt to a dark brown in the heat of the sun. His grubby white vest clung to his body in several places with the sweat which slid down his throat swishing steadily along its neckline. He bent his head and glanced down at his neck. A prominent black mole shone over his left collar-bone. Home and country all appeared to have forgotten him, but that inherited mole had accompanied him to this alien land.

His father had had a similar mole at exactly the same spot, and his father's uncle, who had adored his trips on opium, had had it too. His father, the dutiful nephew, would provide him with a shot of opium every morning and every night, no matter how difficult it was for him to do so. The addiction had reduced his uncle to a bag of bones, his chest had sunk inwards, his cheeks had contracted deep into his palate, his bloodshot sunken eyes would only stop watering for the length of time it took him to puff at the cigarette, whilst his father was constantly losing weight because of the incessant pressure of having to obtain those cigarettes for him. Besides that uncle, he had other relatives to support too.

'Aah! Those countless relations of the Chinese and their rights! Maybe it was a pleasurable duty in times of plenty and abundance, but now, sadly, in this age of terrible hunger and poverty, they have become just another one of life's tragedies!'

So, the relative with a mole on his collar-bone at exactly the same spot had become an incurable disease for his father. They all rode on his weak and bent shoulders like an unbearable weight. Whatever the circumstances, they continued to receive a bowl of rice, cabbage soup or some equally inexpensive dish, whilst his shoulders bent lower and his hair fell steadily, without his even noticing it.

'Oh, it's so hot,' Safdar Yaaseen began to fan himself with the clumsily crumpled newspaper. Except during their working hours, the employees were not allowed to use the electric fan in the shop. Li Yang and the other lads who worked there would nevertheless put it on whenever they got a chance to do so, on occasions when Sang was not around. But Safdar would never use the fan. He was not prepared to tolerate the obscenities Sang used for Li Yang and the other boys.

He dropped the newspaper on the floor once again, feeling extremely restless. That inherited mole had revived a lot of painful memories along with the memory of his father. How his father's health had declined and how his intelligent and self-respecting father gradually became irritable and ill-natured! Then he remembered his mother's quiet and faithful obedience and the hard work of both his sisters. Especially, those unfortunate days when his father had become obsessed with the idea that by talking, making speeches and through writing he had to convert as many people as he could to the view that the starvation and poverty of his nation stemmed from foreign domination and the desire of a handful of people to emulate foreigners and to achieve the same standard of living as them. Sometimes he would get carried away and as loudly as he could emit a painful wail from his starving and thirsty body and shout, 'For God's sake stem this foreign tide. Or, else *you* will come to an end and it will overtake you: this standard of living doused and drunk with wealth.'

All this took place when any such emotion or feeling was considered highly objectionable. Then, of course, one day it came to pass that a short, stout and crabby Police inspector knocked at the door of an old and decaying house. When that skinny, pale man with stooping shoulders stepped out, the inspector made a sign to his men and they clamped handcuffs on his wrists. Safdar remembered very well how he had looked that day. His tangled brush of a beard was motionless and his eyes were peaceful, unlike those of many of his countrymen.

His father, Yaaseen Liu, was released from prison several months later. In that time he had become a spectre, as if he were God's vengeance itself which had assumed a bodily form to visit the earth. A turbulent sea of hatred and contempt stormed in those hungry eyes. The contours of his face had deepened and then arched upwards with the intensity of grief, anger and the need to restrain his emotions. The depth of thought had converted the veins in his forehead into tangles. The tongue which had remained silent for months was now loosened so completely that the predictable happened.

The streets and alleyways of the inner city never saw Yaaseen Liu wandering around again. He simply disappeared off the face of the earth. No one knew what had become of him. But his wife knew very well that her lord and master, that carcass of bones, slept peacefully in the deep well which stood in the gardens behind the old mausoleum, along with several other learned men and sensitive students. He had worked extremely hard and endured many sorrows. Now he had been rewarded for those pains with eternal rest.

Then everything took on its own momentum. Safdar left college.

Dressed in a faded blue coat and trousers, he began to look for work until finally one day he boarded a ship, which was leaving Shanghai with a cargo of silk and rice for London, as a labourer. From there he had been brought to Karachi by a Chinese trader where he was snapped up by Sang who travelled around for two years to various places with him in tow, before coming to live in this place. Thus, Safdar's experience had widened considerably, even though he was still very young.

Now he earned enough from his work at Sang's shop and from various other jobs in his factory, quite apart from the money he made from his door-to-door selling, to be able to send a fairly tidy sum to his mother every two or three months. This sum, combined with the money earned by his mother and sisters through their own hard work, was sufficient to provide enough rice for their drowsy opium-dependent uncle and other relatives.

Whenever he thought of his family and his home, he also thought of the dark alleyways and the starving people of his homeland. Here, in this foreign country, watching life in the throes of the same distress and confusion, he would think, '*Arrey*! I'm not really alone or a stranger here. This is the same familiar environment and exactly the same life that I have always known. There is poverty, starvation and illness here, too. Here, too, there are people whose bodies are naked and whose hearts are shrines teeming with unfulfilled desires. Here, too, people spend years longing to eat the food they fancy, or to wear clothes which would impress the world. Here, too, there is another kind of life, which exists far away from the narrow and melancholy streets – that reserved for the rich and the privileged. A life where all the necessary comforts are within reach, where needs do not appear as vague desires but assume the shape of reality, where children are free of all anxieties about the present or the future and where girls are as carefree and happy as birds, like Cuckoo.'

The thought of Cuckoo was out of place in this context, but it was true that Cuckoo, whose real name was Gaythi Ara Begum, in her very person gave meaning to the words freedom and abandonment.

Safdar yawned and shut his half-closed eyes as he thought, 'She is also spending her holidays at the moment at her father's ancestral home. I wonder what that house is like!' Safdar Yaaseen Liu Chu, the young and unknown representative of Fa Hsien and Megasthenes' homeland felt inexplicably curious. 'Would that house have the same heavy carved wooden doors? Would it also be divided into passages and tiny court-yards? Do they also look after their relations and kinfolk? However their women are not all like Cuckoo, who looks so amazingly Chinese. They seem to have arched foreheads, wide and bright eyes.'

Irrepressibly, his heart yearned to peep into their houses. 'How do they live? Huh! It could be any old way! I'm certain Cuckoo and her family do not live in the same manner at all. Just as an outsider would not be able to appreciate real Chinese culture or lifestyle by observing any modern and rich family in China.'

He laughed to himself, 'Those times have gone when Fa Hsien, Megasthenes and Ibn-i-Batuta could gauge a society with great ease. Culture now falls simply into two categories. The culture of that class to which Gaythi Ara Begum Cuckoo belongs, and the culture of the inhabitants of the narrow houses which stand in the tiny alleyways, that is, those who belong to the same class as Safdar Yaaseen Li Chu.'

He laughed audibly in the midst of his thoughts and reflected quietly, 'Did you hear that, Cuckoo? There is a monotony and a monochromatic quality in this culture of yours, no matter what part of the world it might belong to! Whereas, there is a colourfulness and variety about mine. Every hungry and struggling being has his own style of living.

'Now, why should you wish to address all of this just to Cuckoo? After all, you go to countless homes like hers.' Safdar Yaaseen raised the question to himself and found the answer to it too. 'Maybe, because she is the kind of girl who appears to be very close to everyone she meets. When you see her your heart simply longs to tease her, to make her cry and even to confide in her without fear, when she is in the right mood. Because, she is one of those who does not give away someone else's secrets, who would not disclose that which they do not wish to, even if they were being tortured by the worst and cruellest oppressors.

'Yes, I speak the truth, Gaythi Ara Cuckoo, you are a very strange girl indeed!'

Calmly he leaned his back against the wall, spread out his feet before him and fell into a deep sleep.

22

She was impatient and honest. She could not conceal anything for very long. The moment she thought of something it would possess her mind. Every emotion of hers was truthful and intense. That was why she had looked at Masood that evening and laughed.

It had not been a week since she had returned from Dadi Ammah's house. Her father had been too busy to bring them back from there and had written to their grandmother saying that the girls should be sent with someone else. Masood was on holiday from his college and, after some thought, Dadi Ammah chose him for this duty. He set off the very next day with Gaythi and Arjumand.

Now he sat on a large stone by the rim of the well and Gaythi stood in front of him, peeping inside it, where the water-pump was throbbing with great regularity, emitting the noxious smell of grease and chafing steel. She looked at Masood closely and laughed.

'*Arrey*! Why are you looking at me and laughing like that? Is there something written on my face?' Masood lit a cigarette.

Gaythi took the cigarette out of his hand very calmly and laughed aloud, 'Since when did you start smoking?'

'Why are you looking at me and giggling like a nutcase? Give me back my cigarette.'

'Here, take your cigarette, then.' She grabbed both his shoulders and shook them as she said, 'Do you know, you're very sweet. I think you are really lovable. Do you understand what I'm saying?'

'Nutcase!' Masood felt cross. Not because this girl had said something objectionable to him, but, after all, why was she so hasty? Why had she been the first to say something to him which he had been wanting to say to her for so long? This wretched, nonsensical girl had shown him up completely. He felt like slapping the witch right across her face so she would sit there shedding crocodile tears through her slanting eyes. 'Pig! Bitch!' In spite of his years he swore at her inwardly like an angry child.

'Now what's shut you up?' she laughed even louder at his silence.

'Gaythi,' he said in an admonishing voice, 'are these things for a girl to say?'

'Well, are they things for old women to say then?'

'You are quite indecent!' he was determined to avenge himself.

'Why? Where's the indecency in this? Just suppose that you liked me and you became very fond of me, would you not have told me? *Waah*! It doesn't make sense that you should fancy someone in secret and not tell the very person whom you care for! That would be sheer lunacy!' Gaythi pouted, and then spoke in a sulky voice, 'D'you know I'm dying for you.'

'No, you're not dying for me. You look absolutely fine sitting there.'

'Masood! What do you want then, would you like me to die for real? Turn into a real corpse, you mean? I'm just saying it figuratively. All the girls in school talk like that. They "die" for the school, for the nuns. And you, Masood! You're really pig-headed. Quite mad!'

'You're the one who's mad. You're not old enough to get into things like this. And I'm a lot older than you. You should be polite to me.'

'That's right! You're my father, aren't you? Such an ass!' She thumped his back with her fist.

'Go away. You ill-mannered girl. Now I know what kind of girl you are. No wonder you fail with such regularity.'

'I do well to fail. Are you my tutor, then? *Waah!* What does love have to do with passing or failing? Lovers don't sit and talk about studies.'

'Oh what a great lover you are!' Masood ridiculed her.

'That's a good one! I swear to you, Masood, I think you're very sweet, and specially at this moment, sitting on this stone, like this. Just the way you are, wearing this grubby shirt and with that bereft face!'

If her eyes had not been so full of truth and her tone so full of sincerity, he would have thought that she was kidding him.

'Gay-thi, Gay-thi, come here,' Arjumand's fine and attractive voice wafted from the porch.

'There, Arjumand's calling you.' Masood changed the subject as he started walking in that direction. Gaythi walked behind him. She was neither anxious, nor blushing and breathless, nor were her eyes lowered. She was peaceful and content. She had done her duty. Like an honest trustee, she had offered to Masood the emotion concerning him which she had felt rising from the depths of her heart. It was not possible for her to change his heart and force him to say that he adored her too.

'Well, yes. It all depends on what he wants now,' she thought very calmly, and then her own sense of inferiority surged, threatening to submerge her. 'And yet, I am the worst. I fail, and I look plain. Ammah Begum always criticises me, and so do Bakhtiar Bhai and Saulat Apa. It was only Sheharyaar Bhai who cared for me a little, and he's decided to go and live in England. He doesn't even write a single letter. So why should Masood be the one to suffer, to fall for me? After all Kaamni is better looking, and she is a better person than I am.' A pang of jealousy and privation grew like a pain inside her and seized her being.

Arjumand was dressed in pink. Her cheeks looked as pink as her outfit. Her eyes, as wide open as cups and full of innocence, looked as though they were crammed with pearls.

'Aren't you coming to Jenny's birthday party?' She was holding a present wrapped in coloured paper and tinsel.

'Yes, of course. Oh God! I forgot to get a present for her.' She hung her head. 'Never mind, I'll get it later. It's not necessary to give it then and there, in front of everyone.' Gaythi managed to calm herself with her own reasoning.

Masood was considering whether his reaction would have been the same if Arjumand had made a confession of love to him instead of Gaythi.

'Huh! Who can guess what my conduct would have been like? The question would only arise if she had done it.' Masood felt indifferent. Both the sisters went inside, one after the other. One, pretty, cautious and innocent as an angel, the other, plump, plain, dressed absurdly, clever and illogical like the devil.

That night, as Masood lay on his bed, which stood by itself on the front lawn, warm tears trickled from the corners of his eyes involuntarily and soaked into his pillow. 'I am not thinking of anything, nor have I wanted to do so, so why were those tears flowing like that? Why am I in this strange state? Why am I struggling against a boundless silence, an unfathomable chasm? Curse Gaythi! I hope she'll have to pay some time for my endurance.' He turned on his side, hid his face in the pillow and dropped off to sleep.

Both the sisters walked past him talking and laughing, walking on hushed feet. They had just returned from the birthday party.

Gaythi came to a halt near him and bent down to look at him. Masood had woken up, but he lay still.

'Don't you think he's looking nice, Arjumand? Isn't he lovable?' She spoke exactly like a child.

'Hush! He'll wake up,' Arjumand said gently. 'But Gaythi, you should not have said the things you said to him. What if he tells someone?'

'What can I do if he does? What harm can he do me, anyway? The thing is, Arjumand, if I, you, or anyone else becomes aware of something then we do have to disclose it to others. Look, we don't think our thoughts only to strangle them inside our hearts, now, do we?'

Arjumand stood there a little shocked at Gaythi's impulsiveness. Masood lay there thinking, 'Gaythi is such a strange girl, she is a real witch!' For some reason his heart began to beat wildly and then, suddenly, he felt calm and fell asleep again.

23

He had not seen her around anywhere for a very long time. Her face had been sullen and grumpy since that morning. No one knew why.

He had not yet given a reply to what she had said to him. He did not really know what to say to her, but still he was going around looking for her. He found her at the back of the house, near the fields of fodder and corn. She was seated in the lean-to where the buffalo was kept. He approached her.

Raju stood to the side watching her milk the buffalo expertly, with complete concentration and diligence.

'Bibi, don't squeeze the teat so hard. If you hurt it, gradually it becomes useless.'

'All right, Raju!' She immediately loosened her grasp according to his instruction.

Masood stood watching her from a distance. She was dressed in a blue striped shirt and a white *shalwar* and she sat upright but at ease. She had hung her headscarf on the side of the lean-to. The ground below her was covered with hay. The fodder stood ready-mixed in a vat. She seemed to be lost in a world of her own, oblivious of the pungent smell of the blend of cottonseed, hay and mustard seed husks, or even that of fresh cow dung. Masood felt a pang of envy as he went and stood near her, 'Move over. I'll do the milking now.'

She jumped as if she had been caught red-handed.

'Move,' Masood nudged her, 'you clumsy fool! Your clothes are all hanging about you.'

'Huh! So you've come here to bore me to death,' she grumbled as if she really felt extremely bored with him.

'And why are you sitting here like a dead duck? I've been looking for you for a whole hour now.'

'Why should I be a dead duck? I hope to God you die. What have you got to do with me? You're only Arjumand's cousin, aren't you? You look at her when you're telling jokes, you bring her sweets and you've even bought her a book.'

'Because she reads, and you're a useless ninny.'

'You're not my dad, Masood! You don't need to lecture me about studies all the time!' She forgot the buffalo, the milking bucket and Raju in her temper and walked out of the shelter. Masood was right behind her. There were a few guava trees beside the shelter; she came to a stop near them and resumed the interrogation, 'Tell me, do I ever tell you to study?' She raised her hand and picked a greenish, half-ripe guava and started nibbling it hastily. 'Have I ever accused you of being useless?' Another guava jumped and fell into her hands and she started munching on it loudly. Then she picked another two guavas and sat down on a large stone nearby.

'Tell me, have I ever asked you to tell me jokes or present books to me?' Having said that she sat silently eating the fruits one by one.

81

'Why are you eating so many guavas? You'll die,' Masood took them away from her.

She pushed his hand away and screamed, 'I'm going to eat them. You know why? Because I'm frustrated.'

'*Arrey*! Whoever told you that?'

'Why? Am I a complete ignoramus? I read so much that you don't know about. So what if I fail? I don't enjoy the syllabus.'

He laughed, 'So why are you frustrated?'

'Because no one loves me. Everyone criticises me, except for Abba Mian. And he never has any time to spare. And then, of course, I am very bad anyway so I know that you, too, will love Arjumand instead of me. I know it all.' She seemed disillusioned and disappointed in every living human being. 'But, look here, Masood, whether or not you love me, promise me something: promise me you will not love Arjumand. She always manages to grab everything that's mine by right without ever having to ask for it, or pine for it . You don't know how she has managed to usurp all of Ammah Begum's affection that was rightfully mine, leaving none for me.'

She lifted up her face to Masood. It was filled with such pain and torture, her eyes were so full of hopelessness that Masood could not contain himself. He took that anguished face in both his hands and looked at her closely. Her black, almond-shaped eyes, the pale colour of her skin, so very like the Chinese, crimson lips and flat nose were all fascinating but strange and mysterious too. He bent forward and looked at her straight, relatively thick and black hair, which had a natural fragrance. All these things about her were quite unfamiliar and unique. He drew his hands away from her face slowly and hid his face in that mass of black hair, saying, 'You can rest assured, whatever happens I'll never fall in love with Arjumand.'

A gentle breeze infused with the sweet smell of corn fanned her and she asked him, very hopefully, 'And with me?'

'I'll think about it and then tell you.'

'All right, never mind.' She stood up calmly as if she were telling him that she did not need his reply, that she had already made a gift to him of her own feelings. She flung the remaining chunk of guava in the narrow stream of water swishing past them.

The fields were a deep, thriving green and the lean-to was stacked untidily with golden hay. The air reeked with the mellow fragrance of mustard and cottonseeds. He looked at Gaythi, she seemed to be an integral part of the scene: vast, generous and content like Mother Earth herself.

*

'Huh! God knows what you'll be up to at this moment in time, Gaythi Ara!' Masood pushed away his books with sleepy eyes and a weary heart and lay down on his bed. 'Did you notice how cleverly I evaded you? "I'll think about it and then tell you."

'That's right, Gaythi, I wasn't such an idiot as to not comprehend the meaning of your supplicant eyes seeking mine every morning over the breakfast table. But you tell me yourself, what could I have said in reply to your question? What was so difficult to understand about it? It wasn't a chemical formula. What else is left to debate when something is already well known and well understood? When did I ever not like you? Not liking you cannot possibly make sense. It isn't every day that girls as cheeky and fearless as you are born.

'And you, you have possessed me so completely, that I wonder if it is actually possible for a living human being to become a poltergeist and take possession of others, only to harass them. But, Gaythi! I will not answer your question until I have really thought about it. Or, maybe I shall never answer it because the walls that divide you and me, the walls of wealth and deprivation, cannot be scaled. You, may God protect you from the evil eye, are wealthy and I am a man of limited means. We are worlds apart. Our worlds are so different that your overwhelmingly innocent and straightforward mind cannot even comprehend this difference. And even this is an interesting coincidence: how did you ever come to think this thought which sets you apart from your class? Girls of your rank and status do not regard people like us as human beings. The very thought of receiving attentions and admiring glances from men like me would send shivers through them.

'I wish I had never heard all those comments full of hatred and contempt which girls and people of your class make about mine, and I might have confessed my love with great hopes. I might have stayed at your feet to try and light the lamps of my affection. But how shall I tell you that I do not have the courage to do so? And then people of your class claim that my less privileged class prides itself in false prestige and self-deception which it has chosen to describe as self-respect.

'All right, Gaythi! I deliver this passion, that is rearing its head now in both our hearts, into the hands of fate.'

Masood turned on his side and dropped off to sleep.

'He is gone. He promised me he would think about it and then tell me. I don't know why he seemed so silent and terrified. Did he fail to love me in spite of trying to? But why should he have felt so sad about it? He could have said that he couldn't help it. Anyway, it has to be whatever he wants.'

Gaythi pulled the exercise book closer to her and started writing her answers to the questions. She had to do her homework. After all Sister Eliza would not entertain the excuse that she had started thinking of Masood, not because she had meant to, but quite involuntarily.

'Don't know why all these worldly thoughts begin to intrude when you are praying or trying to work on mathematics.' Then she lost interest, laid her head on the table, resting it on the exercise book with her incomplete homework, and dropped off to sleep.

'After several years Sang and his mistress are going to China. They shall return to their homeland, breathe in the beautiful odours of that beloved atmosphere. They will be able to see and feel all the joys and pains of that place in their own flesh and blood. I wish I could go there too. My sister is getting married next year. Along with clothes and all the other gifts, her in-laws will send her transport from their distant village to fetch her, and she will be carried away to another world, where her husband-to-be is busy working in the paddy-fields, dressed in a blue coat and trousers, a straw hat on his head. That is how it is. The fatherless daughters of learned men end up marrying ignorant peasants. And . . . and . . . well, never mind. What I am concerned about is how they will manage all the formalities of an engagement and wedding without me being there.'

Safdar Yaaseen, who was filing entries in Sang's ledger, paused for a moment and picked up the letter from the table. His mother had written very briefly to inform her son, who had come to live thousands of miles away to be able to support them, in a few beautifully and expertly written words, about the first wedding in their family. She had revealed nothing of her anxieties and worries to him, aware that he was alone in a foreign land. But even those few resigned words and serious sentences betrayed the state of her feelings.

'Do not be sad, my son. Wherever you might be, we feel that you are close at hand. You have had to go and settle so far away on our account. Pray for your sister's well-being. Do not grieve.'

'No, Mother, I shall not grieve. I am happy that my father's daughter is not going to become the wife of a cheating usurer or a corrupt officer. The blood coursing in her veins has been the blood and sweat of hard-earned and honest wages. She will be safe from the illicit comforts obtained through cruelty and oppression. Mother, you should be grateful

84

to God too, that she is marrying a peasant. A peasant is the one who nurtures the world.'

But he still felt sad and miserable. His hard-working, fatherless sister would be leaving for her own home, leaving behind the home which had never offered her any comforts, nor enough to eat. The home where she had had to work hard as far back as she could remember. How able and skilled she is – like countless intelligent and needy women in China! She has never enjoyed days of carefree peace like the daughters of the rich. Now she would be leaving for her own home and her brother would not be there even to say goodbye to her.

He had given an assortment of inexpensive gifts to Sang's mistress to deliver to his mother.

His heart felt wildly restless. In all these years he had never longed so intensely to go back home. He was desperately missing that land on the banks of the yellow waters of the River Yangtse, those decaying crumbling areas of the inner city, the whiff of opium and that drowsy existence. And he was well aware that he would not be able to travel home for several years yet.

He was longing to talk to someone who was sympathetic and supportive, who would share his confidences and dry his tears. 'But is there anyone really like that? Li Yang? He is too miserable and astringent, surely, like a dried date. Sang's mistress? Huh! He may as well confide in the statue of Confucius, or that of the Buddha. After all, what's so wrong with talking to the cross-legged statue of the Buddha, with his long ears, absorbed in his search for knowledge? Then, again, the streets of this city are no worse than that either. Why should I not simply loaf around the streets? Just watching people talk and laugh, absorbed in the sheer hubbub of life completely erases the feeling of deprivation!'

24

After wandering purposelessly along the streets and highways, his bicycle came to a halt next to the wall at the back of the house which resembled a rest house bungalow. Clusters of flaming red flowers hung from the row of Gul Mohar trees, peeking at the road over the wall along which they had been planted. The afternoon had not quite departed. It was early August and the sky was overcast.

Everywhere was silent as usual. He looked around, startled. Why did I come here? I am not even carrying any goods for sale as my excuse for being here.

Her placid Chinese face appeared over the other side of the wall and peered across. Safdar Yaaseen, China Man stood right in front of her. She was seeing him after several months. She completely forgot that she had been unhappy and mournful since that morning and as soon as she saw him, she laughed without really meaning to.

'*Arrey*! Hello, Cheena!' she addressed him in a comical tone, 'What are you doing standing here?'

'Nothing,' he said, pulling a long face.

'So why don't you come inside? I needed to buy a sash for myself. And, listen, Saulat Apa has written for several things. She is living in a really primitive place at the moment, where there are no China Men selling things. So she's written, "Ask Safdar to paint me a scene of a sunset, on silk".'

She rattled off all that without stopping for breath.

'Well, you beautiful girl! I see you've developed an interest in sunsets very quickly,' Safdar thought.

He spoke with the same mournful look on his face, 'I am not carrying any goods at the moment; shall I come in? If you want me to!'

'Why not? Do come in. Why are you standing there, as if you were dead?'

'You are so rude.' He came in.

She laughed again, 'Sometimes I really want to be utterly rude. I feel like fighting someone and talking back at them.' She sat on a concrete bollard under the shade of a Gul Mohar tree.

'Why, Cuckoo? Why do you feel like that?' He noticed that her taut almond-shaped eyes bore dark shadows of sorrow, even though her cherry lips blossomed with laughter.

She evaded the question and said, 'You're really quiet today, Liu Chu! What's the matter? You didn't bring anything today, and you haven't fought with me either.'

He sat down on the grass close to her, silently chewing a blade of straw.

'Are you ill?'

'No, Cuckoo, I'm not ill, but I am worried.'

'What's happened?' She bent towards him sympathetically. Her manner was so sincere and intimate that Safdar could not hold himself back. He felt impelled to tell this girl everything.

'Nothing. I and my entire family are unlucky. Whenever I think of it I feel miserable.'

86

'Then don't think of it,' she said simply.

'How is it possible for a human being to never think of himself, but to think of others all the time? Sometimes, you have to think of yourself, perforce.'

'Why? What's making you do that, today?'

'Lots of things. For instance, my sister is getting married in a month's time and I can't go there.'

'Then so what? Go another time.'

'You're very unkind. Do you know how many years I've been here? And there's no one there to share my mother's worries with her.'

'So why did you ever come here, then?' She felt irritated.

'Really, Cuckoo! You just can't understand all this. If I hadn't come here how could I have supported my family?'

'Why? Is there no money to be made in your China that you had to come here to send them money?'

'Huh, this girl says such stupid things and I still go on answering her questions.' He felt annoyed in his heart, but in reply he said to her, 'Too true, Cuckoo! There is neither money for people like me, nor food, in my China. What can I say to you?' His small eyes filled with tears.

Gaythi's heart yielded and suddenly she looked very sensible. 'Tut. Ah! When will people's hardships ever end?'

'Never, Cuckoo! . . . Unless, unless . . .'

'Unless, what?'

'Nothing. You're still very young. You can't understand these things. And then anyway, how can you understand what life is like for people like us?'

'I understand everything,' she shook her head seriously. 'You think I am far removed from the world of troubles and woes, that I am crazy and do not understand anything. That is up to you. You can think what you like. But, then why don't you go now?' she advised him.

'How can I go now? If I had been lucky you wouldn't have seen me around these parts at all. It was my father's desire that I should become a doctor; he didn't know that I was destined to roam the streets of your country, Cuckoo!'

His black eyes brimmed with real tears. Straight, black hair massed heavily on his forehead. His face was puffy like that of a grumpy child.

She completely forgot that her status and rank were considerably higher than this foreign peddlar's; that to talk to him so freely and to try and give him support in that way was considered highly objectionable. Her hand shot out, she touched his shoulder absent-mindedly, and spoke as if to cajole him, '*Arrey*! Chin, chin China Man! You're really crying.

Arrey waah! You are a brave boy. You've come to our country to earn some money for your mother's sake. Don't be disheartened like this. Here, try some tamarind.'

She opened the small paper bag in her hands and handed him the little packets of salt and chillies along with the red, ripe ends of the tamarind.

'Huh!' He laughed in the midst of his tears, 'She is crazy!'

He too was inclined to forget that she was the young daughter of a wealthy family who had now commenced her journey on the road to maturity. He wiped away his tears and just to please her, tried to eat the stewed tamarind.

Arjumand came on tiptoes, stood quietly behind Gaythi and asked her suddenly, 'Gaythi, you haven't seen my key, have you?'

Gaythi stuffed the tamarind covered in salt and chillies in her mouth and clicked her tongue with relish as she said, 'It must be on my table.'

'Come and find it for me. I can't find it myself.' It seemed from Arjumand's manner that she needed Gaythi more urgently than the keys.

'OK, then, Liu Chu, I had better go. You won't cry now, will you? Make sure you don't.'

He rose quietly, picked up his bicycle which was leaning against the wall, and left. Seeing Arjumand appear suddenly like that seemed to have frightened him a little.

On her way in, Arjumand started talking to Gaythi, 'What has got into you, Gaythi? Only the daughters of cooks and bearers flirt with people like him in secret.' Arjumand reckoned that she was acting in a very serious and sophisticated manner.

'Eh, Arjumand! I swear to you, I wasn't flirting with him.' She was amazed at what Arjumand had said.

'Then what else were you up to?'

'Get lost! That poor chap was in tears because he was missing home – all I did was try to comfort him a little.'

'Did he have to come here, all this way, to miss his home? And even if he did, why did you have to bother to go out of your way to comfort him?' These days Arjumand had taken to mixing with the grown-ups.

'Why, why shouldn't I have bothered? It was my duty to do that . . .'

'*Waah*! Why was it your duty?' Arjumand quizzed her again.

'Yes, it was my duty, Arjumand. The point is that I was the one who broke my leg, not you.'

'What's it got to do with breaking your leg?'

'It's got everything to do with that. When I broke my leg I was lying trussed up in hospital. You've no idea of how upset I felt at times. And then he was the one who used to come to entertain me, every day after finishing his work.'

But Arjumand, who was unwilling to be persuaded to change her censorious attitude, refused to listen to her reasoning.

'And what if Ammah Begum had seen you?'

'What if she had, it wouldn't have been the end of the world! Whatever she sees becomes evil in her eyes.'

Late at night, the headlights of a car shone on the porch before going out again. The sound of the car door as it opened and shut with a dull thud, echoed into the distance. Three shadows came forward in the dark.

'You go ahead, Abba Mian,' she said in a frightened tone.

'Yes, yes, I'm coming. Why are you so frightened?'

She turned round quietly and said, 'Come, Masood.'

Shareef stood at the door to the hallway. 'Shall I serve dinner, Sahib?'

'No, *bhai*. We've already eaten. Is Begum Sahib sleeping, or is she still awake ?'

'Maybe she has gone to sleep. She was very worried at the delay.'

'Yes, we are very late, indeed.' He went in, treading quietly. 'And, listen, Shareef! Make up a bed for Masood Mian in the room at the far end.'

Holding her breath and petrified at the sound of her own footsteps, she bumped into a chair when she entered the room.

'Who is it?' Arjumand started fearfully.

'Hush, go to sleep. It's me.'

'So you decided to come back at last?'

'Did you expect me to stay there?'

Arjumand sat up and spoke in a drowsy voice, 'What is the matter with you, Gaythi, I ask you? You insist on doing things which offend Ammah Begum.'

'Why? What did I do today that is offensive?' Gaythi asked, lighting the lamp.

'Abba Mian was going to Anand Pur to hunt, why did you have to insist on going with him?'

'It's nothing new. We often go with him.'

'But was it really necessary to go specially to see Hashmi Phupho, today?'

'What was wrong with that? I thought she was visiting there, and it would give me a chance to call on her. Do you know how hospitable they were? They did not allow us to leave without dinner. That's why we got back so late.'

'Got back late!' Arjumand said angrily. 'You know Ammah Begum does not approve of just going any old where.'

'It's not just anywhere! Aren't they related to us?'

'They are not really close relations, you know that. You just went off, but I was the one who ended up getting scolded over every little thing all day long because she was angry with you.'

'What was she saying?' Gaythi asked anxiously.

'She's right. She said that all these relatives and kinfolk do not deserve to be encouraged to come all the time.'

'But I've brought Masood back with me!'

'That was clever! Now she'll be in a worse mood. You know that these things upset her but you insist on doing them. And then you complain that Ammah Begum does not approve of you, and that she says this or that.'

'Well, after all it isn't a mortal sin, is it? Masood is not a criminal that his visit should cause so much offence.'

Gaythi would start talking like that when she got really terrified.

'Well, it's nothing to do with me! All I'm saying is that I end up getting a lecture for no rhyme or reason.'

'Then don't listen to it. Just say to her, "Please tell Gaythi off when she returns".'

'I'm not insolent like you.'

She turned the lamp off quietly, crept under the quilt and started thinking, 'I am truly insolent. Arjumand thinks that I am, too.' Then, she secretly regretted bringing Masood back with her without any excuse. I do do things that are out of order, Arjumand is right. I should neither talk to Safdar Liu Chu in that intimate manner nor . . . nor . . . suddenly, her eyes filled with tears and she turned on her side.

He was a bit uneasy during this visit, although he did not know who was offended by his arrival, and to what degree. That evening, Gaythi, observing that he seemed a little fed up, had asked him, 'Will you come with me, Masood?'

'Where?'

'I want to go to the Chinese shop. I've taken my shoes for repair.'

'Let's go.' He stood up.

Both of them set off on bicycles.

'Gaythi!' Masood said to her on the way.

'Yes?'

'Tonight, over dinner, if you could get me Mamoo jaan's permission, I would like to leave in the morning.'

'What's the rush? You're still on holiday.'

'I am, but I'd best stay in Anand Pur.'

'God forgive us, but why should you be so restless?'

'Well, the truth is, that I have a slight feeling that Mumani jaan seems to be unhappy about my visit. Except for her response to my greeting, she has not addressed a word to me since the day I came. . .'

'Why should she be unhappy? Maybe there was no opportunity to do so.' She tried to evade the issue.

'Well. It may be that I am imagining it. But anyway, my heart isn't in it.'

'All right then! You can go. Why should you stay because I ask you to?'

She looked at him with reproachful eyes and Masood felt as if she were insinuating that he had not answered her earlier question. The memory pained him for some reason, and they travelled the remaining distance in silence.

When they entered the shop, Safdar, who was assisting a petite blonde Memsahib as she tried on a pair of shoes, glanced at them out of the corner of his eyes, lowered his head and concentrated even more on what he was doing.

She handed in the repair slip at the counter and started chatting to Masood. The man at the counter said something in Chinese and Safdar stopped in the midst of writing an invoice for the blonde. He looked at both of them in silence, brought the pair of shoes from inside and handed them to her.

'Listen Safdar! Saulat Apa will be arriving soon. Now you must come with your goods,' she said.

'I stay at the shop now,' he said drily.

She looked at his face in amazement. Then the two of them went out of the shop.

For some unknown reason, Safdar felt deeply disturbed. Several times he scolded the young Chinese boy who worked in the shop, without any reason, and then thought sadly, 'What is the matter with me?'

25

Although Gaythi had not asked him that startling question again, on several occasions, Masood had felt that her trusting and confident eyes were probing him, 'Will you ever be able to answer my question, do you think?'

'The answer to the question is very simple, but, I don't know why, my mind trembles in fear each time.'

That day too Masood moved away from where she was and went to sit on the lawn outside. He tried to drown his thoughts in the smell of earth and manure rising from the flowerbeds, and the grinding noise of the lawn-mower.

A staff car came to a stop on the porch. Its door was opened by a respectful and handsome commissioned officer. For a moment, Masood watched the style and pomp of the woman who stepped out of the car in amazement, then he remembered, '*Arrey*! It's Saulat Apa.'

A healthy and firm-bodied ayah got out of the back of the car carrying a little girl in her arms. Both of Saulat's sisters had arrived on the verandah by this time. In the flurry of their meeting and chatter not one of them even glanced at the handsome commissioned officer who was seeing to the luggage like a humble servant. When he paid his respects to Saulat Apa before leaving she responded very casually and went inside.

'So these are the honours a daughter of this house expects.' Masood felt mortified. He was unsure whether he should remain sitting by himself on the lawn, ungraciously, or whether he should join them and inflict his unwanted presence on them like the buzz of a contemptible and annoying little insect. He had stayed there in a state of uncertainty, and when Gaythi had tried to introduce him after a little while, no one had taken any special notice of him. Inexplicably, he had felt out of place and unwelcome. He rose from the spot and slowly walked to that part of the back garden, under the guava trees, where he had promised Gaythi that he would never love Arjumand. The water in the stream by the guava trees was swishing loudly. You could hear a millstone grinding wheat in the distance. He sat for a very long time on the stone on which she had sat senselessly arguing with him. Each and every particle around him appeared to be taunting him.

'That girl, who has, at least, done justice to her sentiments and feelings, is better than you.'

*

The heat had affected Gaythi and she had been lying around listlessly for several days. It was intensely hot that day, too. A strong gust of hot wind reminded Masood of the severity of the weather and he went inside.

Everyone was still asleep when he woke up after his siesta. It was absolutely still everywhere.

'I wonder how she is now?'

He went towards Gaythi and Arjumand's room on tiptoes, and gently knocked on the door. Arjumand called out, 'Who is it? Come in.'

He opened the door and went inside.

She was sitting by Gaythi's bedside reading something. Her face looked even more innocent, attractive and dignified in her simple outfit. In contrast with her was the face of her twin sister. Extremely simple, typically Chinese, but sincere. He stood silently for a few moments looking at both of them. He thought, 'You are extremely simple-looking in comparison, but you are extremely interesting.' Then he decided to give his answer to her question.

'Arjumand!' he said softly.

'What is it?' Arjumand looked at him in surprise.

'Listen!'

Not wanting to disturb Gaythi, she stepped out quietly and walked behind him. When he sank into a chair which lay on the verandah outside, Arjumand felt obliged to sit down too.

'Can I ask you something? Will you give me a truthful reply?'

'What,' she seemed surprised.

'If I said to you . . .'

'Said what?' she felt flabbergasted.

'If I were to say . . . that . . . I . . . that . . .' Then he began again, in English. 'If I were to say to you that I love you, would you like it? Would you agree to marry me?'

Those beautiful and innocent eyes were wide open with amazement, watching his face. A gleam flashed in them for an instant, and then a terrible storm of contempt and pity rose slowly and enveloped her being.

She spoke in a voice that was almost calm, 'But, Masood! Why should you say something like that? And if you did, it would be a great folly on your part. Are you confident that a girl would prefer you and turn down someone more handsome and . . . shall I say . . . better off, than you? And I do believe that it would not be good for you either, that you . . . What I meant was, that one should marry a girl whose lifestyle is not very different from one's own.'

For an instant, Arjumand could not believe that she was able to answer this boy, in whose presence her own heart would begin to race in secret, so easily.

'I am sorry, Masood . . . !' Then she apologised for the relative severity of her tone.

'Never mind. You are absolutely right. I wanted to find this out.'

He was neither sorry nor content. The revelation of certain realities can be quite shattering.

He left for Anand Pur that evening.

When Gaythi came round after her bout of fever she was totally unaware of the fact that Masood had departed the day before. She lay alone in the bedroom. The last rays of the setting sun were kissing the window panes goodbye. Perhaps the family were all having tea in the dining room. There was silence everywhere. She felt lighter but still a touch feverish, and as if her heart were sinking. She heard footsteps and then Arjumand entered the room.

'How are you feeling now, Gaythi?' she asked seeing her face buried in the pillow.

Gaythi did not answer.

Arjumand shook the thermometer on the table, came closer and said, 'Here, take the thermometer.'

She turned over, took it and put it in her mouth without saying anything.

Arjumand looked at her temperature with surprise. It was below 97 degrees. She placed the thermometer back in its case and went out returning after about ten minutes with some hot milk. She stirred some cocoa into the milk and placed the cup gently on the table. 'Drink this, you're feeling weak.'

She rose without protest and raised the cup to her lips. Gently, Arjumand tidied the table, straightened the creases in the bed and rearranged the flowers in the vase.

Gaythi felt slightly better after drinking the milk, and she looked up at Arjumand. Did a strange smile play on her flower-like lips?

'Is everything all right?' Gaythi asked with some surprise.

'It's nothing . . . Masood's gone.'

'When?' Gaythi's heart sank.

'Yesterday.'

'Did he say anything?' Gaythi's voice trembled.

'Yes. He said something to me.'

'What?' She sat up.

'Huh! He's a real fool.' Arjumand looked coy. 'He said . . . he said to me . . .'

Gaythi flared up and spoke irritably, 'Why should you feel shy if he said something?'

'He said, "Arjumand, I love you",' Arjumand ventured, a little intimidated by her scolding.

'Liar. You're so cunning. You're jealous of me.'

'Gaythi, when am I ever cunning in my dealings with you?' Arjumand looked at her innocently.

'But I cannot believe you. He could never have said that to you.'

'But why, Gaythi? Do you think I am that bad?'

'When did I say that? But Masood would never say such a thing to you. He promised me, that whether or not he loves me, he will never ever love you.'

Arjumand was staring at her with wide, bewildered eyes. 'Do you hate me that much, Gaythi? I had no idea.' She felt aggrieved.

'It's nothing to do with hatred. Tell me, could you tolerate it if someone you fell in love with, loved me instead?'

Arjumand was watching her in silence, this half-crazy sister of hers, who always talked like this. But Gaythi was not to be put off. She continued her inquisition. 'All right then, you tell me the precise words that Masood said to you.'

Arjumand always yielded to Gaythi, and she knew that she always had to obey her orders, so she lowered her head and said, 'He said to me, "Arjumand, tell me something. If I were to say to you . . ." then he stopped and said, "If I tell you that I love you, if I ask you to marry me, would you mind?"'

'Was he also a little concerned and sad, when he said this?'

'Not really. And when I said to him "Masood, if you did that you would be quite wrong, you should not even say this to a girl whose rank is much higher than yours", he said very calmly, "You are absolutely right".'

'That's enough. Arjumand Begum! Don't labour under the delusion that he said all this for your sake. He really meant , "If I were to say such a thing to Gaythi, would you people not mind?" He understands the difference in rank between himself and us very well. But you should not presume that he was, in fact, addressing you.'

She was a strange girl. She was saying all these things with great ease and calm, as if this were not at all significant. Her face was completely peaceful now.

26

The holidays were over and the school had reopened. The car was needed for Abba Main's tours so both of them rode their bicycles to school. Gaythi had not recovered her old robustness since her illness, which had now become an ancient tale; and once again she became the target for invective against her ill-mannered ways. An extremely disappointing report had been sent home from school, and she felt deeply disheartened.

Arjumand had not been to school for the past two days because she had a bad cold and Gaythi felt even more despondent and miserable than usual. After a long interval, she had thought of Masood several times during that day. When the school day ended all the girls headed home but somehow Gaythi's bicycle turned in the opposite direction. She parked it upright on a patch of greenery in a small, quiet and tidy park and sat down beside it with a thump. She sat under the shade of a dense moulsari tree, leaning against the trunk, and must have been dozing there for quite some time when Safdar Yaaseen spotted her as he walked past quite by chance. He was amazed. Why is this sixteen- or seventeen-year-old mature girl sitting here, dozing like a vagrant? Huh! But, of course, what can you do with Cuckoo? She is truly wild at heart. She is capable of anything. He bent down and looked with ridicule at that face which was capable of several familiar moods. She looks ill, grief-stricken and broken-hearted, he noticed with surprise; and felt genuinely sorry for this girl, whose father had a limousine, considerable property and authority as an officer in that area.

If it had been some other girl he would never have dared to do what he did, but this was his own Cuckoo. Just as innocent and simple as she was six or seven years ago. He whistled to attract her attention, and she looked up with a start.

'*Arrey*, hello,' she smiled sadly.

The tiny camphor buds of the moulsari had been falling steadily and in several places had become tangled in her dark, straight hair. She looked very pale and dejected.

'What's the matter, my little friend?'

'Nothing! What are you doing wandering round here?'

'I come here quite often, Cuckoo! But how come you are here today? You should not be here.'

'Why not, Safdar? Don't human beings come here, or do you not regard me as a human?'

'How simply this girl makes these comments,' he thought, before he spoke again. 'Human beings do come here, but not the big shots and especially not their daughters!'

'Safdar Liu Chu!'

'Yes?'

'Tell me something. Are the walls between the territories of the big shots and those of ordinary people as high in China as they are over here?'

'Yes, Cuckoo! Even higher than the famous Great Wall of China!'

'And everyone is content with that?'

'Whether they are content or not that is what has been happening since time immemorial.'

'And will it always go on happening?' Safdar could see that her face was pale and her eyes were full of fear and bewilderment.

'How can I say that? I am only an ignorant and poor Chinese who has not visited his country for the past seven years. I have not seen my mother for the past seven years. Although I had never been able to sleep without her being next to me before I left. I miss the yellow earth of my country, the smell of paddy-fields and my mother's body every day.'

'Then why don't you go back? You're always whining about it.'

'How can I go back? My country is very poor and unfortunate. Poor countries fail to provide shelter for their children. Their own lands become too crowded to accommodate them.'

'Why does that happen?'

'What can I tell you now?'

He sat on the soft green turf very close to her absolutely without any decorum. His trouser leg was still held in a clip. The neckline of his yellow silk shirt was open and he wore a tiny silver locket on a delicate chain round his neck.

'*Arrey*, Chu! What's that locket you've got round your neck?'

'Sometimes you call me Chu, and sometimes, Safdar!'

'So you call me Cuckoo, too? Why are you hedging the question? Tell me what's that locket round your neck?'

'Silly! Is this a locket? It's the Holy Quran.'

'Liar! Where could you have got such a tiny Holy Quran from?'

'Here, have a look!' He clicked open the locket, drew out a copy of the Holy Quran the size of his finger-tip, kissed it and placed it in Cuckoo's hand.

'My mother placed this round my neck with her own hands, when I was leaving. For my protection.'

Safdar Liu Chu's almond-shaped eyes were moist with tears.

97

'Can I see it?' She kissed the tiny sacred book in imitation of him. 'Have it then. Put it round your neck,' she said respectfully and fell into deep thought.

'What are you thinking, Cuckoo?'

'I was thinking that perhaps religion is a good thing, from this point of view,' she spoke as if from a great distance.

'From what point of view?'

'Just that a lot of people, whether or not they are big shots, believe in the same thing and do the same things. My Abba Mian wears a copy of the Holy Quran in a silver case, exactly like this one, round his neck. He says that my grandmother gave him that to wear for his protection when he left his home for the first time to go and live in the hostel. And, even now, when he goes to visit her she opens his collar to satisfy herself that he is still wearing it. And I saw the cook's son wearing the same thing too.'

'You think more than you should, girl! No wonder you keep failing at your exams.' He laughed innocently, and Gaythi laughed with him.

But she became morose again and gazed into the distance in silence.

'So, Cuckoo. You still haven't told me why you are sitting here so sad and quiet.'

She thought for a moment and her lips which never lied, which never strove to say what was expedient, poured forth all the bitterness of her feelings. 'Because I feel really disgusted with my own family sometimes. I don't like anything about them. If my father did not live in that house, I don't know what I would have done.'

'What's the matter?'

'Ouf! What shall I tell you?' she broke down.

He heard the call for the evening prayers in the distance and shook himself. '*Arrey*! It's so late. See, what a bad thing you've done! Does a young girl ever stay out of her house this late? Come on, get up; and I don't want to see you in this park ever again.'

'Why not?'

'Because . . . the underprivileged avenge themselves against the big shots who try to keep them at a distance, by making themselves dangerous in the end, so that sobriety and decency are afraid to come near them. Come on! I should be returning too. We can leave here together . . .'

He stood waiting for her. He did not wish to leave this stubborn and silly girl sitting there like that.

'You go! I'll come in a minute.'

'No. You come too.' He seemed offended.

She picked up her bicycle and rose to leave the park. They both climbed on their bicycles and set off together.

The darkness of dusk had settled on the roads. People appeared to be going round happily, busily. Some of the shops had turned their lights on, and it struck Gaythi for the first time that Safdar was right. It was wrong of her to disappear from home like that.

It had become cooler. Safdar glared at her once again. 'Button up your coat properly. You've been so ill and you're being careless now.'

'Huh! The worst that can happen is that I'll die.'

'Don't talk nonsense and go home quickly now.'

He turned his bicycle towards the centre of town at the fork near Mall Road, and waved goodbye to her.

The anxiety and vexation which had surrounded the house could even be felt at the gate. As usual, everywhere was quiet, but to a fearful extent . . . The lights had been switched on in the rooms but the porch and the verandah were dark. Someone sat in a chair on the verandah. She jumped off the bicycle at the gate and dragged it slowly round the back, entering the house through the back door like a thief. Arjumand stood on the verandah inside. Her face was pale and her eyes were red. When she got closer to her Arjumand seized her in an embrace, started kissing her and sobbing at the same time.

'What's the matter with you, Arjumand?' she asked as if nothing had happened.

'Where did you go? Do you know how angry Ammah is with you? Mali told us that you were going round with China Man.'

'Mali is a liar. He wasn't there. I didn't see him . . .'

'Anyway, you were with him. What can Mali have against you?'

'Why should he have anything against me? But Mali could not have been in that park.'

'So were you in the park? Everyone was looking for you. Mali saw you and him on your bicycles. See how contemptible and wretched this China Man is.'

'You are contemptible. Why should he be that?'

'Gaythi you deserve the treatment you are going to get from Ammah Begum. You are calling your very own twin sister contemptible for the sake of that mean and evil man.'

'So what? What else should I say? You should thank him. If he had not scolded me you would still be waiting here for me.'

'Why ever did you go there?'

'Because I felt like it. I wanted to.'

'Wanted to! You corrupt creature. Come here and I'll give you "wanted to"!'

Ammah Begum, who had come up from behind, dragged her by her short hair, and slapped her on the face.

'You can't hit me like this, in front of everyone,' she roared angrily.

'I'll bury you alive,' Ammah Begum pushed her and as she fell on the slippery floor she took off her slipper quite literally and fell upon her, beating her with reckless fury.

She neither screamed nor moved but just lay there on the floor. Arjumand was speechless with horror. Then, after much begging and persuasion, she dragged Ammah Begum into her room, where she sat panting for a very long time.

And, Gaythi, who had been so humiliated, and about whom everyone had made the worst and most demeaning assumptions, just lay there quietly on the cold, slate floor of the verandah.

When something unusual occurs somewhere, whether it is in a small house or a huge bungalow, everyone who lives in the vicinity comes to know of it. That is exactly what happened with this incident too.

'Now I never see Cuckoo around,' thought Safdar one day, as he stroked a new canvas with his brush. He was leaving for home soon and was extremely happy. 'If I never see Cuckoo around, what does it matter?' But he did not know that he had been seen riding his bicycle alongside her, and that this had been given such an objectionable significance that she had been stopped from attending her school. She was now preparing for her matriculation examination by private study.

When she has time, there is a heap of mending before her and she darns clothes, and embroiders initials on bedsheets. Early in the morning she sits before Moulvi Sahib, with the Holy Quran on a stand in front of her as she reads it, rocking gently, her head covered.

If he had come to know of this state of affairs, he would have laughed so much and said, 'That's right, Cuckoo, you deserve this.'

27

Experienced and sensible mothers create a strange and mysterious chasm between children and their fathers. They themselves become the wall between them, and then act as the link themselves, too. On the one hand, through their practical wisdom, they turn the father's position into that of the heir to the British throne, and on the other they create a sense of terror against him in the hearts of the children, 'What if your father hears of it! You know your father's temper!'

However the fact is that the children never really discover the truth about their father's nature. The words, 'Your father', become the manifestation of fear and terror which steadily separates and distances the father from the children and the children from the father.

Begum Jehangir had created something very like this kind of separation and distance between her children and her husband. Both her sons and two of her daughters had accepted this distance without protest. If there was anyone reluctant and unwilling to believe her version of this state of affairs it was this girl who was different from everyone else.

When she added her usual piece after criticising something about her, 'If your father comes to hear of it, then you'll be responsible. You know his disposition,' in her dark and deep voice, Gaythi would say to herself, 'You're wrong, Ammah Begum! I know my father's disposition very well. I wish he had his rightful privilege of having a say in our education and upbringing, and then there would not have been this huge chasm between him and me.'

She was the only one amongst his children whose heart communicated with his and in spite of the remoteness engineered by the constitution Ammah Begum had formulated for governing their offspring, and his own heavy outside commitments, sometimes she would quietly manage to get very close to her father. She had never forgotten that night when her father had called her very close to him and told her gently, 'Do you know? Of all my children, you are the most beautiful.'

Now she had come to realise that he was referring to the beauty of her temperament, endowed so abundantly with truth and sincerity. She was not merely aware of this quality in herself but also very proud of it, and had been since she was very young.

That evening, when she was held in such ignominy and disgraced, even before the servants, she did not feel particularly concerned because immediately she told herself very calmly, 'What does this matter? I am not at all what they consider me to be, and I do not know how Ammah Begum could decide to associate such an awful calumny with me.

'It is a blessing that Sheharyaar Bhai is so far away from here in England or else he might have believed it, too. And Saulat Apa! She would, of course, be the first to believe it. Arjumand had already believed it. Well, OK! They can all believe it if they want to. What can I do?' she thought wearily, and then immediately called to mind her father.

'As soon as Abba Mian returns from his tour he will receive, if not the full version, at least an edited version of the incident.'

The thought upset her. 'Would Abba Mian now never claim that I am the most beautiful of all his children? And say as he often did to calm Ammah Begum's temper, "Begum, my girl is not bad at heart. Do, at least, try to understand her". Now, would he never say things like that in her defence?'

She grew morose at the thought. That afternoon she seemed to be quieter and sadder than usual and finally she gained access to the outside verandah where he sat every morning and every evening smoking his hookah and reading his newspaper. He was lying in an easy chair with the silver pipe of the decorated low hookah in his mouth. His eyes were closed and he was in a deep reverie surrounded by the mild fragrance of the tobacco. On the table before him, along with the papers, stood an open copy of Maulana Rumi's epic poem written in Persian. The wind had teased its pages open. She came forward on tiptoes and as the breeze turned the pages Gaythi's eyes fell on a verse,

'The strings of the lute are dry, so is its skin and the wood
From whence do I hear then the voice of my soul mate?'

This was her father's favourite couplet. He used to read it in his beautiful, steady and sonorous voice. Gaythi had asked him to explain the meaning several times.

She stood for a moment, hesitating, watching the man who always reminded her of jasmine and bela flowers, the cool rays of the moon, beautiful open spaces and powerful pillars.

Suddenly she became impatient to discover whether her father's crystal clear heart had also clouded with doubts against her. She bowed impulsively and leaned her head against her father's chest. She could hear the beat of a heart which she knew was loving.

Startled by the wetness of her profuse tears, he laid his hand gently on her head. Her heart melted further against the warmth of his hand.

'It's not nice, child!' he remonstrated gently, 'you mustn't weep like that. Look at me!'

She looked up at him, tears in her eyes. His eyes were not reproachful but were full of pain.

'So have I really hurt my father?' she thought fearfully.

'Abba Mian!'

'Yes, child?' he answered abstractedly.

'Did you believe as well what Arjumand and Ammah Begum said?'

'Gaythi! You mustn't suspect others.'

'Well then, Abba Mian?'

He understood the query in her eyes, 'Ammah Begum told me nothing. But when something happens, others report it too.'

'Abba Mian!'

'Yes.'

'You don't think I am a liar, do you?'

'No! I am certain that my daughter never lies.'

'Then please believe what I tell you.'

'Say it.'

And she narrated the whole story very simply. There was no hypocrisy or deception in her tone, only the sincerity and innocence of truth. Then she asked him in a tearful voice, 'Abba Mian! Could you be persuaded to believe that your daughter is so evil?'

'No, child. Daughters are like a sacred vow for their fathers.' Her father's tone carried the same depth of sincerity and truth as hers.

He sat thinking for a little while, then he spoke gently, 'Gaythi! Will you listen to me?'

She fixed her weeping eyes on his face in reply, and he began to speak in his typical, measured and gentle tone. 'Look, child! It is possible that a mother and her children may not think alike, but it is impossible for a mother to be deliberately unjust to her children. I know that your mother's views are quite different from yours, but, according to her lights, she thinks only of your welfare.'

Gaythi bowed her head with shame and he continued to speak, 'Children and their fathers are both obliged to venerate mothers, child! Especially fathers who are always under a huge obligation to them for rearing their children with tremendous endurance. That household where the mothers understand their daughters, and where the daughters respect their mothers' sentiments is specially blessed.'

He became silent after that and looked away sadly. He did not say anything else but it grieved him deeply that his children and the person he loved and to whom he had entrusted his all were not close and did not understand each other.

He had revealed only one of his thoughts to her in very gentle words but the tears flowed from her eyes once again. She placed her head on his knees and said slowly, 'Abba Mian! I promise you that I will never hurt your feelings.'

'Nor Ammah Begum's.' He stroked her head.

Gaythi raised her head and rose without answering him, 'You are not angry with me, are you, Abba Mian?'

'No, child!'

She turned to leave.

'Gaythi, shall I say something?' he called out to her.

'Yes.'

'Remember this. You're older now. When one grows up one has to give up perforce lots of the casual ways and habits of childhood.' He took her hand in his and kissed it affectionately before letting it drop. 'Yes, you can go now.' She left his presence with sorrowful but confident steps. He put the pipe in his mouth again, but his hookah had got cold. He pushed it away. The pages of Rumi's poem were flapping in the wind. This time, his eye caught one of his favourite lines:

'From whence do I hear then the voice of my soul mate?'

'Ah! this voice of the friend.' He had heard it several times despite his worldly preoccupations and his purely material style of living. In the wilds, in uninhabited places and sometimes even in the hubbub and crowded company of others this voice would reach him. And here was yet another strange coincidence that, sometimes, suddenly, he would hear a faint echo of that familiar voice in the disjointed discourse of this remarkably strange, and to quote Begum, uncontrollable daughter of his.

28

In the first instance this was not simply a question about whether or not Sheharyaar would ever return. The hopes he had raised in Chachi jaan's heart by adopting a certain manner towards Ismat had been wrecked by his mother's conduct and that of his maternal relatives, immediately after Saulat's wedding. There was nothing else left there but the grand ruins of Pompeii buried under the cold lava, to be preserved forever. But besides that she had heard that Sheharyaar did not intend to return. And now, for the past two years, he had even stopped asking for money.

Very gently and indirectly she revealed this state of affairs to Ismat too. That girl, who according to her, had her dead father's carefree disposition, heard the entire truth in her characteristically casual manner and swallowed it so surreptitiously that no one could assess how much it had affected her.

Sometimes she suspected that this brief romance and failure in love was not a tragedy of her daughter's life but her own. Although she felt sorry at having lost such a good match, she was also glad that her daughter was not as affected by losing Sheharyaar as she had expected her to be. She was not in any special hurry to get Ismat married. She believed that to marry a girl off without preparing her for life was a little selfish. It is true that such haste ended the parents' responsibility for the girl but it put her in conflict with an uncertain future for the rest of her life.

'Yes, of course. If I had been fit for anything I would not have been a burden to my mother-in-law! *Arrey*, a life without any self-respect is not worth living.' Often, the self-respecting and honourable woman inside her would feel enraged at her own incompetence and she had decided that whether or not others objected, and however hard it might prove, she would make sure that both her daughters were able to deal with life before she decided to separate them from herself.

It was a blessing that her mother-in-law agreed with her views. Despite her old age and traditionalism she believed that the real dowry of a daughter is her achievements; everything else is for show and for others to use, only her achievements remain her own. Secretly she was unhappy with her middle son's wife for having married Saulat off to a middle-aged man without letting her achieve anything herself.

'*Bibi*! I do not approve of a half-baked education. A woman should either be illiterate or highly educated. You have to be one or the other, or you remain without peace forever.'

Nevertheless, proposals for Ismat would come quite often. Her mother found it hard to fix her heart on anyone after having thought of someone as handsome, decent and splendid as Sheharyaar in that capacity, even though she had not compared them with him consciously. However, he entered her thoughts unconsciously the very moment she considered the subject. The very first thought that troubled her was her certainty that wherever he might be, and however happy he might be, he would be saddened by the news of Ismat's wedding.

She would see the grief-stricken face of that boy who was so distant from her now, but whom she had loved since his early childhood. He had been attached to her too, from the very beginning. The truth was that Sheharyaar had been very fond of his uncle. And his uncle had always regarded him as a son.

After his uncle's death, this special place had been occupied by Chachi jaan, who always treated him as special, knowing that her late husband had loved him dearly. This was the reason why she had disliked all those proposals in spite of careful consideration.

On the day Ismat took the last paper for her BA final examinations such an unexpected proposal came for her that it elevated her even in her mother's estimation. She smiled with pride and happiness, quite contrary to habit, right in front of the people who had conveyed the proposal.

This was not a proposal from an ageing colonel or a person who owned property but from that low-ranking journalist with a sad face who was known to the world as Zubair. But they all knew well that he had been a god in Saulat's eyes. She had worshipped him right up to the time of her wedding, and that was the only reason why Chachi jaan quickly accepted this proposal for her daughter, rejecting others who were far superior to him in terms of status and looks. Her very first reaction was that Saulat Begum would be left watching in helpless astonishment, as she holds everyone else in such contempt. The second thought which surfaced in her head was that her older sister-in-law would smoulder with jealousy for she had assumed that if Zubair did not get Saulat he would spend the rest of his life grieving for her like a yogi.

Ismat was a strange girl too. That girl – who had so often carried missives from Saulat Apa to Zubair Bhai – wore the ring which had come for her, from his house, and smiled in private for a very long time, thinking that this was indeed a comical situation. '*Bhai*, I shall tell Saulat Apa, quite plainly that I can't help it. It was you who failed to keep the man you had loved.' Then she looked at Sheharyaar's photograph on the mantelpiece and thought, 'You can see for yourself, Barrey Bhaiya, how could I do anything now? You can't blame me for any of this! You know everything yourself.'

But, in spite of consoling herself in this way, and shedding all the blame, her eyelashes had become rather moist. 'Who knows where Barrey Bhaiya is, and what he's doing right now!' she thought again, and left the room.

That same evening she saw her mother standing beside Sheharyaar's photograph, full of sadness. Her beautiful, large eyes looked red. When she saw her daughter she turned away towards the bathroom. Ismat felt extremely sorry for her mother at that moment.

In reality, these were all concoctions of Chachi jaan's own mind. Her older sister-in-law held only one of life's achievements in any regard. That was wealth, in fact, unlimited wealth. There was no room there for such follies. Nor was there any provision for smouldering in jealousy. She felt absolutely satisfied with the proposal she had picked for her daughter, Saulat, after considerable thought and reflection.

As for Begum Saulat Asif Jah, she had risen above all these things so the question of her watching in helpless astonishment did not even arise.

What her heart had had to endure had already been endured. A long time before now she had learnt a lesson on the occasion of her own marriage,

> 'Whatever is ordained for me,
> I must endure, anyhow.
> Even the heart broken by malice and enmity
> finds respite from all its griefs eventually.'

That lesson from a young Chinese boy had also slipped very far out of her mind's reach. She had found that statement very sweet and convincing then, but now, if she remembered all this even by accident, she would laugh at it very lightheartedly and say, 'How foolish one is at that age! What do people mean by the term "fate"? These are all proofs of my good fortune. Now I am truly deserving of the title "the children of emperors". And this Li (the beauty of conduct and good character) and Cin zi (the virtues of decency) are all inventions of those who are less fortunate and unlucky, created only to escape reality.' Her Chiang Kai Shek had given her a house like a palace to live in, and a royal life to lead. He had given her the support of his rank and power which she could use to do whatever she pleased. Power which was so terrifying that no one could point a finger at her.

The news of Zubair's marriage with Ismat had presented itself to Saulat like a joke. 'It would be an interesting after dinner joke,' she thought, carelessly putting the brief and simple invitation on her writing table, and sat down to write an elaborate letter of congratulations to Chachi jaan on her husband's special monogrammed writing pad.

'One thing is certain, I shall definitely be attending this wedding,' she thought. She did not know why the news of the wedding had made her extremely happy. 'There was certainly no need for Ismat to marry Barrey Bhaiya as she wanted to. Nonsense. These are all foolish notions. After all *I* got married to someone against my express wishes.'

She had come to her mother's house in order to attend that wedding. When Ammah Begum discovered her intention she opposed it quite strongly. Firstly, she did not think that her appearance at that wedding behoved her standing. Secondly, the marriage was taking place with Zubair, and she thought fearfully that this could wreck her peace of mind for no rhyme or reason, when she was quite happy with Asif Jah now.

Saulat understood her doubts well. She sensed her anxiety and really relished it thinking, 'Ammah Begum thinks that I am a real fragile darling! As if my heart were made of glass. *Arrey*, I am not that inexperienced and simple-natured Saulat Jehangir. Ammah Begum, this is Begum Saulat Asif Jah, who makes her own decisions and whose innermost feelings do not concern even Asif Jah himself. I can kick ten men like Zubair if I want to and Asif Jah dare not breathe a word. This is the only great advantage of a modern set-up.'

Having thought all this, she spoke very gently but very decisively, 'No, Ammah Begum, I will definitely go. This is the only wedding which will take place at Dadi Ammah's house. Everyone who has ever been part of our family will be there and all the old rituals will be observed. I would like to see them. No one even bothered to hide the bridegroom's shoe when I got married.'

'Who could have stolen that old fatso's shoe?' Gaythi, who sat on the wooden divan embroidering initials on pillowcases spoke up.

Saulat looked at her with deep malice and hostility, 'This evil-tongued girl always speaks in this manner and knocks my pride and dignity.' Saulat hated this kind of perversity and freedom of spirit.

'God punish you for that tongue,' Ammah Begum scolded her and ordered, 'Go and tell Shareef to make some tea and bring it here.'

'I wonder if Ammah Begum will take me along or not,' she wondered faint-heartedly. She had only recently finished her matriculation examination and now found herself free of those hated studies. These days there were so many strictures on her that a lot of her old habits had vanished. For instance, she had not sat on the wall for several months now. She had not climbed the mulberry tree to pick mulberries, but she did not touch the ones Mali had picked for them either. The worst deprivation, of course, had been the fact that although she had been longing to slap the good-looking son of Ammah Begum's favourite acquaintance, the Chief Engineer, because the wretched boy flirted with her so brazenly, she had not been able to do so. That was exactly what Ammah Begum wanted him to do, because he was planning to take the civil service examination in the following year.

If he had tried this a year ago she would have hooked her leg in his and toppled him down so badly that he would have fallen flat on his back. But, these days her spirit felt as though it had been crushed. Nevertheless, she would think, 'Just wait till my results are out.'

Who knows what the result would have achieved. Now she was not even bothered about whether or not Ammah Begum would let her go to the wedding.

Thus, these days she seemed surrounded by the dark clouds of disappointment and loneliness, and in the midst of those clouds that intelligent and dark face would appear as if it were asking, 'Well, Gaythi!

Won't you come even with this wonderful opportunity within reach? Who knows whether you will ever be able to come again or not? Are you not interested in me at all now?'

'Yes, why not, Masood? I am not interested in anyone else but you. But you are so awful that you proposed to Arjumand; wretched man! If you had said all that to me, I would have given you a completely different answer. But I don't care. You can propose to anyone, for all I care. The thing is, you and I never made a vow which required that you should love me too.'

Her mind would be busy with these thoughts when her hands were occupied with uninteresting tasks.

29

As soon as the excitement of the wedding stirred the house with the arched doorways and the platform seats, the old memory of Ismat's father, Khaquan Mirza, who had died a young death, yawned, stretched and awakened too. On this point the mother-in-law concurred completely with her daughter-in-law and her two girls. On any occasion, their eyes would brim with tears on the slightest pretext, and they would have to struggle to restrain their sighs. This wedding was different from Saulat's wedding in every way. Their eldest uncle's family could not attend, nor did he himself arrive in time from Madras.

But Jehangir Mirza's family had arrived several days in advance, and he came three days before the wedding. He stood in for her father for the purposes of all the ceremonies and the songs. He was fulfilling his role in all of these with great sadness but with his fullest attention. To tell the truth, the business of living had made him a stranger to the memory of his brother, but on the occasion of his niece's wedding that memory had come very close to him, to live in his heart. He almost felt as though any minute his brother might just appear from nowhere, his head bowed, his eyes smiling in his characteristic absent-minded manner.

Sheharyaar was still abroad and Bakhtiar's holidays had not yet begun so the only boy who seemed able to take on any errands was Masood. At his uncle's insistence, Masood had to move in with them until the wedding. After running around the whole day, when the girls sat down to sing with the *dholak*, Masood made sure he insinuated himself into the group. He would make a sign to Talat, Arjumand and Kaamni to stop singing, so that Gaythi was left alone to raise her voice. She would carry on unawares before suddenly realising that the other voices were not accompanying hers, and would get cross, 'Waah, I'm not a comedienne that I should be expected to perform alone.'

'What else are you then?' Masood would speak up behind her. She would simmer, fume and slink away from there.

That moonlit night before the wedding day they all sat on a gleaming seat, singing, under the moulsari tree. Gaythi was losing her voice and she had a handkerchief tied round her throat. Everyone asked Kaamni to start the singing. She beat her long delicate fingers on the *dholak* and hid her large eyes under silken lashes. A very attractive blush played on her dark face. She cleared her throat and had just sung the first few notes when someone came up behind her and placed a hand over her mouth. Then he leaned close to her and said, 'Watch it! Are you an entertainer that you should be singing by yourself? You should sing only when the others join in.' She glanced casually at Gaythi.

And Gaythi felt as if she stood alone in a wild, scalding desert, surrounded on all sides by a yellow, shameless sun which glared at her with its pupils wide open. Ouf! The terrible silence and solitude! Masood appeared to be very close to that girl. Their complexions were similar, the shape of their faces bore a marked resemblance and, worst of all, that unfortunate reality of all times: they belonged to the same class, whilst she herself was way beyond their world. She rose quietly and disappeared from there.

Everyone had gathered in Dadi Ammah's part of the house. There was no one in Chachi jaan's little courtyard at that time. She went and lay down on a charpoy, face downwards. Silent tears poured steadily from the corners of her eyes, soaking her pillow. Her throat was dry and painful. She looked up helplessly at the sorrowful moon and then lowered her head again. A shadow emerged from behind the weeping nyctanthes tree in front of her and came to sit stiffly near the edge of her bed.

'*Arrey*, you crazy girl! What's the matter with you?'

The crazy girl went on drying her tears without answering.

'You haven't gone mad, have you?' He grasped her short hair and tugged at it.

She stayed silent.

'Gaythi!' Masood's voice was heavy and tearful. She planted her narrow eyes on his face instead of replying.

'Give me an answer.'

'To what?'

'Do you think I am made of stone?'

110

'What difference does it make, whether you're stone or flesh and blood, Masood?'

'Wretched girl, she talks as if she were a philosopher,' he mused. 'You're a great philosopher, aren't you and I an utter fool?'

'What else do you want?'

'Idiot, fool! You should be ashamed of yourself for suspecting me like that.'

He wanted to call her worse names than that for having lost her faith in him and weeping so.

Slowly his face had drawn close to her head, and he could again inhale the bewitching fragrance emanating from her straight black hair. He rose and left in a panic. As he was leaving, it struck him, 'Why should she act in this manner which signals defeat and failure? Weeping like this was beyond her once. She could fight. Crying was not something she was even capable of!'

Saulat's participation and interest in the wedding was fascinating for the entire family. She had been raised to such a different and relatively higher level than the rest of the family that her condescension from that superior position on this occasion was strange in itself. Especially for the relatively lower class and less fashionable members of the tribe, who were not even aware of how the world had progressed in recent years. The women were impressed by everything about her and worshipped her with their eyes. They would drag their shy and embarrassed children to introduce them to her.

'Ay, pay your respects, she is your older sister, or aunt. . .' And those poor things, inhibited, withdrawn, dressed in crude satin yellows and blues decorated with contrasting braids or dressed in shorts and blouses, would double up with embarrassment.

How could they embrace this beautiful and imposing goddess wrapped in wonderful fragrances as their mothers expected them to? If, instead of her, they had been asked to embrace her sister with short hair and Chinese features they would have done so, winding their arms round her neck without hesitation.

Saulat would laugh inwardly at their ardour. They were not aware that she had only come to see the possible varieties that this old traditional culture was capable of, and having arrived there, felt that there was no point in her staying aloof to establish her own dignity and stature. When a god climbs off his pedestal for some reason, he does not strut around only to demonstrate his superiority. For this reason, she mixed freely with them. Her opinion informed every aspect and detail of the wedding.

111

When the lawyer and the witnesses came in to seek the bride's consent, all the women who had surrounded the bride moved out of their sight to maintain their purdah but she remained right in the centre, her head uncovered, supporting the bride's bowed neck. After listening to the terms of the marriage contract, detailing the alimony etcetera, for the very first time, she entreated the bride in a heavy, philosophical tone, 'Come on, now. Say, "yes," my very own sister!' The bride responded to this insistence a trifle too promptly as well and said, 'yes'. Then very strongly she began to urge the bride not to weep, asking her why she was crying, when, after all, there was no real reason for tears on this occasion.

The bride paused in the midst of her tears, and wondered at the fact that she herself did not know why she was crying. True, there is no reason why I should cry! But this tradition of weeping has been handed down through generations and has possibly become instinctive to every bride so that she begins weeping effortlessly, despite her knowledge that there is no reason for tears. She was secretly offended at what Saulat had said. But the bald-headed and short-sighted witnesses who seemed weary of life were extremely pleased with Saulat and grateful to her for making their task easier. Otherwise, they would have had to parrot those sentences a few times in their phlegmatic voices, and would have had to cock their ears to try and hear the bride's muffled, 'Hmm.' One of the older men who was hard of hearing went to the extent of remarking that she was a very obedient girl, keen on observing the laws of the Shariat, for the most venerated course is speed when it comes to saying 'yes' to marriage vows, or when it is a matter of delivering a coffin to its last resting place.

Saulat had expended all her artistry in adorning the bride for the occasion. She had spent three full hours on getting her ready. Zubair, who was sitting amongst his friends, waiting to be called in after the wedding ceremony had ended, heard that the reason he had not yet been called in for the ritual first glimpse of his bride through a mirror was that she was still being made up, by Begum Saulat Asif Jah.

At that time, just thinking of Saulat's manner, self-assurance, and awesome dignity, Zubair felt intimidated. '*Arrey*. Forgive me, Lord. What a fool I used to be. "It is indeed a blessing that I escaped!"' The memory of the Persian proverb brought a smile to his lips.

It was true that Asif Jah's Begum had taken enormous time and trouble to adorn his bride. That delicate and pretty girl had been transformed into a fragrant and enchanting dream.

Her aunt, Ismat's mother, felt a pang of bitter reproach in her heart, as she watched Saulat's dedication, 'Why, Saulat! Why couldn't you take

112

her back as a bride to your own home, dressed and adorned like this, with your own hands?'

Today, she had missed Sheharyaar several times and for several reasons.

<h1 style="text-align:center">30</h1>

No one was likely to have been happier or more contented than Gaythi at the festivity surrounding that wedding. That arrogant but lovable man had said such a wonderful thing to her: 'Idiot, fool! You should be ashamed of yourself, suspecting me like that.'

It was the very thing she had been desperate to hear for the past two years. After saying that, Masood had assumed his earlier indifference. He would tease Kaamni all the time and ask her to do various chores for him, but Gaythi remained happy and content. In fact, she felt sorry for Kaamni.

'Poor thing! How sweet she is, and how fond of Masood! Masood, who was made only for me.'

She was truly generous and big-hearted. She was not jealous or envious of that girl at all now. When she saw him teasing her during the afternoon, she said, 'Masood! Isn't she sweet? A lovable creature.'

Masood looked at her as if to ask, 'Can there be anything sweeter than you, silly girl? Full of love and self-confidence. Rude and self-willed like Satan, but big-hearted like Mother Earth.' But he did not utter a single word. A strange fear and anxiety stirred in his heart.

When Gaythi's family started to prepare for their departure she said to Chachi jaan, 'I would so like to stay behind with you.'

'Why, yes! It would have been nice if you could have stayed.' If there was anyone amongst her brother-in-law's children she loved, besides Sheharyaar, it was Gaythi.

'Then make me stay, please.'

'I am afraid, eh? Is it possible that your mother would listen to me?'

'She will, but if Dadi Ammah says it with you. And she will leave me if you say it in front of Abba Mian.'

'I shall say it today. I have been so depressed since Ismat left.' She felt close to tears. 'It would help to cheer us up if you stayed behind.'

She raised the subject over lunch that day. 'This house will become unbearable when all of you are gone. It will get so silent!'

'What! God forbid that this house should seem silent. God protect it from the evil eye, but an ordinary day here feels like a party in other people's homes,' Ammah Begum said laughingly.

'Nevertheless, that's all taken for granted,' Dadi Ammah said. 'When guests depart even a full house feels empty.'

'That's true,' Chachi jaan agreed, placing the sauce boat in front of her. 'I really want to keep Gaythi here for a few days. She has already finished her examinations.'

'By all means, keep her,' Jehangir Mirza consented. 'She has been extremely bored over there, recently.' Then he glanced at Gaythi, 'Well, my friend! What do you think? Will you stay with your Dadi Ammah for a few days?'

'I would like to stay, but . . . '

Ammah Begum stared at her with raging eyes, and she stopped mid-stream. But Abba Mian just then spoke up, 'OK, then, it's settled. I won't order a ticket for Gaythi. You can keep her for as long as you like, so long as you send her back a few days before her results are out.'

Noticing that his wife seemed a little disconcerted, he expanded, '*Bhai*, my children should also look after my mother sometimes.'

This time, when she stayed behind, Dadi Ammah observed her very closely. How friendly and simple this girl was: this girl, whose mother was always out of humour with her. She never objected to anything, never refused to do anything, and she was specially attentive to her needs.

'I did not realise that of all Jehangir Mirza's children, this is the most valuable gem,' she said, embracing her one day.

It occurred to Gaythi that this was an expression used most often to describe Arjumand. Does this mean that Dadi Ammah thinks like Safdar? He is the only person who has always considered me to be more worthy of attention than Arjumand.

Masood had not discovered that she had stayed behind. He came that way after several days to find that the girl who lay face downwards on a little bed, under the dense shade of the moulsari tree, was neither Talat nor Kaamni. He came nearer. Gaythi lay with her face on the open book.

'*Arrey*, this dormant head carries a passion for me!' Masood's heart leapt for joy. He felt like bending over to shower kisses on that mass of black hair but he stayed at a slight distance from her, picking the buds of the moulsari, and called out instead, 'Hello, Chinese! You're lying here, like the dead! I'd heard that you people had left. When are you going back?'

She raised her head and said, 'They've all gone, and I stayed behind.'

114

'Why? What madness kept you behind? I hope you'll make your own arrangements to travel back. I'm not going to ferry you around.'

'Who are you to ferry me around? I can go by myself.'

'Sure. If you go by yourself, Dadi Ammah will kill you.'

'She won't. D'you know she really loves me.'

'Get away! Who can love you? She must be saying things to humour you. Have you ever known anyone to love people who are crazy?'

'Not even you?' She was being irrational again.

'What do you mean? Have I been bitten by a mad dog?' He pushed her and sat down on the same bed.

'Move over, you wretch. Creeping into a tiny space like that,' she moved to the edge of the bed.

'All right. Tell me why haven't you gone back?'

'What do you lose by my staying behind, Masood? I am not taking up room in your house. What's the harm in my staying on? At least, I don't get told off here all the time.'

'Why should you get told off all the time?' he asked sympathetically, concerned that she might be suffering because of suspicions about him. 'What's the matter, Gaythi? You look worried, this time.'

That great big fool had always been very vulnerable; if someone spoke sympathetically, she would spill out everything. Her eyes filled with tears immediately and she repeated the whole story, not even concealing the fact that she had been beaten.

Masood heard her in silence. He felt that it was highly objectionable that Gaythi should have stayed out for so long in the park with Safdar Yaaseen without seeking anyone's permission, or telling anyone about it.

He remarked drily, 'That was really out of order, Gaythi! One has to say that you get down to some quite shameless things.'

'Huh! What's so shameless about it?'

'Why did you have to sit in the park with China Man?'

'So what! Did I go to find him, do you think? It was just a coincidence.'

'Yes, but still.' Masood was certain that it was only a coincidence, but he did not agree with her somewhat simple attitude that there was nothing at all wrong with sitting around chatting to people of the same ilk as China Man. He tried to explain things to her again, 'Girls are always in a delicate position, and these people are never fit to . . .'

Gaythi made no effort to listen to what he was saying, and started thinking morosely instead, 'Truly, no one understands me except that Safdar Liu Chu. Allah! Why are so many things in life unsuitable and objectionable? The position of girls has been made delicate without good reason.' She sat feeling deeply disconcerted and preoccupied. Masood found it very interesting to watch her in that state.

Chachi jaan suddenly noticed that Masood was spending rather a lot of time in their house. It occurred to her that they never used to see him for months at a time and now, for some reason, he spent most of his time there. As soon as she observed that she also guessed that Gaythi's conduct with him was different. That deduction gave her special pleasure.

'It is a strange coincidence that as much as the mother has always hated poor relatives, three of her children, one after the other, have leaned towards them. Two of them she managed to restrain, but this girl has the spirit of a genie. Let's see how this new story will conclude!' she speculated.

So she deliberately encouraged Gaythi during this short stay. A hidden desire would nudge her heart, 'God punish this woman for her pride, for she insulted me and my daughter during Saulat's wedding. It would be great if this girl of hers insists on getting her own way. All I want is to see her mother defeated.'

But the notion that she was responsible for consolidating what was a passing fancy, was merely an illusion on Chachi jaan's part. In Gaythi's mind that thought had become firm the very first time it had emerged with clarity. She had managed to influence Masood's inclination with her own will, without his having a clear sense of that. In her own mind there was no confusion or complexity surrounding the question, 'Whatever I have thought, I have considered thoroughly, and that's it.'

Her staying on had livened up the house considerably. She was completely informal and generous. Besides Talat, Kaamni was also fond of her. Masood would come round and the four of them would have a boisterous time together. Listening to their chatter, arguments and passions, Chachi jaan would forget her years.

Those days felt as if they were winged, and were simply flying by. There were now only days left before her result was due. Submerged in her fears, Gaythi forgot everything else and prepared to leave. At least if she failed she would not have to face people other than her own immediate family.

That afternoon when he came he found Gaythi preparing for her departure. She sat folding and packing her clothes. He came and stood nearby. He had been feeling glum all morning without reason and his worst fears came true. He saw her from a distance and guessed that she was leaving.

'What a strangely clumsy girl she is!' he thought as he sat down near

116

her, and addressed her. 'Are you folding clothes or just trying to ruin the ironing?' She raised her eyes and glanced at him, 'What does it matter to you? As if you're any good at housewifely skills.'

'Huh! Is this a suitcase or a squirrel's hoard!' He bent down and dragged out a handful of packed clothes. 'Look at Arjumand, what a contrast! She does everything so perfectly.'

'Curse you! You've just gone and pulled out things which had already been packed.' She sat down grumpily, '*Bhai*, Masood! You're so ill-mannered.'

'As if your packing showed any ability or good taste. And what's this insolence? Aren't you ashamed of calling someone who is older than you ill-mannered? You incompetent! God forgive me, now I shall have to teach you how to pack a suitcase.' He undid all the clothes she had folded.

'Go away! Learn some manners yourself first,' she spoke irritably.

He went off to sit in the verandah and sulk. He felt deeply pained at finding her suddenly busy, preparing to leave.

Talat had gone to see Kaamni and Chachi jaan had gone to visit Dadi Ammah just a little while earlier. Gaythi was alone sorting out her packing. With great difficulty she shoved back all the clothes Masood had pulled out and scattered, into the suitcase and then went to look for something she had misplaced.

'*Arrey, bhai!* I'll be gone soon, and you're sitting here sulking for nothing.'

'Go, away! No one asked you to stay. Why didn't you leave earlier?'

'I'll leave when I feel ready to go.'

'Go, then. Who's stopping you? But you've taken away my peace.'

'Do you think I should just stay here forever? Never go home?' She looked at him in surprise, '*Bhai*, what madness!'

'Have I said as much to you?' Masood could not come up with an answer.

Gaythi gave him a searching look. His face looked pale, he looked defeated.

She laughed, 'You look so nice when you get cross.'

'Fool. Silly ass! Don't talk to me. This is what I was afraid of.'

'Look here, Masood. Just listen to me', she spoke seriously now. 'It doesn't follow that I should stay here forever. Doesn't make sense, does it?'

'It's nothing. You go now. Get yourself admitted to a college and stay happy. And after a few days you can tell your friends a joke with relish, about a certain fool, called Masood. Tell them, "I played a joke on him and he was completely taken in. He didn't even stop to think that there was no match between us. Look at the splendour of Rajah Bhoj, and . . ."'

She put her hand across his mouth suddenly and said, 'Masood, look at me. Do you think I'm that low? Don't you trust me at all?'

Masood looked at her. Her small eyes glinted with resoluteness, and her Mongolian face glowed with honesty.

He kept gazing at her without saying anything and then that naive and short-sighted girl suddenly started explaining to him very soberly, adopting a very realistic tone. 'Look! One should be practical in every respect, whether it's a question of your heart or your mind. To think beyond the promise that we have given each other is nothing but foolishness. Of course I am not a quiet and compliant daughter like Arjumand. As soon as I get back I am going to let Ammah Begum know that when she is making a decision about my future she should not even think of anyone else except you, until the time when you are able to support yourself. And listen. I promise you now that I will work very hard and will never fail. So we should both be able to manage somehow. Isn't that right?' She spoke as if he were a very young child, whom she was trying to cajole and persuade, very gently and mildly.

She was saying all these things so casually, as if it were only child's play. She was talking just as she used to when they used to play together, 'So, we'll do it this way. Yes, and so that will happen.'

'That's right, Gaythi! You went away and you can see what happened. All the joyous splendours of the rainy season fled with you. Dark rain-clouds come thundering and spilling over and the nightingales sing in the groves of mango trees.

'Even when the sky is azure and the breeze is cool, I feel as if I am alone in a solitary blazing wilderness. You had reassured me. But my heart does not accept that. Your family are used to aiming for the heights.

'You've done something wrong, Gaythi! This was my final year. Your joke has snatched away my peace of mind.' Masood brooded over and over again, as he shut his book.

31

It was as if a storm had blown through the house. Ammah Begum remained shocked and stunned for two days. Just imagine Gaythi's cheek and daring! There was no limit to her rage.

Then suddenly she steadied herself. An express letter was despatched to Saulat and an express letter came from Saulat to her, and her anger abated.

She called Gaythi to her room, looked at her contemptuously but said to her in a gentle tone, 'This isn't the right time for these things. You should only be concerned about your studies at present. After that you should think about your decision once again and then tell me.'

'I haven't asked you to hurry things at all,' she spoke without raising her bowed head and left the room.

Ammah Begum could not help smiling ironically at her good luck. Whilst raising her children she had tried her utmost to make them above the ordinary and set their sights high. But her children loved lowliness. 'God only knows, why they all struggle to fall into the very depths of degradation! Well, never mind. If life and death are insistent upon playing pranks on me, I too am not willing to be defeated.'

God had already helped her to succeed twice, so why should she have felt any despair the third time round?

Ammah Begum's letter, detailing Gaythi's follies and seeking Saulat's advice and help, lay open before her on her dressing table. As she clamped her beautiful hair into curling pins she thought, 'I see. So Gaythi Begum is going full throttle. Wonderful! Look at her guts and gall – being able to speak so shamelessly about these issues to Ammah Begum which neither Barrey Bhaiya nor I had considered appropriate to discuss! But then she was always rude.'

She looked at her wide, gleaming forehead in the mirror and then dropped her eyes to examine her lovely eyelids which were naturally dark, so that she never felt the need to darken them artificially.

'I must say Gaythi's deeds and thoughts were always petty! Since she was little her habits have always been different from the rest of us. It is true that Ammah Begum's strictures have confirmed her in her head-strong ways. She was always stubborn, the wretch; and then she has neither good looks nor attractiveness.'

Suddenly that pale colouring, the wide face and narrow eyes flashed before her in her imagination and she smiled to herself. In any case, it was unlikely that Gaythi would have many golden opportunities thrown her way. 'If she were to listen to me, I'd say that she should keep her head down and quietly agree to whatever Ammah Begum suggests. She will appear to be mindful of her filial duties and she will also enjoy the other advantage of being able to live her life the way she wants to. As for all these questions of morality, various principles and strictures, these are all the inventions of people who are powerless. Look at me now, the Begum of General Asif Jah, I have no problems!'

She smiled and glanced at her full-length reflection emerging in the purple light which filtered through the lampshade. In the transparent pink nightgown, her glowing pearl complexion carried a hint of gold like whisky. She stretched and once again her eye fell on Ammah Begum's letter.

'Huh! What a nuisance! There were so many more important things than Gaythi and her wretched Masood. This is not the time to be thinking about them. In truth, one can sort them out when the time comes.'

At that time, what she felt most preoccupied with was the person of Colonel Sajjad, who would be sitting in the mess, laughing and talking. Or he might be bent over his favourite drink, seriously absorbed in his vision of her, Saulat Asif Jah.

'Ah, Colonel Sajjad! What a powerful and attractive person!' Was she truly and sincerely interested in Colonel Sajjad this time? She herself had not been able to decide. For a long time before this, she had been possessed by the attractive personality of Nawaz. For ages she pretended to be an admirer of Indian classical music, just to please him and go up in his estimation. With the greatest devotion she would sit by his side and listen to the ragas and their declensions, to which she could not respond at all. To her ears they sounded like the screeching of lambs at the slaughterhouse. Her spirit would resist but she struggled against all these trials with the greatest patience and tolerance because that was the only way to appease the god whose name was Nawaz. He would either be completely immersed in purely technical talk to do with his profession or, when he was at leisure, he would attempt to drown himself in Indian classical music. He would be in raptures over each and every beat, in ecstasy over each new melody. Sometimes, in the excitement of the moment, sitting in a quiet corner of the club lounge, he would try to explain it to her, 'So, Begum Saulat Aa . . .' He would never finish saying the name of her husband. 'What I mean to say is, this raga, the Asawari, is a raga for the early morning. Its notes are linked with the waves in the atmosphere. It holds the reins of the forces of the supernatural. Its spirit

120

manifests itself in the shape of the lotus flower. The goddess of this raga is dressed in saffron-coloured robes and its colouring is blended with the ashes of cow dung.' Listening to all of this, she would heave a suppressed sigh 'Oh!'

'Why, what's the matter?'

'It's nothing,' she would say in a mysterious tone. 'Nawaz! In that instant I felt as if this goddess of the Bhairveen was standing before my eyes.'

'But I wasn't talking about the Bhairveen.' He would get annoyed.

'That is the problem! You're talking about something else and the Bhairveen insists on coming to stand before me,' she would try to persuade him very innocently. And at that moment Nawaz' beautiful eyes would strive to drink in those eyes before which the Bhairveen and the Asawari appeared in person.

'An intelligent woman is a blessing,' he would reflect with a deep sigh. Then he would immediately launch into an emotional tirade against his wife's and General Asif Jah's lack of good taste. He would elaborate on this in an impassioned manner, forgetting himself; and Begum Saulat Asif Jah would sit before him, an expression of patient helplessness on her face, as if she were truly distressed by Asif Jah's lack of refinement. Although in fact it was the only certainty in her life. Asif was an extremely simple person, if rather plainly solid like the bare stump of a tree. Her husband, Asif Jah, was a very different human being from the personality assumed by General Asif Jah.

Well, no doubt it was an important matter to deal with this Gaythi business, but the appointment with Colonel Sajjad was more important. She could only decide once that rendezvous was over. At that moment, it was ten thirty at night and the most important issue facing her was the problem of saying affectionate things to Asif Jah when she returned to her bedroom. Things like, 'Dear heart, why do you let yourself get so tired? I say, Asif, you must give some time to your wife and children too. Now look at Seema, for days on end she longs to see your face. Yesterday she asked me, "Mummy, is Daddy annoyed with me, he never takes me on his lap?" I just told her, "My darling, your dad has time for everyone except his wife and kids."' She would say all these things and many others in the same vein, without stopping for breath, and so innocently, that all Asif Jah's complaints and doubts would remain unaired and he would feel so ashamed of his neglect that he would succumb to drowsiness. And then Saulat would heave a sigh of relief and fall into a deep sleep.

Slowly she folded Ammah Begum's letter and locked it in her drawer.

She turned off the light in her dressing room and walked towards her bedroom.

32

Her results came. She had secured a pass in the second division. This was not a great achievement for her. Pupils who are preparing for a Cambridge University School Certificate are certain to pass the matriculation examination if on the spur of the moment they decide to take that instead. This was, in fact, another one of Gaythi's petty foibles. In the first place, she had to be stopped from attending school, because of her objectionable behaviour, and then, when the question of taking an examination as a private candidate arose, she agreed very happily to take the matriculation examination. To the sum total of all the woes she had caused to Ammah Begum's heart she added yet another – all her other children had earned Cambridge University credits, and this blessed girl had to be the one to take the local matriculation certificate.

Despite her unexpected success she seemed unhappy and preoccupied. Masood too, had not taken any notice at all of her success. He couldn't even write a few congratulatory words to her. For several days it rankled. If Talat had not written to her she would never have discovered the whole story. Talat wrote her a lengthy letter:

'One day we were all having breakfast when we saw Saulat Apa coming over to see us. Her daughter was with her. Dadi Ammah had a shock seeing her turn up suddenly like that. "Is everything all right, child? How is it that you suddenly come unannounced like this?" All she said in reply was, "I needed to change trains here, so I thought, I'd spend a few hours with you."

'But she was concerned and extremely angry about something. She came to our end of the house after lunch and talked to Ammah in whispers, in response to which Ammah said aloud, "No, child; whatever you want to say you must say yourself. Firstly, I don't wish to get involved. Secondly, who is going to believe me? They'll all assume that I sit here making things up by myself."

'That afternoon she took me and Ammah with her when she went to Masood Bhai's house. The scene she created there was worth watching. She insulted Hashmi Phupho extremely viciously. She said very harsh things, even things like, "You can't change the fortunes of boys by snaring the daughters of the rich." When Hashmi Phupho expressed her ignorance of the whole affair, she told her, "In that case, talk to your son."

'Hashmi Phupho was extremely upset and said, "I am not responsible for that dishonourable person, nor can I assume that responsibility. Whoever wishes to talk to him can do so, if they want."

'Saulat Apa got up, went to Masood's room and said such humiliating things that I could not believe my own ears.

'Then she left to board her train straight from their house. After she had gone Hashmi Phupho said countless nasty things to Masood Bhai. "I expected to earn respect, not dishonour, through you. You have caused me to suffer the most terrible humiliation today. If you are a man of honour, Masood, don't even let their shadows fall across your path ever again." He rose and left without uttering a single word.

'Gaythi! I hope you won't mind if I say that this is entirely your fault. You should not have pulled a stunt like this. Nevertheless, for some reason you people enjoy playing with your lower-class relatives. To tell you the truth, I feel angriest with you over this business: why did you start something like this? I would not have written all this to you but I do know that you are different from all the rest of your family. So I'm writing to let you know that if you care at all for Masood and his mother, then don't do anything which will hurt their self-respect or their feelings. However don't assume that I am annoyed with you. I am still your own,

Talat.'

Talat's letter lay on the table before her and she sat with her head between her hands. Not a single tear had fallen from her eyes. But she felt as if a fire of rage and hatred consumed her entire being. Sparks exploded through every pore of her body and she felt dizzy.

After some time she rose and her feet advanced towards Mali's hovel. It was not something new for the young mistress to visit them. Since she was a small child she had maintained the habit of walking straight into any of the servants' quarters. She would sit on their charpoys, talk to them, eat the *paans* they offered her and play with their children. But now it was almost a year since she had visited them. She had not been allowed to do so. Maalan sat on a bed breast-feeding her baby in the tiny courtyard put together with bamboo poles and thatch at the front of the little hovel, glossy with a fresh coating of unbaked clay. The eldest girl, who was around ten or twelve, sat in the cooking area, cooking the vegetables.

Maalan put the baby down, rearranged her veil and said, '*Arrey*, our young daughter has come to see us today! Would you bring out the cot woven with the new rope, Basanti, and put it down here for our *bitya*?'

'What are you doing, *Bahu*?' Gaythi sat down on the old bed.

'What a lovely little hut,' she thought, looking at the pale yellow flowers on the pumpkin vine which covered the bamboo trellis.

'What are you cooking, Basanti?' Gaythi asked, her wide nostrils gathered up the fragrance of the methi being fried in oil for seasoning the vegetables.

'Spinach with potatoes; will you have some, *bitya*?' Maalan knew her habits well.

'No, don't bother. It's too much trouble.'

'No, *bitya*. Here. I'll cook a chappati for you in a minute.' There was sweetness and warmth in Maalan's voice.

Maalan went behind the screen, poured a couple of pots of water carefully over herself to wash, wrapped a dhoti round her wet body and then entered the cooking area. Basanti ran off to fetch a tender new banana leaf and washed it.

Maalan took the hot chappati off the fire, coated it with some fresh ghee from their village, stored in a small black pot suspended from a frame on which hung various pots and pans. Then she laid it all out beautifully on the leaf for her, spinach with potatoes and tamarind relish, with a slice of pickle.

Gaythi, who had not tasted Maalan's cooking for a long time, fell upon the hot chappati with great enthusiasm. She went and sat by the hand pump when she had finished. Basanti worked the pump for her and she drank the satisfying sips of cold water flavoured mildly with the smell of grease which had been recently applied to the pump. She washed her face with the same cold water and the clouds which weighed upon her heart dispersed. Those flames raging inside her died down. She went and sat on the bed.

'Bring a *paan*, for our *bitya*,' Maalan ordered Basanti, who promptly opened the brass container.

'Do put some of the minty stuff in mine, Basanti.'

Gaythi made Basanti sit by her when she brought her the *paan* and asked her, 'How do you make the tamarind relish? I've asked Cook so many times but he always laughs it off.'

'Well. It is not really difficult. You soak the tamarind pulp in water then rub it. Then you add salt, chillies and sugar, and then finely chopped mint leaves.' The coolness of the peppermint in the *paan* had numbed her mouth. She looked out of the corner of her eye. In a corner of the courtyard stretched the washing line on which hung dhotis. A small brass bucket and shining metal pots were arranged on a raised platform built with bricks and mud reinforced with straw. There was such harmony and peace in all those things.

Gaythi was brooding. Whether it is Mali's house, or Cook's, life is so simple and easy in these homes. With her sore sleepy eyes, she watched the pumpkin vines scattered on the trellis in the shade of the dense and tall kachnar tree. There was such satisfaction to be had from all these things, such comfort. She also knew very well the pains which haunt that life forever. But at least it had not been polluted with haughtiness and false pride. It was free of that tortured atmosphere generated by the polite cold war of nerves. The people who live and breathe here free their hearts of venom by arguing and fighting if they want to. This atmosphere was silent, it seemed full of lullabies. She stretched out on the bare charpoy, under the weeping nyctanthes tree, and dropped off to sleep without intending to. Mali came in wearing half his dhoti, the other half was wrapped round him, a sacred thread hung round his neck. Seeing her asleep, he thought affectionately, 'This *bitya* of ours is a yogi by nature! It is almost as if Mahatama Gautam's restless spirit graces her body. It is as if that man who escaped from his palaces and devotees in disgust had taken abode in the body of this little daughter of ours, who looks such a cheeni!'

Every gust of wind quietly and gently sprinkled the white flowers with their saffron stems off the shivering branches of the nyctanthes on to her. Wells of peace and comfort sprang inside her sleeping body.

She neither gave up eating, nor wept; nor did she sulk and skulk. When she went inside, after having slept there for a long while, Ammah Begum did not question her at all. She had already seen the opened letter which had been left carelessly on the table. Her ends had been achieved and she did not wish to provoke her any further.

Gaythi spent that week very quietly and calmly. Then one afternoon she went to her father's room. 'Abba Mian, I have to say something to you.'

He looked surprised. According to the traditions of that household, to talk to him was indeed a novelty. There had never been any direct communication between him and the children.

'Yes, daughter!' He raised his head to look up from the file of important papers, 'What is it?'

'I have to decide about my admission, now that colleges are opening up for admission.'

'Yes, that's very pleasing. Talk to your mother.'

He pulled the papers towards himself again and put her off in the same dry tone which he used for supplicants at his office when referring them to the officer concerned.

'No. That's not possible. I want to speak only to you about this matter,' she said gently, in a decisive tone.

Her tone was so serious that he became alert. He pushed the papers to one side, took off his glasses, put them in their case and turned his attention towards her.

'What is it, child?'

'Abba Mian I will not take admission here. Please send me to Lahore.'

'Why?' He was startled. 'What's come over her all of a sudden that she should want to leap across a whole region and go to Lahore. Why? And only to study in her first year at that? Wonderful!' If she had not appeared to be as serious as she did, he certainly would have laughed.

'How did you come to think of Lahore?'

'Just like that,' she lowered her head and replied.

'What's the logic behind going to study in a strange and distant city? Let me send you to your grandmother. You can choose to put your name down for any college you want, and then go to a hostel at your convenience.'

'No. I will never go there again.'

'Why? Did you have a row with your grandmother? That's bad, child. She is old and frail. Even if she criticises something you should think that her time is now past: she can't think like you now. She hasn't many days left of her life for us to waste them getting annoyed with her.'

'I? Annoyed with Dadi Ammah? Is that possible? Abba Mian you do not know how much she loves me. I found so much peace there that I never wanted to leave her.' Her voice trembled and tears swam in her eyes.

'Then you must have had an argument with Talat. But, child! She is your sister too. I really wanted to have her stay here with us, but never mind . . .' He did not want to say things to her which would make her aware of the differences between her parents. 'Differences between parents have a terrible effect on children's minds,' he believed.

She did not wish to complain about her mother either. In spite of the differences with her on matters of principle she was aware that whatever she was doing was dictated by her convictions as a mother. To tell the truth, she harboured real venom in her heart only against Saulat Apa.

'I have no grudge against Talat, Abba Mian! But there are some things which we do not want to do without particular reason . . .'

He looked searchingly at this daughter of his, whose twin, Arjumand looked much younger than her in terms of age and experience. She looked very serious and much older at that moment. Her countenance manifested her determination. He heaved a deep sigh. He had always felt that this daughter of his had never been treated justly in that house.

'All right, my daughter. What we'll do is we'll get you admitted at the Kinnaird College in Lahore. Now you can stop worrying.'

She looked at him closely without saying a word. Tall, handsome, Mughal features, a splendid moustache and a very dignified streak of silver rippling though the blackness of his hair – in spite of those splendid good looks, he seemed to be simply her 'Abba' just then.

'What a dear thing a father is,' she thought looking at him fondly out of the corner of her eye.

'If you are keen to stay at a hostel, I'll definitely send you.'

She left him, feeling reassured.

'This is the first time that I shall be intervening between Begum and her children,' he thought. 'But I feel that I have to take an interest in Gaythi's affairs. If she is different and more difficult to understand than the rest of our children it does not automatically follow that she should be completely ignored or systematically opposed.'

He pulled the papers closer to him, and thought, very calmly, 'Gaythi, my daughter! Never mind if your mother finds you difficult to fathom, your father will do his best to understand you.'

33

She opened the doors of the wardrobe and started tidying its contents methodically. Then leaving its doors wide open, she sat down on her bed. There was only one bed in that room now, instead of two, and only one wardrobe. Only one girl's books and possessions lay on the table.

She looked up at the French windows facing west. Lightning leapt through the black clouds gathered across the horizon. She could hear a nightingale singing. A gentle breeze wafted in and Arjumand shivered. It was a year since she had left.

'I had never even imagined that you'd become separated from me like this, Gaythi! Your absence has made me feel utterly desolate. You used to wreck the room with your chaotic habits, and use everything that was mine with a vengeance, and I used to row with you. Now, I really long for you to wreak disorder on the room, to scatter your clothes untidily in the bathroom, and leave things in such a state that I'd be unable to find a pencil or a pen when I need them. Your habits annoyed me so much Gaythi, but I never wanted this kind of peace!

'I know that you left because you're angry with the whole family. That's what you wrote in your letter too.'

'I'll never forgive Ammah Begum and Saulat Apa for the heartache they have inflicted upon me. They exceeded their rights and attained their objective, and nothing can now make up for the irreparable loss I have suffered. I am certain, Arjumand, that if it had been you instead of me, you would have accepted this silently. Maybe I would have done the same if they had not insulted Masood on my account. What right did they have to hurt someone else's feelings because of my folly? It is my duty to make them realise that they have done something wrong. And it is up to me now whether or not I forgive her, I mean, Saulat Apa. Time heals everything. It is possible that ultimately I might forget that they hurt me so, but Arjumand, please do not try to pacify me, or justify their conduct in your letters. If you do, things will get worse, and you know better than anyone else that I am very stubborn.'

The contents of Gaythi's letter which had arrived several days ago were before her eyes verbatim. She fell into deep thought again, 'True, Gaythi. No one knows better than I do that you are very stubborn and very sincere. I have always considered you much superior to myself and I have always remained very impressed with you. So much so that I could not always find the strength to emulate you. But tell me, for what sins am I awarded this punishment? You don't know how my personality has diminished through separation from you.

'That's right, Gaythi. No one has lost anything. Abba is involved in his own work, Ammah Begum is busy with her thousands of jobs around the house. Saulat Apa is in her own home and Bakhtiar Bhaiya is at his hostel. There is, of course, no point in mentioning Barrey Bhaiya. But I? I feel as if my very person has been divided into two.'

Arjumand blinked her angelic eyes as silent tears slid down her cheeks to be absorbed in her handkerchief. Her body shook as she wept profusely, even though she managed to strangle many sobs, for Ammah Begum did not approve at all of her weeping in that choked manner, like someone repressed. She dried her tears and rose again to tidy the wardrobe. A fresh stream of salty and stubborn tears slid down her cheeks and she bit into her wrist to suppress the sound of her sobbing.

It was at exactly the same time, and on the same Sunday, in her dormitory that Gaythi felt deeply perturbed . The girls who were with her seemed preoccupied. Atia was playing records and Phool, who was preparing for her bath, her hair down and a towel on her shoulders, was demonstrating the Manipuri dance to the beat on a record.

Ruth was needling her as she lay flat on the bed, '*Bhai*, China Man! Why are you lying like this? Get up, now.'

'Yes, that's right. Why are you spreading laziness around?' Atia changed the record and all of them started singing along rapturously.

Gaythi felt deeply lonely. She jumped up, pulled a floral dressing gown over her dark beige nightsuit and dashed out of the dormitory. The wind howled through the empty corridor. You could hear the symphony orchestra being played on the radio in the common room above the noisy laughter of several girls. The sound of the piano floated out of the music wing. Absorbed in dedicated study, several of the fourth years were seated on benches under the shade of the tall eucalyptus trees dotted all round.

She returned to the corridor and sat down on the stairs, leaning against the wall, thinking, 'God! Where can I sit and think about you, Arjumand? Can you see? No one can even dare miss anyone here. Oh, yes, except the memory of Masood, which has clung to my life like an evil spirit! I don't get the chance to miss anyone else. Truly, there is no solitude, nor opportunity to do that in the hostel. Well, Arjumand! Old girl! Another time. Wait till these moonlit nights and the hullabaloo is over then one night I shall lie quietly in my bed and remember you to my heart's content. But right now, shall I tell you the truth, tell you what I'm longing for most? I'm feeling really quite upset . . . I'm longing for home . . . you think that I don't miss home at all . . . Well, never mind . . . you wouldn't understand all these things . . .'

Gaythi's eyes became moist and she deliberately shook off the thought of home, brushed the dust off her clothes, stood up and returned to the dormitory. She pulled the yellow check sari which lay spread out on her bed and started changing right there.

Atia screamed, 'Miserable wretch! Are you changing in public again?'

'You can shut your eyes.'

'I should shut my eyes, but you insist on changing in here!'

'What else can I do? Phool is in possession of the bathroom and Aqueela seems to have the title deeds to the dressing room. I have to go out. I can't wait.'

'Go to hell, shameless wretch!'

But Atia's tone had changed instantly, 'Where are you going, Gaythi?'

'Where do you think? The only person on my visiting list is Chachi. That's where I'll go, and I shall go to see a film.'

'What film?'

'Whatever I can get into.'

'Will you go by yourself, you wretch?'

'What else shall I do, take you along, to hear you recite, "wretch" to the telling of a rosary?'

'Who are you to take me along? In any case, I don't want to go. I have to do my notes.'

'Do them, then.'

She dressed and went out, had her bicycle taken out of the store and headed towards Chacha ji's house.

34

She had visited this narrow, quiet and leafy street off Mason Road for the first time with Abba Mian. He had brought her there to introduce her to Chacha ji after getting her admitted to the college. His was the only name on her visiting list.

'This Chacha ji and Chachi ji are quite all right,' she had thought.

Chacha ji belonged to that area but he had been to the same school as Abba Mian and had spent his childhood in Abba Mian's home town. He was a master of Arabic, Persian and Bengali, besides English. He used to work in a section of the Department of Education. He had rented a bungalow on Mason Road which he shared with a Bengali Christian. His only child was Noor-ul-Huda, who had been sent to Aligarh University. Now, he kept himself occupied in his little garden during his leisure hours.

Gaythi was very fond of Chachi, who was tall, fair and slim with large eyes. She and Chacha ji were the only ones who used to be there. Gaythi had not seen Noor-ul-Huda yet.

Why did she like Chachi? She had been unable to answer that question – since Chachi remained absorbed in her obsession. She spent her days and nights in rituals of purification. She would even wash the spices. She kept the servant in such constant terror that he too had become somewhat obsessive about having to wash his hands and to purify things again and again. If ever she managed to find time from her washing she would start worrying about her imagined illnesses. Or she would sit on a prayer mat reciting verses from the Holy Quran.

It was a small, scantily furnished, informal home, and the two of them were cut off from the rest of the world. For this reason, this house suited Gaythi extremely well. Chacha saw her and laughed, 'How are you, my girl?' He always inquired about her health jokingly, in Punjabi. She would bow to greet him and he would stroke her head before returning to his chores.

Chachi would comment immediately upon her health, 'You look really pulled down. You should look after yourself, girl!' She would shout for Azmat, 'O, Azmati. Bring some milk for the babby.' She would give Gaythi a glass of milk or a yoghurt drink and then ask her, 'What would you like to eat?' before lapsing into her washing and scrubbing again.

After that Gaythi could sleep on an unmade bed or sprawl on the straw matting reading a book, no one would disturb her. Whenever she wanted to she would take the bicycle and go off shopping or go to the cinema. Chachi never had time to investigate or obstruct. Sometimes Gaythi would think, 'If Chachi had not been such an obsessive person, her house would never have been this peaceful. She would never have been free from back-biting and gossip, and she would have been hypercritical. So it follows that it is better to be slightly crazy than to be entirely in command of your senses.'

She leaned the bicycle against the verandah and went inside, 'Greetings, Chachi!'

Chachi replied without looking up from the wheat she was cleaning, 'Long life and blessings to you. You've arrived very late today. I thought you'd decided not to come at all.'

'Yes, Chachi! I wasn't feeling too well today. I felt lazy.'

A wave of happiness and delight surged through Chachi, 'Aren't you well? Give me your hand, let me take your pulse.'

'No. I'm absolutely fine now, Chachi, I've come late. I hope that won't be any trouble.'

'In God's name, my daughter! Does anybody cook to precise quantities in a home?'

When Azmat had laid out the tablecloth on the matting on the verandah, Gaythi felt that the food was not only abundant but also elaborate. After they had all sat down to eat, Azmat called out in a loud voice, 'Babu ji, come and eat your food.'

She was surprised because Chacha ji was already there. But someone else emerged from the corner room, drying his hair on a towel, clicking his heeled wooden clogs. He sat down on a corner of the matting without greeting her, and started saying something to his mother in a quiet voice after he had finished scrutinising Gaythi.

'Without a doubt he's saying something about me,' Gaythi thought, as she considered him briefly: very tall, masses of shiny black hair and a strange expression of bad temper and acerbity on his face.

Chachi started pushing the plates towards them without answering him.

'Gaythi, child, this is Noor-ul-Huda,' Chacha ji said with great pride.

'So what's so great if he is Noor-ul-Huda! He seems so bad-tempered,' she thought to herself.

Noor-ul-Hoda was a lot older than her. He did not take any interest at all in this girl with Chinese looks and continued to eat with relish and drink glass upon glass of drinking yoghurt. Chachi claimed that he was a little unwell and was on holiday for two weeks, but he looked fine.

She slept till two thirty. When she woke up she washed, picked up her bicycle and prepared to leave.

Chachi did not always make a point of getting tea for her. In fact, Chacha ji himself was used to having tea at that time and Chachi always ensured that something spicy and special was prepared for her at teatime.

'Won't you have any tea?' she asked, seeing her leave.

'I'm going to the cinema, Chachi. I'll be late.'

Huda, who stood on the verandah, saw her leave and commented, 'This girl seems to be terribly footloose.'

'These days all girls are, and she is the daughter of a rich and fashionable family,' Huda's mother answered very casually. She had no objection at all to the freedoms Gaythi enjoyed. The truth was that there was no other girl in their family and she really liked her coming to stay with them. If she was in the mood for it, Gaythi would do hundreds of little chores for her. She stitched a tea-cosy for them. Sometimes she would mend Chacha's clothes and, once, she embroidered names on to the shirts, shalwars and bed sheets which Chachi was sending with someone to Huda.

But Huda did not like his mother's laxity on the subject. He said with irritation, 'Does this mean that too much freedom does not hurt girls from rich families?'

'That's right, son! It is true that freedom is harmful for girls from low status families. These girls are brought up differently. They are cleverer than us . . .'

Noor-ul-Huda's father intervened, pushing aside the newspaper before his eyes, 'Then this girl is quite remarkable. Her character is stamped on her face. By nature she is simple and peace-loving. I feel envious of her.'

'So you would have no objection to her roaming around like this?' The boy got angrier without reason.

'Not at all! This girl's taking her bicycle and going off to the cinema is exactly the same as your going off to see a film.'

'Wonderful!' Huda said bitterly.

It was an interesting irony that the representative of the younger generation was taking a conservative attitude whilst the old father revealed a progressive outlook.

35

The Plaza was quite crowded. She stood reading the posters whilst she waited for the crowd to disperse. Someone looked over her shoulder at the same picture and the smoke from a cheap brand of cigarettes invaded her eyes.

She turned round in annoyance and then laughed a moment or so later. '*Arrey*! Is that you?'

Safdar Yaaseen stood in front of her. He seemed paler and thinner than before.

'*Arrey* . . . What are you doing here, Cuckoo?' He noticed that she was a lot thinner. Her mischievous, careless eyes looked serious and mournful.

'I am at the Kinnaird Hostel.' She experienced an unfamiliar feeling of joy.

'Where have you been for so long?'

'I had gone home.' He turned round. The crush at the box office windows had reduced.

'*Arrey*, is that so? So you've been home?'

For some reason she felt very pleased to see Liu Chu. She did not know why she felt closer to home seeing him standing next to her like that. Seeing that foreigner had reminded her of the verandah at her home, the garden and the part of the wall on which she always sat astride. He reminded her of everything. Today she had been feeling homesick since the morning, and seeing him now was a strange experience. She felt as if she was already back home. As if Ammah Begum was saying her Zohar prayers on the wooden seat. Arjumand was asleep, and the bearer in the dining room was laying out the crockery for tea with a noisy rattle – not as if he were angry about something, not even as if someone had offended him.

She felt an uncontrollable urge to luxuriate in tears. But she moved forward silently. It was the end of the month. She had finished her pocket money and had very little money on her. She had arrived in a fit of madness in the hope of using her concession and so she went to the manager's room with her ticket.

'There are no concessions today. It is the first day of the film's run,' the manager interrupted in a dry and unconcerned tone.

When she emerged from his room Safdar was leaving the window, having bought his ticket. She was a little worried. She should not have come. The thought of sitting and watching the film by herself with all the strange characters who occupy the lowest class of seating was worrying her. She called out to Safdar who was walking towards the door.

'Listen.'

He turned.

'I couldn't get a concession!'

'Which class ticket have you bought?'

'The same as yours.'

'Why?' Safdar asked annoyed.

'I've run out of pocket money. I had thought I'd get a concession.'

'Then return the ticket.'

'How?'

'It will get sold.'

Suddenly her rational self rebelled. 'After all, what was the harm? The people who sit and watch films in that class are human too. What is the great difference between us and them? Why should we worry about sitting alongside them even on the odd occasion. After all, why have we presumed that all those who sit in the cheapest class are evil and horrible, but all those who sit where people like myself sit are, as a rule, somehow good and superior.'

As she was apt to do, she had once again started thinking along unconventional and nonconformist lines. '*Waah*! Why should I sell it?' she retorted, 'I am definitely going to watch the film. I have been waiting for this movie for so many days and next week I shan't get permission to leave the hostel. What does it matter? You can sit next to me.'

'All right!' He was in a hurry and he had no right to force her to do anything. The newsreel was already rolling. Moving carefully in the dark, they went and sat on the chairs in the middle. As soon as they had sat down, Safdar attacked her, 'You are still the same unruly creature. Why do you roam round by yourself? The world over, college girls go out to

134

the cinema – or for other kinds of recreation – in groups, and you go out by yourself, like this.'

'Safdar! There is no harm in going out alone. And what is the guarantee that all the girls in such a group will be good and virtuous. Do you know girls can be such a bad influence on each other, Chu. That's why I avoid going out with them. Some of them are real bores!'

She was trying to persuade him quietly, in a very simplistic fashion, that if she had come to the cinema on her own it was because she did not consider it to be a bad thing, and that there was no harm in it.

'But people regard it as something bad.'

'People!' She heaved a sigh. 'People truly do. People have filled human lives with bitterness. They are strange and incomprehensible! In fact, they are not interested in good and evil *per se*; they are only interested in ensuring that individuals should be seen to be performing those *acts* which they have declared good or evil.'

How could she instil all these thoughts into this dumb Chinese man's brains when he himself was a representative of 'the people'? There is only a slight difference. His heart is truly affectionate and sincere. She sat thinking silently as she ate her potato crisps. Whenever she had to confront opposition or was faced with a dilemma she immediately succumbed to food.

Until the interval Safdar could not reflect on the situation very seriously. As soon as the lights were turned up he thought of what people might think seeing her sitting with him like that! He went out for a drink of water and she sat there all the time feeling nervous of the strangers around her. It occurred to her that Safdar was right; it really was not appropriate for her to roam around by herself, like this.

That interval felt longer than usual. The bell rang and as the lights went out he came back to sit near her again. His eyes were on the advertisements for soap, tea and phenyl running on the screen, but he felt the weight of responsibility on his shoulders for some reason. His heart was no longer in watching the film.

She turned towards him and said, 'Thank God you're back. I was feeling very awkward. Scared.'

'I thought of what someone might say if they saw you sitting with me.'

'What could they say? We could say that I didn't get a concession. It's better that I should sit with you rather than by myself in this class.'

'You're quite crazy.'

'Why? What's crazy about that?'

'No one will come to ask you. Cuckoo, people don't ask, they just think.'

'Hah! So, nothing can be done about it now? I certainly won't take this kind of ticket ever again.' She could only fume. Safdar had really bored her, as thoroughly as if he were Ammah Begum's emissary. Then she became involved in the film again.

The film ended. They stood outside the cinema holding their bicycles.

Safdar told her everything relating to his visit home and all that had happened since and Cuckoo told him, with the greatest fluency and ease, the entire story of how and why she had decided to come and study so far away from home.

'Cuckoo, shall I ask you something?'

'Yes, go on.'

'Have you said all this to the girls at the hostel too?'

'What! How can it be of any interest to them? Am I crazy?'

'So why did you tell me?'

'That's a nice one. I've always known you and I know that you really care about me. Do you remember the time when I broke my leg and you used to come secretly and amuse me?'

'*Arrey*! This girl still remembers such an insignificant thing! And she is still grateful for it. To remember such a minor detail to do with such a worthless and lowly foreigner as myself . . . !' Safdar Yaaseen felt a surge of tears waver in his narrow eyes only to become still again. He had felt so pleased to see her again. As always, seeing this simple and silly girl had made him feel that he stood at the door to his own house and not on alien soil.

'*As-salaam-ulaikum*!' someone called out from behind and both of them jumped. Akbar, the good-looking son of their engineer neighbour, stood before them, smiling absent-mindedly, feigning indifference. She asked him politely how he was. Liu Chu had taken his bicycle and now stood, respectfully, quite far away from them.

'I saw you in the hall,' Akbar's eyes laughed mischievously.

'Then you should have joined us there.'

Akbar laughed aloud.

Gaythi felt riled deep down in her heart by the mischief in his eyes and she thought, 'Safdar was right. I really should not go round like this.' But this does not make sense. We know and understand ourselves better than others. Why do people begin to speculate and object? She had a strange temperament. She would lose her way just when it seemed as if she might be getting on to the right track.

Abruptly, she turned. Without saying another word to Akbar she climbed on to her bicycle and left. She did not notice Safdar Yaaseen who stood in her path.

36

'Do you see it now? The result of the self-willed little madam's rebellious-
ness? So you let your daughter have her way!' She started harping on the
same theme the moment she set eyes on him again. 'I did not want her to
stay at a boarding house, so far away from home. But no! You had to
oppose me.' As soon as she saw his face she started taunting him and
repeating this saga in a triumphant manner through gritted teeth. As if
she were heartily delighted with the overwhelming defeat her husband
had suffered. It was the first time in his life that he had rebelled against
her and taken the affairs of one of his children into his own hands, and he
had lost on that score. He had stumbled and fallen on his face with the
very first step he had taken.

Now he was filled with regret as he came in. On the surface he seemed
absolutely calm, stretched out in an armchair dressed in his white shirt
and pyjamas. But there was pain in his eyes and remorse on his face. His
handsome and forbidding face suddenly seemed older than it should have
done.

He looked at his wife in silence. Despite the extremity of her anger and
anxiety she was dressed immaculately in a white silk sari as she sat on
the wooden divan, dangling her feet. The thin gold bangles on her wrist
looked very appealing. The servant came in just then to place his hookah
near him and then went out again.

Jehangir Mirza shook his leg restlessly and drew the nozzle of his
hookah closer to himself.

'This hookah or cigarettes are your only reply to everything.'

'That is because I do not know what to say to you, Begum,' he said
gently and drew on it.

'So, that means, in your opinion, I am talking nonsense whilst that
unfortunate creature is following the right course, bringing honour to the
name of her forefathers . . . ?'

At this point Jehangir Mirza reached the limit of his tolerance and
patience. He pushed his hookah away in anger. 'I don't know whether it
is nonsense or not but what seems quite certain is that you are giving
credence to a piece of nonsense. You chose to believe whatever a loafer
came and told you.' Although his tone was low he sounded extremely
angry.

'Is Akbar a loafer, in your opinion? After all, what do you think he has
against your daughter?'

'Without a doubt, I believe that boys like him are loafers. You might think that an expensive outfit and belonging to a rich family guarantees someone's character, but I don't. I think someone who is far superior . . .' he stopped midstream and started again. 'What he holds against my daughter is the fact that, like myself, she dislikes him too.' He started shaking his leg restlessly and then grumbled to himself, again. 'When a boy or a girl's name is tainted foolishly by his or her own family, without any reason, then why should others hesitate to make allegations about them? Only once did she come late from school and what a fuss you made!'

Just then Arjumand peeped onto the verandah, drawing aside the curtain in her room. It was so silent everywhere. A milk-white sheet was draped across the wooden divan, covered with a small yellow carpet and a spotless gleaming bolster leaned against the wall. A vine with bunches of red flowers clung to the delicate pillars of the verandah, and in its farthest corner stood a cage full of budgerigars on a white table. All these things were so familiar and endearing. This house which was so beautiful and exquisite in every detail was her own home. But for the past few days it had felt strange – quiet and lonely. Slowly, bit by bit, it had been drained of its liveliness. Saulat Apa had left after her marriage. In the early days she visited quite often, then the intervals between visits grew longer, and now she hardly ever came. Barrey Bhaiya had decided to stay in England for good. Chachi jaan had stopped visiting too, and then Gaythi got this idea that she must move away from home.

She said Gaythi's name to herself with great difficulty, swallowing the tears which welled up in her eyes. 'How painful a Sunday can be! A day when it is impossible to free myself from her memory, and she hardly ever writes!'

She looked at Ammah Begum and Abba Mian in an attempt to forget her, but they both sat looking silent and sullen. She was certain that they were talking about the same unpleasant subject which had arisen several times in the day, since Akbar had returned from Lahore, and which had caused considerable unpleasantness and unhappiness in their home.

'What a wretch Akbar is! He came and said one little thing and upset everyone here. Just think, even if he had seen something like that, he should have had the grace to keep it to himself. God knows why people don't mind their own business.' Today, swept along by that tide of feeling, she was thinking like Gaythi.

The hookah had gone cold and the two of them sat silently like two strangers who had just been introduced very casually and were now finding it hard to think of things to say to each other. Then he rose and went to sit in his own room.

'Maybe Begum is right. I made a mistake, sending her to a hostel because she wanted to; now, if she gets into bad habits I will be responsible. . . . But who is to blame for Saulat? I kept absolutely quiet when it came to dealing with her affairs. To such an extent, that even though I knew that she disliked Asif Jah intensely, I did not say anything against Begum's decision. She argued then that all dislikes and differences get erased, except the difference in material wealth. I knew very well that Begum had not assessed the temperament of her own offspring correctly. Those dispositions for whom all dissimilarities can be erased are different. I knew that my children were not so insensitive and unintelligent that all their feelings could be wiped out. The results are obvious. Saulat has embittered life for Asif Jah by putting him aside like a broken toy . . . whilst she herself . . .' His face flushed with shame and anger. Saulat had become the subject of a deep sense of shame for him. She was very domesticated and housewifely on the surface but in spite of that there were scandals about her. More than those scandals he hated her duplicity. In his book hypocrisy was the worst sin against humanity.

Besides Saulat's affairs, those of Sheharyaar were completely beyond his comprehension. Only God knew why that boy, who was so obedient, good-natured and happy, had become so weary of his parents and his home that he had abandoned the very idea of returning at all. Sheharyaar's staying abroad really grated on him. As if he had insulted his love, affection and all his hopes.

It was a question of instinctive pride and familial dignity for him so he conducted himself through this defeat and loss with admirable distinction and courage. No one could have guessed, seeing the way he laughed and talked and kept himself busy with his hobbies, about the grievous scar he carried on his heart, the insecurity he felt, his sense of loss and of shattered dreams. In his solitude he would hum sadly to himself with tremendous poignancy:

'Listen to the lamentations of the flute
As she tells the story of her painful separation from the tree . . .'

'The eldest son is a milestone of achievement for human beings, a shiny jingling coin which is a welcome currency in the market, which does not have to bide its time in the suitcase like a bad penny. And if he should take offence without even disclosing why, is it not inevitably a back-breaking, heart-rending loss?'

His bright, hooded eyes were moist with tears. He looked outside the window. The mango trees were covered with blossom now and you could hear the nightingales in song. The damsons had turned black and the bela and jasmine were in flower. His heart felt alienated from the world. A despondent silence and a sense of surrender inhabited all his movements.

37

After a long time she had received a letter from Talat and she had opened it with tremendous quietude. Gaythi's temperament was getting very calm. She now did everything slowly and with great tranquillity.

'O-ho! So you thought of me again today, Talat Begum.' She smiled as she opened the envelope very carefully.

'Gaythi! Lots of kisses!'

She was quite surprised to read this. Does Talat still not think ill of her and has she not yet heard the rumour put out by Akbar? 'Though Akbar Mian has done his best to ensure my disgrace!' She smiled. Arjumand had written all the details to her in her letter.

So, Talat had written the whole story this time.

'Gradually Dadi Ammah found out why Saulat Apa had come here. She became very angry. You know that when she gets cross with one person, she takes it out on the entire family. All day she kept getting cross with all of us. She is not at all displeased with you. She is furious with Saulat Apa, "because she has destroyed the reputation of this family," she says. "This family had a reputation for its wealth and modesty. Its men and women had never been arrogant. She has probably forgotten that her father's mother is from the poorest section of the family. In my father's house they used to put out the lights early in the evening. They served only cups of sweet drinks for my sisters' wedding receptions. My family home was cramped and located in the most crowded inner city area. But on that very threshold your grandfather and great-grandfather, commanders of seven thousand men though they were, stood, to seek my hand; and then, everyone knows, in that same household the respect and glory that I enjoyed no other daughter-in-law had ever enjoyed before me. But Saulat has humiliated my niece's son so badly."

'That is it, Gaythi. What else can I tell you? All her rage against

140

Saulat Apa was vented upon our heads. Just listen to what happened next! Dadi Ammah called Hashmi Phupho. They talked all day, then the two of them went to Choti Nani's courtyard. Hashmi Phupho left after talking to them for a long time. The next day Hashmi Phupho came round at about ten without announcing it beforehand and placed a ring on Kaamni's finger. Choti Nani rummaged through all her bundles and boxes with her trembling hands and produced a faded velvet case which she handed to her. How shall I describe it, Gaythi? It was such an impressive glowing ring. Ammah says it is regal. Choti Nani and Hashmi Phupho embraced Kaamni one by one and wept. It is something worthy of tears. She has neither a mother nor a father. She was weeping herself. Though I do know very well that she does like Masood a lot.

'Hashmi Phupho looked quite upset. She asked me to go back with her. I was in a strange state myself. You may not believe this but your face was before my eyes and my heart was bursting with tears. You know that there are no tears in my eyes, I always go round dry-eyed. Ammah forced me to go with her.

'He had just got back from the University. He smiled when he saw me and said, "I remember my long-lost friend whenever I see you. I feel like telling you not to come to my house."

'"Is that why you have stopped coming to see us?"

'"Yes, Talat! I am interested in human beings who are alive and sensitive. I don't believe in cemeteries."

'"So what do you think? Shouldn't I visit you?"

'"Are you following in the footsteps of that ill-mannered creature? You know I am older than you and her. Both of you address me by my name and use the informal address when you talk to me." He evaded the question.

'"That's true. She used to call you by your name, so I started doing the same," I replied.

'"You don't have to say 'used to' with reference to her, she hasn't died, Talat! Indeed, she is one of those who live on even after they are dead. And I am troubled by her spirit even whilst she is alive."

'"Now you should get rid of her spirit," I said.

'"Has anyone ever been able to get rid of spirits?" he laughed.

'"Come here, Masood!" Hashmi Phupho called him and he went to her room.

'I stayed in the courtyard.

'I could hear them arguing inside. In the end, I heard Hashmi Phupho say in a loud voice, "Don't you even care about my word? I

141

did not expect you to disgrace me like this, Masood. Have I not been humiliated enough at the hands of Saulat because of your stupidity? Must I suffer a second humiliation because of you now? Sons should bring honour to your name, earn you respect, but you are becoming a source of discredit for me."

'Then they both talked quietly. I could not hear their words but I could guess from the tone that she was explaining something to Masood. After some time they both came out. Their eyes were red. He was extremely upset and sorrowful but in his hand he held that ring which had emerged from Kaamni's grandmother's bundle.

'As he went past me I said, "Congratulations!" just like that. He descended into bad language, like you do. "God punish you for that. Who are you to congratulate me? If you laugh, by God, I'll slap you."

'I just looked at his face.

'Then he called me from his room. He lay on the bed still wearing his shoes. He sat up when he saw me.

'"Ay! Tell your Kaamni that she's wasted her education. Did the cat get her tongue? Could she not have said that she did not wish to get engaged to a man of poor taste who fancies a pale-skinned, Chinese-looking flat-nosed face? And ask her to swear if I didn't say to her that she should not deceive herself with the idea that I cared at all for her. And didn't she spit back at me over that, saying, 'I know, tasteless people like you go for plain faces and teeny weeny eyes?' All right then, Kaamni Begum, you shall pay for my endurance. She is a deep one to have just sat there, silent and limp, to have worn the ring.'

'He was talking disjointedly in a deeply sullen tone until I said, "Enough! Stop talking like this now and pull yourself together."

'He then sounded terribly helpless, "I am together, Talat. But I do curse that wretch who treated me like this."

'"Who?" I asked.

'"That wretch, Gaythi. How I tried to put her off, and to explain things to her. She did not lose out; but now I shall suffer for the rest of my life. Tell me what's going to happen now? What shall I do now?"

'I thought that was a good opportunity to say, "Look, drink this water and go to sleep."

'"That's not a bad idea." He drank the water, lay down and shut his eyes. All evening and all night he slept. He was fine when he woke up the next morning, but was absolutely silent. After he had left for college I returned home too.

'He did not come to our house that whole week. Despite being sent for, he did not come to greet his mother-in-law to be. Kaamni was totally petrified about this. She knows everything. He came early in the morning and stayed at his in-laws', that is, in Choti Nani's courtyard. When she moved from there he came to sit under the shade of the moulsari tree where Kaamni and I sat. He smiled when he saw her.

'"Why is there mourning on your face? I haven't died. Learn how to laugh and stop behaving like a widow."

'I noticed that her pale face bloomed when she heard that tiny comment. She lowered her lovely eyes with tremendous style. But he kept picking the moulsari flowers with great tranquillity. Then something occurred to him and he threw away all the flowers in a fury. He turned to leave, then turned back again. "Let me see the ring too, please, the one your mother-in-law gave you."

'When she withdrew, feeling shy, he pulled her hand roughly. "*Bhai*, let me see. I swear to God, this is the limit – that I don't even know the colours of the stones on my fiancée's ring. Do you remember which century we're living in?" Then he spoke again, "Forget it! You're not going to deal with problems like that. For you all the centuries and moments are alike."

'So, Gaythi! Such are the ways of the world. What I want you to know is that Masood will fall in line in a few days and forget everything. So why should you stew over these useless things without any rhyme or reason?

'Ammah sends you her blessings. We've had a letter from Ismat Baji, they're fine and so is their baby . . .'

Gaythi read this detailed letter calmly, word by word. There was no question of the letter slipping from her hand and falling to the floor. Nor was there any rush to shed tears. She folded the letter and put it back, saying to herself, 'You did well to get engaged, Masood. I wish to God that you get a really good position and can buy a limousine to bring your wife with her beautiful eyes to our house, so that Ammah Begum can see that Masood could find a girl who is so much better than her own daughter.'

For some unknown reason, she felt neither upset nor grieved after reading that letter and the news it had brought to her.

38

When she woke up that Sunday morning, for no reason her heart was pounding away discordantly. Everything wore an expression of fatigue and wistfulness. The weather was fine but the atmosphere felt vaguely mournful.

'I don't know what's come over me today!' she said to herself, since the other girls were all busily involved in various chores with their usual cheerfulness. After breakfast was over she came and stood dejectedly in the corridor. The silvery green leaves of the white poplars looked extremely beautiful against the clear blue sky.

The crystalline azure of the sky, the green of the trees and and the inky blackness of the flock of crows – together created a blend of strong contrasts which she had found extremely pleasing ever since her childhood. And just at that moment, the skies were a flawless blue, in perfect contrast to the green of the trees and ... a mere dot of ink, a solitary crow ... Her anxious heart felt a further tremor of fear. 'Instead of a flock of black crows, just a lone crow ... a bad omen, according to the English. God save us!'

Influenced by the European nuns at the convent where she had been educated, she experienced a panic. But then under her breath she said a brief prayer mocking the devil.

'If the superstition had even a grain of truth, then I should have seen this lone crow when I received Talat's letter.' Although two months had now elapsed since she had received that letter, several lines from it echoed in her head.

'But was that really bad news? The truth is that these are just incidents and events which often occur in one's life. Surely, if someone whom we love can overcome the difficulties in his life, then that is not bad news? Surely, Masood's life has become simpler and will now progress more easily? To be honest, it is possible that my existence could have become a kind of hell for Masood. The difference in my status and his would always have remained in some form or other and I am certain that he would have succumbed to a sense of inferiority and lost his personality, if not at my hands, then at the hands of my family, and so he would have lost my respect too.

'That's right, Masood! I have no grudge either against you or against the accident which has changed the course of events.' That girl, who was known as Gaythi, thought with the large-heartedness and generosity of Mother Earth.

She kept watching the solitary crow wandering in the bluish heights of the sky for a long time in spite of her dismissal of the superstition and a strange restlessness weighed on her consciousness.

The head girl used to distribute the post for the hostel after she finished her other duties. Gaythi received Arjumand's letter after eleven o'clock. It was a brief, distressed letter. Its first line ran thus:

'We received a telegram about Dadi Ammah's illness. Both Ammah Begum and Abba Mian have gone over and I am here alone, picking the thorns of desperation. Let's see what happens!'

There was a postscript to the letter which said that she had only just received the news that what was expected had transpired. Now Abba Mian and Ammah Begum would not be able to return soon.

Who knows how much and in what way Arjumand would have been affected by that news! But, broken as she was and so far away from the others, Gaythi felt that the news was deeply tragic. Dadi Ammah, who had liked her very much, with whom she associated the arched doorways, the 'royal' seats and the little alcoves around the courtyards, the bela and moulsari flowers, whose very existence had symbolised the old courtesies, the unlimited, insoluble links of relationships and powerful pillars of support, was now no more. The traditions of a whole century had departed with her life which spanned three quarters of it. Gaythi could not imagine her rambling, beautiful and lively home without her large and imposing person.

She peeked at the blue horizon out of the corner of her eye. That single crow was no longer hovering above; several eagles wheeled round like faint dots.

'That's it! My heart had sunk seeing that crow.' She dropped the letter on the table and lay on her bed, face down. Her pillow was soaked in tears. Her eyes felt sore with weeping, her throat became parched and she felt feverish.

'It's good that there was no one else here; people's sympathies and condolences can be even more of a nuisance at a time like this.' When her room mates returned to the room they found her sleeping soundly.

None of the girls found out that she had received bad news from home and had suffered a shock, even after she had woken up. Indeed, there was no need to express that. This grief was entirely her own. 'Why should others have to share the distress and pain which is private to one's self?

And that grief, which one endures utterly alone and in silence, is also very sacred and precious.'

39

'After all, how long does one need one's parents; there must be some limit, some way of adding it up?' Jehangir Mirza pulled the hookah closer to himself and wondered, as he put its silver nozzle to his mouth.

He lay in a reclining cane chair on the verandah. The entrances to the verandah were hung with clay pots, their edges frilled with clusters of pretty but tiny leaves. Dwarf palms which stood in large wooden planters swayed drunkenly in the April breeze.

'Several times I had thought of my mother as dispensable. She had fulfilled all her duties and, in fact, one hardly ever felt the need for her. How amazing that now when she has departed from this earth, I should feel that I need her so badly just at this moment. I have had to face so many deaths, lost so many friends but, I don't know why, no one's death has ever made me feel that the very springs of life have dried. I have never felt before that the clear, sparkling stream which flowed through the green fields of life has suddenly dried up. Ammah jaan you have been truly cruel to me dying on me now. I have been suffering such pain recently and have been planning for some time that I will go and spend a holiday with you, just by myself. That I will lie and sit beside you and find peace by confiding in you. Tell you all those things with which only a mother's true heart can sympathise. Just seeing you feel my pain would have healed my wounds.

'When I got hurt as a child I would wander all over the house, looking for you. I would lean on your knee and shed a few tears, and when I saw you suffer in sympathy with my pain, it would ease. Now, when I am facing the worst trial of my life you have deserted me. I am really annoyed with you, Ammah jaani.'

He smiled to himself at these thoughts, pushed the hookah aside and strolled away from the verandah towards the garden. Mali, who was turning the soil in the flower-beds to plant the new seasonal flowers, rose when he saw him walking towards him.

'Greetings, Sahib.'

'Greetings. *Arrey*, Mali! What arrangements have you made for some new Chausa mango cuttings?' he asked in his characteristic manner, steeped in kindness and calm.

'Yes, Sahib. It is important to arrange for the new cuttings,' Mali said in his low, husky and philosophical voice.

'Yes! We must check on them now. One of these days the winds will change and become the blazing *loo* of summer. Come let's look at the mangoes.'

He held his hands together behind his back as he usually did and walked slowly with Mali towards the square where the mango trees and their cuttings were planted. This part was quite separate from the main garden and was towards the back of the house. On the dense and healthy mango trees the blossom had given way to miniature mangoes. The trunks of the various types of trees were marked with different notations in lime or white paint to signify whether each grove was dusehri, sufaida or sandoori. But he and his gardener could tell just from the shape of the leaves and the growth of the trees whether it was a langra or a fajri.

'This year this langra should have a lot a fruit.'

'Yes, look.'

'This langra I planted because Barrey Bhaiya had ask-ed me to. Then himself he goes off and sits himself down in Lon-dhon!' Mali's voice was full of regret.

'Hum.'

'Sahib, call Bhaiya back now.'

'How, Mali? It is impossible to call him back now. Haven't you heard how bad the fighting is over there? Now he has enlisted himself in the army there.'

'So, let them all fight. Why should our Bhaiya have to fight in their war? He should just get on to a ship and return.'

In spite of his own anxiety, he laughed at Mali's innocence and lack of awareness. Now such innocence and naivete were vanishing from the face of the earth.

'Life is changing in every possible way, not just in terms of innocence. What is happening today will no longer be there tomorrow. Those loves have gone and the joys of living. Take this, for example: the communication and control which existed amongst our elders is no longer there between all three of us, two real brothers and one sister. For some reason, I feel as if life itself were becoming weary.'

These days if he started thinking along certain lines, he just went on and on. To bring this stream of thoughts to an end he directed his attention once again to the cuttings of the chausa mango.

'These are ready now. What do you think; they will take, won't they?'

147

'That's it, master. If they survive this heat then we could reckon on them. I've made some straw shelters, I'll put them up on top of them in a couple of days.'

'I say! I've been looking for you all over the house, and Bhai Sahib is standing right here,' Azam Baig rebuked him in his sharp tone which rather broadly declared an intimacy with him.

He was startled and turned his gaze towards him. 'Welcome, Bhaiya! When did you arrive? I just came this way to have a look at these cuttings.'

'I thought of that immediately. If Bhai Sahib is not in his room or on the verandah then he must be near the mangoes,' Azam Baig laughed a slightly embarrassed, obsequious laugh, 'because our brother is such a lover of mangoes.'

Jehangir Mirza looked closely at Azam Baig who was related to him, even though the nature of that relationship was not at all clear to him. In his sparklingly clean pair of baggy pyjamas, brilliant white frothy kurta with embroidery round the front opening neckline and black Saleem Shahi slippers, this man of medium height and slight build looked quite impressive. Although Jehangir Mirza knew quite well that he had been wearing that particular kurta and pair of pyjamas for quite some time, and despite its crisp and sparkling whiteness, the kurta was now betraying some signs of its age and decline, he never failed to be impressed by his delicately rolled sleeves, the scents he wore – in accordance with the season, rose, jasmine or cuscus – and, finally, the fragrant whiff of first class tobacco which wafted from the *paan* in his mouth. When he saw him, he would completely forget that, unbeknown to his wife, he paid a monthly sum to this relative, with whom his kinship was vague and undefined. And, that all this was merely a show. His stationery business was hopeless. Indeed, it was not much of a shop at all. Its total stock consisted of a score or so of wooden writing tablets, twenty-odd slates, special clay from Multan, powdered black ink, bamboo pens, exercise books made of smudgy paper and some tablets to make blue ink. But Azam Baig, who was generally known as Baig Sahib, never really raised the subject of his stationery shop. His conversation was so elaborate and was conducted so artistically to suit the taste of his addressee, or whoever was presiding over the gathering, that no one would remember the wooden writing tablets or the slates in his stationery shop.

'*Arrey*, Baig Sahib. You came at a very good time. I was just talking about you.'

'I am always on cue. At least, that's what you always say. It is the ultimate in courtesy and affection, Bhai Sahib, to make your visitor feel, that far from being a burden, his visit is precisely what you desired.'

'Oh, no, Baig Sahib. You have come at the right time today. For several days now, I have been thinking that I should mention to you that the stone of our dusehri mangoes is getting rather big.'

'The stone of the dusehri? The dusehris from your garden, you mean?'

'Yes, yes. This one, off these trees here!'

'It is quite amazing considering you look after your trees so well!' The veins in Baig Sahib's neck were beginning to swell with excitement.

'No, sir. When do I ever get a chance to look after them?'

'It used to be more of a hobby for our Sheharyaar,' Baig Sahib rolled his eyes round, 'and now he appears to have settled abroad.'

'And you know, I am hardly ever home.'

'That's right. Most of your time is spent on tours of duty – and our dear brother likes to spend whatever time is left, exploring forests and wildernesses.'

'You're referring to my hunting?'

Baig Sahib laughed.

'That is my only hobby, sir. Bridge and hunting account for all my vices. I score nil on all other counts.'

Azam Baig laughed again.

'So, you haven't told me how to solve the problem with the mangoes. I have really gone off these trees. I feel like replacing them with new cuttings.'

'That's always possible. You should always have all the cuttings on the go, anyway.'

'So, there's no cure for these now?' Jehangir Mirza said with some disappointment.

Baig Sahib was really beginning to feel important now. 'The truth is, Jehangir Sahib, that if there is a problem with the stone you can be sure that the roots have become diseased. And there are several causes for the problems which arise in the roots.'

Chatting with Baig Sahib and strolling gently, he returned to the verandah.

'*Arrey*, Ghafoor. Could you refresh my hookah and bring it? Use the best tobacco, from the tin which is kept specially for Baig Sahib.'

Jehangir Mirza came back to the room with him. He never resented anyone at all visiting the house. Despite the adverse effect on his wife's mood, he would be delighted at the sight of a visitor. But he paid special attention to Baig Sahib so that he would not feel the distance of their relationship, or the relative lowliness of his status.

149

'Bhai Sahib, I've never found taste and flavour to match the mangoes I had from a certain gentleman's garden.'

'You can only breed quality in a mango with hard work and industry. We are mere amateurs in this respect. The cultivation of mangoes is an art requiring constancy.'

'Absolutely, absolutely.' Baig Sahib wagged his neck. 'It is an area of expertise.'

'Tell me, Bhai Sahib, is there any news of when Mian Sheharyaar will be returning?' Baig Sahib enquired with some anxiety.

'News of his return!' He laughed. 'So that means you are not aware of the mood of the war.'

'Well said, Bhai Sahib, very well said! We are the ones who are having to endure the trials of the war. It's our share of food that has gone. The government has taken control of everything.'

Jehangir Mirza picked up the newspaper. In fact, the mention of Sheharyaar's name irritated him a little now. That's right, things were fine when he left, and then he just decided to stay there. They could not establish a reason. And now the young master has gone and offered his services to the war effort. Now he would be plagued by all kinds of anxieties the moment he heard his name. The doubt which had taken root in his heart amongst others was, that although Sheharyaar would most certainly return, he himself would not be lucky enough to set eyes upon his son's face.

When in spite of his insistence, Baig Sahib did not agree to stay, he got up, took a sealed envelope from the drawer and placed it in his hand. It had four notes of ten in it. 'It was the fifth of the month, was it not?'

Every month, on the fifth, a sealed envelope like that one slid quietly from his hand into Baig Sahib's. No one had even a whiff of this secret.

He went and stood near the window after Baig Sahib had left. Beyond the window he could see his own house, his own land, stretching from one end to the other. The garden was in full bloom. His favourite trees were loaded with baby mangoes. Only a few days ago their buffalo had delivered a female calf. An electric pump was whirring in the well and the household was ticking away with a quiet regularity. There was peace and tranquillity everywhere. Except in his grieving heart. His children were scattered and disturbed. He was not content or happy about any of them.

'I wish I did not possess all this but instead there was understanding between my children and their mother. I wish I was not a stranger in their eyes. How right Baig Sahib was when he said, ". . . if there is a

150

problem with the stone you can be sure that the roots have become diseased. And there are several causes for the problems which arise in the roots."'

40

Gaythi's examinations were now very close. As time was slipping by she was getting impatient to return home. She had not been home for the whole year. Since she had insisted on leaving in the first place, Ammah Begum had not sent for her in the spring or winter holidays. She had spent all those vacations at the hostel. In the beginning she herself was deeply disaffected and felt she had a grievance against them for having insulted Masood and hurt him instead of criticising her when it was entirely her fault. But, as time went by, that transient anger and reproachfulness was washed off her heart. She would write to them regularly, every other week, and she received replies to these letters. When she found out that Ammah Begum did not intend to send for her during any of the holidays she understood that, as was her way, Ammah Begum was punishing her for her disobedience so that she would quietly agree to attend a college of her mother's choice now, if she were told to do so. She knew that Ammah Begum would not like to send her anywhere except to IT College. And the truth was that she was now willing to accept all those things from the depths of her heart.

'After all,' she wondered,'was it really possible for any girl to annoy her parents, to contravene their wishes, and still remain happy?'

Then when she had received Talat's letter and found that Masood had got engaged and that after a brief tantrum, he was now happy, so much so, that he had requested Kaamni not to go round with a look of mourning on her face, since he was not dead yet, she had become perfectly content. She was genuinely happy that Masood had not wrecked his own life or given up the world for her sake. For if it had turned out like that how ashamed she would have been. And as far as the other fact was concerned: that Masood had given up thinking of her, and that now there was no room in his life for any thoughts or memories of her, one could only remark that these are matters and affairs of the heart which can be slowly erased and healed.

So, what transpired was that now she had no complaint against anyone, and she was no longer angry with anyone. She was only waiting

151

for the examination and the holidays which were to follow. Even Abba Mian had written to her saying, 'You should just come during the summer holidays. What you and I have done against the wishes of your mother is enough to annoy her. Now the only way to make her happy is to do exactly what she wants. Truly, you and I have been unfair. We should all respect each other's counsel and wishes.'

And Gaythi was willing to show that respect. Staying so far away from home for so long had made her aware of the importance of a mother. She had stopped going out at all because her examinations were approaching. She had not visited Chachi for several days either. She was now absorbed in anticipation of her return home, keeping count of each and every second, and of each passing minute.

'Forgive my sins! How lazy time is. It moves like a tortoise,' she had thought many times with boredom.

'Her holidays will begin when mine will be coming to an end. *Waah*! That doesn't make sense,' thought Arjumand bitterly.

She did not know that the demands made by the climatic conditions in the Punjab were quite different from those of her area, despite the fact that Gaythi always wrote a couple of lines pertaining to the weather at the end of each letter. For instance: 'Arjumand, it is so cold here that you would never believe it. At most you will be wearing a long-sleeved cardigan, but here we wear a sweater as well as a coat and still go round shivering.'

Then at the end of March she had written to say, 'It is night time and I am imagining all your beds made up on the verandah inside. We are still sleeping in our rooms here.'

But whenever she thought of Gaythi's arrival, something akin to fear rose in her heart. 'That wretched Akbar has got Ammah Begum into a rage for no reason at all. Now when she comes, there will be such a row. Even though much of her anger has now dissipated, and Gaythi seems so very happy at the thought of returning too!'

Unpleasantness and rows were as much a part of life in that house as the golden-haired Arjumand with beautiful eyes hated them. Ammah Begum was extremely short-tempered and practical. She could not forgive the tiniest aberration on anyone's part. So much so, that even one word which transgressed against her wishes pricked like a thorn in her side until she had a showdown.

But this was merely apprehension on Arjumand's part. One of the expressions of Ammah Begum's rage and annoyance was that she would completely ignore the transgressor and stop communicating with him.

Over this particular issue she had grumbled and bickered so much with Abba Mian that most of her anger had already been diffused.

Then again, apart from Arjumand, all her children had been far away from her for so long that she had started having restless nights over them. Moreover, she had dreamt so often that that wretched Gaythi was ill and became extremely worried. In spite of her extreme annoyance with her she would recite a special prayer almost every night and, together with Sheharyaar, also cast a protective halo round Gaythi's image. And now that she was returning, she decided that Gaythi had stayed long enough in the hostel, and that she would not send her back again. If she were to decide not to stay at home then she could be sent to Bhai jaan's place in Bombay. But Arjumand was not aware of her mother's inner feelings. As the day for Gaythi's return was drawing near, her fears were deepening.

Then Gaythi returned, unannounced. On her way to the bathroom to perform her ablutions before her morning prayers, Arjumand saw her. She had hardly any luggage at all, a roll of bedding, a suitcase and an attache case which stood on the verandah, while she counted out the change from a small leather handbag for the *tonga* wallah.

The jug of water slipped from Arjumand's hand and fell with a crash. Petrified, she peeped through the half-open doors. Contentment was apparent from Gaythi's face, though she was a lot paler and thinner than before. She came quietly out of the bathroom on to the verandah. Without saying a word she embraced her sister, kissed her on the throat, and then on her forehead.

'Arjumand!' Tears flowed from Gaythi's narrow eyes.

'You should have let us know. The car would have come to fetch you.'

'Would the car really have come for me?' Gaythi asked with some surprise.

Arjumand was not entirely certain herself so she did not consider it wise to answer her . She held her hand and led her into the room. The prayer mat stood on the wooden divan waiting for her but she stayed by Gaythi's side asking questions.

Suddenly Gaythi asked her in surprise, 'Arjumand, you were probably going to say your prayers, weren't you?'

'Yes, that's right. I had gone to the bathroom to wash when I heard the rattle of the *tonga*.'

'Then go ahead and say your prayers.'

'Yes, there isn't a lot of time left. Let your luggage come in first.'

'Do you say all your prayers regularly?'

153

'Yes, and you?' Arjumand said with some embarrassment because Gaythi used to laugh at all her good habits.

'Yes, I do say my prayers but not all of them. I can never wake up early enough. But I always say my Ishaa' prayers at night.'

'And why?'

'I've just got into the habit of it.'

Arjumand looked at her face in amazement. Like everyone else she had also lost faith in Gaythi. She had presumed that Gaythi had given up everything and adopted a path that was different from everyone else's. Despite that, she considered her worthy of boundless love.

Arjumand was now confronted with the problem of Gaythi's luggage which still stood on the verandah. Although a moment ago she had been saying to Gaythi that the car would have come to fetch her if they had been informed she could now no longer find the courage to ask one of the servants to bring her luggage in for her. Nor did she want to reveal to Gaythi that throughout the previous week Ammah Begum had been proclaiming that she was quite displeased with her. She was not certain what her attitude to Gaythi might be at a time when their father was away on a tour. Who knows! So, she slipped out of the room quietly and with great difficulty carried her bedding into the room through the bathroom.

'*Arrey*, why are you carrying this on your back?' Gaythi understood a little and asked in some surprise. 'I can bring my stuff through.'

Staying away from the house for so long had made her a lot more astute and wiser than Arjumand. Both of them carried the suitcase in and then sat down on it. Neither had the courage to discuss with the other what was clear to both of them.

Arjumand was thinking, 'But how long can this go on? She has to deal with the unpleasantness at some time. After all this is her own house. Why has she come here like a thief or an uninvited guest?'

Meanwhile Gaythi was thinking, 'Is there still no place for me in this house in spite of my having repented over the past year for my defiance and inordinate obstinacy. And I had intended to conform to Ammah Begum's will. . . So where else can I go after all?'

'Come! At least have a wash,' Arjumand said to her.

'Yes.' She was immersed in deep thought. 'That's right. I'll have a bath. You say your prayers in the meantime.'

Arjumand's attention wandered during her prayers as she kept hearing the sound of water splashing round the bathroom, 'She will come out of the bath soon. In just a little while Ammah Begum will finish her prayers and go to the breakfast table. Then the bell will ring ordering members of the household to go to the table at once.' \

These days there was no one else in the house except her and so she was the centre of Ammah Begum's attention. She would sit at the table, during breakfast or teatime, for long hours, her head bowed before her empty plate and teacup, playing with her beautiful pink nails, her large luminous eyes filled with tears, as her mother subjected her to tirades against Gaythi's disobedience and infamy.

What precautions could she take to avert the fuss that was likely to be caused by Gaythi's arrival? Instead of once, she prostrated herself before God three times and then quickly started her prayers again to rectify the mistake. This too is an escape route from unpleasantness that, after the prescribed prayers, one should extend all available opportunities to bow and prostrate oneself before God.

Whether or not Arjumand derived any satisfaction and pleasure from these extensions of her supplication may not be very certain, but clearly Gaythi was enjoying her cold shower after her tiring night-long journey. An exhausted, terrified and anxious body and state of mind seeks tenderness and coolness.

Listening to the sound of Gaythi's voice, humming gently, interspersed with the splashing of water, Arjumand thought, 'I am stretching my prayers because of my fear of Ammah and Gaythi is playing for time by taking longer over her bath. Forgive me God!' She had to say her salaams all over again for she had recited a verse incorrectly. 'This is why they say that one should be virtuous and compliant. Now my prayers are getting messed up again and again because of Gaythi. A pointless sin!' she thought, feeling nettled. Gaythi felt the cool and pleasant swish of the water and thought, 'What a deep sense of pardon and forgiveness resides in this softness and coolness. Such sanctity there is in water!'

The wetness had made her short strands of straight dark Chinese hair even darker, scattering them into her eyes. She felt the rivulets of water flowing down her face and then, sucking them slowly off her lips, she thought, 'Maybe this is why Hindus feel that their sins have been washed away after they have bathed. I sinned too, by disobeying my mother.'

And, although since that act of disobedience she had bathed countless times, it was only after she had washed in the cool, pleasant water in her own home that she began to feel that she was innocent. 'Just like a dip in the waters of the Ganges and the Hardwar rivers induces a sense of purity and sacredness in the pilgrims, making them content. There cannot be a bigger pilgrimage than that to your own home! As the saying goes, "The Ka'aba of the heart can only be in the home . . ."

She emerged from the bathroom feeling light and peaceful. She saw that Arjumand had her hands raised in prayer, her eyes were closed.

'*Arrey*! What can she be praying for at this time . . .?' She smiled.

Finally that bell, the very thought of which was affecting Arjumand's prayers, rang. In a panic, she looked at Gaythi, who appeared to be very content in her pale green silk baggy pyjamas and headscarf combined with a white kurta.

'I am wearing a *gharara* after a very long time. It feels really good.'

'Do you call a pair of baggy pyjamas a *gharara* now?' Arjumand objected only to conceal her agony.

'Yes. It's fine to call it that. Come on, Arjumand, the bell has rung for breakfast,' she said calmly, as if it was not her but Arjumand who had returned after a long absence.

Feeling aware of the dread on Arjumand's face she was secretly amused. That is how it used to be. She was the one who would do something naughty and Arjumand would feel frightened. They both entered the breakfast room together and everything that happened was contrary to Arjumand's expectations.

Ammah Begum was inwardly shocked to see Gaythi suddenly, but she continued to sit calmly on the side of the table where the teapot and cups were laid out, behaving almost as if Gaythi had never left the house. As if both sisters had been coming together for breakfast just like that every day. Both of them greeted her when they got nearer. She embraced Gaythi silently and asked her in a gentle voice, 'When did you get here?'

'Just a little while ago.'

'Yes! I did hear the clatter of the *tonga*. If you had informed us the car would have come for you.'

Gaythi's tears brimmed over with that little remark. Her mother kissed her black hair and turned her attention to the tea.

'What a strange thing your wretched brood can be. And their father really does speak the truth when he says that strictness pushes them towards obstinacy.' Her beautiful eyes became moist unobtrusively too, and her throat felt choked.

Arjumand noticed that the teapot trembled in her hands. She kept offering the various humdrum breakfast dishes to both her twin daughters attentively. How wonderful it is to have your children sitting around you at mealtimes and eating with you. How young they seem to you even when they have grown up. After a very long time she ate her breakfast with appetite and enthusiasm. That morning breakfast took ages to finish.

'Allah Mian listened to my prayers. In fact, he fulfilled even those

156

wishes and prayers which I would not have had the courage to utter,' Arjumand lost her regrets over the blunders she had made during her morning prayer.

'Yes! Home is the most sacred place. The Ka'aba of the heart must be in the home,' thought Gaythi as she sat on the wooden divan near the trayload of vegetables to assist her mother in preparing them.

That night, before she retired to bed, Ammah Begum instructed Sharif, 'Remember to give the young mistress a drink of milk and Ovaltine before bedtime tonight, and every night. She looks so pale.' And Sharif felt confused, 'Oh? I'd heard that our Begum Sahib is annoyed with the young mistress! Isn't this cook good at spinning yarns?'

41

The atmosphere was imbued with the smell of incense. All the verandahs, both inside and outside the house, had been covered with dhurries and white sheets. The cardamom candy and toasted grams had been put away. The chapters of the Quran, which had been distributed for reading, had been collected and placed safely on a high shelf. In the rooms towards the interior of the house women were dotted about, dressed in sober but expensive clothes. They were all busy talking. Outside, in the men's section, the Mullah had departed, and, slowly, so had many of the visitors' cars: because there was no one there for the men to visit, except Bakhtiar, who had only returned last night. Barrey Abba, their father's eldest brother, had also only just arrived. This sudden incident had affected him so badly that everyone had advised him to rest. Bakhtiar sat next to him now, silently watching his closed eyes and exhausted face.

Ammah Begum lay on her bed, half-asleep, dressed in white. The fan was on full speed and the mild scent of cuscus with which someone had perfumed her clothes, in the hope that it might help to sustain her spirits, pervaded the entire room. Arjumand sat on a round Egyptian leather pouffe, drawn close to her mother's bed, gently massaging her shapely wrists, which were without her gold bangles today.

Gaythi lay on a bed face downwards in a room set apart from the others. She raised her face from the pillow in which it had lain buried. The rims of her small eyes were swollen and her face was puffy. She was the only one in the entire household whose clothes were dirty. Today, already half-gone, was the third day since, but her heart was still in torment. She looked out of the window through her bleary eyes.

'Whoever heard of such a thing before? That instead of someone returning from tour himself, his corpse should return, Abba Mian! You really are the limit! Did you have no desire at all to see me again? And I had counted each and every day of the year, waiting to see you.'

Suddenly she remembered that day when she had stood before him mulishly insisting that she wanted to become a boarder. His voice echoed in her ears. 'All right, my daughter! Let's do it like this: we'll get you admitted at the Kinnaird College in Lahore. Now you can stop worrying.'

His tall, handsome person flashed before her eyes. Mughal features, an imposing moustache and the glimmer of a dignified streak of silver in his hair. All that beauty and splendour was before her . . .

'Oh, my father!' She hid her face in the pillow again. 'If I had known that I would not see you again I would never have left you. I am truly a wretch.' Her heart was beating madly. She felt terribly alone and insecure. It had been a loss for the entire family but Gaythi was taking it as an individual and particularly personal loss. She felt that no one was sharing her grief. Bakhtiar and Arjumand had been shadowing Ammah since it had happened, whereas she had stayed distant and aloof from all the others. Even through the depths of her own grief her mother had remained aware that she was mourning apart from everyone else. When Barrey Abba arrived, someone suggested to her that she should cry on his shoulder, but she regarded that advice as hopelessly misguided. 'What did Barrey Abba care about him, or about us? He never came for years on end, nor asked after his brother. He'd be pleased when they met, but if they didn't, it did not matter. If I embrace him I shall miss Abba even more.

'And now Saulat Apa will come and upset everything. Take control of things, for no reason at all,' she thought, when she saw the telegram announcing her arrival.

Ammah Begum, who had shown exemplary patience until then on account of her younger daughters, cried at the top of her voice when she met her mature married daughter. Arjumand had put aside her own pain and grief and was busy looking after everyone else.

After her bout of weeping Saulat collapsed in exhaustion for a little while before recovering her senses. Then, she showered and dressed, and took over the responsibility of running the house. Ammah Begum was now like a toy in her hands. She was still in shock. For one thing, it was a sudden and unexpected tragedy, and for another, the person who could have ably looked after her and the household had taken umbrage and was out of her reach.

When Saulat took over the management of the house, Arjumand got a chance to turn her attention to Gaythi and herself. She was amazed at herself. Under normal circumstances she was very weak and prone to become anxious and apprehensive. Yet, in the face of this incident, she had proved to be the most strong-willed and unperturbable of them all. She had accepted it as an inevitable and natural thing, and until Saulat arrived, she had been running the household as well as supporting her mother with considerable patience and fortitude. In contrast to her, Gaythi, who was fearless, adventurous and physically stronger than her, had lost all control of her senses. Now that she was free of everything else, Arjumand felt that Gaythi was the one who deserved the most attention. Sorrow had not merely affected her outwardly, it had actually proved to be detrimental to all her faculties.

Visitors from out of town had only now started arriving. Once again after a long interval, the house was full of relatives from both sides of the family, just as it had been when Saulat Apa had got married. Gaythi thought to herself, 'Dadi Ammah and my father are missing from this crowd. It almost feels as though both of them might be out visiting elsewhere. Yes, and Hashmi Apa is missing as well, even though she is still alive. She and her son, too. Both of them have not come.' Gaythi felt bitter only for an instant, and then she thought, 'Yes, it was right. I would have done the same thing myself. What's the point in keeping up pretences?'

Her mother's brother and his wife, Mamoo Mian and Mumani jaan had come from Bombay. He left the next day, she stayed for a week but she was very worried about her children. Before she left, once again she urged Ammah Begum to accompany her along with both the girls, so she could observe her four months of ritual mourning at their house.

When she heard that said, Ammah Begum burst into floods of tears again, something she had not done for several days now. 'No, this mourning has to be done here! On this threshold.' Then she addressed her sister-in-law, 'You go. Ammah jaan is ill as it is, and my suffering must have made her worse. Look after her, and when she is better, send her to me. I would like to be close to her now.'

'Certainly! Why not? And she will not be happy there any more without you either. At the moment we have only told her that Jehangir Bhaiya is ill, otherwise God only knows what kind of a state she would be in right now.'

Ammah Begum's tears flowed again.

It had taken Ismat a week to arrive. Her baby was still young and she had no help. In spite of that, she came as fast as she could. She glowed with better health than ever before. Zubair's income was limited and she had to manage within that. She was as simple as she used to be before her marriage. Content, quiet and, like always, forgiving towards everyone. She had been very fond of her uncle, and she had completely forgiven her aunt, Chachi Ammah, who used to chafe at the very sight of her face once upon a time. Ever since she had become aware of things she had seen her mother dressed in white, devoid of jewellery and bangles, and this had never anguished her. But when she saw her Chachi Ammah's beautiful wrists bare, she lowered her eyes to them and wept so profusely that they were soaked in tears. She wept soundlessly, without a sob, for so long that her aunt raised her to her breast with her trembling hands, saying, 'Take courage, my child!'

She hid her face against her aunt's breast and wept like a child, even more piteously. And the tormented heart fluttering inside that chest suddenly softened towards her, 'She is a memento of my Sheharyaar, the mausoleum of his quiet and speechless love.' She bent down and kissed Ismat's shiny hair and her tears slid and scattered round both of them like countless pearls.

'My mother is not malicious at heart,' Gaythi thought as she watched them from a distance. And then, after a very long time, she ran towards her mother. She put her head on her lap, both her hands round her waist and, for the first time, clung to her, as she wept, because, today, her mother was crying not merely for her husband, and the comfort and lifestyle she associated with him, but also for that son who was far away from her, because her hopes of his return were now becoming dim.

'And if Barrey Bhaiya had been here today I would not have been so powerless,' without saying another word Gaythi moved her head from her mother's lap to Ismat's.

These days she behaved as if she were possessed. So much so that sometimes Arjumand would have doubts about her sanity.

Ismat's baby was still very young and Zubair had not been very well when she had left. Consequently, she went away on the third or fourth day, partly also because Chachi jaan did not think that it was right to keep her there for too long.

Bakhtiar accompanied her to the station by himself. After he had found her a seat and arranged her luggage he came and sat down beside her, and said as he played with her baby's fist, 'Ismat Apa, was it not obligatory on this occasion for Talat to come too?'

During her stay of three or four days Bakhtiar had not paid Ismat any special attention or mentioned Talat. So she was startled when she heard what he said and could not reply.

'She has always used the excuse that she was unable to come because of Dadi Ammah. But now, is this not her real uncle who has died?'

Tears welled up into Ismat's eyes. 'Bakhtiar! Can't you guess how badly she must have been affected by this?'

'Who knows? It is true that Abba Mian never managed to look after you people properly, but nevertheless!' Bakhtiar's voice trembled.

'Don't talk like this. Looking after someone is a separate matter. Chacha Abba had a vast, generous heart,' Ismat's tears spilt down her cheeks.

'Not as far as Talat is concerned,' Bakhtiar's tone was reproachful. 'The thing is, we deserve this punishment. I know everything.'

'It isn't so,' she embraced Bakhtiar. 'Don't even think of it, my *bhaiya*! One doesn't need to come to a special place to grieve. The sorrows which are our own, we wish to keep to ourselves.'

Suddenly Ismat's baby started crying and kicking his legs around. Bakhtiar separated himself from Ismat as he commented, 'There you are! You embraced me and your son became jealous.'

'You little rascal! Are you jealous of my brother then?' Ismat picked the baby up and placed a hand on Bakhtiar's back, 'Do you know how much I love my brother?'

The train whistled and Bakhtiar jumped up hastily kissing the baby. 'Give my regards to Zubair Bhaiya.'

'OK. But you'd better let go of this bar and move back. It's crawling now.'

'God be with you,' Bakhtiar jumped on to the platform.

'In the name of God! God be with you. God protect you!' From the moving train she looked towards the crowd in the midst of which her brother stood.

'In truth he is the only brother we have. God protect Barrey Abba's sons, but they actually don't even recognise our faces. And as for Barrey Bhaiya! She was afraid even to think about him. Who knows what the memory of him might prompt me to think!'

42

She had been in the store all morning moving suitcases around and sorting them out in accordance with Saulat Apa's instructions. God only knows what she wanted to achieve through all this. When all the guests had departed she rearranged the room, and now she had started all this upheaval. Arjumand was completely worn out separating Abba Mian's woollen suits from his summer ones, sorting his guns and bullets, and putting them away. Besides, just the sight of the things which his dear hands had touched and used several times, was causing her heart to sink. She was exhausted with the effort involved in suppressing her tears and sobs. She felt annoyed with Gaythi too, who was just resting in bed, like a queen, instead of lifting even a finger to help.

Saulat Apa sat on an easy chair beside her looking through and sorting out ancient group photos from individual ones, whilst giving her instructions at the same time. The smell of naphthalene balls and neem leaves infused her hands and her brain and now only one desire throbbed with life within her, that the work should finish quickly so that she could get away. But to achieve that was impossible in Saulat Apa's presence. She had to ensure that each crease and fold was perfect.

When she was finally free of the work she felt extremely hungry, and as if the smell of naphthalene had pierced through her hungry innards like an arrow. After making her lock the suitcases, Saulat Apa got the store room locked, and gave her the bunch of keys. 'Tell Ammah to keep it somewhere safe.'

'Saulat has dealt with so much work, God bless her,' Ammah Begum said piteously. 'I didn't even think of all this.'

'But what was the rush? The store could have been sorted out one day. My body is falling to pieces.' Arjumand's heart protested silently as she left the room.

Her blood boiled as soon as she entered her own room. Books were scattered all around in total disarray. The bedlinen was creased and crushed. Her writing table was covered in dust and the doors and windows had been flung open. Gaythi lay in bed contentedly reading a book, with three pillows under her head.

'*Tauba*, Gaythi! You are the limit! Couldn't you at least get round to tidying the room?'

Gaythi lowered the book without saying anything and looked at Arjumand as if to ask her, 'What did you say?'

'Just look at it. The whole room is in a mess. You could have tidied up a little. If nothing else you could have asked Sharif to come and do it for you.'

'I thought that you would do it yourself when you got back. I was waiting for you.'

'I didn't have the time! Saulat Apa had me in harness, slaving away in the store room since morning. You never ever take the trouble to help at all.'

Instead of telling Arjumand how ill, distraught and disaffected she felt, how she could not settle down to doing anything, that whatever she took up began to irritate her and drive her crazy, she sat up. She dropped the book in her hands and said, taking offence, 'Yes, you are right. My existence is absolutely meaningless and useless as far as this house is concerned. I am no use to anyone and my presence is a nuisance for you, too. All your things are upside down.'

She had never thought or spoken in this vein before. Arjumand was stunned to hear what she said.

'I didn't mean to imply all that, Gaythi ! And how can your presence be a nuisance for me? This room is as much yours as it is mine. We've always shared it.'

'Nevertheless we haven't been sharing it for the past year or so. You have got used to peace and orderliness,' she laughed sarcastically. 'The thing is, I am the only wild barbarian in this house.'

'Now you are making an issue of what I said for no rhyme or reason. I just said something unthinkingly. Never mind, I'll tidy up myself.'

She started picking up things and tidying them.

Gaythi began to feel that she was doing this to express her anger against her. She rose and started snatching things from Arjumand's hands and putting them away herself.

'Why are you doing it? Your room's been spoilt because of me so *I* will do it.'

'You're getting annoyed for nothing,' Arjumand also spoke sharply and snatched the dirty towel, which had lain crumpled on the table, from her sister's hands.

As soon as she lost her grip on the towel, Gaythi lost control of herself.

'Take them, take them.' She knocked all the books off the table. 'I understand perfectly. Everyone is fed up with me. No one needs me in this house any more.'

She fell on the bed pathetically and kept repeating at the top of her voice, 'No one needs me, no one needs me. Everyone is fed up with me.'

Ammah Begum heard the sound of the heart-rending screams which poured forth from Gaythi involuntarily. She did not have the strength to go to her; she just sat there trembling. Saulat who had just emerged from the bathroom sat before the mirror untangling her hair. The comb fell from her hand and she thought , 'Oh, that Gaythi! Why did that wretch have to be born into this family?' She went towards their room stamping her feet in anger. Gaythi's hands grew cold as she screamed, her face was white and her lips dry. But her condition did not induce the slightest sympathy in Saulat. To her, Arjumand, who now stood near the table, ashamed and apprehensive, her face pale, her eyes full of tears, appeared to be much more deserving of sympathy. This girl, who was a picture of patience and silence, seemed truly worthy of pity in her eyes.

'What happened?' she asked Arjumand gently. Arjumand told her in the briefest possible manner and admitted her mistake.

'You poor girl.' She looked at Arjumand with kindness and affection. With what patience and courage she is facing up to things. How helpful she is towards everyone in this crisis. 'No. It isn't your fault. She has changed her disposition so that no one should dare say a word to her.'

She had said it softly but Gaythi had perhaps heard her, because now her screams had changed to, 'I've done everything wrong, I've done everything wrong.'

Saulat looked at this girl whose fists were clenched and who was screaming with all the strength in her body so that her voice had become hoarse, with disgust and contempt. Thank God everyone had left. Then she addressed Arjumand aloud, 'Now look at her. You always take her side. I don't even talk to her very much because of all these tantrums she throws. Whatever I need to ask or say, I address to you.'

This was, indeed, a fact. Since the day Saulat had arrived she had not acknowledged her existence, with the exception of the first day of her visit when she had embraced her. Arjumand was thinking to herself, 'But she has never behaved like this before today.'

Gaythi's screaming and sense of helplessness intensified as she heard those harsh comments about herself. In her own room, Ammah Begum's condition worsened proportionately. She wept bitterly, 'Please God, let no one have a child like that.'

Bakhtiar, who was on the verandah outside looking through some important papers, could hear those screams clearly now. He lifted his face to catch the sound. 'Someone is losing heart. Dear God! Give my mother and sisters the courage to bear this,' he thought as he went in quickly.

Contrary to his expectations, this was Gaythi, who had not wept aloud like this even on the first day. He stopped for an instant to look at Arjumand and Saulat, and understood that, undoubtedly, one of them had said something to her which she could not endure.

'*Arrey, arrey*, Gaythi! Listen to me. At least look at me.' He bent over her and held both her hands which were cold as ice.

'Arjumand, don't just stand there, gawping. Go and fetch some water.' He sat on the edge of the bed and addressed her, 'Gaythi! How did you get the idea that no one needs you? Everyone needs you. Look here! More than anyone else, I need you.'

He gathered her unkempt hair and pushed it behind her face, stroking her cold forehead affectionately, and she was silent for a little while.

'What's the matter?' Bakhtiar cajoled.

'The matter?' She burst into floods of tears, 'Something awful is the matter, Bakhtiar Bhai!'

'It's nothing.' He gave her water to drink, dried her tears and soothed her. 'It's nothing. The only thing is you're not feeling well, my doll! Look, you should be quiet now, and go to sleep. You're worrying me; everyone is worried on account of you.'

'All right . . . all right. I shan't worry anyone now.' She hid her face on Bakhtiar's lap and held his hand tightly. He stroked her head with his other hand gently, as he patted her to sleep. Slowly, she gave in and dropped off.

He rose quietly from where he sat, called Arjumand and upbraided her, 'Do please try to be a little tolerant towards her and show some patience.'

'But it wasn't anything really, Bakhtiar Bhai,' she said with surprise.

'Maybe not. What can I say to you? Her mind and body seem affected by this, even more than her heart. And the feeling that everyone regards her as reprehensible has taken root in her heart.'

'Fine, but never mind that now. Stop your moralising and get all the papers from the bank together; they're scattered all over the verandah,' Saulat grumbled with distaste, and he went out with his head lowered.

Very slowly, he gathered all the papers together and filed them, thinking, 'These papers are being given more importance than anything else. Don't think of the one who died, nor of the ones who are alive; just keep thinking of these papers, keep looking at them. That's right. What could be more important than these? They're papers from Abba Mian's bank, documents about his orchards and lands, all the policies in our names, and, in reality, they are more important than every single person, dead or alive. Because they make someone important in the eyes of others.'

He was starting to think along these lines because he was still a relatively new prisoner. Until today, he had never encountered all these strange forms and incomprehensible documents. He had felt irritated enough to think, 'How fortunate those progeny are whose fathers do not leave them an inheritance of heaps of tangles and documents! They have the strength of their own two arms and sprawled before them is the vast arena of the whole wide world, instead of files of unintelligible papers.'

He was entitled to think all these things. For he was still young and inexperienced . . .

Throughout the afternoon she kept waking up and dropping off to sleep again at intervals. Every time her eyes opened she would feel that she had slept a lot, more than enough. Enough to be rid of all her fatigue and anger. But despite that, she was apprehensive at the thought of waking up. Being awake was, after all, just another name for reality. Not ordinary reality, but reality of the bitterest kind. That which meant confronting the fact that she had been guilty of a deed, shameful beyond her own imagination. To make such a fuss that the entire household should have become alarmed, over a small and insignificant matter, and that, too, something which Arjumand had said – she was amazed at herself! She did not realise how badly her nerves had been affected by the trauma of her father's death and how alone she imagined herself to be. Every time she woke up she felt terrified at the thought of having to face everyone, and so, finding comfort in the solitude and silence around her, she would turn on her side once again, close her eyes for a few instants and it was as if someone would pat her gently, to send her to sleep again. This state of oblivion and somnolence felt immensely comforting.

Arjumand came in once, drew the curtains and reduced the speed of the fan, so that her sleep should not be disturbed. When she emerged from the bathroom after her wash at five, she lit the pale blue nightlight for her. 'If you wake up in the dark you can become alarmed,' she thought, so she did all these things simply because it was her habit to do them. For today, in fact, she felt full of reproof against Gaythi. 'She made such an issue of a mere trifle and embarrassed me without justification. Especially in front of Bakhtiar Bhai, who must have thought I had said God knows what to her.'

That was the whole thing. Gaythi's fear of Arjumand's annoyance terrified her with the prospect of loneliness. When she finally woke up, she felt a slight suspicion that she had slept all night and that it was now morning. But this was just a feeling. It was eight o'clock. The faint light of the lamp pervading the room had produced the illusion of daylight.

'How long can I go on sleeping like this?' She tried to fill herself with courage. 'It would be wonderful if everyone denounced me the moment they set eyes on me. One should be prepared to get what one deserves.' Now she wanted to see herself being tortured.

She rose slowly, made her bed, then came and stood near the window. It was a silent summer night, relatively cool. The garden had been watered, and the driveway sprinkled. Beyond the darkness of the garden the constant sing-song whine of the crickets could be heard. The odd star twinkled in the sky.

Her sense of solitude deepened and thickened as it enveloped her mind. Instead of self pity she felt anger against herself. She wanted everyone to remonstrate against her and be so angry with her that she would begin to feel sorry for herself again, that she would imagine herself to be oppressed. To prepare herself for all this she bathed, changed and, walking through the verandah, entered the courtyard. The concrete floor of the courtyard had been sprinkled with water and the plants in the flowerbeds along the edges had been washed with the sprinkler so that all traces of dust had been removed. In the lamplight, the white half-open jasmine buds smiled against the wet green foliage. As always, beds, made up with brilliant white linen, were lined up in the courtyard, with glowing canopies of mosquito nets above, supported by green bamboo poles clamped round the legs of the beds.

Ammah Begum, dressed in a snow-white sari, sat on the wooden divan, saying her evening prayers. At a slight distance from her sat Saulat, on a low stool, reciting from the Quran. Bakhtiar was stretched out on an armchair reading a newspaper and Arjumand sat near him playing with Saulat's little daughter. It was the entire family huddled together in one corner. The common bond of sorrow and grief had drawn them closer to each other and despite their sense of irrevocable loss there was a certain expression of calm on their faces.

The feeling of loneliness hidden in the recesses of her mind deepened further. Those moments in time which fail to keep pace with the progress of the world, dip into the depths of darkness and drown.

'So am I only a lost moment in time?' she asked herself sadly. 'Is it an awful torture to be unique in some way? If so, how loudly must the solitude of the Maker of this universe echo!'

When Jehangir Mirza's daughter, Gaythi Ara Begum, gave in to reflection, she always carried her thoughts to an illogical extreme. Prepared for all kinds of conversation and for any manner of address, she advanced slowly, and, drawing a chair close to Ammah Begum's seat, sat down on it. Ammah Begum was telling her rosary. When Saulat turned the page of the Quran, Gaythi cursed herself for not having done anything like that for her dear father for whom she was supposed to be engaged so deeply in mourning.

It occurred to her that his chair used to be exactly where Bakhtiar's chair stood now. Near him always stood his hookah, wrapped in garlands of jasmine, perfumed with rose-water and essence. The warm whiff of the mild fragrance which combined the odour of tobacco, fire and the unbaked clay of the bowl had seduced her several times into stealing a few puffs.

'Thank goodness my father did not drink. Or else, perhaps, steeped in the attractiveness of his personality, drink would also have assumed such a charm for me that I would have tasted alcohol as well,' she thought.

'Exactly on the spot where Bakhtiar Bhai's feet rest, my father's feet used to be.' She felt a wild urge to rub that spot with her forehead and let all the dust infuse into her forehead.

Isn't that convention wonderful, whereby people touch their foreheads with dust from under the feet of their parents? Very close to her, her mother sat on the prayer mat. The smell of freshly washed cotton clothes emanated from her. She felt like bowing before those feet. Her heart was tender at that moment, her mood drenched in tears.

Precisely then, Ammah Begum finished her prayers and put down the rosary. Gaythi sat up straight, prepared for her onslaught.

'You did well to have a bath at this time. You don't have a headache, do you?' Her voice was silk soft with forgiveness and understanding. Gaythi was amazed.

Bakhtiar lowered the newspaper at the sound of her voice. 'Maa ji! I am hungry.' Bakhtiar always called her Maa ji when he wanted to make a show of affection.

'Well, yes, you would be hungry by now. Dinner's ready. Would you see that it is served?' she addressed Gaythi who went in to arrange it without answering. Her eyes brimmed with tears and once more she felt like crying out at the top of her voice. For she could see the white flag of a truce in her mother's hands.

43

He shut the file which contained Abba Mian's policies and placed it on the table. He felt tired of all the paperwork. He was relieved that it was the last file; he had only just completed it that day. He was getting to know all the problems now, which had been left for him to inherit. Up to this point, these documents and files had not given him the opportunity to ponder the nature of his loss.

It was not an event which would cause panic from a financial point of view. The problem, resulting from the death of his father, was for him one of the loss of peace of mind and his erstwhile freedom from worries. He was going through that very stage and time of his life when a boy really needs the mental support of his father. If he does not have that, then an older brother's sympathy and attention compensates. 'That I have already been denied because of Barrey Bhaiya's stubbornness and selfishness,' he thought, feeling bitter in the extreme.

'*Waah*, Barrey Bhaiya! This is not an impressive show of character! That you should have fled the field instead of facing the challenges and the difficulties! I know why you chose the path of avoidance and escape. The thing is that from day one all your demands were met, every waywardness endured. You had never encountered opposition or difficulty and when, all of a sudden, your mother decided to oppose you, you ran away. You think you are punishing her, but you have punished yourself, your father and now me. I wish at this point in time, you were not stranded there in a way which made it impossible for the news of your father's death to reach you, and for you to return. Then I would have completed my studies and never have felt so alone and so responsible.'

He looked at his father's youthful portrait which hung on the wall. Large eyes which appeared to droop with intoxication and a dignified smile.

'Barrey Bhaiya really does look a lot like him, and I am very different from my family.'

Indeed Bakhtiar, with his slim body, wheaten complexion, and wide black eyes, was very different from how his father and uncles used to be. He looked sickly and of a meek disposition. He had never enjoyed a great deal of prestige at home nor had he tried to assert his own importance.

'Gaythi, amongst the girls, and I, amongst the boys, are different from my family. They say that the brother who died very young was even fairer and more handsome than Barrey Bhaiya.'

The heat had intensified and Shareef had fixed the curtain of cuscus grass on the tatty and turned on the fountain of water to run against it. The tiny droplets of water swished on to the curtain like a shower. A cool and pleasant fragrance wafted from it casting itself round his tired nerves. Drowsiness overpowered him and he dropped off to sleep at an untimely hour. The clock, striking twelve, woke him up and he fell to thinking, 'What am I doing in this room on this bed, which belongs to my father. What a strange thing for me to do, to lie down on his bed and drop off to sleep like this. Where would he have slept?' He rose in a panic.

Abruptly, he remembered everything. On this visit he had been staying in this room since the day he had come and had been sleeping in that bed. With pain, he looked round at the beautifully decorated room. He had fallen into such a deep sleep that he had lost touch with reality for a few moments. Though he realised his mistake now, the question remained with him, 'Where would he have slept?' The answer was also there, in his head.

'In that open ground!'

The heat of the sun and the scorching intensity of the loo winds must have heightened. He felt like snatching away the cuscus curtain from the door. He wanted to go himself and sit in the sun, exposed to its heat. The coolness of cuscus grass, its pleasant fragrance and the rich perfume derived from it, were all things his father had loved deeply. He felt as if that handsome and well-dressed man, dazzling, in his fine transparent silk shirt, was standing out there in the sun, getting burnt.

Bakhtiar shut his tearful eyes and hid his face in the soft feather pillow. The soft centre of the pillow had absorbed his tears when he heard the bell for lunch, and raised his head with a start.

'Not a single routine of the household has changed. Only that person who had composed this household is gone. God! Doesn't life persevere in its customs with such laughable seriousness!'

Ammah Begum, noticing his red eyes and wet eyelashes, asked anxiously, 'Are you feeling all right. Why are your eyes red?'

'It's nothing. I just dropped off to sleep at an odd time,' Bakhtiar answered, his head lowered, and then thought, 'Perhaps Ammah Begum thinks that I cannot shed tears for my father, and that there should be a special reason for my eyes being red.'

There was meat and Khurfa spinach, yoghurt with cucumber and mango chutney. The choice of menu discomfited him. It was almost as if all the food had been requested by his father. He ignored all those dishes and drew the bowl of dhal towards him. Even that was from split peas. The very dhal, plain boiled rice and tamarind chutney which he loved. The redness in Bakhtiar's eyes deepened, each morsel stuck in his throat and he kept sipping water, again and again.

Ammah Begum felt his silence and studied his red eyes, 'If your eyes were hurting, you should have washed them with rose essence.'

'Yes. After all, it has been terribly hot,' Saulat said, helping herself to some meat and spinach. 'My father used to love this so,' her voice became tearful.

Bakhtiar dropped his head lower.

Tip, tip, two tears dripped on to Ammah Begum's beautiful hands and she heaved a deep sigh as she put some yoghurt on her plate. Arjumand kept eating, without enthusiasm, her head bowed. Gaythi pushed her plate aside and without saying a word to anyone left the table. They all looked at each other, except Bakhtiar.

She lay on the bed in her room weeping, as she thought, 'Saulat Apa has some strange ideas! First she gets his favourite dishes cooked in that combination and garnished, and then, whilst eating, she makes a point of mentioning in a tearful voice, that Abba Mian liked such and such a dish so much! After all, is it necessary to make falsa syrup in the house so that every time one sees its purple hue and smells its peculiar smell one feels almost as if one's heart is bursting with pain. How he adored that drink!'

She started shedding tears again. It was true that falsa syrup had been prepared several times in the house but Gaythi had not let it cross her lips, without giving any reason for this. However Saulat did not do those things on purpose. She just saw them as the patina of everyday life. One cannot recall the past after all, she believed, just by crying out for it to return. And what can you do with someone whose nerves have become restless and whose spirit becomes impossible to assuage? These days Gaythi was becoming over-emotional and suspicious and hostile towards everyone. 'She's started being unreasonable again,' Ammah Begum thought fearfully. These days she was deeply depressed and her stamina to endure things was drawing to an end. She did not want Saulat to start quarrelling with Gaythi, or scolding her about her objectionable conduct. It would create a scene, quite unnecessarily. 'Gaythi is a terribly rude and touchy girl. To take up an argument with her is not going to do her any good at all.'

But she was now also beginning to realise: 'Then again, I think Saulat is becoming quite argumentative and cranky too, as time goes on. She hasn't an iota of tolerance; which is remarkable. She was so quiet and

171

gentle before she got married. Actually, Asif Jah has spoilt her by yielding to her far more than he should have done.' She was thinking this as she tried to cover up what had happened. She pushed the plate of boiled rice towards Bakhtiar.

'I don't know what the matter is. Perhaps Gaythi is not feeling too well?' Arjumand commented with some surprise.

'There's nothing the matter, nor is she ill. But she is going a bit crazy. That is the result of spoiling her too much,' Saulat looked at her mother.

'Who spoils that poor wretch?' Ammah Begum said in her own defence, in a low tone. 'I don't even talk to her very much. I only say to her what is absolutely essential and needs to be said.'

'Why? So, how else do people get spoilt? Your not talking to her only implies that you are frightened of her temper. We never dared to talk back like she does and be as self-willed as she is.' There was a deep bitterness in Saulat's tone, 'And, God rest him in peace, Abba Mian took a special interest in everything to do with her.' Saulat's voice was so sharp and acerbic that Bakhtiar looked at his mother in surprise. She was silent.

'I don't understand why everything is taken to such extremes in this household. A tiny insignificant thing gets so drawn out that it becomes a serious complex issue. If she decided to leave the dinner table suddenly it isn't such a big deal. Everyone is at least entitled to do some things without thinking, to be impulsive in his own home.'

That afternoon lunch ended on a joyless note. Ammah Begum sat near her silver Hyderabadi *paan daan* in her own room, looking absolutely defeated. Her face was white and her eyes were sad. Each and every point of view and principle she had ever valued looked as if it might get violated, without any one actively doing it. All her hard work had been wasted. What high hopes she had had of her children and what had they come to! But the question was, after all, what had she really tried to make them into? And, she herself did not know the answer to that question.

44

On the surface, the question of a reduction in the current expenses of the household was a minor issue, but for Bakhtiar it was a problem without a solution. This problem would have presented itself to Bakhtiar even if Saulat had not offered him her advice, 'Bakhtiar, it's absolutely essential that the household expenses are now reduced. Except for the essential outgoings, you must put a stop to all the unnecessary expenditure. *Bhai*, I'll say it quite frankly, you should sit down and tell Ammah Begum, once and for all, that it is possible to manage without incurring some of these expenses.'

But it was only when this question was raised in earnest that the true complexity of its nature was discovered. After all, which particular expense could he reduce? He could not imagine the house without Shareef and the Cook? The Sweeper and the Dhobi? Which ones could be left out? In the end, perhaps only Mali. Bakhtiar, who stood in the arched entrance to the verandah, looked at Mali who was cleaning the flowerbeds.

The beautiful arches of the porch were supported by delicate pillars adorned with exquisite pink flowers which dangled against them like an elaborate piece of jewellery glistening upon a woman's brow. Behind them, the lawn glowed green, looking plush and moist even in this heat. The strong mango and lychee trees danced in the hot winds. The roses which stood in the wet containers, row upon row, bore white, yellow and pink flowers. The yellowish jasmine which had been trained round the gates was so dense with flowers that its dark green was almost concealed by the colour which glowed like stars against a dark night sky. The pump which watered the garden could be heard throbbing deep down inside the well. All these things blended together to give the atmosphere an aspect of permanence, and of endurance.

Mali stopped watering the beds, stuck the blade of his trowel into the earth which was dark with water and stood up. He walked slowly towards the lychee tree. Green lychees, turning to a ripe purple and yellow, peeped through the long green leaves. Mali crossed both his hands behind his back as he stood attentively, examining the tree bent with the weight of the juicy bristling fruit. Thick black lips, concealed by his dense brush-like moustache, spread out in an obvious smile. His tiny eyes were full of contentment and calm. The sense of achievement produced through his own diligence flooded through his huddled body.

Mali's living quarters were towards the back of the garden, hidden behind the bamboo poles. In that tiny hovel, coated with layers of glistening unbaked clay, his wife, a strong black woman, who looked like a goddess chiselled from stone, whose gait had still not lost its swagger, had borne her nine children. When she walked, the anklets round her feet tinkled pleasantly as the metal clashed with the rattle beans. Since his childhood Bakhtiar had been used to the sound of the strange song which pulsed from Maalan's feet and scattered itself through the air. He had always seen her with a dark-skinned baby in her arms, thick lines of kohl drawn round its eyes. It occurred to him that the placentas of those nine births were buried just beyond the threshold of that hovel.

Dizzy with worry and anxiety, he turned his face away and returned to the chair where he had left the newspaper he had been reading. He picked it up and thought, 'If there had been no newspapers where would people escape to from all their own doubts and anxieties?'

He heard the scraping of someone's footsteps behind him, turned round and stood up, rolling back his sleeve, '*As-salaam-o-alaikum*, Chacha!'

'*Wa-laikum-as-salam*. Bless you! May you live long! I insist on blessing you with my prayers – because you are my nephew – even if you conform to this fashion and say, "*As-salaam-o-alaikum*". We, as your elders, still have to pray for you.' Azam Baig chewed over each and every word.

Bakhtiar looked at him closely. Ruddy complexion, a slim body and a small brown moustache. Had he ever made his acquaintance before now? He had seen him visiting Abba Mian occasionally, during the early days of each month. On this particular occasion, he had heard it said that this gentleman had proved to be very useful, helping to organise the funeral for Abba Mian, whose close friends just sat on the chairs in the drawing room puffing at their cigarettes whilst he did all the running around. He had bathed the body himself and when Bakhtiar had arrived he came to condole officially with him, even though this formality was not in the least expected of him. He did not express his condolences verbally but the deep sadness in his face and his lifeless manner betrayed a sense of personal loss.

The second time he came, he said to Bakhtiar, 'If there is no one who observes purdah visiting inside, then I would like to call on my sister-in-law for a few minutes.' There was a note of fear and entreaty in his voice. Bakhtiar escorted him to the interior of the house but Ammah Begum took no notice of him. She just sat there leaning against the bolster as she chopped her betel nuts with an expression of displeasure. After sitting there for ten or fifteen minutes, he rose in confusion and left, without waiting for a reply to his farewell.

'Why should Ammah Begum have taken exception to him?' Bakhtiar wondered. She did not even know that he visited Abba Mian frequently. Today was the first time he had come since the day he had visited her and it seemed as though he were undergoing real pain of some kind. The kind of pain someone awaiting the final judgement of his fate might experience. He was trying to be informal today. There was a smile on his face but his eyes carried an uncertain mixture of hope and anxiety.

He could not find a way to begin the conversation. After a brief

174

awkward silence he asked a pointless question, 'Have you informed Sheharyaar about Bhai Sahib's death, mian?'

'What can we tell him at this stage? Who knows what he is going through. He won't be able to do anything except agonise over it.'

Bakhtiar spoke gently but he thought to himself, 'A person spending his time in the damp, stinking trenches on the frontier in France, surrounded by cold lifeless bodies and the shivering wounded, a person for whom the greatest luxury is the transient sense of warmth, light and satisfaction obtained from lighting a damp, blood-soaked cigarette fumblingly found in the pocket of a dead colleague – how can a person like that be affected by the arrival or non-arrival of information about the death of his father in the comfort of his own surroundings?

'And who knows, at this moment, in this instant, Barrey Bhaiya . . .' He was amazed at the audacity of his own thoughts and, deciding to change their direction, he continued, ' . . . where he might be. Perhaps imprisoned by the Germans . . . Yes, that's right. There is no harm in speculating up to that point.' But he could not attach any other image to the person of his smiling older brother, whose eyes always looked as if he were intoxicated and whose carriage and deportment were princely.

Azam Baig was now gazing at something in the distance, on the horizon, beyond the verandah. In his anxiety, he could not help shaking his feet gently. Then he drew a tiny box of *paans* and a grubby sequined purse from the left pocket of his kurta. He wrapped the *paan* and tucked it into his mouth, then tossed some chopped betel nut and tobacco from the purse on to his tongue. The tobacco was scented strongly and a whiff of cardamom escaped his breath, dispersing in the narrow space around them.

Suddenly, Bakhtiar remembered something.

'Shall I get them to light the hookah for you, Azam Chacha?'

Azam Chacha's distinctly Mughal light brown eyes appeared to be extremely gentle and friendly. There were signs of pain and torture on his face. He shifted in the chair as if he were in agony and, turning his face away, he said, 'No, mian. I shan't smoke the hookah.'

Bakhtiar rose and went to tell Shareef, 'Light Sahib's hookah and bring it here.'

When that familiar hookah was brought before him, with its shining lid crowning the clay bowl and its pleasant gentle fragrance, his eyes became red. He lowered his head and then helplessly driven by his need to smoke, he held the tip to his mouth. Despite his flowing eyes he puffed away and continued to disperse the smoke in the air.

All of a sudden, Bakhtiar remembered something. On several pages of

Abba Mian's diary, he had seen an amount of Rupees 40 entered against Azam Baig's name in the column for expenses. He thought for a little while. He strolled around then, out of the corner of his eye, looked at Azam Chacha who sat there puffing at the hookah silent and mournful.

He stood in the room thinking for a long time, with four ten rupee notes in his hand. 'Who knows how Abba Mian used to put this money in his hands?' He could not work out how he should hand the money to this man who was his elder, both in terms of age and relationship. He opened the drawer and took a blank envelope from it, slipped the notes into it, licked the edge and stuck it down. Then he thought, 'Whatever happens in the future must happen, but for the moment, at least, today, I will not disappoint him.' He had no idea that his father also used to hand quietly a sealed envelope to this poor relation of his in exactly the same manner .

As he came out of the room, Bakhtiar thought, 'For a decent man to help another decent man can also be a problem.' Then, with his embarrassed eyes lowered, he handed the envelope to Azam Baig, who looked at him as he sucked in the betel juices creeping round the corners of his mouth. The expression on his face was that of a man who has been caught red-handed. When Bakhtiar glanced at him he felt that for the first time since the moment he had come, his face carried a glimmer of calm and peace. He slipped the envelope in the pocket of his kurta without saying anything and went on puffing at the hookah in silence. When the hookah had burnt out and had stopped rumbling, Azam Baig asked him politely, 'Your holidays are coming to an end now. Are you going back soon?'

'Yes. At the moment I need to visit the lands for a little while.'

'And will you go to Aligarh after that? The girls and sister-in-law will be absolutely alone.' He expressed his concern.

'All these old servants are here. And Asif Bhai is at the front. Until now, Saulat Apa was staying at Dalhousie but now we are planning that she should let her own house there and stay here till he returns. When her children come things will liven up.'

'So has Saulat built her own house in Dalhousie?' Azam Baig expressed his joy. 'But why so far away from everyone else? She should have built it in Nainital.' It was a habit with him, to add a clause of objection, whenever he commented on things.

'Don't know why,' Bakhtiar did not feel obliged to give him a reason.

And, he too, could not see the purpose in staying on any longer, 'All right, then. I'd better go now,' he said lazily.

'Stay and eat with us, before you go,' Bakhtiar suggested as a courtesy.

'No, *bhai*. Your Chachi waits for me.'

When he had reached the gates, Azam Baig craned his neck and looked round carefully before drawing the envelope out of his pocket. Slitting it open, he held the four crackling notes of ten in his trembling hands and only then the curiosity and tension in his face abated. Bakhtiar saw him from the window in his room.

45

Before he left, Bakhtiar called Arjumand and Gaythi to his room and said, 'Look! I have some things to say to you. On my way back I shall be staying for such a short while that we may not get a chance to talk. Both of you must look after Ammah. She is alone, and quite apart from this tragedy, she is anxious about Barrey Bhaiya too. Try to come to terms with your circumstances and to cope with them. I shall do my best to ensure that our standard and style of living should change as little as possible. It is only a question of two years. When my studies are over you people will not have to worry any more. But at the moment, you have to take some responsibility.'

He was slowly collecting his belongings and papers. Gaythi sat in the corner on a circular Egyptian leather stool with her knees drawn up in the circle of her arms. Her eyes wandered outside the window where the toy candy man stood, fashioning toy hookahs, birds and bangles for Mali's children out of the warm, soft multicoloured dough made from raw sugar wrapped round his bamboo pole.

'Toy candy man!' A storm rose in Gaythi's wandering mind. 'How enthusiastically we used to buy these toys and when we went after Abba Mian he used to tell us to call all the children round the compound and buy toy candy for all of them. Anyone could have as many as he or she fancied. So much so that all the colourful sugar dough would be finished and the toy candy man would lift his bare bamboo pole and leave, praying for a long and blessed life for Abba Mian. What a lot of toys we had made during Saulat Apa's wedding. Both Masood and I filled a box up with them. Masood!' A pain shot through her. She was not certain whether it was through her heart or her head that that spark of longing had glimmered.

And so she sat looking out of the window, disinterested and unconcerned with Bakhtiar's discourse. Arjumand, comprehending the nature of her responsibilities, was folding Bakhtiar's clothes and packing them skilfully in his suitcase.

Her beautiful eyes were full of tears and she was biting her fine pink lips in an attempt to restrain them. The gentleness of Bakhtiar's voice and his sad and responsible tone had melted her heart. Two silent tears dripped on to Bakhtiar's hand thrust in front of Arjumand to hand her his neck tie.

'Arjumand! Old girl!' Bakhtiar tried to revive his old careless manner. '*Arrey*! Are you crying? Don't be silly.' He kept his hand on her shoulder. 'You really are a sensible girl, aren't you?' He looked into her eyes and smiled paternally, and Arjumand dried her tears quickly.

'Very sensible! Isn't she admirable?' Gaythi's envy rankled even at that moment. She laughed bitterly.

Bakhtiar turned round, 'And yes, Gaythi! I must ask you specially, you must learn to be sensible now.'

'And you should become a clay doll. Very well, sir!' Gaythi, drawn into her memories of the past, was in a mood for facetiousness just then.

'Don't say silly things. I mean you and Arjumand now need to be more sensible.'

Whenever Bakhtiar tried to address Gaythi individually he would lose track of his argument and would be unable to express his worthy intentions with sufficient clarity. This was because she was completely unwilling to concede his seniority. 'What is three years' difference in age, after all? Bakhtiar Bhaiya, we have played games with you. Played marbles, sometimes with pieces of broken bangles; we've done wicket-keeping for you,' she always retorted carelessly.

'I mean to say . . .'

'You mean nothing,' Gaythi spoke very quietly, under her breath.

Bakhtiar continued to talk. 'Saulat Apa will come and stay here now until the war ends. There is no point in her staying alone at Dalhousie with both the children. Her coming to stay here will mean you won't have to worry about things. And yes, Gaythi! Try not to be rude to her too often.

'Listen to her. She says things for your own good. If she criticises you it does not mean that she really considers you to be evil. It is absolutely essential for Ammah's peace of mind and happiness that both of you act on Saulat Apa's and her advice.

'Abba had a really generous heart. Whenever a new crop was harvested he would make sure that the first consignment was a huge cartload. Even the servants in the house would be sated. He loved to see people happy, noisy, simply enjoying themselves.' The news that Saulat Apa would be staying with them long term had alarmed Gaythi and she retreated into the safe fortress of her past.

'Are you listening to me?' Bakhtiar noticed the abstracted look on her face.

'Yes!' She was startled. Everything had got muddled in her head. 'Why is it necessary for Saulat Apa to come and stay here? Her children will also feel displaced for no rhyme or reason.'

'You are a fool!' Bakhtiar lost his temper.

'At least Arjumand is sensible,' her voice was extremely bitter. Then she left the room.

Bakhtiar stood there looking at this girl who was so vulnerable with a mixture of anger and pity.

46

'Oh, dear. It's getting cloudy,' Saulat thought as she covered her head with the border of her greenish-blue sari. She looked critically at the colourful covers on the tiny tables which stood between the cane chairs on the lawn. Then she busied herself with getting drinks, jugs, glasses and food arranged on the large table which stood at one end of the lawn.

'Listen, Shareef! You bring the spices for the yoghurt savouries and put them on the table separately, and also the tamarind and ginger sauce in a sauce boat. People can use them according to taste then.'

Arjumand, dressed in an outfit which was whiter than snow, emerged from the verandah and advanced towards her, her lovely eyes surveying the scene. After depositing a very large attractive box on the gift table she addressed Saulat in a gentle and sweet voice, 'Congratulations, Saulat Apa. I hope to God that you celebrate Seema's next birthday with Asif Bhai by your side.'

'Yes. I hope so, too.' For some unknown reason her voice sounded a bit false. She sighed, true to form, and added, kissing her forehead, 'There was no need for this formality; you people are forever buying presents for them.'

Arjumand got busy with helping without giving an answer to that. Seema, in a very pale pink flower-like dress, her hair tied in pink ribbons, her cheeks red as apples, came running and skipping down the steps. Her dark hair and eyes resembled Gaythi's much more than her own mother's. In other words, she looked more like her father, Asif Jah. She was light and brightly-coloured like a butterfly and despite her mother's tough vigilance and upbringing she was careless and carefree.

'Look at this, can you see it? Your frock's got crushed on this side.' Her mother picked on her the moment she saw her.

'Not at all,' she swivelled round reviewing her skirt on all sides.

'How can you say it's not crushed!' her mother scolded.

Arjumand bent down to smooth out the skirt of her dress evenly and said, 'It's true, Saulat Apa. You're imagining things.'

'Here Arjumand, take this. Can you put up the bunting and these balloons quickly, please?'

'And what would you like to command this humble servant to do?' Saulat turned round. Akbar was bowing low in a dramatic pose, in his usual comic style.

'The orders for this humble servant are to suspend his comic act for the moment . . . and . . .' Saulat tried to think of a job to allocate to this handsome and elegant man.

'I think there is no reason why I couldn't test the sweetness of the guava salad and the salt in the yoghurt savouries.' He made a sign to Arjumand requesting her not to draw attention to the fact that he already held a sweetmeat in his hand.

'OK, then, Akbar Mian. You could take charge of the ice cream machine.'

'That's not a bad deal,' said Akbar, as he headed towards the verandah at the back.

At that very moment Gaythi lifted the latch on the bathroom door and appeared wearing a white shalwar, a brightly-coloured striped voile shirt and a yellow headscarf wound tightly into a rope.

'What a strange route to use to come out of the house. She always takes the wrong way,' Saulat decided.

The pallor of her face matched the colour of her scarf. Contrasting with that pallor was the wet darkness of her hair and her eyes. She came and sat on the edge of a sofa which stood relatively near the end, her body leaning on its back.

'Well, so this it! A splendid arrangement indeed! There can be no doubt about it, Saulat Apa is a superb housewife, and is so inventive!' she thought.

Seema pulled her hand away from Arjumand's and jumped towards Gaythi, 'Where's my present?'

'Seema, that's a lovely dress you're wearing.'

'Maybe! Give me my present.'

'Seema! Talk in Urdu.'

'I will, I will,' Seema spoke crossly.

'All right, tell me, why do you celebrate your birthday? To get presents or to meet your friends?'

'Oh! To get presents and to meet my friends,' she said emphasising the word presents. 'But I don't have any friends here. Mummy brought me here from Dalhousie for nothing.'

'Yes! I think so too,' Gaythi said, gazing into the distance.

'Where's the present?' She opened Gaythi's closed fist which was empty.

'*Tauba*! You'll get your present. Don't be impatient.'

'OK then. I'll be patient now,' Seema walked off feeling a little disappointed.

'Take it then. Take your present!' Gaythi called after her.

'Huh! What's this?' she looked indifferently at the photograph of a little girl smiling in a tiny silver picture frame.

'That? It is a photograph of your mother, when she was your age.'

'Really!' Seema smiled. 'Did you see Mummy when she was my age?'

'No, Seema, I didn't see her but I have seen her pictures. Now, one day I will show you that album which has all our childhood snapshots.'

'Mummy, look! What a lovely present Auntie Gaythi's given me,' Seema called out to her mother from where she sat.

'Seema! You called me Auntie, again!'

'Then what shall I say?'

'Call me Khala, call me Khala bi.'

'My ayah says I should call you Auntie.' Seema imitated the ayah's tone perfectly.

'Shoot the wretched ayah; she's going to turn you into a damn Anglo, getting you to say, Mummy, Daddy and Auntie all the time.'

'Shoot the wretched ayah?' Seema asked in surprise.

'Gaythi, for God's sake don't use that foul word in front of her again, she will repeat it.'

'So what's the harm in that? She'll learn to speak idiomatically.'

'Go away! God forbid that "wretched" and "unfortunate" should be regarded as idioms.'

'In any case, one cannot deny that they are ordinary expressions of emotion and hatred and vehicles for them,' Gaythi shook her head to push the hair out of her eyes and calmly started chewing her gum.

'Well, that should not be the language of decent people.'

'Maybe it is, maybe it isn't. At least one ought to have the power to express one's hatred, anger and love. I feel sorry for the highly cultured who cannot even give vent to their hatred or anger.'

Arjumand felt the old defiance and wilfulness in Gaythi's tone and

181

looked at Saulat in fear. But today there was neither a frown nor any other sign of vexation on Saulat's face. 'This is such an admirable attribute of Saulat Apa's. She can control her temper so well as the occasion demands.' She herself calmed down when she remembered that.

'Gaythi, that's enough, put your philosophy aside for the moment. Go and have a look in the kitchen. And tell Shareef that the pooris he has to fry for the kebabs should not get too big. They have to be small and puffy if they are to be served with kebabs.' Gaythi turned round when she heard Ammah Begum's voice. She had come after finishing her Asar prayers and was now busy telling her rosaries.

This was a very small function to celebrate Seema's birthday, the first occasion to be observed since Abba Mian's death. Saulat, who was used to celebrating her children's birthdays and other similar occasions with tremendous style and gusto, could not see this event as anything more than a destitute sort of celebration.

On her return from Dalhousie, the entire house, with the exception of Ammah Begum's and the girls' rooms, had been reorganised to suit her needs and convenience and those of her children. There were only two children, and she was alone but she was the growing and expanding force of the present. Saulat was extremely sensitive and upset about Asif Jah's departure for the front. For this reason it was important to humour her and Seema's birthday was intended to serve that purpose. No one else had been invited except a few children, Akbar and his mother.

'By what logic are Akbar and his mother included in this party when there isn't a small child in their family?' Gaythi wondered as she stuck five tiny candles into the cake shaped like a beautiful hillside cottage.

'This moment, this time will also recede and settle into oblivion in the bower of the past. These candles will increase in number and life will get reduced, moment by moment, one iota at a time. Without our being aware of it.' She shook her head in alarm, 'Do you remember when we celebrated Abba Mian's birthday the year before last, and Bakhtiar Bhaiya had placed fifty-five candles round the cake, and then, counting them, had said, "Oh! There's no room left on the cake"? And Dadi jaan had taken offence, "*Bhai*, why do you people light these candles and count them? Each year we just quietly add another gold ring on to a ball of ordinary thread without counting, then we say a prayer over a sweet dish and distribute it. God is my witness, I have never counted the rings for my boys. After your Uncle Khaquan died, I counted the rings round his thread, and there were only thirty two of them." And, when Bakhtiar Bhaiya handed him the box of matches, saying, "Congratulations, Abba

Mian! Fifty-five successful years!" suddenly, Abba Mian had become sad, "Who knows how many of these years are successful, Bakhtiar?"'

Gaythi moved away from the cake and the candles.

'That is your own home, but this is the home of your birth. Your childhood and all your dreams are preserved here. That is why you look so many years younger than your age and experience in your pale blue sari . . . ! I speak the truth, Saulat Asif Jah. There is a secret hidden within you. There is a secret there which has remained hidden under thick layers of expediency and necessity. But that veiled secret of your soul can be seen somnolent in your eyes and sometimes it breaks free of every constraint and every stricture to overpower your personality.'

It was Colonel Sajjad who sat with his hands on the steering wheel of his jeep, reflecting on all this in a strange mood, as he watched her. She was completely absorbed in celebrating her daughter's birthday.

'He never comes on time. I've never seen an army man who is so indifferent to time. No wonder the waves of time are reluctant to go near him. Sajjad, your luminous forehead and sleepy eyes hold a promise of eternity, of immortal strength. You'll come, you will definitely come, but you will be late and then you will smile as usual and say, "I am not known as good fortune, but, nevertheless, I am always late."'

These thoughts flitted through Saulat's mind as she stood holding Seema's hand, amidst her guests who surrounded the lighted candles, singing a prayer for her long life. Unintentionally, she looked up. He had remained where he was, his hands on the steering wheel, his neck inclined, watching her through half-open eyes, as if that day he was seeing her for the very first time. She smiled. Her brilliant beautiful teeth sparkled in their characteristic manner and she stopped abruptly.

'So you did come in the end!' she thought and then returned to her singing with the same concentration, 'Happy birthday to you, dear Seema!'

He alighted from the jeep, pulled himself to attention before her alerted eyes, and then mingled with the crowd.

He showered kisses on Seema, held her hand to help her cut the cake, then picked her up and carried her to his jeep. Both of them returned loaded with packets, beautiful boxes and bags of sweets.

'Mian, you shouldn't have gone to all this trouble,' Ammah Begum observed formally.

'This is what he always does. Someone should ask him sometime if he's ever actually been invited to a birthday party,' Saulat said reprovingly.

And Sajjad started teasing Azam without giving her a reply. '*Yaar*,

Azam! I've heard your father is driving a tractor over there. No, in fact, he's gone over to cut the grass.'

'Huh! He is fighting a war over there.'

'What kind of a war? A verbal one? So how long is he going to carry on fighting?'

The call for the evening prayers could be heard and Ammah Begum went in to say her prayers.

'One can hear the call for prayers and the atmosphere is filled with a tremendous quality of calm. But we are busy trading that peace and calm for restlessness,' thought Gaythi as she organised a game of musical cushions for the children.

Akbar's mother sat on the side, busy chatting with Arjumand whilst Akbar waited upon Colonel Sajjad, who was now directly involved in a conversation with Saulat Apa.

'And, something for you, Colonel Sahib?' Akbar asked obsequiously, bending over him. 'Something savoury for you, or a drink of some kind? I mean, would you like a stiff drink?'

'No, mian! I don't drink,' Sajjad answered in his heavy, husky voice and leaned his wide back against the settee.

'*Arrey*! So what kind of a colonel is he!' Akbar, who was young and inexperienced, wondered with some surprise. 'What is the point of not drinking when you have a good position, a high standard of living and a club life? Colonel Sajjad, I hope you are not lying?'

But these were the only two qualities of which Colonel Sajjad could boast. One, that he did not lie, and secondly, his intellect was bright and well ordered, free of all complexes, and he believed in trying to empathise with others.

After responding to Akbar he addressed Saulat again, 'Any letter, any news?'

'Whose?'

'Your lord and master's.'

'What's that got to do with you?' she said pretending to be annoyed.

'No. What I mean is, there should be some kind of news, after all.'

'Is that so? If I were to say that I had received a letter from Asif only today, and that he had mentioned Seema's birthday in it and sent her lots of love, then what would you say to that?'

'Huh! What can I say? It is something to be thankful for that the father of your children should be so concerned about their birthdays, and that today you have had some news about his well-being.' Sajjad stubbed the remains of his cigarette in the ashtray and lit a new one, on which he drew with great concentration.

184

And Saulat was thinking, 'No, Sajjad! That is not something to be thankful for as far as you are concerned. You enquire after his welfare in the hope that I will give you news of his injury, or of his being lost, or taken prisoner. And that is not fair on your part. That poor man is fighting the war over there, admittedly for the benefit of others, but his own interests are included to some extent, and those of his wife and family. You are lucky that you have been appointed to perform some intelligence duties here instead of being sent to the front.'

Akbar's mother had become bored and had left and the children who had been invited were now being collected by their ayahs. Gaythi, who had been distributing balloons and bags of sweets to the children who were leaving, came and settled herself on the chair in front of them, saying to Shareef, 'If you fetch me a cold drink you will be sure to earn a great reward in heaven.'

Mid-sentence, Sajjad caught a glimpse of her, noticing that the blackness of her hair and eyes shone against the yellow of her scarf. Despite the fact that she had laughed a lot with the children, her tired eyes held the poignant grief and anguish of a huge loss. Since the day he had started visiting the house he had often seen her around, but it struck him for the first time that day that she was very different from everyone else in her family.

All the chairs, tables and the rest of the paraphernalia for the party had been collected and put away and both the girls had gone inside. Sajjad sat on the lawn for a long time smoking cigarettes. Saulat kept stepping out to see to him. The clouds which had been threatening rain earlier in the evening turned to a pitch black louring sky.

47

'What's the meaning of this? After all, is there any need for maintaining such warmth and intimacy with Akbar, now? It's true that when bereavements happen both friends and enemies rally round. Akbar had started visiting again when their father died but Saulat should not be paying so much attention to that boy.' This occurred to Ammah Begum without anyone prompting the thought.

'It was such a tiny episode and he went round gossiping about it everywhere, insinuating all manner of things. And she does not deny it. She simply narrated the facts. I admit that she has always been self-willed, the wretched girl. She decides that she has to watch a film, even if it means taking a third-class seat – and then she feels scared and decides to shelter behind that Chinese man. And, anyway, whatever the reason, Akbar should not have talked about it. But Saulat is so quick to say to me, about any and everything: "You don't understand". If she had said that a little while ago, I would have got my own back, but now, in fact, I haven't the slightest confidence left in my own abilities. I feel that until now I have done nothing but make mistakes. True that all of us make mistakes. That one's very life is a huge mistake. The only thing that proves to be right is Time, which slowly and steadily brings every mistake and every truth to light.' These doubts had invaded her after her morning prayers, and, alarmed by them, she opened a special prayer book and kept it in front of her to read.

Gaythi lay on a charpoy woven with coarse rope, without any bedding, which stood on a red-brick platform under the shade of the kamrakh tree planted close to its edge. When, through its branches, she saw the grey birds searching for food in the muddy July sunlight, a wave of unfamiliar happiness flooded through every pore of her being. She looked at the murky sky out of the corners of her tiny half-open eyes. The sky was overcast with clouds, reddish brown, like puffs of raw cotton. Under this sky, the kamrakh tree, with its beautiful, dense foliage and its fragile trunk of medium height, stood protecting her.

Through the clumps of leaves peeped the golden fruits. I am down here and above all this is my God. That Immortal God who lives as long as we have faith. These tiny ashen birds play and forage in the earth, blending with its colour like miniscule muddy balls. And so long as all this exists, I need not harbour a grudge in my heart. For I hate those scenes which are lit up too brightly, caked in dry dust, clouded by sand and grit. And love those misty moments which are bathed and washed to a bright green in the remarkable waters of the rain, so deeply that all this will fuse into me or that I shall dissolve and become part of it. I intensely hate reality in its stark nakedness. That is why I wish to extinguish the lighted candles of those memories which are bitter. I wish that the secrets of fog and mist should cloud my being, so that I could hide behind them, and only view the beautiful and pleasant aspects of life. Go away, Akbar! I forgive you and you too, Saulat Apa, who allowed someone who gossiped about me into the house once again.' Her eyes filled with tears, as a strong feeling of grace and purification moved her heart.

'You are also due to come today. And I know that you will come later than you are expected. But never mind, I never let my eyes cling to the doors, waiting for you,' Saulat was thinking, as she searched for a skein of red amongst the pile of silk threads which lay before her. Azam sat near her, struggling to assemble a picture from pieces of a wooden jigsaw puzzle and Seema was writing.

'Look, Seema. You've started racing your hand along too fast, again. You need to write slowly if you want to produce fine and beautiful handwriting.' Seema jerked her head to fling her hair back and said, 'I want my hand to move slowly, but it rushes along.'

'Huh! She jerks her hair back just like Gaythi.' Saulat felt aggrieved.

Arjumand came out after she had had the bedrooms and bathrooms cleaned out. She spread out the damp towels neatly on the towel stand which stood outside in the sun and straightened them.

'Where's the sun for these towels which Arjumand is hoping to dry out here? However, I suppose slowly the air and this muddy sunlight will remove their dampness and they won't smell. How lazy I am. I really don't do anything. But how can I do anything? I feel so lazy these days . . .'

As he pruned the overgrown creeper with dark orange flowers which covered the farthest wall of the platform, Mali noticed Gaythi as she lay under the kamrakh tree. 'I have never seen anyone in this house lying carelessly like this on a charpoy without any bedding. Sometimes it seems as though she is just like us. She rests as if she were made of the same metal as poor women, who spread out their legs to rest under the shade of the trees when they have cooked, fed others and have eaten.'

'Right. So, Sajjad Sahib is expected today,' Shareef concluded as he considered the menu Saulat had given him for lunch, 'Mango ice cream, meat with potatoes, plain boiled rice and red kidney beans. Sajjad Sahib's visits are not a bad thing at all. The children are pleased too. How quiet the house has become since Chote Bhaiya left. And when there isn't a man about the house, there is nothing to occupy people in the house, nor any liveliness or disorder. You just serve the meal and then the servants are free to take their hookahs and go off to sit and smoke with the idlers in their quarters. But just sitting idle and gurgling away at a hookah thoroughly undermines one's integrity.' Although Shareef could not articulate these thoughts too clearly, the feeling nagged at him all the time.

*

187

As Sajjad alighted from the car, having parked it in the porch, he saw Gaythi enter the verandah. It was apparent that she had just bathed. Despite the freshening effect of the water on her face you could see the fatigue and sorrow in her eyes.

'Greetings,' she raised her hand to him, noticing that Sajjad stood on the steps of the verandah, quite near her.

'Bless you!'

As he walked past her he felt aware of a pleasant blend of odours, fresh cotton, gram flour and Cuticura talcum powder, which wafted towards him, inducing him to think how pleasant and sacred this blend of natural odours was, and how quickly it was dying out. 'Rustling garments, brightly-coloured, soaked in priceless perfumes, colognes and scents fail to penetrate the surface of my brain, but this gentle fragrance feels as if it is sinking into the depths of my soul.'

Sajjad's eye focused for a second on Gaythi's uplifted hand which was wide and strong, with fingers markedly different from the long tapering fingers of both her sisters. Her healthy-looking nails had been trimmed. 'But, but, this girl . . . her features, her eyes which are so black, seems to be very interesting indeed.'

He walked past her.

These days Ammah Begum would go and lie down straight after lunch, staying by herself until it was time for the afternoon prayers.

'It's good. Her exhausted heart and mind appear to find peace by doing so,' Saulat believed.

Slicing the langra mangoes after lunch, Sajjad spoke up, 'Right, now we have to see who ate the most food.'

'What's the need for that? We all know that whoever was the most starving would have eaten the most.' Saulat, who was far too sophisticated to be seen tackling the stone of a mango, put it aside on a plate.

'That's what you think, madam. We get the most wonderful dishes cooked at our mess. We have a cook from Lucknow these days.'

'I am not naming anyone.'

'So, we shall soon find out.'

Sajjad placed a knife on the table and spun it round. The tip of the knife pointed towards Gaythi when it came to a stop.

'That's remarkable. I had been suspecting this for quite some time now.'

Saulat took a sideways glance at Gaythi, who had for several days now been sitting through lunch with a long face. She had hardly smiled at the funniest jokes, but she was smiling pleasantly now, she noticed.

'Where were you the day before yesterday, Sajjad?' Saulat questioned him. 'That is confidential. That is my secret, Saulat Ara Begum! You have no right to probe. During wartime it is best to ask as few questions as possible. And, I must say, the same applies during the course of love, too.' The last sentence had been uttered in a lowered voice.

'You army men try to be more mysterious than is absolutely necessary. And, yes, Mr Sajjad, may you live long. Why do you forget that you are my younger brother-in-law and to address a sister-in-law who is older than you by her name contravenes the spirit of our culture?' Saulat shot a glance at Gaythi and then turned her attention back to her mango.

Sajjad directed his penetrating gaze towards the mesh on the windows. 'The existence or absence of the relationship bears no significance for me, or anyone else. It is only an act of courtesy that we give people the impression that we are actually related. And it is a great thing, especially as my kinship with your Asif Jah is relatively vague. The thing is, Saulat Ara Begum, that culture, especially our own, is contravened all the time.' Colonel Sajjad, the man with the luminous forehead, thought all this, but said, without offering a rejoinder to Saulat's comments, 'We shall read everyone's palms after the meal, so that all one's suspicions about people can be confirmed.'

'Go on! You can keep your palmistry to yourself. You won't get a thing right . . .'

'Do you say that in all honesty? When I read your palm for the first time, did I not tell you that . . .'

'Shareef!' Saulat called out in a panic, feeling relieved at the sound of his footsteps.

When she saw Shareef she started issuing orders and getting the table cleared. For Colonel Sajjad, who was a very distant brother-in-law, had told her when he read her palm for the first time, quite clearly and in a loud voice, 'You don't love your husband at all. Your entire life is a great but successful charade.' And before the naked truth of his clear and piercing eyes, she could not deny what he had said.

There was an attractive screen covered with creepers in the circular verandah in front of Saulat's sitting room. A camel-coloured carpet in the centre of the room was surrounded by low stools, upholstered in bright green and red leather. At one end stood a low bookshelf, with her own photograph smiling above it, all alone.

Since the rainy season had begun, Saulat would sit on this verandah to read or sew when the children dropped off to sleep in the afternoons. Colonel Sajjad was stretched out on the beige carpet with a cushion under his belly. He threw a familiar glance in the direction of the two girls coming towards him, stubbed out his cigarette in the ashtray, then looked up again as if he did not know them at all.

'So, Sajjad Bhai. We're going to read palms now, aren't we?'

'Not like this. You have to pay a rupee and a quarter each first, and I will tell you a few things. And then if you want to know everything, you will have to pay all of five rupees.' Sajjad lit a cigarette.

'Are you a professional soothsayer?' Arjumand asked, settling herself on a seat.

'Get on with it then, please,' Gaythi sat down on the carpet without much ado. 'Saulat Apa, is he really good at reading palms?'

'Maybe he is!' Saulat was looking for a green amongst the silk threads heaped on the table. 'He is not going to do anything except drive you crazy.'

'Well, the taste of the pudding is in the eating, as they say! All shall be revealed in a moment. All right then, girl, run along and bring us some flour on a plate.'

Sajjad sat up. The buttons along his neckline were open and his trouser legs had climbed up.

'Why? Have you dropped your rate from a rupee and a quarter to a plateful of flour now?' Arjumand laughed.

'Don't laugh about it; bring some flour. Look, it's cloudy today, and so the lines won't show up without the flour.'

Speedily Arjumand brought some flour on a dish.

'Sit down now, I'll look at your hand first.'

She sat down with her palm spread out, innocently enthusiastic like a child.

'Huh! Not this one. You look at the other one for women. Now hold this flour in your fist and then open it. That's right, just tip it back on the plate again. Yes, that's enough; and just keep your hand straight.'

Arjumand felt giggly at the volume of instructions directed at her.

'Go on then, you can have a laugh now.' Sajjad felt offended.

'No. I won't laugh any more.'

'Oh, God. What a cowardly girl. It seems as if they infused the spirit of a little mouse instead of a girl's into your body by mistake.'

He turned over her palm and started searching for the lines for marriage and children.

'Tell me, *bhai*, how far I will get with my education?' she asked eagerly.

'God forgive you. How can you get an education? . . . girls with such a timid spirit can't manage all that.'

'Then . . .' Arjumand's voice became dull, 'then what's going to happen?'

'What can happen? . . . the same thing which has been happening since time immemorial. There is neither tragedy in your life nor any distinction. You are a very competent and kind-hearted girl.'

'And?'

'And what? Nothing. There are thousands of girls like you. Now you can just take to your prayer mat. The lucky man who marries you will enjoy his good fortune . . . how different your hand is from Saulat's.'

'What does Saulat Apa's hand say?' Arjumand asked curiously.

'I don't know what it says. I have not been able to figure it out,' Sajjad said in a low thoughtful voice.

Gaythi noticed that a slight regret appeared in this man's beautiful deep eyes as they reflected on Arjumand's palm.

The drizzle outside had increased to a downpour. Suddenly the gusts of wind became faster and the air much cooler.

'Gaythi could you turn the fan down?' Sajjad issued an order.

'Turn it off, I think,' Saulat shivered, drawing the border of her palest orange broderie anglaise sari round her arms.

'How pleasant the weather's turned out,' Arjumand praised the weather in a very conventional manner.

'Pleasant? Rather interesting, I'd say,' Sajjad glanced at Saulat.

'Will you drink coffee, Sajjad?'

'Well, yes, why not? You don't have to ask if you're planning a good turn.'

'Arjumand! Where are you?' Ammah Begum's voice echoed in the distance and Arjumand withdrew her tiny soft hand from the grip of Sajjad's strong hands.

'All right, Gaythi. We'll do yours another time.'

'*Waah*! That's not fair! You've got to look at it now.'

'How can I do that? There's such a dark storm brewing now,' Sajjad said, feeling offended.

'So what? I'll bring the lamp which has a day bulb.'

'OK, then. But can you go and make some coffee, first?' Saulat tried to put Gaythi off.

'I think it might be better if you did that chore yourself. Living with two younger sisters and all the servants in your mother's household, you are becoming quite indifferent to work, and will, undoubtedly, put on weight. For a brother-in-law like myself, who is after all related to you, these things can be a cause for concern.'

'I literally tremble when Sajjad Bhai speaks with such insolence to Saulat Apa. It is amazing that she should tolerate so much from anyone!' Gaythi felt fearful.

Without demur Saulat put the unfinished tea-cosy in the sewing basket, gathered the scattered strands of silk slowly and treading silently, went to make coffee.

'Right! So what else do you think about?' Saulat heard Sajjad's voice as she returned to the verandah with the tray of coffee .

'Nothing, Sajjad Bhai! Sometimes I wonder why one cannot truthfully utter what one really believes or feels. I say to you . . .' she stopped mid-sentence, when she heard the sound of footsteps.

'Yes, of course. I understand. I used to think exactly the same thing when I was your age. Even now you resemble me a lot in terms of your nature.' She laughed very good-humouredly under the influence of this feeling of like-mindedness and harmony.

Saulat knew extremely well when it was best to tighten the reins on your temper and your nerves and when to relax them. In spite of her displeasure, she sat on her seat with every appearance of normality, calmly whisking the coffee powder in a few drops of water, studiously looking at its white foam. But Gaythi's sixth sense had alerted her to the slight flush on her sister's face and the thoughtful look in her eyes. She will definitely scold me afterwards. But for what?

'This orange broderie anglaise sari, the pale orange reflection on your face, these wide open eyes absorbed in sad thoughts, this maroon coffee set with its faded gold, the silver samovar, this verandah surrounded with screens draped with creeping bougainvillaeas, the beige carpet contrast-ing with the red and green leather stools, and, besides all this, this sister of yours with her features like the Cappalosto family – all these things combine together to create such a complete and familiar atmosphere. Inside here, there is peace and informality, and outside, the black drunken clouds are turning the green of the trees to an inky darkness. This moment has occurred in my life once before now. I speak the truth when I say that this scene is absolutely perfect. I have known it since the beginning of time. How and when? I cannot tell you this myself. But I do know this that all these are familiar and pleasing details. Who knows I may have seen all this in the solitude of the night when a dream tiptoed through my doorway? Dreams, which tread the paths of our conscious and subcon-scious like strange travellers, whose speed and energy is unrestricted by the manacles of time. Then sometimes a half-forgotten moment, an instant from the past gets caught in your grasp like this; exactly as I hold this split second, this instant in my fist. No wonder that sometimes, when one sees certain people, one feels bound to say, "Here, this is that familiar face which I have always been seeking".'

192

It was not only Sajjad but all three of them who were absorbed in their own thoughts. Finally, Sajjad lit a cigarette and sipped his coffee.

'Well, all right, Gaythi! You must show me your hand again some other time. There are some things indicated on your palm about which I must talk to you in some detail.'

'Anyway, I think she should go now or else Ammah Begum will certainly object. To rest for at least an hour after lunch is written into the constitution of this household.'

'Then you should be resting at this time, too?'

'Me? I am married. My conduct and ways are no longer subject to the rules of this house.'

Gaythi rose and left them quietly.

A little while after she had left them, Colonel Sajjad dropped off to sleep as he lay there on the carpet, face downwards, answering Saulat's questions in the briefest monosyllables.

48

'Once I go to sleep I just go on sleeping. I don't know what's happening to me. Everyone wakes up, but I keep waking up only to drop off to sleep again. What use is my wakefulness, anyway? I just sit there pointlessly, thinking. Or I look in utter surprise and astonishment at something in particular, as if it were remarkably strange and amazing. Sometimes the events of the moment appear to be so familiar and commonplace that one begins to suspect that all this has happened once before. Some completely new faces feel so familiar as if one has always known them — in other lifetimes. And that is what makes us feel intimate and close to some people as soon as we meet them. Take Sajjad Bhai, for example. Since the very first day, one has felt, looking at his face, as if one had known him for years. Sajjad Bhai! He's really good at reading palms.'

She spread out her wide and strong hand before her eyes and stared at it. 'So is it true that my life will be riddled with highly unexpected accidents and events?' She felt a little concerned. 'Huh! Let them come then, if they are to come. What's the point of worrying and getting anxious about it now?'

She dropped her hand immediately and, shoving it under the pillow,

193

turned to rest on it. 'I don't know when Sajjad Bhai will come again. He said he will tell me some other things too.'

'Ah! So your Sahib Bahadur's letter came at last! What does he write?' Saulat dropped the letter she was reading on the table.

'What every letter from the front says.'

'Can I say something?' He laughed.

'What?' Saulat looked at her distant brother-in-law with suspicious eyes.

'Nothing. I worry about one thing: your Sahib could get mixed up with the Japanese and get mistaken for one.'

'Be thankful that the war's not being fought with the Chinese,' Saulat said seriously.

'Yes, that's true,' Sajjad replied with the same seriousness.

'Shall I tell you something?' Saulat laughed mischievously.

'Certainly. I would love to hear anything – which makes you laugh so pleasantly before you narrate it.'

'Do you know what a young Chinese salesman said to me before I got married? He said to me, "Do you like this Chiang Kai Shek? If you were to take my advice, I'd tell you to get him married to this sister of yours." And he pointed towards Gaythi. . .'

'Arrey! Gaythi! Gaythi must have been very young at that time, a mere child,' Sajjad's voice was censorious.

'Sajjad, your sense of humour is getting completely eroded. It's obvious that she was young at that time. It's because her face looks so Chinese, that's why.'

'Yes, that is true. It's a very calm, a very silent face. And that girl is very different from all of you.' There was an element of deep interest in his voice.

'Our entire household respects Arjumand much more than her, and she really does have a lot of good qualities.'

'Yes. Arjumand has some good qualities, all the virtues common to ordinary people.'

'What do you mean?' Saulat asked in surprise.

'Nothing,' Sajjad muttered to himself. 'Arjumand's virtues cannot compare with Gaythi's lack of virtue. Her sense of that shortcoming and her discomfiture about a lack of purpose have driven her soul to such a sense of inferiority, such agony and sensitivity that no virtue can compare with that.'

'What are you muttering under your breath?' she laughed.

194

'Eh? Nothing.' He stopped abruptly and addressed Seema, who was sitting near them, 'Seema bibi, have you seen a candle?'

'Yes, Uncle Sajjad. I have two huge candles, shall I bring them? What will you do with them?'

He laughed. 'All right, bring them. I'll show you a trick.'

Seema leapt up to bring the candles.

'What's this, Sajjad? You just sit there thinking up mischief all the time. Suggesting a trick with candles to children! They'll light them night and day. You'll see, you'll end up getting a fire started.'

'Saulat, my dear! Who has filled your heart with so many anxieties, doubts and suspicions? Beauty is supposed to be just another name for indifference and freedom from care. Think pleasant thoughts sometimes.'

'That means beauty is just another name for insanity. It means one should stop thinking of the past or the future because one is beautiful.'

'You're either too practical, or far too emotional.' Sajjad's own voice was heavy and emotional.

'Here they are, the candles. Show us the trick now,' Seema climbed on to his lap in her enthusiasm.

'Sit a little apart, child, then I'll show you.'

'Shall I bring some matches?'

'No, what do you need the matches for? I have a lighter. That's it: look, it's lit now.'

'And now light the second one too.'

'*Waah*! That's the trick.'

Seema rested her face on her tiny plump hands, closely watching the white wax of the candle turning into a thick whitish torrent, melting and flowing in all directions. When less than half the candle was left Sajjad suddenly blew it out.

'All right then, Seema. Get ready for your test now.'

'OK. I'm ready.'

'Tell me which of these two candles looks pretty? This taller, glossy, clean one which is whole, or, this shorter one which has burnt and melted?'

'This one, Uncle Sajjad, this one.' Seema raised her finger . 'This one which is burnt looks so sweet. The wax has flowed everywhere and hardened. It looks so sweet!'

'Well done! Look at it! It's like the ruins of a deserted fortress, like the eroded rocks along the banks of a river.' Sajjad's voice trailed away. 'Congratulations! Your daughter has the wisdom with which you have not been blessed. Seema, my child, your mother says that she finds this clean, straight, unlit candle more beautiful.'

'Huh! Mummy is such a bore!' Seema rose, wrinkling her tiny nose, and ran away. He laughed with a loud guffaw.

Sajjad was mistaken. Saulat was not lacking in wisdom. Her wisdom was hidden inside her like a secret, and that was why her face suddenly became overcast with shades of sorrow. She looked more beautiful than ever today. So beautiful that Sajjad felt a rage mounting within him against her. He came very near her in the darkening shadows of the dusk and bent over her as if to study some highly mysterious object. Abruptly, she stood up and walked away to sit down again at the far end of the room.

'Sajjad, will you tell me something?' Her voice was strong and decisive.

'What?' he sat down a little helplessly, in his own place.

Perhaps she had changed the direction of her question when she finally asked him, 'What's happening to you today?'

He sat silently for a little while before he replied, 'I feel a bit confused. I don't know. I don't know myself, but something has definitely happened to me.' His beautiful deep eyes really did seem confused.

He left without another word. When she heard his jeep starting up Saulat leaned her head against the back of the sofa and closed her eyes. She felt extremely tired.

'I cannot understand you at all, Sajjad! You're exhausting me, and I feel utterly panic-stricken. Why are you so different from all those people who have entered my life since I got married?'

'Saulat Apa! Have you moved my book from the table?' Gaythi stole into the room quietly.

'Which book?' Saulat asked in a tired voice.

Gaythi glanced round, her eyes alert, 'Gone with the Wind.'

'Gone with the Wind?' said Saulat gently. '*Arrey!* That was in Sajjad's hand when he left.'

'*Tauba!* Sajjad Bhai is awful! I haven't finished it yet.'

'It is your own carelessness, though! Why did you leave the book lying around?'

'I forgot.'

'I forgot,' Saulat mimicked. 'You came to have your palm read, what was the point of bringing the book along? Just to show off how much you read, I suppose. Trying to impress others for no rhyme or reason.'

Gaythi's eyes filled with tears. Curse the idea of impressing others. She had just brought it in absent-mindedly. But if she decided to confront Saulat it would mean further remonstrances and unsolicited advice. She went out without saying anything.

Doubts and jealousy were raising their heads in Saulat's heart. These

196

days she felt lonely and morose. She had enjoyed a long period of independent living and of being used to considerable prominence in the parties at army clubs and messes, and she was now missing the dreamy and peaceful cottage at Dalhousie. At that moment she felt that coming to live here had not been a very wise thing to do.

49

When the train came off the main railway line on to the smaller branch line it would throttle, smoke, whistle at every step, moving exactly like a reluctant child on his way to school, who tosses his satchel up in the air, drags his feet and walks at a snail's pace. And then very slowly at the end came the narrow station of Midnapur, with its white railings and red gravel. Halfway down the platform, it had a tap near the edge and three or four green wooden benches were scattered about.

The 'railway creeper' with its blue flowers grew so thick on the white railing that it had almost completely concealed it at several points. The tin roof supported on wooden pillars provided a cover for the few windows which had been designated as the booking office, the ticketing window and so on. On the red gravel platform was the signpost which had Midnapur written on it in all three languages, Urdu, Hindi and English, in black lettering on white stone. This was one of those stations where the railway staff went round wearing only half of their uniforms. This means that guards, station masters or ticket collectors would wear their peaked hats and the regulation blue or white coats with gold buttons combined with either a pair of pyjamas or a dhoti. At night-time they would carry small gas lanterns on their rounds. Their heavy footsteps and sleep-ridden voices could be heard querying subordinates before they suddenly disappeared again. As soon as they left, the station would feel deserted. And then some battered old hawker, selling cigarettes, *bidis* or peanuts, with the funnel of a kerosene lamp planted on his stall, would call out in a sleepy voice, 'Hot roasted peanuts, *paan*, *bidi*, cig-a-rate!'

Even coolies were a rare sight there; since passengers often threw their bundles and baggage off the train and jumped out as soon as the speed dropped, even before it entered the station. They then walked along the muddy tracks, their bundles and even their steel-tipped shoes tied to the ends of their long metal staffs, used for walking in the evenings.

The road past Midnapur was not metallic and just a couple of metres beyond, it divided into narrow dusty footpaths which led into the fields before disappearing here and there. Beside this road ran the canal road to the Alampur settlement. This was a tiny village with a hundred to a hundred and fifty dwellings. Besides those who were engaged in farming, the remaining households were divided into groups of eight or ten according to their occupations.

There was a huge orchard of mangoes at the point where the canal turned, almost entering the settlement. It was the favourite orchard of the landlord and alongside it stood his favourite thatched cottage. It was known as a cottage but it was a reasonably wide bungalow. Munshi ji's quarters were within its compound. He was old and a well-wisher of the owner. He had written to Bakhtiar Bhaiya saying that now it was important for him to visit and supervise his lands. 'There can be no certainty about me. I am all of ten years older than your father was.'

Dressed in a blue striped shirt and coarse cotton home-washed pyjamas which fell short of his ankles, Munshi ji stood at Midnapur Station sporting his unruly white beard. The left arm of his white spectacles was held in place with cotton thread. His hands shook.

'And this is the man who manages our lands!' Bakhtiar stared at Munshi ji's dirty tennis shoes. His crooked-looking toes peeped out of the holes at the front.

'Wait, *bhaiya*, until I arrange for a *tonga*. The news of your arrival came late. Our own *tonga* is out.'

'No, let's take a buggy. I want to take a buggy.'

If his father were still alive Munshi ji would have swung round and asked Bakhtiar, 'Have you lost your senses?' But now he was here as the owner himself, supervising his lands.

Munshi ji engaged a buggy, turning up his nose at Bakhtiar's suitcase and slim holdall. 'And this is how he comes! Without a gun and without a hookah. Jumps off at the station and stands there, all by himself, pathetic, like a solitary stump. How can you compare him with his father? Himself knew very well that there was an army of serfs here, waiting to serve, their hands folded together, but still . . . he never came without Shareef.'

'Bhaiya! Shareef isn't coming?'

'Munshi ji! What can Shareef do here?'

Now, what was the answer to that one?

'Where's our own *tonga* today then?' Bakhtiar asked.

'The women from the tax collector's family have gone to Karamabad to lay some offerings at the shrine. They've had the *tonga* since yesterday.'

'Hum!' Bakhtiar heaved a deep sigh.

198

As soon as the rattling buggy turned towards the canal road Bakhtiar saw the white minarets of the mosque which served the Sheikh community.

'Munshi ji! What was this row to do with the mosque which we heard about recently?'

'Nothing very much, Bhaiya. The Iron workers' clan were sending their offerings of food to the temple to celebrate something and so they were marching past the mosque, beating their drums and blowing their flutes. This clashed with the time for prayers inside the mosque, too. You know what it is like. You try to stop someone doing something, there's sure to be a fight.'

'Why had there never been a fight before?'

'Forget about before,' Munshi ji said irritably. 'Before now you didn't get the lads going round the cities, looking for jobs every day. Out there, in the cities, they fill their heads with this rubbish. Those old days are gone forever now!' Munshi ji had it on the tip of his tongue to say to him, 'Look at yourself now. No hookah, no Shareef. You just come and stand there like a pathetic, solitary stump, all by yourself.'

'How is Bijli, Munshi ji?'

Suddenly, Munshi ji's voice acquired a chirpiness. 'The mare has been serviced this morning and Ikraam is going round looking puffed up.'

'Oh, yes? How is Ikraam? I've come here after such a long time.'

'He's all right, Bhaiya. His wife passed away.' There was a strange flatness in Munshi's voice.

All of a sudden Bakhtiar remembered Ikraam's mud house next to the stable where his wife would sit, a short veil stretched across her face, frying *parathas*, the thickly rolled dough turning a glorious brown, in pure ghee. 'You don't need to wear your veil for Bhaiya,' Ikraam would laugh, settling down on his charpoy, as he teased him, 'Bhaiya, do you remember the numbers I taught you?'

And Bakhtiar would start repeating them hesitantly, 'One, one alone. Two, faultless, two. The gift of the Twos. The Threes are false lovers. Fours are the ancients Vedas. Fives are the Pandavas. The Sixth is Narayan Singh ...' Then his voice would tremble, 'I've forgotten, Ikraam.'

'Then Bhaiya! How will you pass the exam?'

'You don't get numbers like this in your exam!'

'All right, I'll say it for you now. One, one alone. Two, faultless, two. The gift of the Twos ...' Ikraam would carry on reciting till he came to a stop with, 'Nineteenth, Rani Kanchni, Twentieth, Raja Harbans,' and Bakhtiar would burst out laughing. 'When are you taking us for a ride?'

'We'll put Barrey Bhaiya on first, then you will be getting your tu-rn. Barrey Bhaiya is older, you're the titchy one.'

But Bakhtiar never regretted being the younger one, since Barrey Bhaiya himself never rubbed in his status. He would pull his foot out of the stirrup promptly if he saw him getting impatient, 'Bakhtiar, you go for a ride first.'

Today he had come in place of Barrey Bhaiya. Even the women had peered over the walls and through half-open doors to see him as he came down on the buggy.

'God bless the pair of them with long lives! Barrey Bhaiya hasn't come, this is the Titch. When he came last he was just a baby.' Without Bakhtiar knowing it, the women of his territory prayed for him, their voices choking with emotion.

The entire atmosphere of the countryside was infused with a kind of natural music and song. Early in the morning you could hear the songs of the women floating out of their houses above the whirring, grinding noise of their millstones as they worked them; the gurgling sound of the buckets and flasks as they dipped into the wells; the swishing noise of the rope wound round the pulleys and the whining of the plough as it reeled along; and then in the quiet stillness of the night, the slurping of the canal water and then, contrasting with all of them, the tinkle of anklets, ankle bells and the bells on the women's toes – what was all this? It was the unending lyric, the eternal music, the rhythm to which the hands of peasants work. They slaved to draw gold from the heart of the earth. When the wind, on its way to the cottage, stole the soundless songs from their green fields he would forget all the accounts he had come to check.

'How can I call this land to account? Who could ever call songs and love and abandonment into question?'

Then all the work came to a halt when it was time to light the lamps. All the tiredness and heat of the atmosphere would dissolve in the thump of the *dholak* as it rose from the mud walls of the homes of the Kurmi clan. Innocent and playful songs would scatter to the winds accompanied by a percussion of metal plates and bowls.

'Listen, the goldsmith is here from Aajamgadh . . . dear little sister-in-law
Why does he smile as he gives me these dangling ear rings?
For it makes my true love cross.
But, what makes you cross with me, O goldsmith?'

Almost simultaneously a high note wailed forth from the common shelter where the villagers assembled.

> 'Aalha, and Oudhal were warriors great.
> It is hard to tell their story . . .'

Before the Aalha could finish, Ikraam's comical old voice would resonate in the air,

> 'The others planted this and that,
> Madhu planted millets.'

The voices of the rest would repeat the refrain. Then Ikraam's voice would rise above the others again,

> He reaped and reaped
> for days without end
> and the times for fasting were upon us.
> To be sure it made a lot of trouble!'

'How come Ikraam is so comical?' Bakhtiar would think, 'The pace of time has affected even me, who was once a babe in his arms. My good-naturedness, the pleasantries I was used to and the laughter are all changing to sobriety. But Ikraam's light-heartedness seems to be immortal. The stores and coffers in my house have been filled by snatching Ikraam's and his friends' happiness. But in spite of that, my life is full of fears, regrets and doubts. Here they all are empty-handed, half-naked, but there is faith, happiness and innocent beliefs. Those who are ready to raise their staffs and fight like enemies in the cause of the mosque or the temple, now sit together in the common shelter singing in joyous harmony. And here I am, in this beautiful and comfortable bungalow, all by myself. I suppose, we are the ones who have been all alone through several incarnations; that because our civilised ancestors always stressed the importance of individual life, whereas these people's lives are essentially composed of collective experience.'

A thick layer of depression settled on Bakhtiar's being. His bed was under the thatched roof of the verandah. Outside a constant but gentle drizzle fell steadily, yet another song which circumscribed the countryside. He could hear the jackals howling in the distance, amidst the dense trees in the orchards.

To escape the drizzle he drew his bed further inside and pulled the sheet across his face. When he heard the sound, the night-watchman banged his stick hard on the ground, calling out, 'Stay alert!'

'*Arrey*, Ramu! You're not getting wet, are you? Go to sleep.'

'No, Bhaiya, I am under the shelter. You sleep. I will stay awake.'

'You sleep, I stay awake,' Bakhtiar repeated to himself, pained. 'That, too, is a strange suggestion. Yes, Ramu, we are asleep and you are awake.'

'Ramu, go to sleep,' Bakhtiar said in a commanding voice.

'All right, Bhaiya!'

His narrow charpoy woven with coarse rope squeaked loudly as it got soaked in the rain; and then silence fell all round them.

The mare was now ready for riding. Ikraam had washed and groomed her and prepared her for the ride. He held her reins and led her gently to the verandah for Bhaiya. Then he stopped as he saw him, dressed in khaki breeches and shirt, looking tall and slim. 'God save him from the evil eye. In such a short time this little boy has grown up and has assumed responsibility.' He had come to visit after many years.

'Take her, Bhaiya. Bijli is here now for you to ride,' Ikraam handed him the reins of the horse.

And then Ikraam remembered, 'Both the brothers used to come together, Barre Bhaiya would ride and then this one would get the chance to do so.' Exactly the same thought struck Bakhtiar. This was the first time that he was the first one to be offered a ride on Bijli, when she was freshly groomed and scrubbed and walked with a swagger in her gait. Previously, Barre Bhaiya used to ride before him. That he was so tender-hearted as to pull his foot out of the stirrup the moment he saw the longing in Bakhtiar's eyes, saying, 'Bakhtiar, you have a ride first,' was a different matter. 'And, if he had been around I would not have come here. This would have been his business.'

Ikraam led the mare to the gate of the cottage as he chatted, still holding on to her rein. As he emerged from the white wrought-iron gates which gleamed against the bright green hedge, Bakhtiar felt aware of a wild impulse to hear Ikraam ask him casually, with a lilt to his special, comical voice, 'And Bhaiya, do you remember how I taught you to say the numbers?' But rank and status intervened between them now.

'Since Sahib's passing away, you are the owner, as Barre Bhaiya's delegate, working in place of him. And I am only a humble groom employed by you.' This statement was clearly inscribed on Ikraam's face.

Bakhtiar turned round to look as he spurred the horse. The little bungalow with red tiles and delicately carved wooden pillars, the creepers covered with red and yellow roses wrapped round poles, the gleaming white gates shining through the dark, thick, green leaves of the nirbasi hedge – all these were very pleasing to the eye. Everything needed for comfort and convenience was tastefully and methodically arranged in that little bungalow. And on the other side, behind the bungalow, next to the stable was Ikraam's hovel and shelter caked with mud. Throughout his entire life Bakhtiar had not seen any changes or additions there besides the two charpoys woven with coarse rope, some brass utensils and a few black clay pots. Apart from the clothes which hung on the washing line, there were a few suits of clothing: coloured ones, and some in neutral fabric for occasional wear, which were stored in a large basket woven with paddy fibres. Some pieces of crockery were arranged on the recessed shelves above the stove. Now that his wife is dead, Ikraam will go in, pick up the hookah in the corner and sit quietly on his charpoy to smoke. Now, he will never suggest to him laughingly, as if they were equals, 'Bhaiya, smoke some tabac . . .'

And now he himself will never ask him, 'Ikraam, why do you call tobacco, tabac?'

'I say it out of love.' All these words will not echo again on the resonant air waves because Bakhtiar, rather than Ikraam, has grown up now.

'Why should some people's growing up make such a big difference?' Bakhtiar wondered.

When he returned from the other end of the fields, riding Bijli at a gentle trot along the banks of the canal, very close to the orchard planted with mango trees, he looked round. The platform, on the far side of the milkmen's clan, which was surrounded by bay trees was steeped in its usual atmosphere of contentment and tranquillity. With their faces squat like vats, the gods adorning the roots of the peepal tree, sat with the same old pride and austerity, still wearing those vermilion dots on their foreheads and their inscrutable smiles. Ramcharna, wearing the sacred thread across his body, sat cross-legged directly opposite, naked, reciting the Ramayan with dedication, his rotund belly rocking to the motion.

Bakhtiar's intentions slowed the pace of the horse further. So many times in the past he had run away with these round and elongated gods. Each time Abba Mian had brought him back to make him return them to the spot with his own hands.

His lifeless monotone was scattering the words of the Ramayan in the atmosphere.

Bakhtiar stopped and thought, 'Bharat's mother, Kaikai, who was Ram ji's step-mother, sent him into exile for fourteen years because she hoped to clear Bharat's way to the throne. And the way was cleared for him. But Ram was also obstinate. To maintain his sovereignty he brought his slippers and kept them on the throne in his palace. But my mother, who is my brother's real mother has not done anything with any such intention. My father had made no such promise to anyone. But despite that the eldest son of my father chose exile for himself, without any Sita or any Lakshman for company. And he still wanders from one Lanka to another, fighting Ravan. Ravan, at whose feet lies the sanctity of countless Sitas and the vermilion from the parting in their hair. Ravan who lives through each and every period of history ... And, who knows, Barrey Bhaiya at which front you are fighting now! How will I find your slippers?'

Bakhtiar, who was finding his position and responsibilities far more difficult than Bharat, pondered with deep regret. He's left his slippers on the throne and surrendered his responsibility for everything and I am having to deal directly with the rights of so many people. The rights of my family, the rights of this earth which has gold hidden in her womb, for me and for my family, and the rights of these labourers who, on the basis of their spirit and strength obtain gold from the earth and lay it at my feet. I owe them countless rights and obligations.

'Dear God, how can one ever uphold their rights?' Bakhtiar panicked at the very thought. 'Who knows whether or not my father, and his father before him, felt aware of this responsibility towards them when they inherited this land and became landowners?'

He felt very responsible and important at that time. Even though, in practical terms, people who think like this are considered highly irresponsible. It was quite interesting how he had been lecturing his sisters, especially Gaythi, before coming here about taking their responsibilities seriously. Now he was thinking of things which were well outside the domain of responsibility.

50

His uniform, stiff with starch and ironing, and his boots, glistening with polish, awaited him. The tea sitting next to his bed had got cold. Ashes from his incessant smoking were heaped by the side of his bed, near the end where his pillow was perched. The black particles stood out as they shone against the burnt paper and the washed whiteness of the tobacco.

He raised his head half-heartedly and looked across. There was still a long while to go before morning appeared. 'And have I been awake all night?' All night his sleep had been interrupted and at that time he could not be at all certain whether he had been awake all night or had had snatches of sleep in between.

This was Colonel Sajjad whose brain felt numbed to such a degree at the dawn of quite a pleasant morning. 'Huh! Another muddle now, to complicate things further.' He gnashed his teeth. 'This always happens to me, I don't know why. Why does my heart suddenly change direction, half way in its pursuit of one genuine course? And this time, too, all this mess has been created by you, Saulat Ara Begum. If, at that moment in time, when I was bending over you, you had not moved suddenly to the other end of the settee and asked me, "What's happening to you today?" then perhaps all this might not have happened and this time my heart would never have changed tracks.

'Why ever did you ask me that question which forced me to wonder about what was really happening to me? Believe me, Saulat Ara Begum! I myself was surprised at your question! I had decided that I would wait for you, until that time when you yourself felt fed up enough to create a new way out. But that question of yours startled me and forced me to examine myself. You know that in this matter, like your sister, Gaythi, I think that one should not be prevented from expressing what one thinks. So my assessment was that I had felt something very akin to fear of this sister of yours who looks Chinese; and I had tried to seek refuge from her in the shade of your veil. But you startled me . . . You made me aware of what I wanted and of what was happening to me. A brief question of yours has shown me the way. And if you had not asked me that question, believe me, I would have spent my entire life labouring under the misapprehension that your person is the focus of my attention.'

Panic-stricken, Sajjad hid his face in the soft depths of his pillow stuffed with duck feathers. Ducks which he used to shoot in season during November and December, camping along the banks of lakes and rivers. 'What better use is there for a solitary life?' he often wondered.

And for a long time now these moments of solitude had been a part of his being. It was now several years since Razia had died. But what difference could her life or death have made? Razia had not entered his life like a welcome guest nor did she acquire that honour. 'A beautiful, educated and graceful woman can also fail to become a true companion for life sometimes. Why?' Sajjad himself was amazed at this question of his.

After the death of that woman, whose passing affected him only as much as one might be affected by the death of an acquaintance, he had not even thought again of trying to resolve the question of his loneliness or of starting a family. Possibly because he had no hope of finding someone who could offer him the prospect of intellectual companionship. His family background, personality and rank had attracted, not only

205

young girls, but also married women towards him. He, too, would incline towards them with great seriousness and a sense of irony. But far from plumbing its depths, not one of them had managed to touch even the outermost reaches of his heart. Then, he met the wife of his distant cousin, Asif Jah. He had heard about Saulat Asif Jah, and that she formed liaisons very quickly, and the focus of her attention changes very quickly too. In actual fact, this information was as untrue as the word that Colonel Sajjad was a great connoisseur of beautiful women of good taste.

Sajjad had found nothing in the depths of her soul except a woman who was thoroughly deprived and barren. However, he was gradually impressed by her extremely dignified and Begum-like appearance, her highly sophisticated and refined habits, qualities which elude some remarkably good-looking women. The truth was that, more than of Saulat herself, he was an admirer of the background in which her personality had been cultivated: a milieu achieved by blending several great and beautiful elements.

'All right then, I shall continue to worship you from afar,' he had thought several times, as he watched her absorbed in her children and her household in spite of the fact that she had no interest in Asif Jah's existence, nor any affection for him.

'Although our mental horizons are far beyond each other's reach, within you there is still all the softness, warmth and charm of a complete woman. And one could consider this a great if coincidental blessing in itself . . .'

Colonel Sajjad would lean on an easy chair laid out on the lawn of his distant cousin Asif Jah's house and think with tremendous resignation, 'Even if one had to spend one's life like this, it wouldn't be too bad!'

Then slowly, perhaps not that slowly, it became apparent to him that Saulat looked upon him with great affection and respect. The kind of quiet and awed respect which converts very quickly into love. How pleasing that thought is, how you wallow in it! More especially so for someone who is resigned and willing to please.

'Believe me, before I met you I had never felt any sense of inferiority.' He had thought all this in secret, as well.

Contrary to his expectations, Saulat dropped her barriers of formality and that tongue of his which wanted to utter all that the brain had pondered, loosened. After giving him leeway up to a point, all of a sudden Saulat would tighten the reins, and he would return to his place.

'Well. That's fine too. But I had never felt so powerless before now, Saulat!' And he had never ever revealed that to her.

The war began for them when Asif Jah received his orders to move on with his brigade. This was not something new. Every army man spends his entire life waiting for such a day. But Sajjad was appointed to some intelligence duties which dictated that he should go round freely rather than to the front line. The question of sending him to the front had still not arisen at all.

Since the departure of Asif Jah his heart would sometimes entertain terribly ugly and cruel expectations.

'Have I fallen that low?' Sometimes his conscience would question him with horror . . . On some occasions he felt disgusted with Saulat, with his environment and even with himself. The first time he had noticed that girl was whilst he was in that state. She had just come out after her bath, exuding the gentle fragrance of white cotton, hair washed with gram flour and Cuticura powder. There was grief and sorrow in her eyes. She had raised her hand to greet him in a gesture which amazingly combined confidence, healing and supportiveness, 'Salaam, Bhai!'

'Bless you! . . .' He had said with apparent paternalism but he had started thinking, 'You look young, but there is a centuries-old feeling in your eyes. It seems to me that your thinking and philosophy are ancient. As if your steps were too fast for Time to keep up with you. . . . Gaythi Ara! Is it true that I have always known you? But in what mysterious darkness did you stay hidden until now? Involved in your meditation and quest for knowledge. As people would view it, I am probably almost three times your age. So now I understand the mystery, why Razia and all the numerous women who entered my life after her saw themselves as unwelcome guests. The space in my heart is limited, and that tiny space had already been filled.'

Colonel Sajjad sat up. He pulled a pillow on to his lap and planting his elbows firmly into it, lit a cigarette.

'And that very young girl would be comfortably asleep at this time, in her gleaming white bed.' He smiled.

51

Ammah Begum read the letter and put it under the corner of her prayer mat. She took out her prayer book and started reading it silently.

'Chote Bhaiya has written, "I will not have the time to visit on my way back, and I shall return to my college straight from there".' Arjumand peered out of the window as she addressed Gaythi, who was busy reading a book.

Light brown and maroon clouds were assembling slowly to cover the sky, and she felt an urge to paint the scene but she did not know where all her paints, canvasses and brushes were. There was no longer that calm and placid atmosphere in the house which they had been used to before, in which one can lose oneself and achieve so much.

'Huh! It's good if he does that. What will he achieve by coming here? This house is no longer a home. I don't know, but sometimes I feel as if this were not really our own house; as if we were all guests here. As if even Ammah Begum herself were a guest at Saulat Apa's house.'

This was something Arjumand had been aware of in her own heart but she could never articulate such a strange thought, or even think it through clearly. Fearless thoughts like this fell to Gaythi.

For the past week Saulat had been very unhappy with Gaythi. Why? Gaythi had not understood this herself with any clarity. 'And she deliberately insults me in front of Sajjad Bhai. Well, never mind. He is her brother-in-law. What does it matter to me? I just won't go into his presence any more. It doesn't feel right to be insulted before a strange man,' she had thought.

But that never came to pass because quite suddenly towards the end of that week, Sajjad got himself transferred.

'I've heard Sajjad Bhai has chosen to go to the front.'

Arjumand loved to bring news. She was a cowardly and low-spirited informer. And today she was also a little annoyed with Saulat. For she had scolded her harshly first thing in the morning over something very minor. She was in a really bad mood. She had remembered her husband after such a long time, and she had sat up in the afternoon to write him a letter as well.

'Good. He should go away somewhere.' Gaythi was in no mood for a chat. She pulled up her comforter to her ears and curled up to try and sleep.

'Huh! Look at her – trying to sleep at such an odd time!' Disgruntled, Arjumand moved away from the window. Sometimes she took no notice at all of her bits of news.

When Saulat wanted to discuss something important with Ammah Begum she would pull the basket of betel nuts towards herself, catch hold of the nutcracker and cover her head.

Now Ammah Begum could guess when she was going to broach something final and decisive. For some reason her heart would start beating wildly the moment she guessed it. Her decisive discussions and advice often became the basis for fear and change.

When she saw her in the mood for a discussion she put away the prayer book which she held in her hand then removed her spectacles and placed them on top of the book.

'I think I saw a letter from Bakhtiar, too, in the post today,' Saulat began.

'Yes, here it is.' She took the letter from under the prayer mat and handed it to her.

The letter was brief except for the boring and turgid factual information to do with the land and with ownership issues. He had written that his holiday was over and that he would leave for the University directly from there. As long as Saulat Apa was with them he was not that worried about their feeling lonely.

'It is a good idea, really, for him to go directly from there. If he had come here and then left from here it would have been a pointless expense.'

'That is true. But if he had visited us here I would have felt reassured to have seen him with my own eyes. All these days in the village he probably won't have eaten properly. Who knows what that's done to his health?'

'Ammah! You do worry unnecessarily. God save him from the evil eye, but he is a very healthy lad and then the fresh air of the countryside, all the milk and ghee; you know that better than us.'

'Even so.'

'Even so, what?' Saulat took exception to that. 'The boys are not going to stay here forever, tied to your apron strings.'

She decided it was best not to reply to that. She looked straight in front with great helplessness and fell silent.

'How can you understand this, now? Only someone who has already lost one son can understand what the second son means to him. I cannot even explain it to you.'

Feeling anguished, she put on her spectacles again and picked up her book about the stories of saints, which lay next to the bolster.

'So what do you think now?'

'About what?' Ammah Begum asked in surprise.

'About the girls.'

'The girls?' She seemed surprised. What could one think about them at that moment?

'Yes, who else?' Saulat sounded a little irritated at her lack of concern.

'You tell me what to think?' She sounded powerless. Her grief was so fresh that her heart and mind still felt unable to concentrate.

'Just that Gaythi's college will also re-open in a month or six weeks and then she will have to go to Lahore.'

'Lahore? Eh! What's the point in her going to Lahore now? She can study here.'

'I don't think she'll agree.'

'Why not? Doesn't she understand the pressures on the family?' Ammah Begum felt offended at Saulat's level of prejudice against Gaythi.

'Perhaps she has understood a little up to now, and she may understand a little more then. Have you seen her taking an interest in anything to do with the house these days?'

Some things fuse lies with facts in such a way that it does not seem perverse to credit them. And Ammah Begum also conceded this point a little.

'Well, if she hasn't understood so far, or taken an interest, then she will have to be forced to do so now.'

'That is what I mean to say, too. God bless his soul but Abba Mian gave her a great deal of licence; that should be curtailed now. That time has gone now, when she used to ignore even you. She used to make decisions about herself and just inform Abba Mian.'

The mention of Gaythi's wilfulness reminded Ammah Begum of all those incidents in the past. She changed colour . . . But she sat thinking in silence as she gently painted the lime and catechu paste on to the *paan* leaf she held in her hand.

'And I'd say that the way she has been loafing around in Lahore up to now cannot be tolerated any more. We now have to make her aware that she has to tread very carefully and has to keep her eyes open. There is no longer that protection behind her which used to save her from the disapproval and gossip of others.'

Ammah Begum picked up the smaller chippings of betel nuts from the basket and rolled them into her *paan*.

'No. That's it. I have said it already. There is no question of her going back, so what's the point of saying all these useless things and trying to explain to her? In a few days now the college here will open and I will get them to put her name down.'

'Really! Well I can give it to you in writing that she will never agree to stay here for her studies.'

'So then! How shall I deal with the wretch?' She felt very irritated at her own helplessness and at that miserable girl's bleak future. 'Is there a cure for her then?'

'There is, of course. Only one cure.'

'What's that?'

'She should be married off now.'

'Eh? Already?' She felt flustered. In fact she could not name any suitable boy or match for her.

'Why Ammah Begum! Gaythi is a little baby, is she? And was I really so mature then that I was handed over to a man who was as old as my father, as if there was no other alternative? Even though at the time our father was alive to protect us. And for her, who is fatherless, you make it a question of "Already?"' Saulat said all this without stopping for breath. She dropped the nutcracker into the basket and pulled the *paan* box towards her, though she seldom ate *paan*.

Ammah Begum sat in silence. She felt a little dizzy, impelled by a desire to lean her head on the pillow and howl at the top of her voice.

'Ay, if only I could find some wretch who is willing to take her hand, I would agree. I hear that Masood is into the third year of his Engineering degree, now.'

'Masood!' Saulat shivered as if some thoroughly repulsive cretin had appeared before her eyes. Anyhow, even Ammah Begum had no intention of considering him. And what could Saulat have said about it . . .

'What does Mumani jaan think?' she asked.

'What can she think? In the first place, the opportunity to talk about something like this has not arisen so far. But she has no intention of forming such an alliance with us. You know Bhabi jaan's attitude towards us. She wants to keep the relationship to the level of mere acquaintance.'

'And you should remember that if she did have any such intentions she would have chosen Arjumand. Her thoughts would never even stray towards Gaythi. She has repeated at least ten times that Shah Bano has raised such a wild girl – who can ever manage to live with her?'

'Well, no. We don't want to give her our wild daughter, anyway.' Such comments offend mothers; she also lost her temper.

'That is what I say. If she can only be settled somewhere it would be enough. There is no point in looking for someone for her who is landed and comes from a good background. She should just be married off into some family of outsiders. Into people who can value her.'

'Anyway, child! It would take time to find a match like that too.' Ammah Begum picked up her book again, tired of this ill-timed discussion.

'If the future could be ignored by reading books, then there'd be no need for any strategy.' Saulat took the book away from her hand.

'Then tell me, what shall I do now? At the moment there is no such proposal for me to eye, nor am I ready for this task, either mentally or emotionally.'

211

'There is a proposal which I have, but you must get your heart and mind ready.' In spite of the calmness of her tone there was a bitter edge to Saulat's conversation.

'Then, tell me. What do my heart and mind matter? If you think it is suitable, then you can do what you like. You are not her enemy, after all.'

'*Bhai*! I am afraid of that girl making a fuss,' Saulat said in a quiet voice, her head bowed. 'Akbar's mother has asked me several times.'

Ammah Begum looked at Saulat in surprise, 'Whose mother?

'Akbar's mother. Who else?'

'Who did she ask for? For Arjumand, or for her?'

She asked specially for Gaythi.'

'Akbar had gossiped about her,' she thought, but did not think it expedient to say anything.

'Does Akbar want it too?'

'What do you think? The liberal mothers of today would never propose without the consent of their sons, now, would they?'

Ammah Begum started chopping betel nuts in silence.

'Then tell me, what do you think?'

'Hum,' she stretched the sound as she meditated. She looked deeply concerned.

'Now look, he has finished his Engineering examination and has got employment as well . . .'

'You should find out what Gaythi thinks too.'

'I am not prepared to talk to her.'

'You shouldn't have to. Ask Arjumand.'

'You know how sensible she is. Do you really think Gaythi deserves to have a say? That is a right you can only give to people who can differentiate between good and bad.'

Ammah Begum fell to wondering how that could be allowed to happen. Even if it were only a formality – this was something she herself had been asked. But she could not say this to Saulat.

She knew very well that she herself had only given Saulat the leeway to say 'yes'. Saulat was comfort-loving and desirous of security so like a good girl she had bid farewell to her past intentions and views and had given her mother the exact reply she wanted from her. And now this was the only concession she was prepared to make for Gaythi, that her decision should only be based on one option – that was the kind of space she had been given herself.

'Regrets and careful thought can only be useful if they precede any wrong moves that one is going ot make, and warn one at that stage. It is no use if they come to you when the chugging train has already taken you five stations past home. If regrets, results and awareness advance towards you at that point holding out the yoke of rebukes, they can only drive you crazy. Isn't that so?'

She felt irritated and thrust her face out through the window. The night was dark and warm. The odd star glimmered in the sky. The engine screamed as if in fear of the dark and deserted jungle it had entered. She drew back inside the carriage feeling frightened and alone. Her senses felt stunned and her hands and feet felt paralysed.

'How did all this happen, and why?' She struggled to gather together the scattered sequences of her thoughts once again. All the mischief could be traced to that one telegram which came from Bombay bringing some sad news for Ammah Begum. When she had heard the news of her mother's death she had wept aloud. She left the same day as well. When a grief-stricken person has more sorrows heaped upon him, others may have even less regard for that person's troubles. They begin to lose a sense of that person's suffering.

So this confrontation occurred on the third day after her departure. In the first place there was no way Gaythi could tolerate hearing Akbar mentioned in that manner and then, in that decisive tone of voice.

'Judging by the present circumstances, the appropriate thing to do is to slip a ring on your finger quietly when Ammah Begum returns.' Gaythi's nerves had not entirely recovered when this subject was raised in such a distressing manner, and also at a time when her mother was not present herself. Her peace of mind was utterly destroyed. Saulat's final and authoritative tone had numbed what remained of her strength.

If Saulat had known that Gaythi, once she had assessed the situation and persuaded herself to do something, had this strange capacity to surrender in absolute silence and commit herself so fully that the greatest lovers of peace and expediency would be amazed, then she might have tried to persuade her at a different psychological level. But for some unknown reason, she had never regarded her sister as worthy of her understanding and analysis. She was used to making presumptions concerning her and insisting on their truth.

On this occaion, when Gaythi lost her nerve, she did not succumb to screaming or a hysterical tautening of her limbs, nor did she distress others with her wailing and moaning. She responded and argued gently with great calmness. She clenched her lips with great self control, further inflaming Saulat into making baseless and unfair allegations. It appeared as if the worst that could happen would be that she would let go of herself and shed a few tears when she was alone, and the whole episode would be forgotten in a few days.

But that did not come to pass. When she was alone, she felt intensely unsupported in the absence of her mother.

'Now that all this has transpired in Ammah Begum's absence, I will be the one to blame,' she thought. Everything which could be said and every situation that could arise seemed to be much worse to her than the reality.

As soon as they entered the gates that evening after a comprehensive shopping spree, Arjumand and Saulat noticed that the deep silence and stillness which had descended upon the house and the garden had deepened. It felt worse than it usually did.

'What a sad evening this is!' Arjumand looked ruefully at the signs of dusk behind the sandalwood trees. The dry leaves scattered on the porch crunched under her feet.

The light on the verandah had been switched on but the bedroom and the passageway were still dark . . .

'Now she is sleeping off her anger,' Arjumand thought to herself. 'Good. It brings her round to the right way of thinking.'

'The children still haven't returned from their walk.' Saulat felt annoyed. 'This is the problem with Margaret. She'll be hanging on to the pushchair whilst she stands there, rolling round her eyes and talking to one of her acquaintances. Seema will be getting bored and besides, their dinner will be late. Anyway, one couldn't expect Gaythi to remember to tell her to come back early.' She entered the house feeling quite vexed.

It was amazing and incredible that Saulat should have lost control of her senses. For the first time in her life she had thought, remorsefully, that in actual fact she had been very unfair to Gaythi and that she had always been unfair to her . . . Her face became wet with warm tears as she stood in the dark room. At that moment she did not have the heart to face even Arjumand.

A boundless feeling of fear, helplessness and shame was overtaking her. When Arjumand returned to the room and switched the light on she found Saulat unconscious on the floor. They could hear the voices of Margaret and both the children from the dining room as they argued noisily.

'Baba, if you lot don't eat this pudding, we'll have to tell Mummy.'

'Tell her, go on tell her.' Azam Jah's stubborn voice rang out in protest. Seeing Saulat unconscious like that frightened Arjumand out of her wits. She had passed through the emotions of shock, grief and shame and was now only aware of an abiding sense of being powerless. Her tears had dried and she was extremely worried. Leaning her head against the wall of the deserted and quiet hallway, she thought for a few seconds and then her fingers swung round the dial and she put the telephone receiver to her ear.

'Hello, Akbar, this is Arjumand here,' she whispered close to the mouthpiece.

'Is everything all right?' Akbar's soft and calm voice encouraged her, and she burst into sobbing.

Without asking her anything further, Akbar put the receiver down, got his car and came round.

She had already moved Saulat to the bed with Margaret's help. She was startled to see Akbar rushing in through the hallway. 'I shouldn't have phoned Akbar in my panic.' She regretted the phone call.

It was a blessing that Gaythi had given a very valid reason and excuse to the servants for her departure, 'There's a telegram from Bombay that Ammah Begum is very ill. Arjumand and Saulat Apa can't go right now, so I am going.'

That one excuse covered both events, Saulat's fainting and Gaythi's absence . . .

'I don't think we need the doctor,' she said to Akbar. She was not now prepared to gather a further crowd or to tell them.

Saulat was beginning to come round . . . Slowly, she opened her eyes and looked at Akbar who was bent over her in surprise. She heaved a deep sigh.

'What's the matter Saulat Apa?' Akbar asked her gently.

'Nothing, Akbar!' The tears flowed from her eyes. Akbar dabbed them away gently with her veil.

Saulat's tears caused Arjumand to lose her self control once more and she went out of the room to lean against the wall of the verandah and weep silently. Akbar, who had seen her leave the room, followed her on tiptoes.

'Arjumand you are a very sensible and brave girl,' he cajoled her and sat her down gently on the chair. She sat leaning her head on the arm of the chair, shedding tears.

'Listen, pray to God, and God willing, Khala jaan will recover and return soon,' he exhorted once again.

In her state of loneliness and impotence he appeared to be very

215

sympathetic and a great blessing to Arjumand. She got up to go in again. Margaret was helping Saulat to a drink.

'Arjumand come here. Come closer to me,' Saulat said, taking in her red eyes and pallor. Arjumand rushed to Saulat and resting her head against her breast, sobbed as Saulat stroked her dark, soft wavy hair very gently and started weeping herself too.

'God have mercy on this family. They seem to be suffering one tragedy after another,' Akbar thought, as he stood on one side.

'Margaret, go and put the children to bed. Akbar Mian, I am fine now. May God bless you for rushing to our aid like this when we needed you,' Saulat thanked him.

'If you like I could stay here for now. I can tell Mummy on the telephone.'

'No, *bhaiya*. If we need help we wouldn't call anyone else but you. If something does happen we can get in touch with you on the telephone.'

'Tell me! What's unacceptable about him as a husband? What's wrong with him? Such a sympathetic boy!' Saulat said softly after he had left.

Slowly the routine of the house settled into its normal pace. After helping Saulat into her nightdress Arjumand returned to her room. She switched the light on. The bed next to hers was empty, the bedclothes uncreased. Much more than the rest of the entire house, this room was drowned in sorrow and desolation.

52

Where should she have gone, and to what destination should she have purchased a ticket? She never had the wherewithal to think all this through. And if she had been willing to think things through, then she may have been led into not buying the ticket at all.

Only one sentence kept reverberating through her brain, as monstrous as a huge rock, 'Gaythi! How can I tell you what you're really like? You've always been a headache for all of us. If only you had died long ago it would have been far better.'

Gaythi had taken this comment from Saulat in silence but she had thought, clenching her lips, 'Why should I die, Saulat Apa? What right have you got to give me this advice? This life of mine is not a loan from you. It is a gift from God which has been given to me, only to me, and for me. It is my duty to protect it; and making every decision about this life is also a right which is only mine. Yes! As from today, I shall not be a headache for anyone.'

And now she sat in a compartment of the train as it hurtled through the rural areas, thinking repeatedly, 'This is why people warn you against saying sharp and bitter things to women who are in their prime.'

'And it is also said that you must not allow petty little things to inflame you,' a very faint and petrified voice raised its head in the depths of her perturbed and aggrieved heart. And faced with her wrath and fury, it lowered its head again and disappeared somewhere.

She could have purchased a ticket for somewhere other than Lahore. But the thought that all the colleges and hostels here would still be shut did not occur to her until Lahore was only a few stations away.

When she alighted from the train at nine o'clock at night and stood on the platform, her heart enquired of her, 'But where will you go?'

Fear and dismay suddenly strengthened her nerve and alerted her brains. She came out of the station and gave Chacha ji's address to an inebriated, hunch-backed *tonga* wallah who drowsily held the reins of an emaciated mare. The city was under a complete black-out. As was its custom, Mason Road was already quiet and immersed in sleep. The clip-clopping of the hoofs of that feeble horse and the rattle of the *tonga* sounded explosive to her heart.

'My God! This black-out turns the night into something even more terrifying,' she reflected.

Before then, she had found the whole routine of rehearsing black-outs very interesting. The switching-off of all the street lamps and external lights of houses, the drawing of black curtains against the windows early in the evening, and the sound of sirens, warning against make-believe air attacks – a vague feeling of fear blending with a sense of complete security – it all seemed to be a fascinating and wonderful experiment.

But today the darkness of the black-out perturbed her so that she agonised, 'Allah! This war!' but then her brain abruptly somersaulted to, 'What a good thing this war is! In minutes it wipes out entire communities and economies. It gives no one the opportunity to nurture anger or grievance against anyone, and does away with the need for remorse and shame over one's foolish mistakes. Barrey Bhaiya is so lucky, to be completely engrossed in his own work, to be surrounded by air attacks, canons and bombs. And look at me! Let's see what tomorrow brings for me. And that doesn't just depend on tomorrow.

'*Arrey*! What in heaven's name have I done?' she muttered in surprise at herself. 'I wish these Germans or the Japanese would bomb this city overnight, so I would die.' She saw this city, in which she had sought

217

protection from Saulat's anger and misguided decision, being bombed in her imagination.

The flow of her thoughts came to a stop with the *tonga*. 'And now what shall I do?' This question rambled in her small, worried head again.

'What can you do? Please yourself. Just keep doing the first thing that comes into your head,' she scolded herself inwardly, as she moved towards the verandah on to which Chacha ji's rooms opened, avoiding a confrontation with Joseph Wilson's dogs.

Chacha ji came clicking along in his wooden clogs, dressed in a dhoti and a vest; he opened the door and peeped through it. He was amazed.

'*Arrey*, is that you, Gaythi? Is everything all right?'

'*As-salaam-o-ulaikum*, Chacha ji,' she said in a tired and limp voice.

'*Arrey*, Azmat!' Chacha ji yelled, 'Get Bibi's luggage off!'

'Chacha ji, there is no luggage on the *tonga*,' she said as she paid the *tonga* wallah.

'This girl has come at this time without letting us know, without any luggage, and she looks exhausted and sorrowful!' He looked at her closely. He was not in the habit of asking too many questions and trying to worm things out of people.

In the hullabaloo Chachi woke up and she sat on her bed sneezing and coughing.

As soon as Gaythi entered the room, she said to her, 'If you were getting in at such a bad time you should have wired us. Your Chacha ji would have gone to meet you at the station, child! Has the college opened? Call Azmat now, ji; so he can get some dinner for the girl.'

'I've eaten, Chachi ji,' Gaythi lied. 'I've been a nuisance coming at such an awkward time.'

Another bed stood at a slight distance from Chachi's bed, its bedclothes still undisturbed. She felt intensely sleepy all of a sudden and she sat down near Chachi on her bed.

'Gaythi Ara! Our friend is well, isn't he?' Chacha ji sat down on a stool near the bed. Gaythi stared pathetically at him, her mouth open. Until that moment she had never articulated the words that her father had died. 'How can I form these words with my tongue?' she wondered. Her silent grief startled him once again.

'Is all well, child?' he stuttered a little.

'Maybe passing away is easier than death,' she thought, and uttered the words with great difficulty, 'Chacha ji! He has passed away.'

'Haa-en!' The stool shuddered under the weight of Chacha's slender, muscular body.

'When? How? And you didn't even let me know?'

Her head was bowed now and she was weeping unashamedly. Chacha had guessed a while ago that these tears bore a grief beyond that of her father's death.

'Nee! Haaey! When?' Chachi's sneezing worsened.

'Oh, my girl!' Chacha's peaceful and quiet eyes filled with tears. He stroked Gaythi's head. He thought daughters were very sweet and he did not have one of his own.

He drew his stool very close to her. 'Some relationships are such that they are not affected by time. My relationship with Jehangir was like that. We did not see each other for years at a time, but the connection which had formed itself between us once never broke . . .'

Then he addressed his wife, 'Take this, for example. I was not the only friend he had in Lahore, but he had given his daughter permission to visit my house alone. My father always lived in that part of the world. He was not used to living in the Punjab at all. If ever he had to return because of a wedding or a bereavement in the family he treated it as an obligation and left as soon as he could. Jehangir and I spent our entire childhood together.' Chacha ji's voice became muffled all of a sudden, 'When your childhood friends die you feel as if your youth is gone.' Then he kept talking in his usual calm manner about the mischief he and Jehangir Mirza would get up to together. 'Then time separated our paths and that was inevitable. But our hearts never succumbed to that separation.'

'And where is Noor-ul-Huda?' he said eying the empty bed as if to change the subject.

'He said he was going to the cinema today,' Chachi managed between two sneezes.

'Oh, all right! You go to sleep now, daughter. You're tired.' His voice was full of paternal kindness.

When she lay down on the bed, her earlier panic and fears had vanished.

Noor-ul-Huda was astonished when he returned from the cinema and saw that his bed had been brought outside. Azmat was asleep a short distance away from his bed. He woke him up and asked him, 'What's the matter? Why has my bed been brought out here?'

It occurred to him that his parents had felt annoyed at his going to the late show and maybe that was why they had cast his bed out. But Abba ji never did things like that. In the time that it took Azmat to wake up, rubbing his eyes all the while, numerous possibilities flitted through Huda's head.

'Well, Azmat? How did my bed get here?'

'How could it get here, Bao-ji? I brought it here.'

'Why?' Huda scolded.

'Guests came.'

'Who came?'

'That bibi from the college who comes here sometimes.'

'Haa-en! How did she get here at this time of night? Is there someone else with her, or is she alone?'

'She's alone. How do I know how she's come? You can find out in the morning, Bao-ji! Go to sleep now.' Azmat was anxious to get back to sleep himself.

But Huda felt inquisitive. First thing in the morning, the first chance he got, Huda asked his mother about Gaythi's sudden arrival.

'Be quiet. I was surprised myself but your father gets cross if one talks like this.'

'But still, you should have asked.'

'I could have done that but as soon as she came the subject of her father's death came up.'

'O – ho! When did that happen?' Huda chewed his lower lip. He felt sorry for Gaythi, but he really did want to know why she had come there unexpectedly, all by herself.

Gaythi had lived there for a year and Punjabi was not so very different from Urdu for her to fail completely to comprehend it. She heard all Noor-ul-Huda's suspicions and doubts.

'Chacha ji and Chachi are such wonderful human beings that one could stay here forever, but I don't know how they have a son like wretched Huda,' Gaythi reflected. 'And anyhow his college has re-opened now, why hasn't he gone back to Aligarh? Who knows whether he will go back or not?'

There was no question of Huda returning to Aligarh. He had come over with the Party to campaign for the Muslim League during the elections and was staying in Lahore to do something specific. Gaythi would only have found all this out if she had asked.

'God knows what this wretched Huda thinks about me and what he might persuade his parents to think.' The thought worried her so much that she considered running away from there, too, by escaping through the back door in the bathroom. 'But could one keep running away unthinkingly like that for one's entire life?' She felt as if she were learning to be sensible, but very slowly.

She came and sat near Chachi for breakfast. Chacha ji sat on the chair reading the newsaper and Chachi was busy measuring out her herbal medicine which she took before breakfast. Huda's shaving things were arranged on a small table under the dense pomegranate tree in the courtyard, and he sat on a chair ostensibly lathering his face, but he was observing her every movement from the corner of his eye.

'As if the secret police had specially appointed him to keep a watch over me.' Gaythi felt aggrieved, as she glanced at him absent-mindedly. There was a deep shadow of objection in his eyes and face.

Gaythi felt disconcerted but she went on eating her breakfast, her head lowered. Chacha ji was busy preparing to leave for his office now.

'Chacha ji take me to the office with you,' her heart called out, but her lips remained silent.

'And when he leaves, Huda is going to interrogate me like a police officer.' She felt tearful. 'What a blunder I've committed. If only I had the money left I might have headed back. When I left there, I just went and bought a second-class ticket foolishly. It's the height of stupidity. Does anyone ever run away from home like this?' Now her heart admitted freely that she had run away from home.

She remembered the sweeper's grandson, Dulara, who used to ask every young man very innocently, 'Did you run away to Bombay, too?' Then he would add quickly, 'My uncle has run away to Bombay as well.' She thought that now there was no difference between her and Dulara's uncle!

Curiosity dripped from Huda's face. He was waiting to speak to her alone when he would be able to prise out of her the answer as to why she had come in that way. And if necessary he could proffer advice and lectures. He had a natural antipathy towards girls who were too free and wayward. Then he rose to get ready for going out.

Thankfully he left before Chacha. That part of the day had now begun when children have departed for schools and the men for their offices and the women get busy with their housework. She went to stand by the window. Chachi sat on a low stool on the verandah stuffing fine strips of rolled paper up her nostril to make herself sneeze.

Gaythi noticed that the weather had quite unexpectedly become pleasant. The sky was now covered with darkening clouds against which the lawn, the bushes and the distant trees gleamed fresh and a verdant green. The suffocating humid stuffiness suddenly diminished. There was a kind of silence and an agreeable feeling in the air. Her heart grew heavier. The wind, rustling gently through the trees, appeared to have got into a rage and had started blowing furiously. The green trees shook as if in an earthquake but it all came to no more than a drizzle. She came away from there to sit on the bed again. She had never felt so useless as she did that day. 'After all, Saulat Apa was not doing something so terribly wrong.' Everything now looked as if it would become acceptable to her, without anything changing. 'Actually, this problem has been further complicated by Huda, otherwise it would not be so bad. I could have taken the money from Chacha and returned in a day or so, but this wretched Huda ...' She started thinking along perverse lines again. 'Why do people develop hostilities against each other? Anyhow, that is all right too. This house is Huda's. I should be sensitive to his displeasure and do something about it as soon as possible.'

When Chachi came from the kitchen to lie down on her bed for a little while, she asked her, 'Chachi ji, where did you have my bicycle stored?'

'It's locked in the store room. Get Azmat to take it out for you.'

54

She had left the house without any specific purpose in mind, hoping that she would be able to think about her future whilst she wandered round. But when she saw a few Chinese women walking quietly on tiny footsteps along Warris Road, the thought of Safdar flashed through her head.

'Oh, thank God, there is one person in this city who has treated me in exactly the same way, right from the beginning to the present time, whose heart has not changed towards me, like Arjumand's.

'But Arjumand has the misfortune of possessing a heart which always bows to pressures.' That thought flitted through her head as her bicycle turned towards Safdar's shop. He was at the back, working on the machine. Dressed in a small pair of shorts and a vest, he was drenched in sweat. She locked the bicycle and went straight in. Various ready-cut parts of shoes were arranged on brackets and the smell of leather was everywhere. Rows of shoes were lined up mounted on shoemakers' blocks. Safdar glanced up from the machine.

'*Arrey*! Is that you?'

'Now everyone will be surprised to see me,' she thought, feeling hurt. She had become even more sensitive than before.

'Yes! It is me,' the seriousness and anxiety in her voice conveyed a good deal to him.

'Come, let's go out,' he said, moving away from the machine.

'Maybe another time. You are busy now.' She turned to leave.

'No, I am free. Come.'

They went out into the alleyway. Apart from the poorer Christians, a few Chinese families also lived there. The entire narrow street reeked of leather.

Children with distinctly Chinese features played near the thresholds. The relatively better-off families had ducks outside their houses spattering the filth in the drains with their beaks. Chinese women dressed in short coats and narrow trousers, carrying shopping baskets, walked alongside the Christian women, dressed in cheap, loosely-gathered frocks. Their faces wore an expression of peace and well-being, engendered by a simple, set, routine life. Gaythi watched them with envy and then looked at Safdar, hoping that he would ask her why she was roaming around there, out of term-time. This was no time for college girls to be roaming around.

He stood there silently thinking, 'I know that once again you have been thrown by some extraordinary crisis and anxiety. And this must be the result of your own doing.'

The subject arose of itself. She narrated everything and then asked him, 'Safdar! Do you think I've made a mistake again today?'

He was silent.

'Tell me! What do you think?'

He was thinking, 'What shall I tell you now, Cuckoo? When things have come to this, Cuckoo! Now I have to say that what you did was right. What's the point in blaming you, anyway? The mistake is not yours, but theirs, who assumed their rights extended beyond the prescribed limits, but did not try to understand you.' He was in no mood to condemn her today.

'This is not the time to prove whether you were right or wrong. What we need to think about is an excuse for your coming like this, to offer to those people. In fact, Huda's suspicions are only to be expected. Give them an excuse – anything!'

'Yes. You'll have to find me one.' She sat down on the steps to the shop and looked at him very simply. 'Up to this point, my brain has been unable to fashion an excuse.'

'Shall I tell you something?' He looked at her triumphantly as if he had suddenly hit upon the solution to an unsolvable riddle.

'Yes, go on!' She sat up.

But in that time he had already rejected the sentence he had thought up. Whatever she suggested seemed unsatisfactory to him, and whatever he proposed felt unreasonable to her. The truth of the matter is that it is difficult to find a reasonable pretext for an unreasonable action. Then the big problem was that neither of them was skilled in the art of deception. She sat thinking that all this division into countries, nationalities and areas was a farce. Human beings simply need each other. What is this man, Safdar, to me and what interest can he possibly have in me that he should stand here so concerned about me?

'I think it won't be possible for me to study any more. I should now find some work.'

'Not possible to study! Are you saying this, Cuckoo?' He looked at her and thought, 'You, who are such a young girl?'

The outside wall of their garden sprang up before his eyes, on which she used to sit very confidently. And he would stand for hours, leaning his bicycle against that wall, teasing and arguing with that girl who had an interesting face, only to hear her chatter, which was so different from that of ordinary girls and children.

'What do you think?' and she continued to sit on the steps like she used to.

'What can I say now about what I think?' He stopped. 'What I had thought was that if you agree I will put you on a train tomorrow and you can go back home.'

'No, Safdar! That is impossible now. I can't go back and endure further humiliation. You don't know how much I hate Akbar.' Signs of anger and hatred were clearly apparent on her face.

'Then I think, for the time being, I cannot give you any other advice.' Safdar felt a little irritated with this girl's shortsightedness and obstinacy, and she felt disillusioned with him. 'How crazy of me. To come all this way to take his advice. What sympathy can a Chinese man, who works a machine for stitching shoes, have for me!'

An indescribable feeling of disquiet and remorse saturated her being. She turned quickly and rapidly crossed the narrow alleyway. The black and white ducks pecking into the muck at the sides, scattered noisily, flapping their wings as they dispersed in different directions. A small, plump Chinese girl seated on the steps of one of the houses burst into tears, petrified at the noise. Gaythi looked back before turning the last corner.

Safdar Yaaseen had calmly lifted the girl, who was crying, into his powerful arms. He gently pushed her straight black hair off her forehead and tried to placate her.

'Yes, that's fine. She is your compatriot, isn't she?' her unsupported, jealous heart muttered, blood vessels in her throat aching with her effort to control the tears which blurred her vision. She walked blindly for a long time. At the other end of the alley stood the man with the child in his arms, watching her leave. The same man who used to come and sit in her room for hours when she was in hospital with a broken bone, amusing her with his mimicry and impressions, merely to see her laugh happily.

After she left he did not return to his work on the machine. He just stood there for a little while, feeling slightly dazed, even after he had handed over the little girl who was crying to her mother. Then he went back to the showroom at the front of the shop. That day several of his customers felt that Liu Chu, who was always smiling and laughing whilst they bargained with him, was in a very bad temper. That day he argued irritably without provocation and several people left, taking offence at his tone and manner. Leaving the shop to trainee assistants he went up to his room, contrary to his usual routine.

Even though the room was much cooler than outside, the heat and sweat were driving him crazy. Picking up his towel he went quietly into the tiny narrow and dark bathroom and kept pouring water on his body for a long time before he realised that sometimes cool water can fail to wash away physical and mental disquiet as well. Slowly, he dried his sandy, yellowish body with a towel, dressed, and came out. His straight, dark hair was scattered untidily.

'What is happening to me today? Why am I behaving like this?' He felt mildly vexed.

'Tap, tap,' he heard Li Fan's eleven-year-old knock on the door. Safdar had an arrangement with them for his meals. Without moving from where he was, he asked, 'Well? What is it?'

The little girl thrust her face round the door and delivered her mother's message, 'Why didn't you come to eat today?'

Then she asked, 'Shall I bring you food here? I've been to the shop as well, to call you.'

'Oh, yes, I haven't eaten,' he remembered immediately, and answered without looking at her, 'No, there's no need to bring the food here. I am coming myself.'

The little girl skipped down the staircase and he followed her into the third house further along the alley. A mat woven from coconut rushes covered the floor of the long, narrow room which looked like a corridor. At the eastern end of the room stood a fairly low delicate table on which the steaming food had been arranged very daintily. Its smell pervaded the room. At the western end of the room, leaning against the back of a low bamboo chair, sat Li Fan's wife, darning her husband's coat. She had a quiet disposition, a very broad open face. When she heard his footsteps she raised her head as if to ask, 'Where have you been today?'

Safdar greeted her with a nod of his head and went to the food table

225

without any apology. He knelt on the cushion in front of the food. In the centre of the room Li Fan's newest baby slept in a wooden crib. The heat shed a morose silence all round them.

Safdar picked up the chopsticks and drew the bowl of white rice towards him. There were dried prawns in sauce in another bowl and shredded green chillies pickled in vinegar.

The steaming fish exuded a medley of appetising smells – cottonseed oil, ginger and garlic. Safdar always ate his food with great relish when prawns were served, but today he did not. Each morsel felt as if it were sticking in his throat. He swallowed a few sips of water with great difficulty and stood up.

Noticing that he had finished too soon, Li Fan's wife objected, 'Well? What's the matter today? You've left the food untouched. Prawns in curry sauce are your favourite.'

'I don't know what the matter is today. The food feels as if it is sticking in my throat . . .'

'Someone must be hungry then.'

'Huh, you Chinese women have always been superstitious.'

'Not really. An Indian woman told me that.'

'What difference does it make if she was Indian? What I really meant was that you women, whether you're Indian, Chinese, Russian or Turkish, you're always nursing some fear or other.'

'And I say that you men, wherever you come from, will always regard women as stupid and crazy. I used to think that only Chinese men did that, but an Indian friend of mine tells me that Indian men also think women are thick and unintelligent.'

Getting into an argument with that quiet woman just then made Safdar feel as if that strange feeling of disquiet in his mind had diminished. 'All right! So what does that Indian woman say?'

'You're just going on about it. What's the point in asking, when you don't really believe what we women say?'

'No. How can I not believe it? That is the strange thing. Despite their foolishness, a lot of the things that you people say turn out to be true. Believe me, the things which my mother told me over there often come out true, here.'

'Well . . . the woman said that if food sticks in your throat you should assume that a person dear to you is hungry.'

'Hum . . .!' Safdar stood there absorbed in thought for a little while.

'Someone very dear is hungry . . . well, that is so!'

Li Fan's wife knotted the thread and broke it off, looking at him triumphantly, 'So, what are you thinking?'

'Hum? Hum,' he jerked to attention. 'I think that Indian friend of yours is right. It's not a case of must be, someone is, in fact, hungry.' Without finishing the conversation with one long stride he leapt out of that corridor-like room.

The gusts of loo winds zapping through the alley did not feel at all painful or hot to him. He walked on slovenly feet as if he were trying to kill time. Even when he lay down on the charpoy in his room that unspoken question went on echoing in his brain, 'Who could be hungry, except that silly girl? Who else could be hungry?' To avoid the reverberations of that thought he kept tossing and turning and finally buried his face in the pillow.

'Sometimes I don't see this silly girl who's angry with her family, for ages, and even the thought of her doesn't remain in my head – does she rank as someone so close to me that her hunger should cause morsels of food to stick in my throat?' This question truly puzzled him.

That day he woke up late in the evening. He was soaking in sweat, and his brain still felt numb. He looked around with fear in his eyes. An unspeakable sadness enveloped him.

'The truth is, that that girl's walking out of the alley in such disappointment has been etched into my heart and brain. How helpless and unfortunate she looked! She, who used to sit astride the wall of her garden, making faces at me, came today to seek my advice. Every move of hers used to drip affluence and gay abandon. She would go round as if there was nothing she cared about in the world. What kind of a girl is she? How did so much waywardness and defiance grow within her . . .? Is it possible that this girl is really . . .?'

He could not imagine anything beyond that. He had known Cuckoo for so long and had been interested in her personally since the beginning and so could not associate any evil with her.

'She is a very innocent, decent and truthful girl, who lays her heart bare before anyone and who never understands at all why people should prefer to keep their feelings and experiences secret!'

The sound of church and temple bells rang out simultaneously, mingling in the air. In the distance he could hear the call to prayer chanted in Arabic, 'O, you people! Choose the path of virtue, choose the path of virtue.' Safdar knew the meaning of those familiar words very well.

'Some people seek virtue and some remain in pursuit of evil and

227

destruction like this girl who I always think of as Cuckoo, and whose real name I cannot recall.'

He stretched and rose, lit the lamp on the table and then the stove to boil water for his tea and went into the bathroom to bathe again. When he returned, the kettle was hissing noisily; he made the tea and turned the fan on.

On the shelf were ranged a few books in Chinese, some pamphlets about the political upheaval in the country, the translation of the Quran into Chinese, works by Confucius and Lao Tzu's *The Way of Being*. He picked up the latter and opened it as if it were a set of Tarot cards which would yield a reading. He bent over it and began to read. The first word that he saw, writ large on the open page was,

(Tao) which means 'way of being'.

'Oh . . .!'

Feeling vexed, he turned several pages and his eyes came to a halt automatically on the last few lines of a poem.

'So there is a proverb which goes like this: that there can come a time when an average person can interpret everything to be the opposite of what it really is. It is a time when even those paths seem shrouded in darkness which gleam, with the light shining upon them. When straight paths appear to be uneven. The highest virtues assume the form of evil and the holiest innocence and purity manifests itself dressed in tatters. Good character can look promiscuous and depraved. Solid learning seems to be as transient as restless waves. But the reality is far from this.
A true span is one which has no borders.
Powerful forces come into operation only after a long time.
The notes of the greatest melody are gentle and the aspect of the tallest person cannot be encapsulated.'

The book slipped and fell from his hand. His lips were sealed together and the darkness in his eyes had deepened.

He repeated absent-mindedly, 'When straight paths appear to be uneven. The highest virtues assume the form of evil and the holiest innocence and purity manifests itself dressed in tatters. Good character can look promiscuous and depraved.'

He shut his eyes but that open innocent face, filled with calm, still remained before him smiling like a yogi who smiles sympathetically at the follies of the worldly, having arrived at knowledge through years of patient perseverance. Her face was always like that – exactly like that, even when she was young; and that is why she looked so mysterious and interesting. He opened his eyes in a panic. On the small bookshelf sat a tiny statue of the Buddha, cross-legged, immersed in deep thought in search of the Truth. Safdar also thought, 'When the Lord of Creation is weary of the lack of feeling and evil character of his surroundings then he tries to escape. Sometimes he wanders in the streets and alleys of the Jewish town of Bethlehem, sometimes he sits in a mosque striving towards knowledge, sometimes in search of *nirvana* for his restless soul, he says goodbye to an inheritance of elaborate palaces in the darkness of night. And sometimes it can also transpire that someone turns his back on the tranquil security of his own home and wanders friendless and shattered in the streets of an alien city, assuming the persona of a foolish and reckless girl.'

Without hesitation he gave that ordinary girl the title of 'the Lord of Creation', and became content. Today he had discovered the secret of all the waywardness and follies of this strange girl. He heaved a really deep sigh. 'Cuckoo, after all, who could have advised you to adopt the way of Tao? The way of being is uneven and tortuous. Yes, I mean: (Atao)

55

'If someone else had walked off like this instead of you, without giving me their correct address, then it would have been difficult for me to trace them, maybe even impossible. But this is you, Cuckoo . . .!

'It is not at all difficult for me to guess where I might find you. This is me, and I always come punctually, I don't know how! Only God knows how.

'But when you fell off the damson tree, and again when you had gone to sit by yourself in Company Park, and then the last time when you had bought a lower-class cinema ticket, I was the one who came to your aid.

229

That day I had reflected upon this – that Nature, or coincidence, always sent me to you at the time of need.'

On Sunday morning, when his Christian fellow expatriates had gone to church and the rest were in their houses dressed in shorts and vests, mending chicken coops or playing with their dogs or children, his bicycle followed the direction of his inspiration as it moved slowly along the long, black road. He saw the open-air box office window on the right side of the road flanked by tall poplars and his narrow slanting eyes, gleaming with a strange but faint hope, looked all round into the distance. In various corners, small groups of people sat under trees and bushes, celebrating Sunday. Amongst them were Sikhs with colourful turbans, elaborately dressed beards and hooded eyes, and Muslims and Hindus dressed in different kinds of clothes. There were well-off Anglo-Indians and black Christians; English children accompanied by their ayahs were busy making noise. Happiness and a carefree spirit surrounded all of them. His heart began to sink. She could not be seen anywhere.

'If I find you today, as I expect to, then I will come to believe that there is some unknown connection between you and me, and that Nature has appointed me to protect you. I speak the truth: this will become my faith, because we Asians are superstitious and bound by beliefs.'

She was nowhere to be seen there. Repeatedly, he scanned the benches on the low hillocks covered with ferns, small bushes and naag phani plants. Many nooks of the park still needed to be investigated, he thought, as he climbed that little hill which, in those days, sported a gate covered with red and white creeping roses on its very first slope. He looked around as he leaned against the green railing and then climbed up. On that hillock there was only a Madrasi ayah minding a small English girl as she played.

Dismayed at the whining of the ayah and the noise of the little girl he turned towards the slope to the front of the hill. On that side the water bubbled out of the tap concealed under the rocks, sliding noisily as it passed downwards through them. There she sat, propped against a large rock, and partly shielded by it, reading a book. There was something in her mouth which she was chewing slowly.

When she heard his footsteps she raised her head and looked up at him but pretended to keep her attention on the book, even though her eyes were not looking directly at the page. He went and stood very near to her. It was strange. Despite his finding her unexpectedly like this after his earlier disappointment, he was not at all surprised or startled.

'Yes. This had to happen,' he thought, and that was his only reaction.

He addressed her after a few moments of silence, 'Cuckoo, it's me standing here.'

'Yes, I've seen you, Safdar!' Her voice was dry, reproachful, but most noticeable was the fact that she had, very reasonably, called him Safdar, instead of Chu or Liu Chu.

'But I came looking for you, Cuckoo!'

'Looking for me? Who told you that I was sitting here?'

'Someone did, I suppose. That's why I arrived straight here.'

'That is very strange. I didn't even tell anyone at home. Who is it who was able to tell you my whereabouts so accurately?'

'It's served my purpose this time, so what's the point in my telling you or your asking me? Since yesterday, when you left so suddenly, I have been constantly worried about you.' There was immense sincerity in his voice.

'All right. But you were irritated at the time, and I regretted that I had wearied you for nothing.'

'When we can't solve a problem easily, and can't find reasonable explanations, then we do get irritated.' There was apology and regret in his voice, 'But now I have come with the intention that we should both get together to think of something reasonable. Actually, suddenly hearing all that at that time, truly numbed my mind.'

She put down the book in her hand and shook the hair off her forehead with a customary jerk of the head. Then she looked studiously at Safdar, who was thinking something.

'Today her face wears the same calm and peace which you see on the face of a philosopher who has discovered the meaning of life, and her eyes look content and indifferent, as if she were looking down at the world, seeing it far, far beneath her,' he noticed.

Whilst Gaythi was thinking, 'Liu Chu is truly good and sincere. I should not have become suspicious of him. Now what possible motive could he have in ruining his Sunday, looking for me? Who knows how he has traced me and how many people he has talked to, in his search for me!' The bitterness was washed off the mirror of her heart and her mood changed to friendliness.

'Come and sit here,' she pointed to another rock which stood at a slight distance from her and he sat on that very obediently. Today, she seemed to him to be a lot older than even he was.

'I don't need any excuse or apology any more,' she said, very calmly.

'Why not? Has Huda stopped being hostile to you, then?' For some reason Safdar felt uncomfortable about that thought.

'Whether he stops being hostile or not there seems to be no need for advice in that area.'

'But why not?' He was getting impatient.

'Because . . .' she replied extremely calmly, 'I have told Huda the truth.'

'This means that you and he have come to some understanding.' Safdar felt a little sad at the thought that Cuckoo did not need him any more.

'Just listen to me, you unreasonable Cheeny; I can't talk if you interrupt me so much.'

He looked at her in silence.

'What happened was that Huda got there as soon as I returned to the house. Chachi ji had gone to the doctor's for an injection and Chacha ji was at his office. Finding me alone, he cornered me, firing questions one after the other. I became angry and I said to him in no uncertain terms, "If I had been in your position, Mr Noor-ul-Huda, finding you alone I would not have pounced upon you, and questioned you like this, even if I had thousands of suspicions. And now that you are asking me these questions, here is the answer. I am angry with my family and have come here because I walked out on them without telling them anything . . ."' She laughed after saying all this. 'Believe me, he jumped when he heard this, and then, slowly, I told him the reason too . . . So much so, that he actually became a little breathless, and then he said with great difficulty, "I still don't believe what you're telling me. Girls from such families don't do things like this and to tell you the truth, this does seem well beyond a girl like yourself." I replied, "It may seem beyond me now, but I have already done it, whether you believe it or not." He started lecturing me then, "If you have really done this then you should forget about what is already done and go back now. I will tell Abba ji today, that he should take you back himself." I said to him, "Look here, Mr Noor-ul-Huda! This is my own business, there's no need for you to interfere in this. I know quite well how to judge what is good for me and what is bad. And I will live in this house of yours for several days even if you fight with me and are bored by my presence."'

'What did he say?'

'First he fell into deep thought then he laughed aloud and said, "You're a truly comical and impudent girl. You tried, quite brazenly, to deceive me but then I am studying at Aligarh you know, Gaythi Ara! Did you hear that?" And he went to the other room and started getting his things together. These boys are here canvassing for votes for Pakistan, you know. He had to catch the afternoon train the same day to go somewhere.

232

Bhai, he is terribly busy with his work, otherwise he might have given some thought to what I had said.'

'Is that so? They're here working towards the referendum then?"

'*Arrey*, Safdar, truly! They are working very hard. Chacha ji was telling us that these boys have only held on to the books in their hands, and have given away whatever else they possessed as donations.'

'Blessed are the boys who are making sacrifices for their country and their nation!' Safdar thought sadly. 'And here I am, miles away from my country, banging my head against stinking leather and a machine, day in and day out.' Then, he said, gently, 'Congratulations, Cuckoo! At least you have made up your mind now.'

'Made up my mind! Honestly, Safdar, I had never realised the importance of truth before now. We feel so light when we tell the truth, however shameful and horrifying that might be.'

'But you always tell the truth, Cuckoo! No wonder you stay so carefree and content,' Safdar thought silently. '"Who says that the true path is uneven and riddled with thorns . . . Who says truth is a deep and endless ocean." Someone should ask this girl, Cuckoo, about this deep, noisy and endless ocean at the bottom of which lie hidden pearls, corals and God knows what else, gleaming away.'

Gaythi took a pinch of something which she held wrapped in paper in her fist, 'So! Ha! It's delicious! Want some, Liu Chu?'

'Give it here.' He took it from her hand absent-mindedly and put it in his mouth. Salt, chillies and the sour taste of tamarind paste dissolved in his mouth, putting his smoker's teeth on edge.

'Silly girl!' he thought and scolded her as usual, 'You're eating tamarind? Silly! Don't you realise that Huda would feel even more fed up if you got ill? Throw it down, right now, in front of me.'

She threw the little packet in her fist into the running water.

56

Now, according to his beliefs, she had come into his care and his domain of responsibility.

'Sometimes, without consulting us, life and death hand us responsibilities which we have never desired or anticipated,' Safdar thought, as he cut out the 'upper' for an eleven-year-old's shoe from a large piece of red leather on the table in front of him.

'And these responsibilities received on this false basis for allocation are even harder to fulfil. And I have been targeted right from the beginning by this Will, for the fulfilment of such responsibilities. Or else . . . or else.'

With longing, he remembered the environs of Peking College in which he had spent barely a year and a half of his life.

'Countless boys, carefree and laughing, dressed in uniforms, books and notebooks clutched under their arms, must still be roaming the rooms, verandahs and grounds of the college. Must still be busy with their science experiments bent over the tables in the laboratory, or learning the techniques of various games and the skills of gymnastics, and every year at the convocation, thousands of students will leave, and disperse in all directions, holding degrees in their hands.

'And it will not even occur to anyone that once upon a time a boy named Safdar Liu Chu had left the compound of this college, filled with longing and despair, without completing his courses in order to be able to take over responsibility for his parents, brothers and sisters and numerous relatives. I had neither desired that kind of responsibility then, and nor have I desired this other responsibility which has been thrust into my hands recently or which I have myself taken on.'

Now, at least on Gaythi's account, he was reasonably satisfied. He had arranged some really good students for her to tutor and she shared a room with a Chinese Christian girl at the YWCA, where she was also taking a secretarial course.

'Slowly and gently, I will be able to persuade her to return home. It only needs for her anger and fear to diminish a little more.' He was thinking of her as he worked on his accounts, when he saw her cycle gleam before him. Her yellowish complexion looked cool and tranquil in her simple snow-white outfit. She looked at him with tired eyes and said, '*Arrey*! Are you still busy with your work?'

'Yes! It's a bit like that.'

'And when does your Sang return?'

'There's little hope of my poor Sang returning. He is very ill and there is little hope of his recovery.'

'So then, will you get this shop?'

'God forgive you. What right have I got to this? I am only his employee. But the news is that his older brother's son will come by the end of the year to take over the business.'

'And what will become of you, Liu Chu?'

'Me? The same as ever,' he laughed. 'Well, what brings you here, today?'

'I felt restless so I came, just like that,' she said simply.

'Why did you feel restless? Are you missing home?' He looked into her eyes to catch the truth. She blinked and changed the subject.

'I went to Chacha ji's house yesterday.'

'Really?' He did not like her evasiveness. He had thought that he would now try to persuade her to go back, after introducing the subject of home.

'Huda's gone back.'

'Where?'

'Aligarh. Chachi was missing him.'

'That's inevitable! All mothers miss their children if they are separated from them.' Halfway through his addition of entries, Safdar put the pencil down and gave her a meaningful look. 'Your mother must miss you when you are here.' 'Certainly. Last time when I was due to return she stopped sitting near me three days before I was due to leave and would only talk to me when it was essential, in fact, only when I addressed her. My father's old aunt objected to this and said to her, "In the first place, the boy is going away soon and, then, who knows when he will return next but you have stopped even talking to him!" To this Mother replied, "I want him not to miss my love and my conversation, and not to remember me. He belongs only to God – I hope he is happy wherever he chooses to live." Then she sat down in the courtyard to clean the rice, her face devoid of emotion.'

Gaythi lowered her head. Her eyes were downcast. Suddenly, Safdar asked her a question, 'Gaythi, your older brother is at the front too, isn't he?'

'Yes, Safdar,' she spoke gently; she looked dejected all of a sudden.

'Have you heard any news of him?'

'We had not been able to find out anything up to the time when I left home. We had only one letter in all the time I was there. And that was a very old one too.'

'I saw that brother of yours only once, but I liked him very much. He is very handsome and really does look aristocratic.'

'You haven't seen my other brother, Safdar. He is very nice too, and he has become so responsible now.'

'Who does that brother look like? Not like you, I hope?'

'No one looks like me. In my entire family, both Bakhtiar Bhaiya and I are the ones who don't look like anyone else. His complexion is the worst of all of us. But some people say that he looks much nicer than Barrey Bhaiya.'

'Your other sister is also nice looking. What's the name of your twin sister?'

'Arjumand . . .!'

'*Bhai*! All of you have really difficult names, and what's that name, your older sister's?'

'Saulat . . .!' She spoke a little hesitantly.

'How many children does she have now?'

'Two.'

'Just boys?'

'The older one's a girl and the second one is a boy.'

'They must be beautiful children.'

'Especially Azam, the one we call Guddoo. He is really lovely.' She started narrating anecdotes about him as if there were no quarrel between her and their mother.

Safdar put his pencil down and shut the register. He was looking at her face and listening to her intently. When the young cleaning boy came in, Safdar asked him to bring some tea.

'Well, I'd better go now,' she said when she had finished what she was saying.

'If . . . if it doesn't bother you . . .' he hesitated, 'the tea will be here soon, have a cup of tea before you go . . .' Then he spoke again, after a pause, 'You won't mind . . .? I mean . . .'

'Yes. I know what you mean,' Gaythi thought. 'A very ordinary shop-keeper offering tea to a girl from a well-placed family is considered highly objectionable. And you are feeling embarrassed yourself suggesting tea. But do consider all that you have done for this girl. You have always helped me Liu Chu! Now and on other occasions, even when I did not specially need you. I will never forget your coming to visit me at the hospital on those scalding afternoons, keeping your visits secret from Sang. At that time you used to come every day merely to make me happy and just for my sake you would go out again in that heat to buy things like *paans*, betel nuts and ice for Chachi jaan. And I am also aware that in this world of ours with its worldly principles, there is no value in so much sincerity, decency and love. If there is any value it attaches to status and class.'

Her imagination and thoughts raced ahead but her tongue was slow. She could not urge it to utter even a word giving voice to all that. In truth, when does one ever say things like this?

She thought all that without giving Safdar any inkling of it and said, 'No, it doesn't matter. All right then, I can go after I've had some tea.' She leapt up again to sit on the high stool which stood next to the counter.

'Who are you cutting that shoe for?' she said looking at the scissors which lay on top of the red leather.

236

'A little girl.'

'I've been thinking that I should learn shoe-making too,' she said jokingly.

'Why? Is it such an interesting job?'

'All jobs are interesting. When I was little I used to pester the carpenter who worked in our house, "Give me the saw, I'll cut the wood. What's so difficult about it! Show me how to sandpaper."'

'In that case, instead of shoe-making you should let me teach you how to paint.'

'*Arrey, bhai.* You are utterly useless. You have neither taught me your language nor painting.'

She sat there so relaxed, talking to him half-jokingly, that Safdar forgot his earlier embarrassment over asking her to have tea with him.

When the boy brought in the tea, he rose, poured it with great ceremony and lowered his head with great respect as he handed her her cup, as if he were a servant of hers.

When she had left, Safdar Yaaseen thought, 'Your presence and your personality are so wonderful . Wherever you go, one feels there is nothing but peace, tranquillity and innocence there.'

Today, it was also encouraging to see that she was talking about her home and her family with such fervour and love.

'Her heart is gold, nothing but gold,' he thought, as he got involved again in the tedium of dealing with customers.

57

That August evening was relatively cool and pleasant. The YWCA Hostel seemed fairly quiet and deserted. Most of the girls had appointments with their friends and, bathed and dressed by four o'clock, they would stroll by the gates whilst they waited. Or they would sit on one of the few benches on the lawn, trying to kill time by immersing themselves in cheap editions of novels.

Some women and girls used to come from outside to play badminton and played until the light bulbs on the tall wooden poles were switched on. On days when her Chinese room-mate, Margaret, was on evening duty, Gaythi would find herself alone. On such evenings she either visited Chacha ji or spent the time in her room, reading a book in bed. She was no longer the carefree girl she used to be – who could leave her room in chaos. In the midst of her reading, she would suddenly remember that it needed to be done. She would throw the book aside and get up to gather and rearrange the things scattered around by Margaret and herself, draw the curtains and call the sweeper to mop the bathroom floor. Then she would go and sit with old Mrs Benjamin in her room. She suffered from Elephantiasis and every day she had a new grievance to narrate about her swollen, bandaged feet. Gaythi would listen to everything she said with great absorption and interest and then think, 'Other people's problems are such a blessing, one can forget one's own by losing oneself in them. How cruel those people are who pretend they are happy and do not have any problems and difficulties. They want those who are suffering to stew in solitude. How generous Mrs Benjamin is in this respect! She lays bare all her sorrows before you and you can lose all yours in the overwhelming crowd of hers.'

The gentle, mournful melody being played on the piano in the common room floated adrift. Instead of dissolving and melting away those songs remained suspended in the atmosphere.

'If only every moment of time and every voice could stay trapped like this forever.' Gaythi let her book drop on the table.

'But why? Why did I wish for that? After all, what moments could I be in search of?'

She asked herself the question as she gently drew together the curtains at the window. Behind the wire mesh the jasmine and malathy creepers had tangled together into a kind of dome. Beyond them was an untidy cluster of mulberry, damson and peepal trees. In the twilight everything looked forlorn and weary.

Margaret will be busy at this moment in the Nursery Ward of the Strangers' Home, looking after those children who are the very field of war, who will never have either home or family. For whom their mothers' tender and attentive touch is out of bounds. Whose mothers, in their attempts to forget their existence, dressed in the WAACs uniforms, are busy assisting the fighters with great diligence and discipline.

How well suited Margaret is to this job! Silent, responsible, pale and imposing, her eyes and hair pitch black, she has the attention and stamina of a mother. Margaret was Chinese and was a secretary to the Officer In-Charge of the Strangers' Home. Her behaviour and conduct towards Gaythi were exactly what they were towards a child in her care. This was in accordance with Safdar Liu Chu's special instructions to her. And she could not help it either, partly because of the gentleness of her temperament and her sympathetic nature. She tended to be quiet but sometimes she would step out of this shell of silence and passivity to become talkative.

She was not in today so Gaythi was waiting for her. She wished that someone would talk to her so much that she would forget everything that had ever happened to her. Today she felt frightened of her own heart and did not wish to be alone with it, since it had retorted rudely, brazenly and quite unequivocally to the questions which flitted around in her head concerning her own sense of tedium and uncontrollable restlessness, by saying something like this, 'Gaythi Ara Begum, however much you might pressure me and order me to keep my secret, I cannot endure any more. I will not be prevented from disclosing the fact that you are missing home and that you need it – desperately.'

Gaythi no longer had the strength to resist or deny anyone. She rested her head on the table in resignation and let her tears flow unreservedly. Her heart was bursting with anxieties and worries about each and every member of her family.

Old Mrs Benjamin, disgusted with her Elephantiasis, her spectacles planted on her round owlish eyes, her hair knotted in the shape of a pad designed to balance a basket on the head, said to herself, 'God knows why that girl has not been round to visit me for the past two days. Just talking to her when she comes takes the weight off my heart. How comforting it is to share your pains, blunders and aberrations with someone who does not start blaming you or lecturing you!'

58

'Did you hear that? The war's over,' Gaythi said to Margaret early in the morning, letting the newspaper fall.

'Yes! I heard that news last night whilst I was on duty,' she said in a gentle voice, arranging her hair.

'What a strange, down-to-earth nature this woman has! She's been sitting all morning as if nothing had happened, as if the cat had got her tongue. Even if it stops raining people always mention it to each other.' Gaythi felt vexed at Margaret's lack of communication.

'But I've only just discovered now that the war's ended!'

'That's because you went to bed early yesterday, otherwise you would have heard then too,' Margaret's voice was as gentle and level as before.

'How do you know that I went to bed early?'

'I know, and I also know that you wept last evening.'

'Who told you?'

'Me?' Margaret glanced briefly through the window at Mrs Benjamin's room as she put her hairbrush down and said, 'Well, someone told me.'

'Never mind,' Gaythi waved that aside. 'Aren't you pleased that the war's over?' her voice sounded childishly happy.

'What difference does the end of the war make to me? If the crisis and tussle in my country came to an end – that would be something. And then again, this sudden end to the war may not be such a good thing. You'll see, lots of departments, which had been set up temporarily, will close and unemployment will rise dramatically. And who knows what else will happen?'

'Who knows what else will happen?' Margaret had said those words in that specially mysterious and superstitious tone of a thoroughbred eastern woman.

Gaythi's heart began to pound, 'This wretched Margaret is like that. If she starts telling stories, they're about witches, ghosts and poltergeists to make your heart quake with fear. Just the kind of frightening horror stories which the village naani, Kaamni's grandmother, who lived in Dadi Ammah's house, used to tell.'

'Kaamni . . .!' Gaythi's thoughts strayed again. 'Kaamni, who was Masood's fiancée,' and she immediately reined in that thought. 'But Margaret! You're a Christian. You should be pleased that the fighting has stopped but instead of that you've started moaning about the problems in your own country.'

'What if I am a Christian, Gaythi? This war was not a war about Christianity. And how can I forget the problems of my country? Like the others have forgotten them? Like Safdar Yaaseen's forgotten them? You won't understand him,' she laughed.

'I . . .?' Gaythi found this comment disagreeable. 'Do you know how long I've known him? Since the time when I was a very little girl and you've only got to know him very recently.'

'. . . However long you might have known him.' She rose having finished arranging her hair. There was a special glint of familiarity in her face and her eyes, as if she were saying, 'What do you know about him, you foreign girl? I am his compatriot. I understand his language. I know his beliefs. His problems and mine are the same and what a big thing that is.'

Then she bowed a little towards her and said in a peculiar tone, 'But, yes, I am happy that the war's ended, for one reason: that is, that my

240

little Cuckoo's brother will now return. The brother whose mention makes her very sad sometimes.'

'Why does she call me Cuckoo, like Safdar does?' Gaythi felt exasperated, and said, 'Yes, and lots of other soldiers will return to their homes too.'

'Provided they're still alive,' slipped absent-mindedly from Margaret's tongue. Then she noticed that Gaythi's face which had been flushed with excitement, paled. She clenched her lips together, tightly.

'I see. So that was why she was so happy first thing in the morning about the news of the war coming to an end.' Margaret suddenly realised her mistake. 'I've said such a worrying thing without justification,' she thought. Then glibly said, 'So! You'll treat us to a party, won't you? Myself, Safdar and Mrs Benjamin. Now they will be back very soon.'

'Provided they're still alive. Provided they're still alive!' Gaythi's heart repeated with every beat. Instead of giving Margaret a reply, she lowered her head and hiding her face in the soft palms of her plump hands, she started shedding tears quietly.

59

He stopped tightening the attachment on the machine and looked at her with concern. 'She wept last evening and then so much again this morning, and you still left her alone, by herself?' There was rebuke in Safdar's voice.

'But Safdar! This was my day off. I hadn't been here for so many days. Li Fan's wife has been asking me over for such a long time.'

'But she was worried, and lonely,' his voice carried deeper reproach.

'Then what could I do? She's not a child.'

'She is a child.'

This aggravated her. 'OK, Safdar! Goodbye! I didn't know that these days you're never in the mood for a chat.'

'That's what you think.' He started tightening the attachment again.

She came out of the workroom and as she walked down the alley towards Li Fan's house, she thought, 'I just don't know what the matter is! What's happened to Safdar? What does he think?'

*

When Safdar went over to eat he saw that Margaret was happily seated on the low bamboo chair, Li Fan's youngest boy in her arms, his little three-year-old whose hair was plaited tightly close to her ears, sitting leaning up against her whilst she was absorbed in telling her a story. Her face puffed up with anger when she saw Safdar and her involvement in the story deepened.

'Don't you get enough of children at the Strangers' Home, that you should come here and ignore everyone except the children?' he teased. But she continued to be busy with Zoe.

When Li Fan's wife walked past them, Margaret said, 'I'm bringing a little poodle for Zoe next time.'

Zoe's mother stopped abruptly, 'These children are naughty, Margaret. They'll kill it.'

'No. I'll talk to them. They won't do that.'

'But . . . but. . .' Zoe's mother stammered.

'Why don't you tell her the truth? That she shouldn't bother to bring a dog, that Muslims don't like keeping dogs,' Safdar said in a decisive voice and laughed.

'Why?' Margaret pretended to address the question to Zoe.

'Because the angels of mercy don't visit a house with dogs.'

'Get away! As if you're such a great staunch Muslim yourself!'

'What difference does that make? Don't bring a dog to this house. Zoe! Don't accept it, whatever happens. What does Margaret know? She's a Christian.'

Despite her anger Margaret could not help laughing. Safdar kept telling jokes over dinner to amuse them and Margaret felt that her day off went pleasantly.

That Saturday when Gaythi visited him in the shop, he felt that she looked even more stricken and preoccupied than before.

'How's your course going now?' Safdar asked her.

'It's going well. The instructor thinks I am progressing faster than most of the average girls.'

'Hum.' Safdar glanced at her forlorn eyes, 'These small, black eyes look so interesting when they're full of yearning,' he thought before asking her the question, 'What are you pining for today?'

'What a question to ask, Safdar?' she laughed. 'People like me are always yearning.'

'But why did you cry the other day?'

'Margaret must have told you.' She looked outside indifferently. 'Margaret has this bad habit of spreading gossip.'

'That might be so, but what was the reason?'

'Again? What was the reason? Why do you keep missing the point?' She felt irritated. 'Is this something to quiz me about? There are numerous reasons for these things.'

He was hearing her speak in an imperious tone after a long time, and Safdar liked that very much, 'All right. I won't ask any more.' He went back to stand near the table on which he had laid out the leather for the upper he was cutting.

'*Arrey bhai*! Margaret herself gave me the reason to weep,' she said in a placatory tone. 'The war's ended, hasn't it, Safdar? So I was rejoicing that Barrey Bhaiya would be returning now and lots of people like him. She said nothing about Barrey Bhaiya, but when I mentioned the others she said flatly, "Provided they're still alive." This doubt has lodged itself in my heart – "Provided Barrey Bhaiya is also still alive." And Safdar, if something like that happens, my mother will die. Her problems and afflictions have reached the limit. There isn't a sorrow that God has not given her.' Her voice sounded very pained despite the fact that it was level.

'Yes, some sorrows are sent by God and some by one's near and dear ones. Truly, Cuckoo, anyone like that is terribly long-suffering and pitiable.'

'You're right,' her head was bent low again today. Then she went out of the shop.

'Both my students will have arrived by now.' She turned her bicycle towards the YWCA hurriedly.

Their soft dark brown hair tied in ribbons and their chubby round faces lowered, both the girls were bent over their notebooks, busy with their work. She was thinking, 'Why should I tell Safdar that, apart from other things, one of the burdens on my mind is that the college is due to re-open next week and I won't be able to get myself admitted?'

60

For one thing, Saulat had been ill. For several days she could not sit up because of her bouts of dizziness. And for another, she had been avoiding writing to Ammah Begum because of her own fear and anxiety.

It was frightening for her mother not to receive any news from home for a week. Besides one does start having strange nightmares when one is distressed. So she had started feeling homesick in Bombay.

'*Bhai*, I really must go now,' she would propose to her brother and sister-in-law in her fits of anxiety. On this occasion her brother realised, that once she left them no one knew when she would visit them again. She was deeply concerned about her son and, apart from that, on account of her son-in-law as well. Both these misgivings had filled her with apprehension and made her very tense. She had never been like that before. But her panic was increasing by the minute and she could no longer be persuaded to stay under any circumstances.

'I'll come again, if all's well, God willing,' she assured her brother.

'If only Mumani, Mamoo Mian and Dulhan had persuaded her to stay for at least a few more days,' Saulat had hoped that they would. The telegram lay open before her, and she felt the same sense of dread and disquiet which she used to experience as a child when she had been guilty of a misdemeanor, however minor, in her mother's absence.

In that short space of time she had scolded and spanked both of her children several times without good reason. She had shouted at the ayah without restraint, and today for the first time she had wished from the bottom of her heart, 'If only Asif Jah would return unexpectedly . . .' If only, she could have that kind of life, once again, blessed with security and free of care, which he had firmly placed in her grasp. She repeatedly cursed that moment in time when she had rented out her house in Dalhousie to Wooller's Mem Sahib, and had come away herself. Just to be together, for their sake, and for her own. Anyhow why did they fear being alone that much? In any case what kind of togetherness was this?

Very slowly the moment drew near when Ammah Begum arrived home from the station. Here were the stony white flanks of the gates of her home and the nirbasi hedge, with its beautiful, blackish, succulent leaves. The garden, the lawn were lush green as usual. The machine which pumped the water from the well was on and the buffalo stood grunting near its post. This house looked quieter since the death of its owner, but there was an air of absolute calm and familiarity around it. Even before she stepped into the house she felt as if someone had removed hundreds of needles boring into every nerve and blood vessel of her body.

She entered the house with tremendous delight and tranquillity surrounded by a bevy of girls and servants and went straight into her room to sit on her wooden divan, covered with spotless white sheets. It was as if she had never been away at all.

The container for her *paans* had been refilled with fresh lime and

244

catechu, and the *paans* lay wrapped in a piece of damp red cotton on a highly polished brass platter. When Shareef entered the room wheeling in the tea trolley she thought, with a great sense of contentment and thankfulness, 'What a blessing these daughters are! Just look at that! It seems as if I haven't been away at all.'

Arjumand had been busy getting her luggage unpacked, asking her dozens of questions about the things she had brought with her and getting Shareef to open and sort out her bed-roll and had thus avoided getting within range of any of her questions.

Saulat, who had been sitting near her, started picking on Seema all of a sudden. 'So, you've come out again, now. You should have stayed there till you'd finished studying. You and your brother are driving me crazy. Come, come with me again. You won't let me sit here, I know that for sure.'

She picked up Azam and literally herded Seema out of the room just when Mali brought the post in. Ammah Begum raised her serene and satisfied face to him and asked in response to his greeting, 'Are you well?' 'You must have bedded the tomato seedlings by now?' Then she placed an envelope in his hand and told him, 'Get this letter over to Barri Bitya's room.' She thought to herself, 'Thank God there is a letter from Asif Jah. Dear God, let Sheharyaar's letter come too. Then I shall say my thanksgiving prayers for the two of them, jointly.'

The sound of faint sobbing from Saulat's room rose by degrees to loud wails.

Ammah Begum's hand trembled and the cup slipped and overturned on to her lap but she did not even feel the burns from the scalding tea. Reaching Saulat's room with great difficulty, she found her lying help-lessly on the bed. Arjumand, panic-stricken and anxious, was busy unsuccessfully attempting to give her support.

'*Arrey*! At least tell me what's happened?' Unremitting woes and sorrows had dried up the wells of tears in her own eyes, 'What's the news?' her voice trembled nevertheless.

Slowly and gradually Arjumand told her the story. 'Now, whenever there's a letter from Asif Bhai she gets into a state. It's happened twice before in your absence.'

Saulat's distress intensified and some more time was bought. A reprieve was granted yet again. But for how long could that have continued? In the first opportune moment he could find, Shareef asked, 'Choti Bitya didn't come back then?'

'Oh, yes! Where is she?' said Ammah Begum. 'There was such a crisis on! She didn't come out to see me; she could at least have ventured out to see why Saulat was screaming. God, grant this girl some sense! See where she ends up with a disposition like hers!'

'See where she ends up with a disposition like hers,' Arjumand repeated to herself. 'She's ended up exactly where one would expect her to.'

Then somehow courage and skill surfaced in Arjumand, on the strength of which she could tell her mother everything, slowly and gently. Ammah Begum did not say even one word in answer to all that but just sat there, leaning against the bolster, staring unblinkingly into space. Her face was pale and her lips parched. But she kept a hold on herself with the perfect decorum and dignity to be expected from a lady of aristocratic descent. Bakhtiar's letter lay open beside her, pinned down by her knee. He had written her a letter full of love and affection, on thick, white monogrammed notepaper. Exactly in the manner one would use to cajole a little girl in distress:

'Ammah ji! Don't you worry. If you feel the slightest need for my presence, do write to me. Your son will immediately present himself, like the genie of the Arabian Nights, to deal with your problem and any difficulty. Ammah ji, believe me, I am not the old Bakhtiar I used to be. Now, I am my Ammah Begum's son and a responsible brother for my sisters. My heart is always with you, Ammah jaani!'

His peculiar style of writing, blending both the forms, the informal and the formal address, in a cosseting mood, had recently begun to endear itself to her so much!

61

In her moments of leisure, Margaret always wore a dress made of a very beautiful, pale pastel yellow silk printed with yellow asters. Her mother had made this for her. When she wore that dress, with its high neckline and baggy sleeves, she found herself slipping away from reality. And to become indifferent to reality cannot be a good thing. But then what can one do about the fact that sometimes she deliberately wanted to forget that she was miles away from her own country. Forget that she was serving as a WAAC in a foreign land.

These days she was working in the parachute department, in the dull job of receiving, checking and packing parachutes. When the time for her transfer from this department finally came, after great difficulty she was thrown into supplies. In ordinary circumstances, other WAACs considered themselves lucky to be appointed to this department, but she did not have a home to fill with eggs, butter, powdered milk and dried meat. Especially not, when in her own country her mother and both her sisters could not even dream of all these luxuries. Would Linda and Julie still be going to school? she wondered involuntarily, when she saw healthy schoolgirls walking on the roads, to and from school, their satchels slung round their necks. Now, after patient prayers and recovery from a prolonged illness like typhoid, she had been transferred to the Strangers' Home, which she had found more interesting than all the other departments she had served in. Staying close to people who are suffering and apart from the world makes your own problems seem simpler and lighter.

During this period when she met Liu Chu, or Safdar Yaaseen, through Li Fan's family, she drew a great sense of tranquillity from that too. The kind of tranquillity that comes from a feeling of friendship and concordance – in this foreign land he was also alone and homeless like her. And he was also very gentle, quiet and good-natured. Since she had met him, Margaret had not felt that overwhelming and deep sense of loneliness that she used to feel.

'Safdar Yaaseen is hard-working, responsible and a very decent boy.' When she heard those words about him from her acquaintances her neck would stiffen with pride for no reason at all.

She came from a town far south of his hometown, Peking. Her village was close to the canal. Rains were abundant in that area. But all these minor differences, arising from the distance, language and culture can only be acknowledged when you are in your own home country. When people are far away from their own homeland then such a huge and universally accepted difference as a difference of faith can also seem false. 'Take this, for instance: Safdar is a Muslim and I am Christian but despite that, he seems so close to me, to be such a kindred spirit.'

Safdar had never given her a false impression but still sometimes she found him more than just someone to herself – she felt as if he belonged to her. Especially during her moments of leisure, on her day off, when she was busy tidying her room and doing other such chores in a thoroughly domesticated manner, dressed in her yellow silk gown printed with the yellow asters, she would feel that he was even closer to her. Since the day he had placed that strange upper-class girl into her care with great faith and confidence she had assumed that she had an absolute claim on him. One does not take just anyone into one's confidence.

The shapely fingers of her tiny soft and plump hands were involved in lazily arranging the flowers in the vase and her mind was occupied with these racing thoughts.

'Whatever the reason, why should Safdar care so much for her? This is the thing which is unendurable. Even if Safdar had not been involved in the relationship I would have grown very fond of this girl – simple, straightforward and disinterested as she is! In all this time she has never given anyone cause for complaint. But to crown it all, the other day when I got there to spend my day off with them, the very mention of her ruined Safdar's mood. That much concern on behalf of a girl who is a stranger is unaccountable, I think. In fact, so far I haven't found a proper place in Safdar's heart.'

She felt miserable and a little resentful towards Cuckoo. 'What I'm going to do is say to her, '*Bhai*, you should go to Mrs Benjamin's room ... but ... but that means that Safdar would be thoroughly annoyed with me. She is his guest.' Margaret continued to dwell on that dilemma.

The door opened gently and Gaythi entered holding her notebooks and books on shorthand and book-keeping. She looked tired and pale. Her face was drawn and dark circles of sleeplessness ringed her eyes. All Margaret's plans were tossed away in one fell swoop. Giving her notice to quit the room and advising her to go and live with Mrs Benjamin were a far cry from her impulse to gather that broken-hearted being into the protection of her arms, to stroke her untidy hair into place, to kiss the pale forehead and despairing eyes, and to comfort her. However to express that much kindness so openly can also compromise one's honour. For some reason a person is shame-faced about exposing the drama of the melting of his own heart even before the person who is the object of the warm fires of sympathy which produce the thaw.

She looked at her penitently without moving from where she stood and said, 'You look far too pale and tired. Don't work so hard ...'

Gaythi's heart had been so crushed by grief that now a single sentence of affection or consideration would moisten her dark eyelashes.

'I won't any more,' she said in a spirit of helplessness and surrender, as she threw her books on the table in her old carefree manner. Then she steadied herself and almost immediately collected them up and rearranged them.

'There's a phone call for you, Miss Sahib ji,' the peon from the office came to tell Margaret.

'Huh! Looks as if I've been called back for an emergency.' She rose reluctantly and left the room walking with tiny unenthusiastic footsteps.

She could not believe it when she heard Safdar on the end of the telephone. 'Margaret! This is Safdar speaking.'

'*Arrey*, hello, Liu Chu!' Margaret immediately switched to Chinese, feeling at home. 'Well, what is it?'

'You had your day off the other day. I don't know which one of us was in a bad mood then, and that plan we had of going to the cinema fell through. I can take you today to make up for it. Are you willing to go?'

Safdar's voice sounded cheerful at the other end. He was in a very good mood. She did not want to wreck that mood. She wanted to see him happy forever.

'Well, what are you thinking?' The enthusiasm in Safdar's voice dropped.

'No. I am not thinking of anything at all. Tell me, will you come to collect me, or, where should I meet you?'

'I'll come there and pick you up. We just have to get to the Plaza.'

She could not even replace the receiver properly as she dashed back towards the room to get ready, feeling a little crazed by happiness and the wild racing of her heart. She felt like going out to the cinema with him still dressed in her yellow silk frock, but anyway, she knew she would have to change.

When Gaythi saw her rushed preparations she asked, 'What are you getting dressed for?'

'For the cinema. Safdar is coming to fetch me,' she replied, brushing her short shiny black hair.

'That's good if you're going to the cinema. For the past few days you've looked exceedingly bored.'

'Yes, I . . .' She stopped, and feeling guilty that Gaythi had guessed her secret thoughts, she said 'You come with us too.'

'Who? Me?' Gaythi laughed. She remembered how that day her decision to sit with him for her own safety had led her into such a sticky situation. 'I'll rest for a while, and then my students will come.' She stood in the verandah seeing them ride away on their bicycles, shoulder to shoulder and felt pleased. 'This Safdar is such a good man, he looks after everyone.'

'If you had asked Cuckoo she might have come along,' Margaret said in an attempt to make up for her narrowmindedness the other day.

'*Arrey*! No, no. You shouldn't even ask her something like that. You don't know; she comes from a very important family and this is something beneath her dignity.'

When Margaret heard this, she felt pleased and contented.

62

The letter she had written to her mother sat on her table for several days. And for several more days what continued to happen was that whenever she went out for something she would pick up the envelope and put it in the basket of her bicycle but remember it only when she had already missed the post office and the letterboxes along the way. 'I forgot to post the letter, almost as if I am frightened to post it,' she thought.

So that letter, which she had written with great courage and determination and partly at Safdar Yaaseen's behest, had still not been posted. It was not a lengthy composition. All she had written was:

'I am well here, and hope that all of you are keeping well too. My secretarial course is now nearly finished and I now have four very good tutorial students. Please convey my greetings to everyone in the house.

My salaams to Mali and Shareef.

There was no special need to say where she was staying because the letter was addressed at the top. To write about why she had left home was pointless. 'She will never be prepared to listen to what I have to say and if she were, who would allow her to believe me?' Gaythi had become resigned to that.

'It might have been better if I had given this letter to the peon; it would have been posted. Or to Margaret who would have definitely posted it.' The day Mrs. Benjamin said to her that she was going to the General Post Office, that she should tell her if she wanted anything done, she saw the frail, old lady who walked with great difficulty on her swollen feet, as extremely sympathetic and responsible. There was pride in her eyes and the comforting glimmer born from her sense of being useful to someone else. Gaythi did not feel like disappointing her.

'Yes! Mrs Benjamin. I have an important letter. You could post it for me; it would be a great favour.' She opened her drawer and placed that letter in Mrs Benjamin's hand. Mrs Benjamin removed the bag which was dangling from her wrist and placed it on the table, unzipped it very smartly and deposited the envelope in it.

As Gaythi saw her walk through the gates dressed in her navy blue polka-dotted frock, her hair piled into a wheel-shaped bun, she heaved a sigh of relief. Thank God, this letter which perhaps I would never have been able to post, will now be posted. She lay down on her bed and fell into an untimely sleep.

Her face glowing with a sense of responsibility, her eyebrows arched with pride and arrogance, Mrs Benjamin stood near the letter-box in front of the GPO and opened her bag. She fumbled through the mass of numerous receipts, pieces of paper and old letters, then pulled it out with trembling hands and dropped it into the letter-box.

That evening she stayed up late in her room, her lamp lit, searching through the drawers, her wardrobe and her shoe cupboard for the blank envelope in which Mr. Williams had sealed his letter addressed to the Post Master at the General Post Office. That envelope had not been found in the bag whilst she was there, so she had failed to accomplish the task which she had set out to do that evening. With both her hands she repeatedly pulled out the things crammed in her bag, looking through the papers and receipts.

Then, feeling frustrated, she threw all those papers which included many crumpled old envelopes into a drawer, thinking that she would now have to get another letter for the Post Master.

'But whatever happened to that envelope . . .?' She rolled her roundish eyes as she sat wondering for a very long time.

63

'All right then; you tell me. What else could I do? Issue a description, or file a report? What a scandal it would have been! This family is not in the kind of position where it is possible to issue a "Missing Persons" notice,' she said in a very helpless voice.

'Huh! The position of this family,' Bakhtiar stamped his feet. 'How could it have survived? Where is the position of your family? Show it to me. Where do you keep it safely?'

He stood up and then sat down on the chair again. 'You couldn't issue a notice like that but you could have informed me.'

'No. That couldn't be done either. I myself arrived home ten days after it had happened. What could I have accomplished by calling you? It was something beyond my imagination, it stunned and shocked me so much that I am amazed that I didn't go crazy myself. You can assume that I have only just now recovered enough to be able to call you. And Saulat was under the impression that she would return of her own accord within a few days.'

'You can assume . . .' he grumbled ill-naturedly. 'We should understand everything. Have you ever tried to understand us?'

'No, son! I was never capable of that.' She raised her head above the soft, pure white pillow and looked at his face which had blanched unexpectedly.

'This woman who is my mother has changed so much, so suddenly!' he thought, observing the dark circles round her large beautiful eyes and the lines on her forehead. 'All this has happened because her time is now past. That time which was hers has slipped from her grasp. And when someone loses his grip on moments and instants then he falls instead under their jurisdiction. And I am now demanding from her the answer to the forces imposed by one such moment of powerlessness.'

His head fell, and his tone softened.

'My intention is not to blame you. All I am saying is that if you had called me at the right time we could have put our heads together and come up with a solution.'

She lay there silently, her eyes closed.

He went on saying, 'She wasn't that contemptible or insignificant that her leaving in that manner should have meant nothing. However bad she might have been, she represents the honour of this family – the position of which matters to you so much.'

As she felt the gentleness and remorse in the tone of her enraged son, her tears spilt over. Not because of the cutting edge and fierceness of his tone but due to her own self-reproach. She felt like wailing at the top of her voice and telling him, 'Don't just keep quiet, making allowances for me. I deserve your disapprobation. I did not try to understand any one of you. I have been unfair to everyone, starting with Saulat. And I feel as if Nature, or maybe Saulat, has avenged herself against my injustice towards her.'

But who knows what withholds you from such admissions and emotional expression – keeping you silent, and dignified on the surface, whilst others assume that you still stand by your original rigid stance and your ability to feel things still lies dormant?

'And here you are crying in front of me so helplessly today! You, on whose lap I have laid this head and wept, God knows how often, in the past twenty-two or twenty-three years.' He was a very emotional and tender-spirited boy. 'Ammah Jaani!' He bent over her and let her tears fall on his hands. Then he added a few drops of spirit ammonia which

252

stood on the table to a glass of water and offered it to her as he changed the subject.

'When did Saulat Apa leave?'

'One day. I don't know when,' she said, her voice drenched in tears. Then she blew her nose into a handkerchief and said, 'The day we got your letter saying that you were coming – she left that same afternoon. She had to go, anyway. The people who had rented her cottage were leaving and also Asif Jah is due to arrive by the end of the month. I had even suggested that she should leave the children. "Once the cottage is vacated and you've reorganised your furniture you can come and get them." But she did not agree. She said, "We won't have any problems. We have friends there. And if I don't stay there now it will be difficult to sort out the house."'

'That's right. It's best if she organises the house before Asif Bhai returns. All right. You go to sleep now!' He bent towards her again, 'Sleep well. What I find distasteful is that you were suffering all this alone and you did not let me know. Whilst I am around there's no need for you to suffer like this! I am still alive.'

'Yes! God keep you safe,' she kissed his neck and then took his hand and made him sit down. 'I am perfectly all right. You sit near me.' She kept hold of his hand like a small child, frightened of being left alone, keeps his hand on top of his mother's, forcing her to sit with him.

'Bakhtiar!' she called as if she were calling out from the depths of a well.

'*Jee*,' he said gently.

'Like you said, maybe she is bad, but I tell you the truth, I never thought that for a second. She is self-willed. What I am sorry about is that when I tried to draw her closer to myself, I failed because of a succession of such incidents and calamities which did not give me the chance to make her aware of that feeling.'

'But what do you think? Where do you think she's gone?'

'I think she will have gone to her college.'

Bakhtiar's eyes opened in amazement. 'And in spite of that you did not enquire about her over there?'

Her eyes fell. Then she spoke slowly, 'Whenever I decided to do that, I could not carry out my intention fearing that if a reply came to my enquiry telling me that she was not there, then what would happen?'

'But whatever happened to Saulat Apa's reason?'

'Don't mention her! She just kept trying to persuade me from the day I returned that if this issue had not arisen then she would have found some other excuse and would definitely have gone anyway.'

'I have to say – I don't know for what reason – but somehow this matter has been treated with criminal neglect.' Bakhtiar had become angry again. But this time he rose and left without arguing the point further.

64

When she was told that her brother was waiting for her in the common room, she did not believe it at all.

Nevertheless she went there and when she saw Bakhtiar in the room, her footsteps came to a halt in the doorway. Stronger than her fear of rebuke and disapprobation was her sense of pique and mortification at not receiving a reply to her letter. Beyond that was her own disbelief at what she saw before her, with her own eyes.

Seeing her rooted to the spot, Bakhtiar walked towards her himself. He embraced her, took her by the hand and escorted her in.

'What are you thinking, Gaythi?' he asked her, noticing her silence. 'Do you think I should not have come to see you?'

'No. I'm wondering how you found me since no one answered the letter I wrote. And I did not have the courage to write a second one.'

'No one had a single letter from you. Did you post the letter yourself?'

'No, I gave it to someone to post. Then how did you trace me?'

'I didn't even know that you were here. It's only when I got back home from college that I discovered that you were not there and I just came here following a hunch. You weren't at the college which really disappointed me. This afternoon I was standing near the Plaza when I saw you coming this way on your bike. You whizzed past so I could not call out to you but I turned this way and when I saw you enter the gates I was relieved.'

Gaythi judged from his tone of voice that at least he harboured no contempt or hatred against her. With great courage she enquired about everyone in a superficially calm tone.

Each pause between the answers felt awkward as she would start wondering if Bakhtiar was going to ask her questions about why she had come away. But Bakhtiar did not ask her a single question along those lines because Arjumand had already told him all the details in her truthful and non-partisan manner.

'What time do you return from college?'

'I am not at the college.' She lowered her head.

'That makes sense. How could she have gone to college?' He did not ask her any further questions.

She volunteered herself, 'I have three tuition jobs and I am attending a secretarial course. I wrote all that in the letter.'

'That will no longer be necessary. It is late but however difficult it may be, I will get you admitted into the college before I go back.'

She looked so silent and woebegone that Bakhtiar felt pained. 'Whatever her failings might be, obstinacy, wilfulness and disobedience, she is the same Gaythi who, the moment she set eyes on him, would demand of him, "And what did you bring for me?" Then go through his pockets to find the bar of chocolate.'

'What is the last film you went to see?'

She looked at him in surprise, 'Who? Me? Bakhtiar Bhai, there has been no question of that.'

'There is now. Go and get ready quickly. We'll go to the cinema now.' He desperately wanted to erase from her heart the feeling that he was annoyed with her, or that she had done something out of the ordinary.

When he was leaving he went to see her at the hostel and reassured her very affectionately, 'Don't worry about exams or anything like that. All I wanted was for you to get admitted to the college now. There's no question of your taking the exams this year. I'll feel easier if I know that you are at the hostel. Don't do anything irresponsible. You know your admission would have been impossible without the help of a big "push" from someone.' Then he said, 'Our circumstances have changed. We'll be getting Arjumand married soon.'

'*Arrey*, Arjumand! Old girl! You're getting married? But to whom?' she wondered, but could not bring herself to ask.

Bakhtiar himself said, 'Arjumand does not have any objections to marrying Akbar. Then there are other considerations. He has come to know so many things about our family that everyone thinks this may be the best thing.'

Gaythi lowered her head, '"He has come to know so many things about our family and Arjumand agrees with what everyone thinks . . ." Truly, Arjumand! I admire the qualities you possess. But I lack them, and somehow there is no desire in me to possess them either.'

Then Bakhtiar started saying with great difficulty, 'What can I tell you? Circumstances have changed. We are now at a stage in our lives when we have to have the strength to face and endure every reality. Barrey Bhaiya is never going to return now. His name is not on the list of

255

those missing in action but on the one of those killed in action. We have hidden this news from Ammah, and that's a mistake as well, but news like this, to do with the war, can be hidden for a long time.'

Gaythi felt dizzy. But she stood there, dry-eyed. Her brother saw her face whiten and he placed his hand on her shoulder, saying, 'You are a very brave girl. Pray for me. I hadn't the slightest inkling that I would have to shoulder everyone's share of responsibilities. And now, look; don't allow yourself to be intimidated ever again. If you have a problem, talk to me. You were so devoted to Abba Mian. Don't you remember how calmly and with what fortitude he faced conflict and opposition to his own views?'

Then he stopped, looked at Gaythi and said, 'It is a great thing if people have the capacity for sympathy and being supportive, but I don't believe that one should be above receiving sympathy and support oneself.'

Then he placed a hand on her back and said, 'Goodbye!' before adding, 'I have spoken to Chacha ji. They are very kind and decent people. I have put their names down again as guardians, but you should not go there too often either. They'll call you whenever they want to. That's all right, isn't it?'

She nodded gently and her brother set off on his return journey. Enormous tears poured down her face.

'How wretched I am! My brother has departed from this earth. My mother has had to endure tragedies and a huge shock merely because of my impetuousness and unyielding attitude – dear God, Who is worthy of honours, You let me be twinned with Arjumand, but did not make me at all like her!' She went to her room thinking about all this.

65

He had been standing in the corner nearest the window for a long time, painting an elongated bamboo screen woven with very white glossy reeds. His brush moved rapidly. And she had also been sitting silently watching him for a very long time as she leaned against the strong willow chair.

White, maroon, light brown, bright red, green and black struck out along with the deep shiny blues, gold and a sharp turquoise. A constant shower of colours rained forth from his brush which had only three or four fibres on it.

And these colours scattered on the bamboo reeds which almost stuck together, were causing chaos and confusion in her head.

One of the features of boredom and disgust is that the clamour inside your head grows louder but you continue to tolerate that noise, the disgust and the irritation with immense calm and quiet. So much so that the onlookers assume that you are perfectly calm and in absolutely no hurry at all.

Although in fact at that moment what she really wanted to do was to get up in irritation, snatch the brush from his hand and throw it away, and with her fingers smear and smudge together the damp paints on that nearly complete screen.

And then to push his strong fingers stained with paints into the bowl of turpentine oil and clean them with her own hands. To brush back his straight grey hair which fell on his forehead, look into his eyes and ask, 'Have you gone mad? I am sitting here and you are immersed in something which does not exist.'

But she did none of these things. Instead she asked him a question, 'Why don't you paint on silk or satin?'

Safdar looked back at her in reply, 'Because I hate the softness of silk and the sheen on satin. I don't know why but the glossy sheen on satin drives me mad. I find it satisfying to see shapes appearing on rough and hardy surfaces.'

Despite her misery and amazement, very calmly she kept watching this man who sat before her, half turned towards her, dressed only in shorts and a vest. Slowly the words rose to her lips, 'I think you're certainly a little crazy.'

'Crazy!' He laughed as he bent down to take some more paint from the cup. 'What's crazy about this?'

'If this isn't lunacy then what is it? You hate the sheen of satin and the softness of silk puts you off.'

Safdar did not respond to Margaret's comment. He was now painting the cock's-comb with the brilliant red of fresh blood, which carried traces of blackness along some of the edges, whilst he thought, 'These are the secrets which you do not understand, Margaret, which you are so quick to link with madness. And what would you say if you saw my painting on the bark of a fig tree? But why would I show you that? The only person who can appreciate it is the one for whom I made it. I took so many days to settle on a subject for it and now that it is ready, I have not had the opportunity to show it to her. She came here for a few moments in such a rush before she got herself admitted to the college.'

How pleased he had been to hear of everything that had happened.

Thank goodness, the second letter had managed to reach her home. He had felt so relieved of the burden of responsibility for her, as if an enormous weight had been lifted off his shoulders.

'Ouf! What a great responsibility it is to be entrusted with the care of a girl who is not your own!' he had thought.

He had not seen her since. Except for once when he saw her sitting alongside her brother in a green car. The person who was driving the green vehicle was certainly her brother's friend. Then he saw the three of them get out and go into a confectionery shop.

She appeared to be quiet but content, dressed in a slate grey shirt and a white dupatta. He could have stopped there to have a word with her. But he moved immediately and went in a different direction, impelled by an unnameable emotion.

'There! He's lost again. With such difficulty I'd found a subject to attract his attention. So this means that I have to sit here until the evening and ruin my Sunday; and these fried prawns, sliced fish and grated carrots which I brought for him, which I have worked so hard over, will sit here getting cold and stinky.'

She sat for a little while seething and disgruntled, then stood up very calmly, and said, 'All right then, I think I'll go now.' Then she went over and stood near the table on which the stove was kept, 'Take the food from the lunch-box and warm it up, and leave the lunch-box at Li Fan's place. I'll come and pick it up sometime.'

Safdar left his paint-soaked brush in the cup and wiping his hands on a brownish towel said, '*Arrey*! I thought you were enjoying watching me so much that you didn't even want to chat. Otherwise, I'd have stopped right then. And anyhow, it isn't as though it's late now!'

'It's nearly one o'clock,' Margaret glanced at her wrist, and then watching him rubbing his fingers on the towel said, 'So you've cleaned up your hands now?'

'You start boiling the rice, my hands won't take a moment to clean.' He lifted the cup full of turps which stood on the shelf and immersed his fingers into it. When he came out of his bath, the food was already laid on the table.

'Where did you put the books which were on this table?' he asked rubbing his head with a towel.

'There they are, your books.' She pointed to the shelf.

While he was tucking into the food enthusiastically, Margaret said, somewhat abruptly, 'Cuckoo is such a thoughtless girl, she hasn't enquired even once in a great many days.'

'About whom?' Safdar asked without looking at her.

'Forget about me, but she hasn't even asked about you. That's what people in this country are like, you know. And well, I'll be honest, she seems to me to be a really spoilt girl – intractable and stubborn.'

Now that the girl did not need anyone's sympathy, Margaret felt that there was no harm in talking about her in that vein. Sometimes she did feel really jealous of her.

'If women stopped talking about others it wouldn't do any harm,' he said with a smile.

'If women stop talking about others, they wouldn't be able to manage.'

'Why's that?'

'Because, to tell you the truth, Safdar, if women stop talking about others their own future and the survival of the family would be at risk.'

Safdar laughed loudly.

'What does it matter to you? You can carry on laughing. OK, tell me then, is it wrong to talk about someone even if he is that selfish and uncaring?'

'Certainly, you can do that. But she isn't like that, like you think she is.'

He observed Margaret's colour changing and her thoughtful eyes and spoke seriously, 'Actually, if you appreciated the fact that she does not belong to your class or mine, then you would definitely not raise objections like this against her. The fact is that there is nothing in common between us and her.'

This brief statement comforted Margaret a good deal. She no longer felt peeved with that churlish girl.

She left the chopsticks encrusted with rice in the bowl and looked at his face. He still looked tired.

'Why do you work so hard?'

'Do you think I've come here to relax?' he smiled.

'No, but you don't rest even on your day off. You've been struggling with that painting since the morning.'

'The indulgence of your passions is satisfying, Margaret!' He looked fondly at the painting which was nearly complete. 'And I have taken up the paintbrush after a long gap this time. Don't you like it?' Then he stopped. 'Oh, yes, you're not really enthusiastic about all these things!'

'Why? Whoever said that? Why ever not?' She scrutinised the picture closely to demonstrate her enthusiasm. She felt a sense of revulsion against the images – the squidgy exposed flesh of the cockerel which had lost its feathers in the fight, and the white and black quills of the plucked feathers.

'"The Plucked Cockerel" might be a good title for this painting.' She expressed further interest.

'I've already decided on a name.'

'How repulsive this wretched bird is,' Margaret could not help stating the truth in a momentary lapse of attention, and then she panicked. 'But what I meant to say was . . .'

'That's all right.' There was a glimmer of satisfaction on Safdar's face. 'You feel repulsed, don't you? That's what I wanted.'

'What is the title?' Margaret was trying her best to take an interest.

'It's called, "After the War".'

She laughed a meaningful laugh. But Safdar was well aware that she had not understood anything.

That evening when he went to the YWCA to drop her there after they had been to the cinema, he took her in his arms and looked into her eyes as they stood near the building. Then his face which was drawing slowly closer to hers stopped abruptly. His arms slackened their hold. He swung round quickly and mounted his bicycle bidding her goodbye and left.

That Chinese girl, dressed in a green skirt and a white blouse, said to herself as she entered the gates, 'People are so right when they say that we Chinese are mysterious and difficult to understand.'

66

After the games were over, they all sat on the lawns, on the grass, under various trees or on the benches. As the dusk waned, its redness was dissolving slowly into black. The church bells were ringing. Then a very faint and vague sound of the muezzin's call to prayer echoed through the atmosphere, and Gaythi's heart was plunged into grief. Whenever she sat idle at times like this, she would remember Sheharyaar.

'Barrey Bhaiya, I haven't seen you for so many years. And I hadn't missed you that much but now it feels as if we've only just lost you.'

She went to her own room intending to pray. When she raised her hands in supplication she could not pray for the deliverance of her brother's soul. 'It would make me feel that you really have departed,' she wept bitterly.

Then she lowered her hands and sat on the prayer mat thinking, 'It seems to me as if this large scale war occurred only to take my brother's life. I can't even share my grief with anyone in this hostel brimming with people. I could not endure it if this anguish which is torturing my soul was met with a superficial show of sympathy. The kind which is forced or half-hearted – for that would be an insult to one's distress, wouldn't it?'

She longed to relieve her sorrow by leaning her head against her mother's breast, and sobbing her heart out, by making her cry in unison with herself. 'Or else . . . or else . . .' her brain hesitated. She could sit on her bicycle and head straight towards Safdar Yaaseen's shop, reeking of leather and shoe polishes, go and sit on the salesman's stool, amidst the shoes ranked in the showcases and say to him, 'Did you see that, Liu Chu? My wretched heart proved to be right in its fears.'

That man, who was not her compatriot, who did not belong to her class, was well versed in the art of respecting other people's grief. But this was no longer possible.

'The intelligent only need a clue,' Bakhtiar's words echoed in her ears. 'It is a very good thing if people retain the ability to sympathise and be supportive, but what I do not approve of is that one should lose the ability to receive sympathy and take support.'

Even beyond that was the hint which was concealed in the several pairs of shoes Bakhtiar had bought for her, quite unnecessarily, and in the words he had said, as he gave them to her, 'I am sure that I have bought you so many things that for several days now you will not need to wander round the shops or bazaars in search of things you need.'

'No, even if I need to now, I will endeavour to do so as little as possible. I will definitely not add to the problems of this brother of mine who is trying to meet all his responsibilities with the utmost grace. How generous and forgiving my brother is! Bakhtiar Bhaiya, your big-heartedness and consideration has cast chains round my feet.

'It does not matter if you believe that I am ungrateful and churlish, Safdar! What harm can it do? This is how we are trained into understanding and maintaining our status and dignity. He could thank Chacha ji in every possible way and appoint him my guardian but in spite of my telling him everything, he could not feel that you were my best guardian. He could not bring himself to say even one word of thanks to you. Now, tell me, how can I deal with that?

'Whatever happens, I will not hurt his feelings now.'

She folded the prayer mat and put it away inside the wardrobe and glanced round her small, peaceful room. She was not in a dormitory this time. Bakhtiar had managed to get her a room which had become available by chance.

He had bought her a lot of things: her favourite packets of chocolate, packets of biscuits, jars of jam and pickles. She kept remembering the new untamed mare which had broken free and escaped because of the mistreatment of the new stable-hand who had replaced their old groom. Two days later, she had strolled back and started grazing close by the gate. Abba Mian had gone and stroked her flank, breathed deeply against her nostrils, and then tied up a front leg and a hind leg and placed some soft hay and a bucket of clean fodder near her. Later she stood in the stable, groomed and scrubbed, dipping her head to graze on the soft grass as if she had never left the place.

She could see the blackened boughs of the trees dancing through the window panes. Beyond that was the kohl-darkened sky, covered with the deepening dusk. The bell was ringing in the dining hall and clusters of girls were heading towards it. Security and peace of mind had found her, cajoled her and brought her under their own protection once again.

Through the straying folds of the thick dining room curtains and the gleaming window pane smiled a pale and pathetic moon. Spotless table-cloths draped over the long tables, the pleasant fragrance from the flower-filled vases which stood amidst the shining cutlery and the plates, gentle laughter filled with gay abandon, soft conversation punctuated by the clink of knives and forks against china, all these things were guarantors of protection and of freedom from worry.

In spite of this, several times she missed the environment of the YWCA overflowing with care, responsibility and hard work. And she found the weight of the heavy chains of love very hard to endure. She prayed before she went to sleep, 'Dear God, give me the intelligence and the conscious-ness I need to stay on the path which is straight and narrow.'

67

The date for Arjumand's marriage had been deliberately chosen to fall during her college term time, because her good sense and her resolution were still suspect and no one could be certain that her presence would not occasion some kind of problem or unpleasantness. She had received the letter confirming the date. Even now it was only Bakhtiar who wrote to her. It was the warmest morning of the summer and she woke up feeling extremely hot. In the middle of her bath she remembered that it was Sunday the next day, and that Arjumand would be getting married and that she wouldn't be there.

The fixing of that date could be construed to mean that perhaps they did not want her ever to come home. It was quite possible that Bakhtiar Bhaiya had come looking for her entirely on his own initiative and got her a place at the college. And that brief letter from Ammah Begum which she had received after she had joined the college may have been written at his insistence. That would explain why she had not received an answer to her own letter.

The text of that brief letter reverberated through her memory. She had written that it was a relief to hear about her admission to the college, that she should write to them for anything she needed besides her fees, and now that she had lost so much time, Bakhtiar thought that perhaps it was best if she came back only during the summer holidays.

She had not had any letters from Arjumand and she kept thinking that she would write after Arjumand had written to her. There is no way I will write to Arjumand unless I know what she thinks of me.

'And now she is getting married tomorrow. If only she had written me a letter! Never mind, I wish her every happiness.'

She could not envisage who would attend the wedding and what it would be like. 'Well, whether others come or not does not signify. I, for one, will not be there,' she thought, again and again. In all that time, she had never before missed her home so much.

'Who would have thought that I would not be there at my twin sister's wedding?' She could not settle down in class. She had not mentioned to anyone that her own sister was getting married the next day, on Sunday. On Sunday morning she had stood in the bathroom and wept to her heart's content. Deeper than her anguish at being unable to attend the wedding was the hurt caused by Arjumand's indifference.

Then she tried to console herself. 'That's all right! People like me deserve to be treated like this. In fact, I deserve worse punishment.'

That Sunday Chacha ji came to fetch her after a long period. He had had parathas stuffed with potatoes cooked for her. After consuming the steaming buttery parathas and mango pickle, and drinking a glass of *lassi*, she thought contentedly, 'Well, at least this is a blessing. When I come here I feel as if I am in my own home. And the best thing about being here is that no one bombards you with questions. Huda is inquisitive, but he doesn't live here. Sometimes questions appear in Chachi ji's eyes but never dare to emerge on her tongue for fear of Chacha ji.'

She stretched out on the small cot woven with cotton tape and went to sleep not caring about anything at all. Chachi ji sat on a low stool, close to her bed, rolling strips of paper into tapers to induce sneezing artificially.

68

That Sunday morning was also hot and silent like every other day. There was no noise, activity or any signs of panic in the house.

Saulat, who had been there for a week now, was busy getting her children bathed and changed according to her routine since the children's ayah, who was sick, had been left behind at Dalhousie. Asif Jah reclined in an armchair reading a newspaper on the outside verandah. Bakhtiar, who had only just woken up, was taking his breakfast in Ammah Begum's room. Chachi jaan sat on the wooden divan close to Ammah Begum sewing a tinselly edging on to a brash turquoise *dupatta* which had been rolled tightly into a wavy rope. That was the only evidence of the wedding which was under way in that house.

Arjumand had woken up very early that day, like every other, and had bathed and said her prayers. Then she took Ammah Begum's tea to her bedroom and left quietly when she found that she was still praying.

In fact she was feeling intensely shy of her but this wedding was being solemnised so quietly and on such an ordinary scale that she could not sit huddled in a corner. There was only one guest for the wedding. This was Chachi jaan who had come because she had only heard the news fifteen or twenty days ago that Sheharyaar was missing and thought that this was indeed the case.

She had come to give support to Ammah Begum but had been persuaded to stay for Arjumand's wedding.

'It's not a wedding really, only the ritual ceremony!' Ammah Begum had said with a resignation steeped in unfulfilled longings. She felt thoroughly disheartened. Two or three times in the day she would come up with the words, 'A fine war that was. It took away all our peace of mind. What a fight that was which should have had nothing to do with us.'

Arjumand was going round getting the rooms cleaned. Now she entered Ammah Begum's room. She felt a little embarrassed at the sight of the *dupatta* on which Chachi jaan was working.

'*Arrey, bhai,* come here.' Chachi jaan took the duster from her hand and pinned it down under her knee. 'We've never seen a bride like this who goes round on her wedding day getting the house cleaned.' Her head lowered, Arjumand sat down between her and Bakhtiar.

'Surely this is too much? However simple the wedding might be, the bride should get her rest.'

'Yes. Why have you been wearing yourself out since the morning? Go and take a shower. See how hot it is! You could have told Shareef to do this, but you are quite unable to say anything,' Bakhtiar commented.

'This girl of yours is so passive,' Chachi jaan pretended she knew nothing about Gaythi, but she knew everything.

'This girl is such a good girl!' Bakhtiar embraced her and then said, kissing the top of her head, 'I shall have to worry about the house when she leaves. I was completely relaxed about it because of her.'

She remained seated, her head lowered. Her eyes were moist and looked even more beautiful when she raised her head.

'You really should have rested. Come, let me take you to your room.'

She leaned her head against his shoulder and started crying. 'Don't weep now. You'll feel ill,' Ammah Begum said, wiping her own eyes dry.

Bakhtiar took her towards her room, 'Look, don't be silly. You are such a sensible girl. What's there to cry about? Look at me – there's a smile now, there it is!'

She smiled. 'You go and have your breakfast.'

'Right. Promise me you won't cry any more?'

'I promise. Please go.' But as soon as he stepped out of the room she laid her head on the pillow and began to shed tears.

'They tell me not to cry. You miss everyone so much on occasions like this. How is it possible for me not to miss my father, think of my brother, or that wretched, loveless Gaythi? She left because she was angry, but what wrong did I do her? She did not write to me. Now she writes letters to Bakhtiar Bhaiya and Ammah. She could have written a few words to me too. But she does not love me at all. And even after hearing about my marriage, she did not write a single word. And I wanted to say so many things to her. Maybe, she is annoyed with me anyway.'

She picked up Akbar's photograph which stood on the table and looked at it, 'I am getting married to someone she dislikes – but you are not that bad . . .' She looked at his picture and smiled.

'I wonder what you'll look like with a *sehra*, its veil of flowers cascading across your face!' Her tears then stopped of their own accord and she went into the bathroom to take a shower.

After lunch, however, the house felt as if activity and chaos were descending upon it. Marquees were being erected on the lawn outside now. Inside it was still relatively peaceful because only tea was to be served and that, too, in a mixed gathering of both men and women. There can't have been more than thirty or forty people, including the bridegroom's party.

'Oh, it's such a shame. You've had a really quiet wedding. It needn't have been this quiet, surely?' Chachi jaan kept repeating endlessly.

'You cannot guess how anxious my heart is, sister. My heart and mind can no longer take the strain of entertaining. You need calm and peace of mind for all that.'

'Yes. That's so true. God bless you with peace of mind.' The depth of the sighs which accompanied that remark did not accurately reflect the relative lack of depth of her emotions.

When the time for the arrival of the wedding party came near Saulat also became tearful. She hid from Ammah Begum and wept for a long time. Then Asif Jah tried to console her, 'Look, what will we do if you lose heart like this? Think of your mother. And you should be with that poor girl at this time! I feel really pained at the subdued and forlorn manner in which this wedding is being conducted.'

Saulat dried her tears and looked at that man who was trying to explain things to her very simply and honestly. The man who had returned to her alive and in one piece after a very long absence. But he had become extremely despondent, and now, in comparison with her, looked even older than he used to before he left. But now Saulat had a great deal more patience and tolerance for him than she used to have.

'You're right.' And she went to see Arjumand, who was alone in the bedroom.

Arjumand's hands were cold, she felt confused and overwhelmed by a wild desire to call out aloud, 'Gaythi, where are you? Come here. Give me some support.' Saulat Apa entered the room just then.

'Now you should steady yourself. Be strong.' She placed a hand on her back and then started weeping again.

She started sobbing with her, thinking, 'How strange our ways are! If people around you did not create this atmosphere, the bride would not feel so confused. If Gaythi had been here she'd be sure to comment on this; I've only dared to think it.'

'*Bhai*, we must have the "viewing ceremony",' Chachi jaan started demanding the moment she saw her dressed as a bride. 'We have to have some of the rituals! What's the bridegroom going to think?'

'Yes, certainly. Do get it done . . .' Ammah Begum gave in, though she found it all tiresome and painful.

Akbar looked at her open eyes in the mirror under the shade of the red canopy enmeshed with sequins and thought, 'I used to prefer Gaythi's looks but right now your familiar face looks very new and endearing in the mirror. The truth of the matter is, that you are the one who is really beautiful. This piece of jewellery on your forehead suits you, the glitter shining in your hair looks lovely; it may not have suited her straight and very black hair.'

69

She stood inside the old familiar station, in the dusky darkness of the evening, all the doubts and fears of an uninvited guest crowding into her heart. It was one of the last few days in June.

Before the holidays had begun she had received a money order with a note on the coupon from Bakhtiar which said, 'I'm sending your fare. You should set off the day your holidays begin and send us a telegram announcing the time of your arrival.'

'I sent a telegram but I can't see anyone.' Now her suspicion was solidifying into crystal clear certainty that all this warmth and conciliation emanated only from Bakhtiar Bhaiya. No one else wanted to retain any relationship with her.

'*Arrey, Bibi*! Here you are! And there I have been, look-ing, and look-ing all over the platform for you.'

She swung round in surprise, '*As-salaam-ulaikum*! Shareef!'

'May you live long, Bibi! But where were you hiding? I thought that maybe Begum Sahib had read the time wrongly.'

'Who is at home?'

'May you all live forever but who else would you expect to be at home – but us and our Begum Sahib?' Then he said with a start, '*Arrey*, you're standing there, holding your ash-atte case yourself. Please give it to me.'

'No, Shareef. The attache case is not that heavy. And also we ought to be in the habit of doing our own work.'

'Yes. You ought to be. But, child, we're still alive, *haan*!' He took the attache case from her hand. There was sweetness in his tone, and paternalistic affection. Gaythi took heart.

When Shareef had had her luggage stowed on the *tonga* and sat down in the front seat himself she asked, 'Shareef, how is Ammah?'

'Well, you'll see for yourself, *Bibi*! She's been completely broken by her anxiety about Barrey Bhaiya. God Almighty will solve her problems. I have promised to make offerings in the name of our saint, Barrey Pir Sahib. When he returns I shall cook a cauldron of sweet rice and send it up to the shrine, and I shall light a lamp at the *mahjid*.'

'Do you still say *mahjid*, instead of *masjid*?' she tried to change the subject.

'What d'you expect, child? Can we start talking different now? It's all downhill now, what is left of our time on this earth.'

She looked up at him. His hair was besmirched with grey.

'*Arrey*, Shareef! How grey you are!' she tried to distract his attention since she did not have the strength to hear such hopeful statements about Barrey Bhaiya's return.

'You're saying that to us, wait till you've seen Begum Sahib. Let alone all of us, Saulat Bitya's bridegroom has gone so aged. I was shaken when I saw him. I'll say this, if Barrey Bhaiya . . .'

'Is that so, Shareef? Has Asif Bhai started looking really old?' she interrupted him hastily.

'What else did you think . . . now he really does not look a match for *bitya*. Even before now it was always more a question of . . .' He became silent.

'Who came to attend Arjumand's wedding?'

'*Arrey*! Who? – I swear upon my honour, *bitya*, there were more people around when our Sahib died. The only guest who came to stay was Chachi jaan.'

'Really? Chachi jaan came?'

'*Arrey*, yes. It was a kind of a visit – she had heard the news that Barrey Bhaiya was missing and so she came to reassure Begum Sahib. *Bhai*, she used to be very fond of Barrey Bhaiya too. I swear to you, she used to cry in secret so that Begum Sahib should not worry. *Arrey*, what I say is . . . '

But she interrupted him again, 'Shareef, what did you think of the bridegroom?'

'What do you think? He's a boy we've seen and known. God protect him, he looked so good, you needed to worry about the evil eye, and the truth is, *bhai*, that there are few brides who can look as wonderful as our *bitya* did. What a light from heaven glowed upon her face. She looked really beautiful. It seems like yesterday when I used to take both of you riding on my shoulders, as I went about the house doing my work.'

'After how many days did she leave for Delhi?'

'*Arrey*! She left our house the very next day. They were going up to the mountains first and then to Delhi – *Bitya* cried so much when she was leaving. Then, she took me aside and said, "Listen, Shareef, don't let Ammah suffer in any way." '

Gaythi sat quietly listening. The station was quite close to the house. The rest of the journey was spent in silence.

'This house and everything in it seems so changed that one cannot believe it!' The deserted verandahs and rooms ranged from one end to the other in silence grated upon her. Despite the fact that the house was as clean and orderly as before, there was a numbness and silence everywhere. She was utterly shocked at the sight of her mother. Some people get so cruelly crushed beneath the tread of time. She had gone completely grey and her skin sagged but, worst of all, the frailty of age had crept into her temperament. There was a decline in the majesty which had surrounded her. It seemed as if in that one year she had aged by ten years.

Who knows what had contributed towards that process but she only held herself responsible for all that. She prayed once again in her heart to stay resolute, 'Dear God! Give me the capacity to think and live according to their expectations. And what is the harm if one does live according to the wishes of others? In fact, that is the easiest thing to do.'

Both of them were trying very hard to avoid even mentioning the unpleasant memories which lay in the past.

She started looking after the house the very next day. At first she made a few changes in the rooms. The shifting around of things can help to alleviate the sad lifelessness infused in the environment. She instructed Mali to arrange flowers in the vases every day or just foliage if there were no fresh flowers in the garden.

And this helped to reduce the emptiness which had become part of the house. Sometimes she would think, 'This house is really a sieve. Its entire life is riddled with gaps and empty spaces. And even now that the two of us from this family are here together, there are distances and voids between us. Although we are both trying our utmost to be very considerate towards each other, and both of us try our best to ensure that there should be no occasion for disagreement between us, yet this very warmth and caution is in itself the real void. When we are discourteous to each other and careless in our behaviour, that signifies our mutual trust and the filling up of those voids in between.'

She picked the purple berries from the back garden and took them to Ammah Begum.

'Did you see these berries? This time they're bigger than ever.'

'Yes,' her mother's eyes filled with tears, 'the one who had them planted did not have the good fortune to taste their juice. And what will we do here with so many berries?'

All her joy evaporated. She looked at them dejectedly.

'What you should do is send a few to Shareef's household and send some to Arjumand's mother-in-law. Akbar really loves them, God protect him, but he is not here either.'

She picked up the basket and went to the pantry. They seemed quite useless to her now.

After she had left the room, Ammah Begum opened the Book of Five Prayers and started reading it. Gaythi took her sewing into her mother's room and came and sat on the wooden divan in there. If the only two people living in a house that size choose to sit in different rooms it can seem even more desolate.

'It might be better, Ammah Begum, to let this house. A small bungalow would be sufficient now.'

'Oh no, God forbid that a small bungalow should suffice! Don't say things like that.'

Along with all his other work, Shareef did all the cook's work now too. For that reason she had had to get the rooms cleaned one by one. Today she was going to do Ammah Begum's room.

'If you say your prayers on the verandah I can get your room cleaned in the time it takes you to say your rosary.'

'The room's quite clean. Poor Shareef sees to every corner without my even telling him.'

'I meant to rearrange things a little. If this bed is moved over to this side and the table into that corner there'll be a bit more space and it will look a little different.'

'Forget the "different look". It drives me mad. Let my room be. It will stay as it is. When I sit here I feel as if the house is full as it used to be. Himself will emerge just now and sit on his favourite chair. And when I go to sit over there on that wooden divan to have my breakfast, the boys will turn up and will be sure to eat something with me.'

She looked at her mother with pained eyes, thinking, 'Ammah Begum avoids saying Barrey Bhaiya's name now. Whenever the need to mention him arises she uses the word "boys".'

And Ammah Begum wondered if she had offended her by opposing her plan, so she added by way of explanation, 'The thing is, child, when you get old, you just get used to having things a certain way, and if anything changes in that routine, then your very soul becomes perturbed.'

'And how stupid I am to be advising her to leave this house and move to another one, in which her soul would be utterly restless.'

270

Ammah Begum was not so old, or old-fashioned, as to be alarmed by the arrival of the mail, let alone telegrams. But Gaythi had noticed lately that she would be restless when it was time for the post to arrive.

She read Arjumand's letter and gave it to her daughter with trembling fingers. It said right at the beginning, 'I am not so concerned as I was before, knowing that Gaythi will be there by now. I am longing to be there at the moment. She'll go back and God knows when we shall be able to see each other again.'

'Really! So this is how it is.' She began to regret the fact that she herself had not written a letter to her. 'And I should have been the one to write. She was getting married. How false and mean-hearted we humans can be! Why does each of us always want to have the upper hand in relation to the other?'

70

Thick clouds besieged them from every direction. It looked as though the breeze had scattered kohl whilst it strolled drunkenly across the sky, which darkened by the second. The green of the trees in the compound and beyond that, of those lining the street, turned inky black. She sat on the front verandah reading a book. It was then only eleven o'clock in the morning. 'I'll have to go inside and switch the light on,' she thought, looking at the dark clouds spilling across the sky.

'Now, let's see how long it takes Shareef to get back from the station. I've popped into the kitchen twice to check on the cooking; I hope the food won't get burnt because then he'll tease me for being such a nincompoop. I don't even know when you add the water to thin the sauce.'

She could not follow a single word she was reading because of her fears and concern. She took a hairpin from her hair and stuck it in to mark her page, left the book on the table, and went into the kitchen.

The curry spices for the sauce were singing with a loud hiss and their fragrance as they roasted at a high temperature filled the kitchen. She fumbled in the bread box and pulled out a piece of stale bread to eat with a piece of meat and the sauce, then removed the saucepan from the fire and placed it on the table.

'Is there anything more delicious than the spices roasting at this stage

271

of the cooking?' She was eating slowly with relish, as she kept a look-out through the window.

Rattle, rattle – she heard the sound of the trap outside.

Shareef's trap entered through the gate in the back yard. She felt amused seeing him huddled amidst those tall wicker baskets which filled the trap, and almost looking like one himself. The vehicle stopped near the shelter for the buffalo and Shareef jumped out. One by one he unloaded the baskets covered with pieces of sackcloth sewn round the edges, and then paid the driver.

'So there's pilfering going on in the kitchen behind my back?'

'Pilfering going on, or me minding your cooking? You went off and glued yourself to the station. I thought the ticket collector had appointed you to check the tickets.'

'*Arrey, bhai.* It's no joke getting clearance from the railway staff these days! This bitch of a war's over but she's left her curse behind. Difficulties everywhere, problems everywhere. After all, we used to clear fifty baskets at a time even when the land had not been divided and then within minutes we used to send them off to your Chacha Abba and Phuphi Begum in Madras and Calcutta.' Shareef always referred to the past with great gusto and enthusiasm.

Mali had taken the baskets inside. She came through the pantry on to the verandah. Ammah Begum sat on a chair, the straw scattered around her on the floor of the verandah. The flavours of the various types of mangoes blended, wafting through the entire house.

'Do you see how silly Munshi ji has been! He could have sent these mangoes directly from there to Bakhtiar and Saulat. Now we have to go to the expense all over again, and the trouble, too.'

Shareef separated a few of the unripe langra mangoes which still needed to be kept in the straw while Ammah Begum was arranging them on salvers for distribution amongst their friends and acquaintances.

'I'll keep these separately in the straw. Barrey Bhaiya is specially fond of these. Who knows he might even come in the next ten days or so.'

Her face blanched – Gaythi took the mangoes from Shareef's hand and mixed them with the others.

'All right. Here, take this tray and tell Mali to deliver it to Arjumand's in-laws.' Then she took him aside and said, 'Shareef, why do you always keep mentioning Barrey Bhaiya? If he does come back, we can sort things out. It just upsets Ammah for nothing.'

He looked at her face and became silent.

After lunch Ammah Begum took dusehri mangoes and kept them on her plate.

'Have a langra, you like those,' she said.

'No, you eat that. I prefer lighter things now.'

She guessed why Ammah had not taken the langra mango.

It was drizzling outside, and a very gentle pleasant breeze rustled through. Ammah Begum had retired to her bedroom. Gaythi brought the book into her own room. 'It was an afternoon exactly like this one when Sajjad Bhai read our palms as we sat on the verandah at the back.' When the weather is as pleasant as this, all your old scattered memories assemble in the corners of your mind to refresh and adorn themselves. Different conversations and various events link and slot together with each other, falling into place. 'And it was after that day, for some reason, that Saulat Apa started behaving tersely with me. Although, he hadn't even quite finished reading my palm.' Along with that thought all those bitter memories started surfacing and she decided to go to sleep. That day, and all the days which had gone before it, had been spent so quietly but peacefully.

The sky was overcast once again when she woke up and it felt almost as if it were dusk already. Ammah Begum had come out on to the verandah to say her Zohar prayers, and now sat on the prayer mat, her palms uplifted in supplication.

Her hands were trembling she noticed as she sat close to her in an armchair, looking at her through half-open eyes.

'Does this mean that my mother will spend the rest of her life with her hands lifted up in prayer, hoping for the safe return of her dead son, seated right here on the prayer mat draped over this wooden divan, on this verandah? How and when will this routine change? I can't understand this.'

A flood of tears threatened to burst out of her eyes but she held them back with such skill that her throat felt choked with the effort.

When she finished praying Gaythi asked her, 'Shall I order tea?'

'Yes, do. What's the matter with your voice, and your eyes look a bit red too?'

'Feels like a cold coming.' She walked off towards the kitchen in a hurry.

'How different she is now! It is true, one changes with time. Let's see if this mood continues.'

'Begum Sahib, congratulations! Pakistan has been made.' Mali's teeth showed in a grin and there was happiness in his voice.

'Is that so?' Gaythi put down the teapot.

'What are you saying?' The cup trembled in Ammah Begum's hand.

'Mali, you haven't had a dose of opium, have you?' Gaythi laughed.

'Listen to that! I've had a dose of opium – and the news is rattling round like mad on the roads you know. Syed Sahib's bearer heard it with his own ears.'

'Oh, well. Then it must be right. Well, it's been in the air for so many days. In our house it seems no one bothers with the newspapers or the radio any more. Even you don't bother to open the papers to look at them.'

'Well, if Pakistan were created, Mali, why should it please you?' she asked Mali.

'Why shouldn't I be happy? Our Sahib and Bhaiyas wanted it so much. And Sahib used to talk only about Pakistan to all the people who came round.'

'Sahib was different. Pakistan has been made for the Muslims, Mali!'

And Mali became confused. His happiness had never been separate or different from his lord and master's, for him not to be happy today. Each and every plant in this garden had lived in his and his master's eyes; they had prayed for each and every leaf which had unfurled, and waited together for each and every bud to bloom. So what was so new about today that he should have sat with a grumpy face?

Someone was whispering silently inside Gaythi's heart: 'A revolution is upon us, a very big revolution.' She rose and went towards the garden steeped in the mild perfume of moulsari and frangipani which were in bloom. The dense bushes of kaamni twinkled with tiny stars. Under the shade of the thick moulsari tree stretched out a blanket of tiny cups of delicate flowers and thousands of pistachio green budding leaves were bursting into life in the grove of bamboos. A black and white crested cuckoo sang in the distance. Another one in the garden chirped in reply.

'I know, someone should be here soon, re!' the thin voice of Mali's youngest daughter, Sukhdai, wavered in the air.

Gaythi noticed the three tiny reddish-brown leaves, ready to unfold, rising from the top end of the pink stem emerging from the stone of a mango planted at the base of the sandalwood tree. Her hands moved involuntarily and she pulled out the stone which lay on top of the earth.

All three tiny leaves and the pink stem snapped and fell on the grass. She stripped the outer, mud encrusted casing and drew out the '*bijli*,' the soft core of the stone, the quickening hidden in its heart.

'Barrey Bhaiya would squeeze that so easily, held between his thumb and forefinger and ask it, "*Bijli, re bijli!* Which way lies the house of

Gaythi's in-laws?" Pop! the *bijli* would hop away and hide somewhere and all of them would look for it desperately in order to discover the location of the house she would go to when she was married. He used to investigate where the in-laws of all the girls lived. Then when he asked that question about Ismat Apa's in-laws, the *bijli* would disappear and both of them would be left desperately looking for it.

'Huh! Why do these memories leach on to people's lives to harass them forever? Will I ever be rid of them?'

She felt irritated and scraped down the *bijli* against the rough trunk of the sandalwood tree. One end of it got rubbed down, turning it into a whistle and Akhawa Phowey, the special mysterious odour which the *bijli* of the mango emits, escaped and besieged her senses. It is a strange spell-binding smell which makes you want to dissolve into it or bite into it so that you can chew it and absorb it into your own being.

The thought of the sharp taste set her teeth on edge. Then, absent-mindedly she held the whistle of the *bijli* to her lips.

'Peep . . . peep . . . peep!'

And she forgot that a revolution had come to pass, which she had described as a 'major revolution'.

The cuckoo in the garden sang, 'I know . . .' she heard Sukhdai's voice waver again as she pushed forward the swing.

And then she came in, frightened by the sudden leap of lightning in the sky.

71

There were strips of inset lace on the shoulders of Shareef's shirt. He wore a two-sided cap planted tightly on his oil-plastered hair and sported a checked handkerchief on his shoulder. His old polished shoes peeped through his loose-flared pyjamas. His grin stretched from ear to ear.

'Begum Sahib, I'm off to say my Jumma prayers,' he announced his intentions, as was his habit every Friday.

'*Arrey* Shareef! So early today? This is the limit, really!' Gaythi objected. 'And to look at all your preparations and dressing up, one would think it was Eid prayers you were going out for.'

'What else do you think? This is more important than Eid prayers,' Shareef's voice was louder than usual and his eyes were shining. 'It is the first Friday since Pakistan was made. You should see the marquees Moulvi Sahib has had put up in the *mahjid*. He says that the real work has only begun now.'

'Does that mean your Moulvi Sahib is going to Pakistan?'

'Who's going to Pakistan, *bitya*? We're only celebrating. Neither I'm going, nor is Moulvi Sahib.'

'So what does it matter to you?

'Tut! You're still a child; what do you know? Begum Sahib will understand what I mean. What do you think, Begum Sahib? If we ever set eyes upon a stamp or a note from Iran, or Turkey or Arabia, we would kiss it with our eyes; and I'm not talking just about myself, I'm talking about our betters too. Even Sahib would kiss their currency. You know why? Because it was from an Islamic government – for they're all our own.'

Shareef's voice had acquired a note of preaching. 'So, Begum! You say it: could we have thought even in our dreams that in our own country, as near as you like, there will be an Islamic government. *Arrey*! We will celebrate and pray for it. When did we ever have such good fortune before now?' His voice broke, scattered and transformed itself into sobs.

'That's true, Shareef!' Ammah Begum dried her tears on a corner of her *dupatta* but they welled up again. 'Now that it has appeared on the face of this earth, we'll keep it alive. Shareef! People like us will pray for its survival.'

That day Shareef left to say his Friday prayers without eating his lunch. Until four o'clock in the afternoon the food sat rotting in the saucepans and the dirty dishes in the kitchen.

As Ammah Begum went to say her Asar prayers she said, 'That is the trouble with Shareef. He must be going round the city making speeches and offering up his life in his mad enthusiasm.'

When she turned her head to say her salaams towards the end of her prayers, a dubious-looking young man who was looking around respectfully, came and stood in front of her and without any preliminaries started saying, 'There was a riot in the Neem tree Mosque during the sermon. A lot of the people who had come to pray were martyred. Your servant Shareef was also a casualty. Please tell his woman. I'm going now.'

She just sat there stunned. Then she called out, 'Gaythi, come and ask him what he wants to say?'

When Gaythi asked him, he repeated the same news in a flat, unemotional manner.

'And how did you survive?' Gaythi could not believe what he was saying.

'I didn't go to say my prayers,' he said drily.

'Where were you?'

'I? I was playing in the alley next to it.'

'Who are you to Shareef?'

'I am his sister-in-law's relation.'

'Why didn't you go to his quarters?'

'Just didn't . . . You convey this news.'

He sounded quite rude. Then he spoke again.

'Don't worry about the body. There's no point in bringing him out here, in the middle of nowhere!' His voice was heavy, then his eyes reddened, 'Whatever happens, the bodies shall be buried properly.' And he slithered away quickly, like an evil spirit which enters and then exits.

The presence of mind which Gaythi showed in the boy's company vanished with his departure. The earth seemed to cling to her feet as she realised why Bakhtiar had hidden such a major piece of news from his mother: 'It is extremely hard to convey news of this kind.'

Even so she went towards Shareef's quarters. His wife lay on a cot under the kamrakh tree, feeding her baby. When she saw Gaythi, she spoke, 'You must have come asking after him. He is not here. He must be going round with people of his "paalty". Since the day Pakistan's been made, his head's been in a whirl. He's been gone for hours now, to say his Jumma prayers . . .'

She sat down next to her. 'Bahu, listen to me! There's been a big feud at the Neem tree Mosque.'

'Oh, my God! *Bitya*!' She clamped her hand over the child's mouth and pulled her breast away and just sat there with her shirt still rolled up.

'Yes, Bahu! We've only just got the news. Come with me, Ammah Begum is calling for you. Where's the older boy?'

'He's at his maternal grandparents' . . .' She spoke as if she were miles away. She was staring at the door. Her child was crying with hunger and her shirt had become soaked with the milk which was still flowing from her breast. 'Bahu,' Gaythi shook her by the shoulder. 'Hum, *bitya*!' she said with a start. 'Ammah Begum's calling you.' 'So is your Shareef never going to return from the Jumma prayers, now, *bitya*?' She slapped her thighs and then stood up, the child held to her shoulder. The tears spilled over from Gaythi's eyes. 'Bahu! Take your *dupatta*, at least.' '*Bitya*, is the body going to be at Begum Saab's door?' There was not a single tear in her eye. She wrapped her *dupatta* round herself very carefully and drew a

277

short veil across her face, like she always did when she went into the house.

Gaythi held both the girls by their hands.

She threw herself at Ammah Begum's feet and brought the heavens down with her cries, 'Begum Saab! Get the body at least. Won't you send your Shareef away from your own threshold?'

Ammah Begum broke into helpless sobs, '*Arrey*, Bahu! Who shall I send for it? May God keep my sons alive, it was Shareef who was the man of this house. Haa-ey, Bahu! I have no legs to stand on any more.'

Mali came in, his head bowed and his footsteps silent, and Gaythi retreated behind Ammah Begum's back. Bahu stopped screaming and Ammah Begum paled.

'Dear God. Keep our honour safe,' she said softly.

Mali's heart sank, as he thought to himself, '*Bitya* took fright at the sight of me. And when Shareef used to be away, Begum Saab used to send me in the car with the girls to take them to school.'

He felt like saying to Gaythi, '*Bitya*, why are you scared of me? I am the keeper of this garden, I have learned only how to nurture and raise plants. How can I bring myself to say, "As long as Mali lives, you needn't fear anything"?' He gathered his courage and said, 'Begum Sahib, tell Bahu, whilst I'm alive Shareef must be sent from this threshold. Don't worry, all of you. I haven't died yet.'

'Yes, you are our only hope now, Mali,' she said, tactfully. 'You should go out now. Shareef will be buried with the people with whom he went.'

'*Arrey*, Mali, why don't you stab a knife through us too? Why should you spare us?' Shareef's wife was keening.

He was remembering their chat about Pakistan. The other day when Begum Sahib had asked Shareef laughingly, 'So, Shareef! Are you going to Pakistan?' he had answered with a lilt to his voice, 'Begum Sahib, me go to Pakistan? *Arrey*! My father's and grandfather's bones are buried here. And then, how can I go and leave Murli behind. If Murli comes along then I'll go too.'

Thick tears blurred his path and he just stood there, leaning his back against the sandalwood tree for God only knows how long.

Spirit ammonia and all the other medicines stood there useless, for Ammah Begum did not feel the weight on her heart at all. At around nine o'clock Gaythi made some tea and forced her and Bahu to drink some. The box with the straw and the langra mangoes stood in the pantry.

'Haa-ey, Shareef! You had wanted to save these mangoes for Barrey Bhaiya, and then you left to join him, empty-handed.'

She sat for a long time shedding tears before the dirty utensils.

The doors had been shut early in the evening but she did not have the courage to go round and check them to reassure herself.

'You sleep here, next to me,' Ammah Begum insisted and she brought her pillow and bed-sheet.

At some time during the night, amidst her tears, Bahu dozed and stretched out on the floor near them.

Gaythi laid out the cot woven with cotton tape and put the girls to sleep on it. She lay herself on the wooden divan for a little while before she asked in a hesitant voice, 'Can I come to your bed, Ammah Begum?'

'Yes, I was going to say so myself.'

She was lying close to her after many years, and she felt strange clinging to her mother's breast as she told her to, 'Go to sleep,' and placed her hand over her back.

All night Ammah Begum did not shut her eyes even for an instant. All night she had heard the shout of, 'Hear! Hear! Stay awake!' accompanied by the tap tap of a stick, sometimes close to her own room and sometimes next to the other rooms.

72

'Almond trees
Cool sweet springs of water swagger by the mountainside.
The morning breeze
rocks the green weeping willow gently.
The girls on their way to pluck water-chestnuts by the lake down
    below
happily sing songs from the ancient past
And the happy and joyous crowd laugh boisterously,
Whilst they row their boats.'

His hand was moving expertly on the soft brown downy suede leather whilst this timid melody of spring from Ming Yun Ching slid by itself from his brain to his lips.

The pair of shoes had already been cut and lay separated from the leather spread out on the table. 'And now this leather no longer bears any relation to, or has any connection with this pair of shoes . . .' He removed the template of the shoes from the gap, and then hummed again,

'Cool sweet springs of water swagger by the banks of the mountains.
But my attention wanders to my country
I wish I could go there . . .
Yes, I wish I could go there . . .'

He sat down on the stool and started staring at the shoes which had been made to order arranged in the showcase.

'I don't know why my heart is so restless! I don't know who needs me today. And I don't know why the food was sticking in my throat today.'

The crammed shop and its leathery atmosphere were wearing him down. He felt like leaping out of the shop and wandering round the streets without any purpose. But the streets were not worthy of that any more either. The tension which for a long time had been integral to that city was beginning to snap now and to scatter itself as it broke. This was not his own city but nevertheless, when disaster strikes such a place, it affects everyone who lives in it. His heart was heavy and careworn and that was why he had remembered the song of spring from his own fatherland.

The sound of dragging heels made him think that a customer had walked in. For the past four days things had been so unsettled that the arrival of a customer seemed amazing. He was so fed up that he thought, 'Let him come if he wants to. I'll see to him when he calls for attention.' He remained seated on his stool.

But this was not a customer. A familiar smiling face and hopeful pair of eyes were looking everywhere for him with a completely casual air.

'I see. So, it was you!' he said, still remaining seated where he had been. 'Someone has rightly said that think of the devil and . . .'

'And he'll be there. But you're lying. You weren't thinking of me.'

'Is that so? Then who was I thinking of?'

'How do I know who you were thinking of, Safdar! If at this moment in time I believed that you were really missing me I would have gladly accepted being the devil.'

'And if I wasn't missing you, then how did you come? That's why I'm saying that . . .'

'You're the devil,' Margaret completed his sentence for him. 'And now you should not try to lie any further. In fact, you should get up from that stool and come here, in front of me.'

'Anyway, Margaret, you did well by coming here right now. I was really feeling forlorn today.'

'Are you happy now?' She smiled unenthusiastically. This man's existence or absence did not matter to her at all now. She had given up deluding herself about him. She knew very well that she did not have a place in any corner of his heart, which she had so desired.

She understood very well that he would never consider her to be more than an interesting and passing friend. But in spite of that she looked for chances to come and be with him, stay and spend time talking and laughing with him. Not because she expected him to change towards her but because this brought her happiness. And this tiny, temporary and makeshift happiness is not a mere trifle either.

Finding him lonely just then pleased her. Who cares what the reason is, she thought, at least he was pleased that I came.

'Why are you feeling lonely? Is everything all right?'

'Why am I feeling lonely? I don't know myself. But, tell me Margaret, do you not feel the misery and desolation in the air?'

'Yes. The atmosphere is silent. Just think what a huge event has come to pass – the government has changed.' She was not very well acquainted with politics and nor did she want to discuss it. '. . . What a nice day it is today!'

He kept looking outside silently as if he were trying to assess the virtues of the day. Then he spoke, 'Margaret, you shouldn't wander about too much these days. The atmosphere in the whole city is extremely foul.'

'But I am not a native, nor do I belong to any of their religious groups.' Then she laughed, 'Safdar Yaaseen, *you* should stay on your guard, you belong to one of the sects here!'

'Is that true?' He laughed and fell to thinking, 'But did that sect ever regard me as one of them? Did it ever take any notice of me? They just see me as someone Chinese. How can I tell them that there are so many similarities between the lifestyle of our people and the common people in this country?'

'There's far too much chaos here, Safdar. It would be better if one could leave this place.'

'I was going to say just that. Why don't you go back? Things are changing really very fast now.'

'I have received orders to go, and I am leaving very soon. But you should also go back home. You haven't taken a holiday for ages.'

'I don't want to go back just yet, and I won't take a holiday either.'

She started staring outside the shop. The silence on the road had deepened. She was not in the least bit interested in the atmosphere or in the people here. She was not even specially interested in the people whose war she had come to fight. Once they had claimed victory though, she

281

sometimes felt as if they had won such a huge war on the basis of her support and her neck would stiffen with pride. Nevertheless, a worrying despondency was beginning to seize the whole atmosphere of the place.

'What kind of freedom is this?' she asked. 'You used to say that your mother is a widow and is very old. Do you have such faith in her long life that you expect to find her still alive, waiting for you? And then you also claim that you love her very much.'

Her last words were emphatic, and angry as well. Safdar knew why she wanted so intensely to persuade him to leave too.

She was right. But, in spite of that, because of several reasons, the likelihood of his leaving soon was possibly nil. Together with all the other reasons, one inscrutable one was that quite unaccountably his heart was unwilling to bid farewell to this land.

After remaining silent for a little while, he said, lighting a cigarette, 'Do you know what I was humming to myself before you came in, Margaret?'

'You tell me.' Margaret looked at him.

> 'Almond trees
> Cool sweet springs of water swagger by the mountainside.'

Margaret recited the second stanza and the first was left incomplete:

> 'The girls on their way to pluck
> water-chestnuts by the lake down below
> happily sing songs from the ancient past
> And the happy and joyous crowd laugh boisterously,
> Whilst they row their boats.'

She became silent but her eyes seemed to be saying, 'All these things have to do with the motherland.'

Safdar drew a long puff on his cigarette and said, 'But you left out the last verse. Let me finish it for you:

> 'But my attention wanders to my country
> I wish I could go there . . .!'

The evening was upon them now. Both the salesmen had come into the shop but only a couple of customers had come so far, one of whom had only wanted to find out the prices of various pairs of shoes.

Safdar went out with Margaret.

73

He stood there stunned and petrified. He could not believe what he could see with his own eyes, because all this had happened right in front of him. The shelter for the buffalo stood vacant, half-eaten fodder in the vat, the bare post and desolate shelter, everything seemed incredible; because all this had happened not in the darkness of the night, but in broad daylight.

A small group had broken in through the gate in the back garden and had very calmly untethered the buffalo and taken it. Then some people climbed down the well and smashed the water pump which meant that now the garden could no longer be watered.

'And only the other day I had made such a tall claim, "Begum Sahib, so long as I am still alive, you don't need to worry." How can I face her now?'

He went and lay down silently in his hovel. Since Shareef's death he had been seeing to a lot of the work inside and outside the house.

That afternoon, when the time for Asar prayers was getting shorter, Ammah Begum asked the sweeper's son, 'Will you go and have a look? Mali hasn't come in at all today . . .'

The boy came in after a very long time. '*Jee*, Maalan says that Mali's gone out somewhere.'

'*Arrey*! Didn't you ask where he's gone and when he'll be back?'

The boy smiled somewhat strangely, '*Jee*! Mali is in there, sleeping. But Maalan says he's gone out.'

It was a strange piece of information. For some unknown reason she felt as if the ground were slipping away from under her feet. 'Gaythi!' she called out.

'*Jee*!' she had just bathed.

'Could you go yourself and see how Mali is, child? I'd sent this silly boy and one moment he says he's out, and the next he says he's sleeping in there.' Deep inside, she really did not want to believe such an incredible story, that Mali should send a message saying that he's out when he is, in fact, at home.

'He talks nonsense, he's always been a bit of a gabbler,' Gaythi said, spreading out her wet towel, and she went towards Mali's hovel, still wearing her wooden clogs.

Ammah Begum argued with the boy again, '*Arrey*, Bundu! Did you see him lying there with your own eyes?'

'*Jee*! On the bed, inside, he was lying there. Maalan was sitting on the threshold. When I went up and spoke he turned on his side.'

Strange doubts entered her mind. 'I shouldn't have sent the girl over there. Never mind, now, God is the One Who is the Protector.'

'So Bundu was telling the truth,' Gaythi realised as she saw Mali lying on his side.

When she saw her, Maalan rose and came to stand near her.

'Well? Is Mali feeling all right? Why is he in bed?' she asked very gently with great tact.

Maalan regretted inwardly what she had said earlier, 'It was wrong to say he was out. I should have said he is feeling poorly.'

'He's fine, *bitya*. He's drunk a little too much, so he didn't come in. Made an excuse.' Her eyes were lowered and another lie was inscribed on her face. And now there was no point in asking any further questions. She returned on slow, thoughtful feet.

'What should I say to Ammah Begum when I go back?' She noticed that you could neither hear the buffalo lowing under the shelter, nor the throb of the water pump in the well.

What a tragic calm and stillness enveloped everything. Her feet stopped suddenly, near the shelter. The buffalo was not there, nor its calf – it was an untimely absence. Her feet dragged even more. Shareef's quarters were locked. His wife had been fetched by her brother. That day the sky had cleared after several days and the brilliant colours of a rainbow stretched colourfully from one end to the other.

When she was little, Shareef used to point it out to her, 'Look, Bibi, that's God's bow and arrow.'

She came and sat down silently on a chair.

'Well, what is the matter?' Ammah Begum asked as soon as she could pause in the middle of her prayers.

'Maalan was saying that he's drunk and that's why she'd made an excuse . . .'

Ammah Begum picked up her rosary.

The discovery of the empty shelter for the buffalo was creating havoc inside her. To keep such a significant piece of news hidden was a matter of great courage. No one could predict what the consequences of keeping it secret might be! And that too, when they knew very well that the incidence of violence had increased in the inner city areas. She decided that the most appropriate way of facing the reality of the present was to face it realistically.

'Ammah Begum!'

'Hum!' She looked at her whilst turning the beads of her rosary.

'When I was returning that way I noticed that the buffalo was not in the shelter.'

There were signs of surprise on her face but she continued to turn the beads.

'Neither the buffalo, nor its calf. And the pump wasn't working in the well, either.'

The rosary fell from her hand. 'So you should have asked Maalan. You're telling me now,' she said irritated.

'What should I have asked Maalan, Ammah? Mali didn't seem drunk to me. However, I did guess that he had turned on his side when he saw me. And Maalan came and stood in my way before I could go any further. It was quite obvious from her face that she was lying.'

'So this means that Mali is responsible for all this . . .'

She rolled up the prayer mat and stood up. 'Look, you telephone Akbar's father and I will just go and lock up the doors.'

'Ammah, shall I call the sweeper's wife inside?' she replied, in terror, reading the signs of danger on her face.

'Don't make that mistake. These low caste people! If they guess at all that we are panicking they'll get bolder.'

Since the day Shareef had met his death, Gaythi had noticed a strange transformation in her mother. That sense of paralysis was vanishing from her by degrees. She no longer stayed immersed in that oppressive impotent silence, absorbed in her routine or her prayers, day and night. She was now watching everything, both inside and out, with great alertness. And she was cooking both meals herself, despite Gaythi's attempts to help. When Arjumand's mother-in-law and father-in-law had visited them after hearing about Shareef and had insisted that they should both go and stay with them, she had reassured them that the feud was only a chance skirmish. That that man who had died was destined for martyrdom. 'And if I leave, who will look after his wife and children? I have written to Munshi ji asking him to send Ikraam.'

She had written to Bakhtiar, Saulat and Arjumand herself to give them the news of Shareef's death. Arjumand was the only one who had responded to it.

She did not panic at all about not hearing from Bakhtiar. She had assumed he must be away on some project. About Saulat she decided that perhaps she was not at Dalhousie just then. Asif Jah had talked about going to visit his mother.

When she returned after securing the doors throughout the house, Gaythi told her that she had not been able to get through to Arjumand's father-in-law in spite of several attempts, that maybe their telephone was out of order.

'Is that so? Then you should have lodged a complaint.'

'No one's answering there either.'

'Try again in a little while,' and she went towards the kitchen.

'Where are you going now?' she asked in a fearful voice.

'Nowhere, child. Let me put on some rice with peas to cook. Don't you worry. God is our Keeper,' she said with great effort.

In a little while, driven by anxiety, she went to join her in the kitchen. It was spotlessly clean. The militia apron which Shareef used to wear whilst cooking was still hanging on the peg. She sat on a stool watching very closely thinking, 'Even at a time like this Ammah Begum is concerned about the chutneys and sauces to go with the rice and peas combination.'

She was going through an elaborate process of chopping green chillies and onions finely in order to mix them with the sour sauce she had already finished preparing.

'You go and lay the table,' she said, 'the rice is on a low flame now and should be ready soon.'

'Ammah Begum, let's eat here,' she was trembling with fear inside.

'All right.' She cleaned the stone slab table top and kept the plates on it, saying, 'Be brave, there's no point in letting your spirits go. God is with us. If your time is not over then Death herself looks after you.'

The rice was hot and delicious. She ate a few morsels and then looked at her mother; tears were flowing down her cheeks. What if all the doors and bolts were closed? The window panes were so long that even if one were to break . . .

They both lay silently on their beds. Ammah Begum was repeating the Prayer of Blessings. A light shone very close to her window and then fell on Gaythi's face through the chink in the curtains. At that moment those gleaming long window panes seemed so flimsy and insecure. She crept nearer to Ammah Begum and said in a whisper, 'Someone is flashing a torch round.' The light moved away and her mother pulled the curtain back a fraction to take a look outside. Several men were walking around.

'There is only one God, Who is worthy of praise.' There was a tremor in her voice.

Then gradually her suspicion was replaced by the certainty that a few people, armed with sticks and lanterns, were on guard outside.

And when she heard someone close to her window clear his throat and call out loud once, 'Stay awake. . .' , Gaythi ejaculated, '*Arrey*, that is Mali's voice!'

74

'Listen to the lamentations of the flute
As she tells the story of her painful separation from the tree.'

The Persian couplet, gleaming on thick yellow paper, flapped amidst the pages scattered in the deserted and abandoned room and then, driven by the wind, it fell at his feet. He looked at the shredded papers, bottles of medicine and various odds and ends with reddened eyes. That scene of this house being plundered was still clearly before them.

The noise of the furniture and other things being snatched and dragged through the rooms, stores and bathrooms. The awesome muddle as the contents artfully arranged in each room were thrown together, the rows over the division of the booty, the fingering of each and every thing; one by one each of those memories had come to cling to his eyes.

When he had seen all the stuff scattered untidily on the lawn and the verandahs, he had wondered for a minute, 'Look at that! Curse the lot of them! They've made such a mess of all the furniture; and how will I sort it out all by myself, and put it all in order again?'

The looting had begun whilst Begum Sahib was still here. The soldiers in the jeep had only managed to rescue her and Choti Bitya with great difficulty.

And what travails he had had to go through to get them to bring the jeep over to the house. He had hurled himself at Kapoor Sahib's feet, had wept and beaten his breast before him. Only then had Kapoor Sahib managed to organise a jeep. It had taken them all of six hours, and by the time he had returned, the looting of the house was already under way.

Both of them sat silently on Maalan's charpoy, and Maalan sat on the ground, leaning against the frame of the charpoy, her veil extended across her face. After all, she couldn't have sat before Begum Sahib with her face exposed, could she?

They had traversed the distance between his hovel and the jeep surrounded by the soldiers, veils extended across their faces. When he saw them sitting inside the jeep, in the protection of those army men, he had felt as though an enormous weight had been lifted off his head. He had felt so happy that he had even forgotten that they were leaving never to return.

When the jeep vanished in the distance as it left the gates he remembered, 'I didn't even say a final farewell to my Begum Sahib.' He stared at the long empty road for a long time. There was a lot of noise inside the house but the streets were silent. It was the second day since the commencement of organised rioting in the city.

When he returned along the red gravel path, the stones had crunched under his feet. The house had been plundered and there was no longer any furniture to be seen scattered on the lawn or the verandahs to worry him. Slowly, he moved towards the silent, ravaged house. In Sahib's deserted room the torn pages of books were flying around like yellow autumnal leaves. What was written on those pages he could not understand. He only knew that these were the pages of his Sahib's books which he used to treasure. They used to be kept tidily arranged in the glass bookcase. Now the shards of that glass lay scattered everywhere. There was a breeze speeding through the room. He looked at the ceiling. Those people had left the ceiling fan on. He switched it off and went out of the room.

75

He stayed there after lunch, playing with Li Fan's little daughter. He was in no hurry to return. When the child's mother came in bringing her embroidery with her, he left the child and addressed her. 'I hear your departure's been confirmed.'

'Yes, we'll know in a few days when we leave.'

'So this means that I will be the only one left here eventually.'

'No, you won't be left alone. Some people will leave this place and some new people will arrive.'

'I meant acquaintances.'

'Margaret's gone too!' She looked at him and laughed.

'Yes, look at that! Even she's gone!'

'She kept begging you to go with her but it had no effect on you at all.'

'And now I'm regretting it,' he laughed. 'This city seems so terrified and grim at the moment that I am finding it hard to settle down to anything here.'

'Yes, it has been through a major revolution. All its business and civic life is totally dead but in a few days everything will be all right again.'

'Well, if it isn't then one cannot guess what else could happen. In these last few weeks so much has taken place; one has probably seen the worst that could happen – looting, arson and a mass displacement of people. There can't be much left now that can possibly happen.' He moved the child's hand away from his face to stop her repeated assaults on his nose, 'Honestly, I've been very anxious these last few days.'

'Hum!' she said in a deep voice, her attention absorbed in finding the right shades of orange and beige as she placed the skeins of silk thread against the black acacia tree. Then as she started threading her needle she spoke, 'Thank goodness we have nothing to do with this fighting but in spite of that, I don't let the children out at all. Whilst I think of it, Safdar, could you make sure you come on time yourself at mealtimes. Before all this happened, I used not to mind sending one of the children to fetch you if you were late.'

'All right. I'll be careful!' His voice sounded preoccupied for some reason.

'Li Fan's wife you speak the truth – thank goodness this feud has nothing to do with us,' he thought, 'but I don't know why I feel that I do have a stake in this upheaval. I'm not sure what is happening to me, but the words, province, city, motherland, sometimes lose their significance for me. And I don't know what is happening to my brain but all these vast distances and differences have faded for me.'

He lifted the little girl off his lap and stood up to leave.

'Are you going to the shop?'

'That is the intention,' he laughed. 'A shop which opens with great regularity amidst all those others that are shut or are locked also seems quite strange. Do you know why I open the shop?'

'Why?' she lifted her quiet dispassionate face to look at him directly.

'Perhaps I want to enjoy the feeling that I am safe and distant from all this violence.'

And he stepped out into the alley. 'But the truth is that I am involved in it, and I am feeling vulnerable despite the fact that I am safe,' his heart whispered to him.

He stayed in his own room all afternoon drinking cups of tea. Today, again, he was sadder than he should have been. Then he fumbled through his few books and picked up one. This was the book which always brought him peace and happiness. He started reading and turning the pages impatiently:

'Therefore the dervish always keeps himself in the last row, and then it is revealed to him that he belongs in the front row.
He looks upon his existence as something newly created. . .'

The pages turned rapidly and his eyes consumed the lines and forms but he could not find peace. He flicked over several pages together and read:

'The dervish lives in this world in peace and tranquillity
For him, all the people on this earth belong to one nation
That is, they all belong to the territory of the heart.'

He repeated that sentence under his breath several times,

'For him, all the people on this earth belong to the one nation
That is, they all belong to the territory of the heart.'

And now it had become clear to him why sometimes the words, province, city, motherland, lose their significance.

He kept reading and smoking but when daylight faded and the darkness of the evening stretched before him, he felt that the wildness of his heart was also stretching with it. He dressed and went out of the room. He did not know where he was headed.

76

Such utter poverty, that you would never believe it! A sudden and unexpected reversal of the kind you come across in legends and fictitious stories. More than for herself, Gaythi would start suspecting that this was a nightmare when she saw Ammah Begum exposed to that strange environment. The odd thing was that she was silent and content. The strength which had surfaced in her after Shareef's death was still there, steady, and possibly increased.

So far they had not been able to find out anything about Bakhtiar or make contact with Saulat or Arjumand. In spite of that, there was neither that restlessness nor fear nor anguish which had wrapped itself round her constantly in the days when she had not heard from Sheharyaar. Now, she did not pray time and time again, drawing imaginary circles of protection built up through repeated recitals of a special prayer for safety. She would sit on the straw and say the most basic prayers, pray for forgiveness after her death and drop her hands to her sides.

When some of the people at the camp heard that her son was being educated at the army cadet school at Dehra Doon and her son-in-law was a general, they tried to make her regret what had happened, saying, 'You could have used their influence and arrived here under the protection and management of the army itself.' But she did not regret her haste and mismanagement at all. She would just open the container for her *paans* and whilst chewing on the remains of her betel nuts with the aid of the dried-up lime and catechu, softened and increased in volume with an added dash of water, she would say, 'It is all a question of kismet. Who has ever succeeded in reorganising a fate devised by God?'

Then she would shut the container which she had brought with her despite the thousands of difficulties surrounding their departure. When she saw the state others were in, she would count herself lucky to have succeeded in bringing with her – along with that *paan daan* – two suitcases of clothes, a jug, her bank book and a small case containing the jewellery which was kept at home in case it was needed for unexpected festive occasions.

On the fourth day, when they had received messages from Saulat and Bakhtiar over the radio, Gaythi remembered that Chacha ji lived in this city too. When she went out, the entire city looked strange to her, as if she had never been there before. There were now no colourful turbans or beards dotted around, nor the faces of happy, carefree Hindus. The city was silent. When she arrived at Mason Road, she found that Chacha ji's house was locked. Some Christians with anxious faces told her that he had got killed trying to save the family of a Hindu friend. Their son was a member of the Muslim League so he had been arrested in India and when his ageing mother had become very ill, her brother had come from Multan to fetch her.

She stood for a long time leaning against the wall, as she pondered this, the lock held in her hand. 'So, Chacha ji, they killed you as well? You, who never liked to interrogate people or interfere in their business. Why ever did you decide to intervene in such a major issue then?'

Then she remembered Chachi who had never involved herself in anyone else's business, be it good or evil. When she had finished her morning prayers, she would get her house sparkling clean and then sit under the arch of the verandah rolling fine strips of paper to make herself sneeze artificially. After all what sin had she committed to deserve this hell of separation and loneliness! No sin at all. 'There is so much chaos and such confusion in this world. Why are people's destinies so full of discrepancies?' She felt confused.

Now there was only one other acquaintance who remained in this city and he belonged to a different race and a different class, a man with a skin colour different from her own.

'But, no. I won't ask him again for any kind of help – that was my business, this is Ammah Begum's. I will not place her under an obligation against her wishes to a man whose help she regards as unworthy of her dignity. Though it has to be conceded that she is under an obligation to Mali too.' The thought of Mali brought tears to her eyes, 'But Mali was different, he had eaten at her table, and he was her paid employee ...' There were, of course, several girls from her college and their families; and she was on good terms with some of them. But to go like this, in these circumstances, to anyone's door for help would really be such a wrong thing to do!

'But then, in this familiar city which looks so alien right now, how shall I find a place for us?'

Her hired bicycle came to a stop near the YWCA gates. 'I wonder what Margaret is up to! But, no. Margaret is a Christian, and she is Chinese. She has no connections with this new country of ours, or with the old one we have left behind. How can I bring myself to tell her that they have thrashed us out of there; that we had no intention of coming here?'

At that point she became aware of the odd change in herself. When all their dignity, prestige and arrogance had died she found in herself a growing pride. I am that same person who, without hesitation, never considered it objectionable to say anything in front of anyone. I used to sit in Safdar's shop and talk about my family problems without any inhibition. And now I am embarrassed at the thought of talking about the excesses of my compatriots to Margaret.'

The church bells were tolling carelessly. She looked at her watch, it was six o' clock. 'Today has been wasted too,' she thought, 'and who knows when I'll reach the camp!'

77

What is Ammah Begum going to say? 'Is this a mansion?'

A house with two tiny bedrooms seemed to her far too small for Ammah Begum. She stood amongst the torn books, empty boxes and bottles, thinking. Then she strolled towards the dining room. In the centre stood a pot of unbaked clay full of cold water. She was extremely thirsty, having ridden her bicycle all that way, she bent over it and started drinking out of the palm of her hand. The cold water shot through her parched throat and hit her innards. She sat there for some time, holding the pot, then steadied herself and rose. Perhaps this pot has been left by those refugees who were turned out of here by the custodian's men?

'Where would they have gone now?'

She came out of the room. She took her bicycle which was leaning against the pillar of the small circular verandah and started to leave, but then she thought of something. She shut the rooms, using the lock the custodian had given her and went to fetch Ammah Begum.

When the *tonga* entered through the red gates half concealed by the terribly overgrown hedge she noticed the sign. On the flank of red bricks was mounted a tablet of white stone with the words 'Anand Bhavan' written on it in Urdu. Ammah Begum's feet trembled when she reached the verandah, as if she could not believe that here was a roof over her which she could call her own.

Gaythi was wondering when she would complain about the house. She expected her to say that it was not only too small, but also that its design demonstrated a lack of good taste.

But it seemed as though the house had met with her approval. The lawn was bordered all round with different varieties of roses, yellow and white, both indigenous and English which had survived the neglect. The western wall was covered with what looked like a frieze of tiny rambling roses. Looking at those countless tiny roses, she remembered for the very first time, their own creeper which had been trained over the round wrought-iron gates. It was late evening. The khaki birds which lived in the trees and the bushes were hopping round noisily.

Gaythi cleaned one of the rooms with the crude broom she had purchased on the way out to the house, spread out a soft straw mat on the floor and placed Ammah Begum's *paan daan* upon it. It now contained not only lime and catechu but also *paans* and betel nuts.

'While she says her prayers, I'll chop the betel nuts for her,' she thought, opening the tiny packet of tobacco to fill the little box. That *paan daan* had been used to house Ahmed Hussain's highly fragrant ground tobacco and cardamom coated with silver leaf.

All the light bulbs were broken. 'I wonder if the meter is working or not!' She tried switching the fan on. Thank goodness that at least was working. She fumbled in the shopping basket and found a fat candle which she lit and placed in the window.

'She is so far-sighted! I would never have guessed. She has remembered to bring everything that was needed.' Ammah Begum looked at the mat, the candle and the re-stocked *paan daan* thinking, 'This time she has been a son to me.'

She sat on the floor in the middle of the doorway. Her *shalwaar* looked dirty and her shirt had been mended in various places.

78

It was a small cottage with only two rooms but it was extremely attractive, light and comfortable. The best thing about it was that it stood on a slope and she and the children did not find it at all difficult to climb up or down. She had been living there for the past two months and was experiencing living on a mountain for the first time. 'Allah! How beautiful these mountains are! And hundreds of thousands of people who live on the plains die without ever seeing them.' She had often thought this. These days she wrote letters regularly to Talat and Ammah jaan, detailing the weather and the beauty of their environs. She would write in great detail about everything, from the stony staircase of her tiny cottage to the stream of water with its white, black and moss-ridden green stones, which flowed behind their kitchen.

The most interesting and remarkable thing was, of course, that a coincidence had brought her and Saulat Apa together. Admittedly her cottage was located at a great height and it was very difficult to reach. She had seen her in the bazaar, shopping for toys with her daughter. Both of them had been surprised to see each other and had then embraced each other, like real first cousins.

'What are you doing here, Ismat?' she had asked.

'Zubair has been posted here, Saulat Apa! He is in public relations now, you see,' her eyes agleam as she said that.

In addition, she had wanted to say that Saulat would be amazed if she met Zubair himself, who was becoming more handsome and smarter as time went on.

Noticing the glow on her face, the brilliance of her forehead, Saulat had thought with surprise that Ismat was turning out to be very beautiful. Then when she bent down to lift her little boy and said, 'Offer your respects to Khala Begum!' Saulat had asked her with a start, 'So Zubair has moved into public relations? How long have you been here?' She had added in a softer tone, 'Well, yes! This war has given everyone the chance to jump up the ladder in no time at all. What I mean is . . .' But Ismat was so delighted to meet Saulat Apa unexpectedly like this, that she paid no heed to that sentence. Her intention at the time had been to buy something inexpensive to amuse the child, but now, in the presence of Saulat Apa and her daughter she ended up having to buy a waddling wind-up duck.

'I had your address but Zubair has not had the time for us to go looking for your house, and I don't keep that well, here, anyway,' she smiled.

'Yes, that's true,' Saulat forced a smile. 'Well, all that one can hope for in these times are these chance meetings.'

'So why don't you come home with me now?'

'It would be best if you could excuse me for now. I've been out for a while, and Seema's tired too. And also your brother-in-law now stays at home all the time.' Her voice sounded a little tired.

'Well, that's all right,' Ismat bowed her head, feeling furious with herself for her earlier elation. 'There was no reason for me to have got so excited at seeing her.' She went towards the counter to pay.

At that point Saulat spoke up, impelled by something she could not quite identify, 'Ismat Bibi, come, let's go and see your place now, then one day both of us will come round and spend some time with you.'

Ismat was delighted once again. Actually, she did want to show off her little cottage to Saulat Apa, which she had decorated with extremely good taste in accordance with the surroundings and the demands of the climate.

'To tell you the truth, Saulat Apa, I did want your advice about the decoration in the house. I have already done the curtains, but we have not yet bought some of the things we need.'

By saying that she felt reassured that Saulat would not consider the place under-furnished.

Dressed in a yellow check sari and a pale beige smartly-tailored blouse, she looked quite beautiful as she stood in her own house.

'She is a real first cousin of mine, after all,' Saulat looked at her beautiful white feet stuck in the black Burmese slippers.

After handing the boy over to the ayah, she came back to the drawing room and sat down close to Saulat, talking. Zubair entered exactly when the ayah brought the coffee tray in and placed it in front of Ismat. She did not recognise him for a moment because of his blooming looks and startling good health.

'Wonderful! So you found your sister without having to look for her!' he laughed good-humouredly.

'You can see for yourself, sir! I found her myself in the end. You just kept putting it off.'

'Well, what can be better than that? You traced your sister yourself. I think I would have searched in vain.'

She did not want Zubair to hurt her cousin whilst she was a guest in their house so she spoke quickly, 'There were two telegrams for you, Zubair.'

'Is that so? Never mind, give me some coffee first. The telegrams never seem to stop.'

'Where's Asif Bhai?' Zubair asked Saulat.

'He's here too.'

'Surprising! We haven't seen you around before now, or else we would have . . .'

'You've changed so much, Zubair.' Saulat could not contain herself any longer.

'Yes! But you haven't changed at all,' he looked at her and smiled. Then he put down his cup of coffee and said, 'Is there some news about Sheharyaar Bhai? The last news we were given was that he was missing. Let's wait and see. It's all down to luck. Anyway, if there's life there's always hope that he might return some time.'

Ismat bowed her head down, thinking, 'He was my brother. I should have been the one to ask about him. But somehow I don't feel like mentioning his name to his family.' She was constantly troubled by a feeling of guilt, without any reason – as if she were responsible for his homelessness. 'If I wanted to, I could tell you right now where he is. But I could never say it in front of your wife: say, that that brother of mine whom she loved and who wanted to marry her, is no longer in this world. And anyway you can see for yourself how happily she is living in your house. The thing is, Zubair Khan, that you are the one she deserved. This tiny, pretty cottage is the one which suits her!' Saulat went on thinking until suddenly her blood was boiling with rage. But she replaced the cup on the table very gently and spoke with sadness in her voice, 'Ismat, could you call Seema away from the children. We should be leaving now. It's going to rain soon.'

They came out to the slope to send her off and they were both absolutely silent as they came back. The clouds were thickening. As he saw Saulat Apa mount the rickshaw holding up her brilliant orange Japanese umbrella, Zubair said, 'Her beauty is indeed immortal. Did you notice how dejected she was?'

'She stayed such a short time that I could not ask anything about

Arjumand's marriage, and about Gaythi and Bakhtiar. Nor even how Barri Ammah is.'

'What happens is that one feels absolutely stunned in her presence,' Zubair said as he entered the house.

'Will you tell me something, Zubair?' Ismat searched the depths of his eyes with restless, anxious eyes.

'*Arrey*, is that all? Is that all the heart you have for it?' Zubair took her into his arms.

79

Saulat had not invited them to her own house but Ismat wanted to meet her again. It would be a topsy-turvy world if two real first cousins living in the same town did not meet each other at least once a week.

It had been raining all morning but they set off the moment it stopped drizzling.

'You are forcing me to go and then you'll suspect me, Ismat Ara. And that is quite wrong.'

He looked so sweet smiling like that! 'I will take you and I will be suspicious too.' She put herself in his arms. 'Do you know how precious you are?'

'Tell me one thing, Ismat.'

'Ask me.' She looked at him very fondly.

'Do you never ever think of Sheharyaar?'

'Who? Barrey Bhaiya? Look at that! Why should I not think of him? I pray to God for his safe return.'

'Women are so very clever,' he laughed, and came out of the room with his arm round her waist.

As they trod the path paved with red stones which led up to the Saulat villa, Ismat felt as if someone had grabbed her feet. She wished she had not taken Saulat to see her cottage, it was surely no more than a hand span. Someone who lives in such a grand residence must have felt claustrophobic in a place like that.

The bell was answered by a bearer with a huge twirly moustache which made Ismat quite nervous. Then he inclined his head respectfully and guided them in.

She was still in her nightdress. She came in on light footsteps, dressed in a light blue flowered dressing gown and fur-lined slippers, looking like a faintly remembered dream.

Zubair was watching her very silently and the moment she sat down Ismat started enquiring about everyone. Asif Jah entered midstream dressed in a burgundy dressing gown with a golden paisley print. Since they had got married, this was only the second time Ismat had seen him, 'Salaams, Asif Bhai.' She rose.

'May you live long, *Bibi*. I see the family resemblance with Saulat in your face, but . . .'

'Chachi jaan's eldest daughter and her bridegroom, Zubair,' Saulat shortened his lengthy introduction. She was embarrassed to a painful extent by Asif Jah's hairless pate, his eyes heavy-lidded with wrinkles and the rotundity of his paunch thrusting through his dressing gown. But he was stretched comfortably upon the sofa, pipe in hand, deeply immersed in conversation with Zubair which shifted from the freedom movement and the violence connected with it to the war.

He offered some interesting information about his war experiences in answer to Zubair's questions and Saulat, who was talking to Ismat, was thinking, 'You are not even ashamed of yourself, Asif Jah, that you are busy talking to Zubair, sitting shoulder to shoulder with him. If there had been a mirror before you, you might have been able to see how ugly and old you look in comparison with him. That's fine. Why should you be aware of it? You have creditable achievements and you care little for your external appearance, but I have no achievements to my credit. Except that, upon my mother's advice, I bowed my head and agreed to marry you. Therefore my outward appearance and the show of my surroundings are very dear to me.'

She thought all that and then raised her extremely beautiful eyes very gently as she interrupted Asif Jah, 'You have taken your tablets, haven't you?'

'*Arrey, bhai*. I'll even take a bullet if necessary!' When he laughed his entire wobbly being laughed with him. '*Bhai*, a wife who looks after you beyond the call of duty is also a problem. What do you think, Zubair Mian, what's your experience?'

'Exactly the same. And the girls from this family look after you like old women. I'd say my mother left me to my own devices more than my wife does.'

'Do you see how these men exaggerate, Saulat Apa? Then you hear them claiming that women exaggerate things!' Ismat laughed and Zubair and Asif Jah laughed with her.

Zubair looked at Saulat's gently uplifted eyes, bemused, 'You are still truly enchanting – a poem, an everlasting spell!'

Lunch was announced just then. During the meal Saulat reminded Asif Jah that he had to rest immediately afterwards since he had an appointment for tea at three o'clock.

Whilst they were washing their hands Zubair nudged Ismat, 'I think we've stayed long enough. These people have to rest and they have to go somewhere later as well.'

'Yes, I thought we should go now when I heard Saulat Apa.' Ismat seemed somewhat embarrassed that Zubair should have heard that too.

As soon as they had crossed the gates, Zubair said, 'Asif Bhai seems to be a really decent and reasonable person. There isn't a hint of arrogance in him.'

'Yes,' she said and remained silent. She was a little tired maybe, for she looked somewhat anxious.

As soon as they had left, Saulat had wondered, 'Does one ever get rid of these relations or not?'

She might not have gone to visit them again for a very long time because she had sensed that Saulat Apa was not especially pleased to meet them. She was therefore surprised to see her arriving first thing in the morning that day.

The first thing that Saulat asked her when she arrived was, 'Have you had a letter from Chachi jaan at all?'

'Why? What's the matter? Is there rioting there too?' She felt alarmed. The news pouring in for the past week had been worrisome.

'No. So far there's no such news. I just wanted to know.'

'None at all. I'm worried. Have you had a letter from Barri Ammah?'

'Not at all. The rioting is already happening there.'

'See! Didn't I say it? And Zubair fooled me, saying there wasn't such a problem. That there would have been only a few incidents in outlying areas and that newspapers always exaggerate things.'

'Zubair possibly tried to cover up because of your condition,' she looked extremely worried.

'Then you should have sent a telegram, Saulat Apa. Zubair wasn't right to try and hide it from me.'

'What could you have done?' Enormous tears shone in Saulat's eyes. 'Do you know you can't get a response to any letter, telegram or trunk call? Today Asif sent a message through Signals. He said he'll phone me the moment he gets any news. When I rang him I felt as if he was just trying to pacify me.'

'What was he saying then?' Tears surged in her eyes in sympathy with Saulat's tears.

'He said "your message will be the first to go when the lines are free",' Then she broke down and wept desperately. 'I feel as if my mother's gone forever.'

'Don't talk like that, Saulat Apa. God is there to protect us,' she embraced her, trying to reassure her.

'What protection can He give? Who has He protected so far? I've lost my brother already. An offering to the war!'

'What?' she said with surprise. 'Don't say that. May God bring him back!'

'He's done it already.' Saulat covered her eyes with her handkerchief. 'We had hidden the news because of our mother.'

Ismat moved away from her. She was afraid that she might shake Saulat and scream, 'It's you, Saulat Ara Begum, who has killed him and now you're blaming the war!' She held her head in both hands. Her tears had dried. As Saulat watched her sitting there with her head lowered, she was thinking, 'You've devoured him, you witch! And how happy you are now and content! The way you talk to Zubair – so affectionately, right in front of my eyes, as if he had never ever mattered to you. That's all right. You can be happy. Zubair is still alive . . .'

She stood up, 'I think I'll go now.'

'Already? Stay for a bit,' Ismat's voice sounded choked and forced, as she spoke half-heartedly. Her face was white.

'No, I'll go and see. Maybe there's been a reply.'

'If you do get an answer please telephone Zubair's office, here's the number.' She put Zubair's card in her hand and held on to the door for support. She felt faint.

Later, when she lay on her bed she remembered how he had shinned up the peepal tree because she had asked him to fetch her the tiny nightingale chicks, but then seeing the nightingale yell and screech she had forced him to return them to the nest, saying, 'This nightingale will curse you.' He had slapped him gently then, saying, 'Why do you pester me so much? First you get the chicks down, and now you want them put back.'

'Barrey Bhaiya, she'll curse you.'

'Then what. I'll die?'

'Waah! God forbid. Why should you die?'

But by the time he had climbed up again to replace the chicks, Saulat Apa had already reported it to Barri Ammah. And that day he had had a real walloping. I wept with him, too, that day.'

She buried her face in the pillow and her entire body shook with her sobs.

80

She had just decided to hail a *tonga*, giving up on the bus after having waited for a long time, when she heard someone call out her name, 'Gaythi!'

She turned round with a start and looked closely at the caller.

The man with overgrown stubble, dressed only in a shirt and a pair of pyjamas, was healthy and attractive despite the fact that his face looked drawn. Her silent and surprised stare pained him.

'Don't you recognise me? But you could not possibly have forgotten your sister?' His voice startled Gaythi.

'Who? Zubair Bhai? Allah! How changed you are!'

'I've changed? Really?'

'Vastly,' she sounded impatient, 'and where is Ismat Apa? When did you come? Is everything all right? How did you come?'

'The way everyone else is coming. Ismat is at a friend of mine's place – when did you get here and who is with you? Where's Bakhtiar?'

He had assessed their situation from her cheap sandals and clothes, and her waiting for the bus.

'Only Ammah and I have arrived here. We've only heard Bakhtiar Bhai's message to us on the radio. It's almost a month since I came.'

'So, Gaythi. Have you found somewhere to stay? Where are you? Is Chachi Ammah well?'

'She's OK. If you're not specially busy then come and see our place, otherwise, how will we meet you again?'

'Yes! That's what happens here. You lose sight of a person once and then you have to go round looking for them.'

'Come, we'll get a *tonga*.'

'Where have you been?'

'To the office.'

'Are you working somewhere?'

'Yes.'

'Where?'

'In the custodian's office.'

301

He looked at that girl from top to toe. He had seen her a few years ago when she had been quite young. 'What work do you do?'

'Stenographer's.'

She spoke as the *tonga* turned, 'I kept wondering, Zubair Bhai, where were you? And where are Chachi jaan and Talat?'

'They're still there. Talat has got herself admitted to an MA course. There was no violence there. However we came here as refugees from Dalhousie.'

'Dalhousie? Were you in Dalhousie, Zubair Bhai? Then you must have seen Asif Bhai and everyone?' She mentioned Asif Jah's name instead of Saulat's.

'Yes, Gaythi! We met your Saulat Apa a few times. Ismat grabbed hold of her and brought her home one day. Then we visited them too. Then one day she came because she was anxious about all of you but I was at work.'

'So there was violence there too?' Gaythi got worried, 'So, where are they? You must have all been together during the rioting?'

'They're all in Delhi, and they're fine. How could we have been at the same place? They're big shots. Whether there's a riot or something else, big shots remain big.' Zubair spoke drily.

'What a thing to say.'

'Whether it is or not, one has to face realities.' Zubair's voice sounded irritated. 'Do you know, Gaythi, when the feuds began we were surrounded by danger, arson and abductions. At that time, I telephoned them because Ismat asked me to. At first their servant said that they were resting. I had wanted them to let Ismat stay at their place until things settled down a bit so I rang them back after two hours. She answered herself and I will remember that tone of hers for the rest of my life. She said very distantly, "We've had phone calls like this from lots of people, but you know how difficult it is because of Asif's position." Then she said after thinking of something, "Look, wait till he comes back. Maybe something can be done." After that we left our situation to God and He brought us here.'

'So you haven't found a house so far?'

'No. I'm going to Karachi in a few days. I'd opted for Pakistan.'

'Anand Bhavan,' Zubair bent down to read, 'the name of the house is sweet, Gaythi. Well done! You've shown great courage for a girl on her own. To have managed all this by yourself. Chachi Ammah must be worried about everyone?'

'Well, don't even ask about it. The truth is, Zubair Bhai, that her sorrows have multiplied so much that she can absorb every new grief and not notice it.'

'What are you saying, *bitya*!'

Two bamboo stools stood on the small circular verandah. There were no curtains at the doors to the rooms. A charpoy woven with coarse rope and a divan for prayers could be seen in one of the rooms. Gaythi called out from the verandah, 'Ammah, look who's here!'

She came out barefoot. Her sari was old and soiled.

'Zubair!' There were tears in her eyes. Who knows what she had been thinking? Her hands trembled as she embraced him. Gaythi went into the kitchen to make tea.

'Chachi Ammah, Saulat Apa is fine, in Delhi.'

'In Delhi? Did you meet her?'

'I met Asif Bhai at the airport and before that we had met in Dalhousie a few times.'

'In Dalhousie? Have you come from there?'

'Yes. We couldn't get in touch with each other over there but we met at the airport in Delhi.'

'Do you have any news of Arjumand?'

'Yes. He told us that she is in hospital.'

'God have mercy on us! Did he tell you why, son? Is she injured?' Today, as she heard news of her being alive, a prayer for her well-being crossed her lips and she felt restless.

'No, God forbid, she wasn't injured. There was something about her being a few months' pregnant. And Akbar is ill himself, too. His father is in prison and they had no news about his mother and the rest until then.'

'Where's Ismat?'

'She's here too. I'm staying at a friend's place.'

She was silent for a little while. Receiving news about the well-being of both her daughters had made her seem a little preoccupied. In those few days she had forgotten how to be happy or amazed at anything. She heard everything with the same inertia and implacability.

'*Beta*! There is a house here. Bring Ismat here, there are only two rooms but we can work round that and manage.'

'I'm leaving for Karachi in a few days, Chachi Ammah. If we leave the people we are staying with now, they might feel offended. But I will definitely bring her to see you this evening or tomorrow morning. She'll want to come the minute she hears about it.'

When Zubair left them she could not help saying, 'God save him from the evil eye, he's in very good health and he looks handsome now. What a shame I forgot to ask where Talat and her mother are.'

'Talat is doing her MA and Chachi jaan is still in Dadi Ammah's house. There was no violence there,' Gaythi told her.

There was no violence there! Talat is doing her MA, and Ismat's husband has turned out to be so handsome and fit. Before her eyes was Asif Jah's head, devoid of hair, his ageing face and flabby body. Arjumand has lost her baby and Akbar is ill. Gaythi could not even finish her BA and is working as a typist at the custodian's office. Everything is getting into such a strange muddle, as if the cards had been shuffled so well that the game had changed unrecognisably.

Zubair had left them. She stood up quickly and commenced her prayers.

81

When two cyclists stand shoulder to shoulder, waiting for the traffic signal to change, they manage to see each other very clearly. The girl on the bicycle next to him, with short black hair touching her face, reaching her shoulders, was someone he could have recognised even amongst a crowd of thousands.

He had recognised her and was now wondering why his heart was beating madly seeing her so close to himself, and why he should have experienced that strange mixture of happiness and fear. Those truths which had been struggling to manifest themselves for a very long time but had been unable to do so because he would not allow them to, were now unveiling themselves to him. Now they were insistent upon exposing themselves, even without his sanction.

'So, this implies that my guardianship and sympathy were being secretly directed by my hopes and desires.'

That man, who belonged to the homeland of the followers of the Buddha, and who himself believed in the religion of those who had upheld the traditions of mysticism, kept cursing himself like a thorough-bred Asian.

As the cycle behind her jogged Gaythi, she looked to her right with a start – and then turned her face away and completely ignored the person who had been a benefactor and a protector to her. And, she was absolutely serene about this action of hers.

When the traffic warden turned and signalled to them, the cycles moved off, one after the other.

Everything that was strange seemed ordinary enough now. Those things which might have seemed absurd assumed a seriousness simply through their daily repetition.

For example, Bakhtiar, who had now reached Pakistan, had traced his mother through a letter from Saulat. He was with them for four days, on holiday from his course at Ghora Galli. When he saw Gaythi going to work, he felt a mixture of pain and satisfaction. It was only a question of six or seven months, then his course would end and he would get an appointment somewhere.

He sat talking to Ammah Begum for the whole day, 'Asif Bhai does not intend to come here. He says, "My health is not up to the upheaval and if I do go, my mother, who is very old and frail, will never agree to go. These riots will not last forever. I will look after my lands".'

She sat in silence, chopping her betel nuts finely. 'Did you meet Arjumand as well?'

'Of course; I stayed there for three days. And those people visited me too. Arjumand looks really pulled down.'

'She doesn't write letters. She's written only two in all this time. Do you think she's happy though?'

'Yes. She seems all right. They haven't been able to trace Akbar's mother and younger brother. His father is in prison and he has become somewhat irritable. Arjumand feels upset that she is the only one left behind. Although Apa tells her repeatedly that she is not alone and that she is there too.'

Her eyes filled with tears, 'But she should write to us.'

'What can she write?' Bakhtiar was forced to utter the truth, 'Akbar says, "If you keep on sending letters to Pakistan, I might be arrested. My father is already a political prisoner".'

'So they don't intend to come here then?'

'How can they do that? With his father stuck in prison. Just leave him there and come themselves?'

'Yes, that's also true.' There was a tremendous sense of helplessness in her voice.

'In actual fact their intention is to go abroad when his father is released. That's the most peaceful way out, now.'

She looked at Bakhtiar in surprise. Gaythi had returned from the office. Today she had brought a young boy of twelve or thirteen with her. She

305

called out triumphantly from a distance, 'Here, Ammah! I've brought you a servant too.'

'God bless you! You've done everything for me,' she answered gently. She felt she owed her many debts but the biggest was that she had never referred to the past.

'Carry on then, enjoy yourself for a few days.' Bakhtiar laughed. 'I'll get you admitted to the college after that. Actually, you are so unenthusiastic about studies that whenever you do get admitted to college, you make such a mess of things that your studies are left in ruins.'

'That's why I tell you that further studies don't agree with me. I've now given up all intentions of going back to study.'

'Have you heard that Talat is doing her MA?'

'I've heard!' She smiled. 'So what can I do?'

'Go back to study. It's only a question of another six or seven months. I met Chacha Abba too, in Delhi; he was there on an official visit. They're all fine. He said that once things have calmed down properly he'll visit our lands, too. Ammah! Munshi ji, Ikraam – all of them have died.'

'But everyone tells me that you can make claims here against property in riot-affected areas.'

'Well, we'll try to do that as well. But first you must change houses. Someone told me just yesterday that people will only be allotted the places where they have chosen to live now. You'll find this very inconvenient then.'

'Thank God, son, that He has given us a roof above our heads. I don't feel any inconvenience. This is sufficient for both of us.'

'How will this be enough for you when we all get together? You'll feel the pinch then.'

'Getting together' brought tears to her eyes. 'How can we get together, son? We're all scattered now.'

'Once again you've started saying those gloomy things. Just wait for a few days, then you'll see how often they'll all come. Even if Arjumand does go abroad you'll see, she'll visit every year. And then, how about me? I'm someone who will come!' he laughed.

'May God preserve you forever.' She placed a hand on his back, 'I don't need anything more now.'

At that moment, Gaythi felt that she had misunderstood her mother a few years ago.

82

'*Arrey*, what are you doing here, girl?'

Her fingers slipped on the keys of the typewriter at the sound of that heavy voice and she looked up. Sometimes people appear before you so unexpectedly that you have to tax your memory a good deal to identify them. The tall and stocky man kept gazing at her for the next couple of minutes whilst she stared at him vacantly. A shadow fell across his beaming face, 'Didn't you recognise me? I am Sajjad.'

'Is it you? Sajjad Bhai . . .!'

'Yes! And I've forgotten your name, even though your face has always remained in my memory.'

'My name is a little strange – Gaythi.' She smiled.

'Yes, that's it. Wonderful! Now, I remember it.'

She scrutinised Sajjad. His complexion had become darker, his fore-head wider because of a receding hairline and there was a strange look of inertia on his face.

'Can I sit down here, if you don't mind?'

'Why should I mind? Do sit down.'

'Is everyone well?'

'Yes. Everything's fine now.'

'And where's Saulat?'

'They won't be coming here. Asif Bhai has been posted there – to Delhi!'

'And your other sister, the one who was very artless?'

'Arjumand? She got married. She is there too. Her husband is planning that they should go abroad.'

'Who did she get married to?'

'You might have met Akbar.' She tried to remember.

'Oh! That young show-off.' Then he steadied himself, 'Forgive me, Gaythi! But that's the impression that boy left on me at the time.'

She said nothing.

'You've taken offence. That is my greatest failing – I just say whatever comes into my head without hesitation. But he was, of course, a very interesting boy with lots of potential.'

'Now don't try to talk yourself out of this embarrassment,' she laughed. She remembered what Sajjad had said the day he had read their palms: that there was no harm in expressing frankly whatever one has observed or thought.

'Where are you people staying? Did you find a decent house? Tell me the address so I can visit you sometime.'

'Yes, we have a reasonable house now. The one we had before was terribly makeshift. Here.' She wrote the address on a piece of paper and was going to draw a street plan for him when the peon came to collect the file.

'Well, goodbye! You are a very courageous girl. I can't believe it is you sitting here.'

'That's all right, Sajjad Bhai! No big deal.' She returned to finishing the letter as fast as she could.

Sajjad lit a cigarette as he was getting into his car, 'Sometimes a tiny tract of time grows into such a vast span and brings such incredible changes!' Then his car started racing along the streets in the cantonment area. There was calm here and quiet. It felt as though there had been no revolution or disturbance there.

83

'Sajjad has changed so much in this short time! I only noticed today that the hair on his temples has turned grey,' Ammah Begum commented after he had left.

'Yes, but then he is quite old,' Gaythi said, lifting some paint on to her brush. She had stopped going to work since Bakhtiar's appointment. She had joined the Mayo School of Arts and now sat on the verandah with the intention of finishing her painting. Sajjad had been sitting there too, taking tea with Ammah Begum.

'Oh, what a shame! I completely forgot to ask him if he had remarried or not.'

'He must have done.'

'I feel as if he's still going round like he used to. I think even now if he finds an older girl who is a reasonable match, he should get married.'

'Who knows, he may already have done that.'

'Yes, that's always possible ... Let's see when Arjumand gets here. It's nearly time for them to return now. At first they kept waiting for her delivery. Now, God bless her, the baby's nearly a month and a quarter. I feel as if they'll go away without visiting us.'

'Did you write a letter of congratulations when Akbar Bhai's father was released?'

'I gave it to you to post.'

Ammah Begum rose and went to lie down inside. She had organised a prayer meeting to bless Sheharyaar's soul on the previous Wednesday. Every month she would have his favourite dishes cooked to be distributed after these prayer meetings. As soon as her eyes grew heavy she heard Gaythi's voice, 'Here we are. Arjumand's telegram's arrived. She's coming tomorrow afternoon.'

She sat up. Her face would pale now even when she was happy.

As they came away from the border, Gaythi held the baby in her arms and Arjumand kept poking her head out of the moving jeep to look at the streets and buildings of this city which was now her mother's and her sister's homeland.

'How are you feeling? Were you ill?'

'No. I'm absolutely fine.'

'Then why are you so weak? There are shadows under your eyes!'

'It's taken three attempts in eighteen months for me to have this baby. I got ill again only three months after the first time. We didn't write to you because we thought you'd worry.'

'But what is the matter with you, Arjumand? Look after yourself. What's the desperate need for children so soon?'

She lowered her head, looked at the baby and covered her foot with the pink blanket.

Gaythi bent down and pushed the baby's dark hair off her forehead and kissed it very gently. A whiff of talcum powder and milk assaulted her nostrils and the baby wiggled and clenched her fists.

'Do you like Pakistan?'

'Hum. I've only seen one street so far,' she answered with a start.

Ammah Begum stood waiting at the entrance to the hallway. Arjumand was ahead of Gaythi who held the baby in her arms. She ran and clung to her mother and wept so much that even Ammah Begum got alarmed. They were meeting for the first time since she had got married.

She brought her into her own room with great difficulty. Every now and again she would embrace her and kiss her.

'Here, drink this.' She pushed the glass into her hand.

'Now take a look at her too,' Gaythi put the baby on her lap.

'What have you decided to call her?' She wanted to play with the baby now.

'Naushaba!' Arjumand watched her with interest.

'Do you give her ordinary milk?'

'No.'

'No wonder you're in such a state. You should eat properly.'

She sat for a long time telling them about her father-in-law's imprisonment and release.

'Is there some chance of Saulat coming too?' Seeing one of her daughters there had given her new hope.

'None at the moment. Until Asif Bhai retires it will be difficult for them to come. You will have to go to visit them.'

'Asif is so stubborn.'

Arjumand changed the subject and started asking about Bakhtiar.

'He's in Kohat. His orderly was here. He left yesterday. I have sent him a message about your being here.'

That night the two sisters shared a room after a long time and lay down next to each other.

'Since we've been here this is the first time we have a third person in the house. Bakhtiar Bhaiya comes sometimes to brighten up our days.'

'You should look for a suitable girl for him.'

'What does Talat want to do? Do you know anything?'

'Know what? Chachi jaan wrote me a letter and invited me, saying that I shouldn't feel all my family were in Pakistan and that I should visit them. Well, I made the blunder of going along. What can I tell you, Gaythi? She avenged herself of all her old grievances, which had piled up since God knows when! In one week she really managed to wound me so deeply. All day and all night, she didn't miss a chance to have a dig at me. When she sat down to condole with me about Barrey Bhaiya's death she went so far as to refer to Ammah as a witch. She repeated to me a thousand times how happy Ismat Apa was. Then one day I just let slip that once Talat finishes her MA we'll get her married off, and Chachi jaan screamed and ranted so much that I was amazed. She used to be so quiet and calm. She's shed her old skin good and proper now.'

'What did she say?'

'She said, "Stop! That's enough! Don't any of you dare even mention Talat's name. When you people were well off you found faults in us and our children. Now that you are biting the dust, all of a sudden you think of Talat. Sheharyaar had to be sacrificed to all that arrogance; how come you've thought of Talat now? Our girl is living like a queen. She has a magnificent and loving husband. God forgive us, he doesn't have skin which sags and a paunch that wobbles!"'

'Well that means Chachi jaan's become quite arrogant; that is obviously a snipe at Asif Bhai.'

'Yes. I think she is planning something else for Talat. Talat went to Madras for her holidays this year.'

'What does Talat herself want?'

'She says nothing. Oh, yes, they talked quite a lot about Chacha Abba and Chachi Ammah this time. He never even writes to us. When I was getting married they made an excuse of his heart attack, but now they've sent a huge bundle of saris for Talat. She was also wearing a very beautiful locket from Madras.'

'So they must have intentions towards Ayaz Bhai.'

'That's obvious. We'll hear the announcement within the next few days now.'

'That's fine too, I suppose. They have the upper hand now. Sometimes the days are longer and sometimes it's the nights.'

'There's been an amazing change in Chachi jaan.'

'*Arrey*, this is what life's like, Arjumand.'

'The revolution has shown us so much of life, Gaythi, that one has come to loathe this world.'

'Yes, the world is a horrible place, but it is beautiful too. There are some very sincere, sympathetic and uncomplaining people in this very same world as well. And how is Saulat Apa?'

'Don't even ask about her. My heart has grown bitter about so many things. She drinks so much, she is so wayward that I can't even describe it, sister! I'd heard that she was planning to divorce. Then Sajjad Bhai wrote her a long letter and phoned her too, saying, "I will consider you to be the cruellest person in the world if you abandon my brother in his present condition".'

'Why? What's the matter with him, then?'

'*Arrey*, it's very bad. She has tortured him so much. One feels very sorry for him now.'

'And you went to Lucknow. How was everyone there?'

'Hashmi Phupho's fine. Masood has become an engineer. I'd heard they're coming to Pakistan. He's got a job with a company. Kaamni's grandmother was very ill and wanted the marriage ceremony to be performed in her lifetime, so it must have happened by now.'

'How is Kaamni?'

'She was so distant with me that I can't even begin to tell you. Talat had already mentioned to me that she has changed ever such a lot since Masood has got this job. Once when we asked her for the recipe for a dish she just said quite brazenly, "*Baji* I don't really know how to cook. I haven't even learnt how to cook rice khichri".'

'So she calls you "*Baji*" now?'

'What else do you think? She only referred to you once, and then she said, "Gaythi Apa".'

'Did you meet Masood at all?'

'No, I didn't. I heard he doesn't visit very often. He only comes when his mother-in-law invites him which she has to do repeatedly and then he sits with them most of the time. Chachi jaan says that he's become arrogant. God only knows if that's true, but he didn't set foot in the place while I was there. I went to call on Hashmi Phupho myself but he never came home all day.'

'Oh, look, she's woken up. You'd better feed her now.'

There was silence in the darkness but for the tweaky sound of the baby's sucking.

'Are you asleep, Gaythi?'

'No,' her voice sounded hoarse.

84

When Arjumand left she took with her all the bustle and cheerfulness which had entered the house with her, albeit, temporarily. Bakhtiar visited twice whilst she was there. Akbar came to fetch her and stayed for a week as well.

Ammah Begum started finding herself busy again after a long time. She chopped betel nuts finely, prepared the seeds of coriander and shredded coconut for Arjumand to take with her. She also made shirts and comforters for her.

Gaythi had found parting with Naushaba the most painful. She would get dressed and leave for college quietly in the mornings and when she returned she would busy herself with finishing her paintings or sculpture. They had a good servant now, and there was not that much housework to do. She would read when she had time to spare.

Ammah Begum spent her leisure time looking after the garden. She complained that the gardener they had employed was so useless that he could not even identify the plants. Then she would miss Murli.

Gaythi had had a severe cold for two or three days. That morning when she woke up, she felt she had a slight temperature too and so she did not go to college. At about eleven when she felt slightly better, she brought a chair into the garden and sat down under the lychee tree to read.

'Wonderful! So you're enjoying your holiday!'

She looked up surprised, 'Salaams, Sajjad Bhai!'

'*Wa-laikum-as-salaam!*'

'You've become so stingy now that you can't even say a prayer in response!' She turned the book over on her lap.

'I'll pray for you, but first find me a place to sit.'

When she went in to fetch a chair he planted himself on her chair and shut the book.

'*Waah, bhai!* What's this? Why did you shut my book? Here's the chair for you.'

'So that means Madam is going to read and I must watch like a dunce!'

'Why should you watch? You came at this time so obviously you couldn't have come to have a chat with me. I should have been in college by your calculation.'

'However, you're not at the moment. Oh, yes, that prayer I owe you, if you like I'll give it to you now?'

'There's another debt you owe me too.'

'What's that? Now you'll keep accumulating debts against me.'

'You might remember that you read Arjumand's palm and mine one day, but you didn't finish mine. You said, "We'll see to it another time," and then Your Highness simply disappeared . . .! Yes, how come you vanished all of a sudden like that?'

She noticed that Sajjad was deep in thought. 'Hum!' He started, 'Give me your hand, I'll look at it now. But why do you want to show it to me after all this time? Whatever I didn't tell you must have transpired by now?'

'Yes, and what hasn't happened so far will soon come to pass,' she laughed.

'Oh, yes! I heard that girl Arjumand was here along with a daughter. *Bhai*, she is a mere child herself!'

'You didn't come to visit even once while she was here. She asked after you several times.'

'Well, yes. I'd gone away then,' Sajjad said softly, and then spoke in a bullying voice, 'Gaythi Ara Begum! I notice that you are getting too smart!'

'Why, Sajjad Bhai?'

'What's this you're reading? Do you know who this writer is?'

'D. H. Lawrence.'

It seemed as if Sajjad could not settle on a topic for conversation. He kept flitting rapidly from one subject to the other.

'Why are your eyes so red? Have you been weeping?'

'I have a cold and a temperature.'

'I can cure them like that.' He snapped his fingers.

'How?'

'With a hot cup of coffee.'

'I can organise that for you right now.'

'What the same old thing again! The guaranteed treatment is a cup from the Coffee House; you'll see, girl! This cold and temperature is because you're very lonely and your heart's restless. One of the extreme symptoms of boredom is that you get a cold.'

She watched him in silence. 'I would come but I need Ammah Begum's permission.'

'Who? Is that you, Gaythi Ara Begum, talking about permission?' He laughed.

'*Jee*! It's me, talking about permission.'

'That permission will be obtained in a moment.' He went inside and she followed him.

'Yes. She's been very quiet since the day Arjumand left; and anyhow she is a little weak.'

'Sahib, she has been enormously burdened, physically and mentally. During the next holidays you should take her to stay with Bakhtiar. She'll have a break there for a few days. She really needs to enjoy herself; how pale she looks!'

'I agree. You take her out then but she said she felt feverish. She may get too tired.'

'No, don't worry.'

Gaythi sat in front of the mirror brushing her hair, thinking, 'I said it to Arjumand, but I myself am looking too sallow without any good reason.' She looked at the dark circles under her eyes and put on a light shade of lipstick to conceal the chalkiness of her lips.

'Sometimes I am amazed Gaythi! Could someone like you, who can't put together an outfit, actually be Saulat's real sister?'

'Why? What's wrong?'

'Such a lovely pink shirt and this stiff white muslin scarf? *Arrey*! You're not a widow! Go and find a pink scarf to wear with this.'

His commanding tone was so entertaining that she went and found a pink scarf and sat down on the car seat next to him laughing.

314

85

All afternoon he had slept, almost unconscious. Even at tea time, Li Fan's daughter had to call him several times to wake him up.

'What is it?' He came round suddenly, and sat up.

'Mama wants to know why you haven't come to eat. What's happened?'

'Tell her I have a temperature.' Then, he lay down and immediately went to sleep again.

When he next came round, it was evening and the room was nearly dark. Someone rested a soft hand on his forehead. He became alert, 'Oh, so you've come?'

That hand which was soft and cool moved away gently.

'How are you, Safdar?' Now a heavy and warmer hand touched his forehead. He opened his eyes and looked round as if he were searching for something.

'What is it, Safdar? Look, we've brought you some tea. Will you have some?' This voice and language were familiar. The words had been spoken in his own mother tongue but they felt strange and unfamiliar and he had difficulty in comprehending them.

'I'll have some water,' he spoke in English, as if the two people who stood near him did not understand his own language.

Li Fan moved forward and held the glass of cold water closer to him, 'You will be able to drink if you lift your head a little.'

Instead of raising his head, he sat up and drank half a glass in one gulp. Li Fan's wife quickly handed her husband the wet towel and Safdar rubbed his face and hair with it. His eyes opened and he lay down.

Then he spoke in a faint voice, 'How long have you people been here?'

'Nearly an hour. When you didn't come over last night we thought you may have eaten out somewhere, as you often do but when you didn't come for lunch today, Zoe came to see you and she told us that you had a very high temperature.'

'You mustn't talk too much though,' Li Fan's wife advised.

'Let him talk. There's no harm in that.'

'Shall I make you some tea?' she said promptly.

'Yes, give me some tea. There's a foul taste in my mouth.'

'I'll put some salt in it for you.'

When he got up he said, 'I feel as if everything is miles away from me. You two seem very far away too. It is as if I've been ill for years.'

'You can lean against me,' Li Fan sat behind him.

'I think you should put cold compresses on his forehead,' his wife suggested.

'No. My temperature isn't that high. I'm not rambling.' He put his cup down after drinking the tea and fumbled under the pillow for his cigarettes.

'Here, take this cigarette,' Li Fan lit one and gave it to him.

'How kind both of you are!' His eyes filled with tears. And then he was sweating again. In that cold sweat and restless anxiety he started rambling once more, 'I feel as if I am in space. That I've got to stay in this very space for the rest of my life. Just see how faint and unreal you two seem to be now. Li Fan's wife! – You should tell me now to go to my own homeland. Do you know what Lao Tzu says? – He says: "The dervish lives in this world with peace and tranquillity. For him all the peoples of this world belong to only one land, the territory of the heart."

'And I say to you that this is all nonsense. Lao Tzu is a fool, or he makes fools of us. Listen to what I say. Man can do only two things: either he can play the fool himself, or fool others – And maybe you don't know this: I have been fooled, and I will guard my follies too. Because Lao Tzu has fooled me. Tell him the land of the lovers is desolate. And now tell us where the dervish must go? What else can he do except secure himself in the fortress of his own follies?'

His voice fell by degrees and his feverishness decreased slowly too. He started dozing and those two stayed watching him and looking at each other, in alarm and dismay.

All night he slept peacefully and Li Fan sat by his bedside checking his pulse every now and then. His temperature and pulse slowly went down to normal.

The next morning he had no recall of the day before. He lay very calmly with his eyes open. Li Fan looked at his eyes attentively. More than the ravages of illness, they bore the look of loss and resignation.

After giving him his breakfast he handed him a cigarette, saying, 'I'll go now. Zoe will come and play here in your room. Is that all right?' He bent towards him affectionately.

'All right.' He shook his head.

'Whatever happened to me? Why did I have such a high temperature?' He strained his memory. 'What was the last thing I did before feeling feverish? – Oh, yes, that's right. I wrote my diary.' He turned on his side and picked up the diary which lay on the stool near the headboard.

As he held the diary unopened in his hand, he wondered, 'What did I write in it? I can't remember a thing.'

316

Then he turned its pages. There was very little recorded in it. He seldom had time to spend on writing. The freshly written pages were before him now:

'I have said so many things to you since you were tiny, but I have always ached to say one sentence. Forget about saying it aloud to you, I have never even dared to think it through in a rational or sequential fashion. And, I have never repeated it, even to myself. But today, I feel as if today I will say it to myself and write it on this page too, "I love you, Cuckoo."

'I love you, and I am human too. That is why the other day when I saw you at the entrance to the Coffee House with that magnificent mature officer, I felt as if everything on this earth was slipping away from me. As if the earth had let go of its axis and run away from under my feet. Now this world, and everything in it, appears to be unreal and unconnected with my being. How can I complain to you? You have had no responsibility for this. My own consciousness respected the reality, in that there had never been any link or relationship between you and me. But what can one do about one's subconscious, which is so foolish and intractable? My conscious mind strove to remain unvexed even when it saw you laughing cheerfully near the door of the Coffee House . . .'

The diary slipped from his hand and Zoe came running to him, 'Look, what I brought you, Uncle.'

She placed her hand on the pillow and opened her palm. A black butterfly paused for a second and then took flight.

'So what does this signify as far as the symbols of our love go?' he wondered, looking at it.

She came and sat before him on the stool like a well-behaved child. 'How are you feeling now, Uncle?'

'Zoe?' Safdar asked, looking at the ceiling above, 'Did you study today?'

'Yes, Uncle.'

'What did you read, tell me?'

'Huh! I don't remember – Uncle, you're not well; shall I dab your forehead?' She planted herself on the stool obediently.

'No, Zoe, these hands are too tiny, they'll get tired.' He took her hand in his own.

'Then what shall I do for you, Uncle?'

'You should sing me a nice song.'

'But I don't want to sing at all.'

'Well, then, never mind.'
'So then why don't you sing me a song?'
'Which one?'
'The usual one,

> "On the rocks,
> a flower,
> a weeping willow
> and a fisherman . . .".'

'Oh, that one –

> "Shining upon the river
> a ray of the sun
> and a bird flying on its wings . . ."

No, I can't sing that song for you.'
'Why not?'
'Because I'm ill, Zoe!'
Then he repeated the rest of the words under his breath,

> 'Half way to the mountains
> He makes a half-broken vow,
> and the worshipper moves ahead.
> In the forest
> a yellow leaf
> rustles
> and falls off the branch.'

'What did you say, Uncle?' Zoe asked.
'Nothing, Zoe! He turned on his side and repeated softly,

> 'He makes a half-broken vow,
> and the worshipper moves ahead.
> In the forest
> a yellow leaf
> rustles . . . and . . .'

Tiny, thick black lashes dropped over his eyes and tiny soft sleepy breaths submerged his being.

As she looked through the pictures in the magazine, Zoe laid her head down on it, and dropped off to sleep face downwards on the floor.

86

They were to set off very early in the morning so Sajjad had slept there that night. Ammah Begum kept reminding Gaythi over and over again about each and every detail. She was doing her best to reassure her mother, but she kept getting tense. 'Look! We mustn't forget my medicines. Check your warm clothes once more.'

'God forgive me, Ammah Begum, but you never used to panic like this before and now you're worrying about such a brief journey.'

She did not answer her and instead started her prayers.

What would she remember of how Ammah Begum used to travel? She never took any baggage with her, nor had to unpack. All of it used to be sent two days ahead, and she always found things unpacked and arranged for her in an orderly fashion, when she herself arrived.

They had to have the lights on when they woke up to drink tea and they set off whilst it was still dark. She and Ammah Begum were travelling for the first time since they had come. Sajjad kept talking to them about the route.

'We'll get you lunch at Wazirabad.'

'Why? Is there something special about that?'

'You'll see when you eat it.'

'Forget it. What do people here know about cooking?'

'You should try it and see, Khala Bi.'

'You can see for yourself. I've had all the traffic stopped for your sakes. It's only you people on the road from here all the way there.'

'Sure!' she laughed, 'who else would be crazy enough to venture out so early?'

'Will there be enough room in Bakhtiar's house, son? Will we all fit in it? I had heard there were only two rooms.'

'*Arrey*, Sahib! If there's no room, you can stay at my place and this girl can stay at Bakhtiar's.'

'That's a new one! I wouldn't dream of bothering you now.'

'What's the problem? If I needed to, I could stay at your house so happily and freely – You'd never guess.'

Then he spoke softly to Gaythi who was sitting next to him, 'Why do older people get so anxious without any reason?'

'Anxious? Yes, I don't know why. But you're getting old yourself now. You'll be getting anxious without any justification.'

'Get away, girl!'

'So! Am I lying? Just look in the mirror, you've so many grey hairs.'

'Hum, hum. That's very bad news you've given me. One of my anxieties will be that I am getting old. Never mind. Now light a cigarette for me please, so I can forget my sorrow over that. Here it is. Look, it's in that pocket.'

Then he addressed Ammah Begum, 'Khala Bi, Bakhtiar invited you only after he'd got a nice house. But I am telling you now, that you'll have to pay me off, too, for my labour in taking you from here to there.'

'Are you going to charge us a fare then?' she laughed.

'*Jee*. You can call it that.'

'Then you should tell us beforehand, so if we can't afford it we should look for some other means of transport,' she laughed.

'No, it's not that much. It's only that you'll have to stay with me for at least fifteen days.'

She laughed but said nothing.

'Well look at that! The traffic you'd had stopped for us has started again. There's a lorry coming, and then a car right behind it.'

'Which one? A bullock cart?'

'That'll come too. It seems to be a car at the moment.'

'Can you tell what make of car it is, girl?'

'How do I know what make it is?'

'Don't you know even that much?'

'I don't go round buying cars. What've I got to do with a car?' There was a whiff of regret in her voice.

'It seems to be a powerful car, and the colour is beautiful too. And, look at that,' he bent towards her and whispered, 'so's the passenger! I think I'll slow down, to have a good look when they get closer.'

'Forget it. So what if she is? What if the man in the other car's saying the same thing.'

'I beg your pardon, Gaythi, but our passenger isn't that lovely.'

She looked away in embarrassment.

'*Arrey, bhai*! This turns out to be our Engineer Sahib.'

Gaythi turned round to have a look at the car. The swarthy face of the woman dressed in blue silk was very attractive and seemed familiar. 'Which Engineer Sahib?'

'There is one – whom I met in Quetta then he went off to Karachi. He's only been here a little while. They may be on their way to Murree.'

'Is he a refugee?'

'He would have been a refugee if he had come when people were being displaced. He only came a little while ago. His appointment is quite new and so is his marriage.'

'So, where's he from?'

'From the same place as yourself, Lucknow. Masood Ahmed.'

'Masood Ahmed!' Gaythi was surprised and as the car drew very near them, it was apparent that the driver was, indubitably, Masood.

'Huh! Go away,' Sajjad said to himself, 'I waved and the gentleman did not see it, he's that busy driving and talking to his wife.'

'So have you met his wife too?'

'Certainly. She's wonderful, Kaamni, both by name and in her looks.'

'What do you mean?'

'She speaks very carefully. A touch nervous, and incredibly intelligent. It seems as if she's come out for the first time, but she grasps everything in a flash. Very few people can guess that she is so green. She makes a few interesting blunders too.'

'That must embarrass her husband.'

'Not at all. He says yes to the twitch of her eyebrow; he's a very compliant husband.'

The car had whizzed past, leaving the jeep behind.

'Well? Should we overtake Engineer Sahib? We'll get you introduced to him.' Sajjad slammed his foot down on the accelerator.

'No, no, Sajjad Bhai. Don't speed; it makes Ammah Begum feel very ill.' Their car was already parked before the restaurant in Wazirabad. She saw Masood open the door for Kaamni who stepped out, the border of her sari carefully draped across her white blouse as she looked up at him with her beautiful lowered eyes. A thick garland of jasmine flowers was wound round the large knot into which she had piled her hair high. Masood moved forward, put his arm round her waist and they went in.

'God protect us! What a place for that romantic gesture!' Sajjad laughed, 'He's still an amateur! So, what do you think? Shall we go in to eat or get the food sent to us out here?'

'Sajjad Bhai, Ammah Begum will not be able to eat here. She'll be very uncomfortable. Why don't we stick to our original plan and eat at Flashmans in Pindi?'

Bakhtiar was waiting for them at the car park.

'Are we going to leave the jeep here?' Ammah Begum asked anxiously.

'No, Sahib! The jeep will take you all the way home. This boy is here only to welcome you.'

As she climbed into his car she saw that Masood and Kaamni were going up the steps. Two coolies, who were carrying their luggage, walked in tow. Kaamni was not thin like she used to be; her body looked rounded and beautiful now.

'Just take a look, madame! Bakhtiar has maintained his garden so exquisitely, in contrast with Gaythi Ara Begum's management,' Sajjad said, driving the jeep through the gates.

'Why should it be my management? Ammah Begum looks after things herself.'

'No wonder, I thought that the garden had started looking a lot neater than it used to!'

When Gaythi had had the luggage put away, she showered and changed before coming down for tea. Bakhtiar asked her as soon as he saw her, 'What's the matter? Are you very tired?'

'To tell you the truth, I made the effort to come on her account. I thought she'd get some rest here; she's getting very run down over there,' Ammah interjected.

'She puts on airs as well,' Sajjad said, pouring himself a second cup of tea.

'Actually, I'm looking tired now because Sajjad Bhai has been picking my brains all the way down here.'

'Fear the wrath of God, girl! That's the limit! I tried to entertain her and she says I've picked her brains.'

After a little while, when Ammah Begum had gone to her own room to rest, Sajjad said to her, 'Is everything all right? Why have you gone quiet all of a sudden? Have I really bored you that much? Anyway, I'd better get going now, and I do apologise for having done so.'

'*Arrey*! No, God forgive me! What are you saying?' Her eyes filled with tears.

Sajjad paused, and looked at her for a moment; and then, he left.

87

'*Arrey bhai*! Are you in *aythikaaf* that you don't come out of the house at all?'

'What's *aythikaaf*, Sajjad Bhai?'

'Look at that! It's the limit – this is the daughter of a Muslim who doesn't know what seclusion for the purposes of prayer is!'

'What's the point of going out of the house? Your Murree doesn't seem to be big enough for a stroll. If you take a long walk you get to the other end of the town. *Bhai*, we've never seen a mountain resort like this before.'

'You can see it now.'

'We've seen it already. Where have you been for the past four days?'

'Me? Nowhere.'

'Is that a reply?'

'I went to Muzaffarabad.'

'Take us round once, to your Muzaffarabad.'

'It's difficult. You have to have permission to enter it. Let me take you to Nathia Galli instead; it's a very nice place.'

'Forget all your nice places. Murree is also supposed to be a nice place.'

'Lo! Again the taunt about Murree. I didn't make it. Whatever we have, we offer to you. And this was given the title of "Queen of the Mountains" by the British Sahib Bahadur!'

She laughed, 'They must have done that to console you lot!'

'Look here, girl. You should be grateful for what is available and try to take it to your heart. I say that if your past can't keep up with you, then you should bury it.'

'That's a reasonably good theory.'

He kept the cushion on his lap and dug his elbows into it, 'So what did you do in all this time?'

'I have finished a painting, and it is the first one I am satisfied with.'

'I think you should forget all that nonsense, girl. Why do you want to labour, or take on problems for yourself?'

'That's a good question. So, what's your advice?'

'Advice? I'm going to give you one piece of advice.'

'O-ho! Sajjad Bhai is here today,' Bakhtiar called out from afar. 'Where have you been?'

'I was away for a little while.'

'You've come and I'm going.'

'Where to?'

'Abbottabad.'

'You're off, but you haven't really done anything for this girl. She looks exactly the same. In fact, she seems a bit quieter here to me.'

'Yes, it's turned out a bit badly for her. I've no time and she doesn't go out by herself. Won't even go to the Mall.'

'Why bother with the Mall? It is so boring. You meet someone and move on and you meet him again in the same breath. Meeting not just one but several of your acquaintances at every turn, repeatedly, and forcing yourself to express delight and warmth again and again, is extremely annoying.'

'Allah! What a delicate darling she is! What can you say?' Sajjad could not suppress his laughter.

'No, truly. You feel as if you've entered the mysterious world of a strange story in which you keep colliding with the same statue at every corner.'

'People who stay alone and brood – end up like this!'

'Meaning?'

'Like you, I mean. I'm going to Nathia Galli for the whole day tomorrow, Bakhtiar! If you like, I'll take her with me.'

'Certainly. We'll ask Ammah.'

The climb was dangerous because it had suddenly started raining. The bends and turns in the road were quite uninteresting. She sat in silence, leaning against the back of the seat, reading the milestones without intending to and staring at the signposts for the next turning.

'It would have been better to have carried a sack in the jeep.'

'Sack? Why?'

'At least one wouldn't have felt cross with it for pledging to silence. The road's become so tricky and you're being so boring. I feel like crashing into a pit.'

'You can do that; I don't mind. But my mother will be distressed.'

'I don't even have to worry about that. There's no one to mourn me.'

'If you'd got married, your wife would have mourned you.'

'So you think I meant it? I beg your pardon, but my life isn't that unimportant.'

'You're strange. Whoever asked you to dive into a pit?'

'Gaythi Ara!'

'*Jee*, do say it!'

'Haven't you changed a lot?'

'Yes, possibly.'

'But why?'

'One is not a lifeless stone that one should never change.'

'You were so headstrong. What's the reason for the change?'

'The reason is that I was labouring under the delusion that my mother does not need me, and that I was an extra piece of baggage which accompanied Arjumand. Sajjad Bhai you have never heard of a pair of twins so unlike each other.'

'It is extraordinary.'

'Sometimes I used to believe it when people laughingly suggested that I was adopted.'

88

She realised, whilst eating lunch at the Paton Hotel, that she liked that place. And she felt as if she had known it all her life. After lunch she wandered around outside without a specific objective and Sajjad sat watching her on a small rock surrounded by stinging nettle.

As she sat amidst a cluster of white daisies with yellow hearts she commented, 'But you came for some work. You'd better finish your work first.'

'I didn't come for any work.'

'Then you made up such a dangerous climb for no rhyme or reason? We should have gone back when it started raining.'

'Why? Gaythi, I brought you here because I wanted to do it.'

'But why?' Gaythi looked at him closely. His tanned face was serious. His high forehead gleaming against his wispy hair and deep eyes combined to make a magnificently attractive image.

'I wanted to bring you here.' She thought it over, fear and panic surged through her veins. She sat silent, head bowed, watching the daisies as if they were extremely important. 'These are things I can't comprehend! Why was I sent out like this with this stranger? And I will never forget how Bakhtiar Bhai had forbade me, quite explicitly, to meet that other man to whom I was obliged. However I did not expect this of Colonel Sajjad who is so much older than me.'

He rose from where he sat and came to sit near her. 'Why are you worried?'

'No, I'm not worried.'

'But your voice reveals something else. This is what I was saying, that you've changed a lot. You don't like to say what you're thinking any more.'

She sat silently.

'Do you consider me to be the lowest of the low, Gaythi? I'm not some young irrepressible boy, but a responsible officer.'

'But sometimes it is the responsible people who prove themselves to be highly irresponsible,' she went on thinking.

'Look at me, don't keep staring at those daisies. They cannot protect you or give you any useful advice.'

She laughed gently and looked at him.

'If you cannot trust a big, tall, mature officer then how can you have any faith in these flowers?'

It was pleasing to see him saying such comical things so seriously.

'But I will repeat myself, Gaythi. I brought you here because I wanted to do it.'

She lowered her head again. His conversation was making her anxious.

'*Arrey, bhai*, again that interest in the flowers! Look at this living human being and ask him, "Why did you want to bring me here?"'

'Why did you want to bring me here?' she said in a lifeless voice.

'Because I love you, and have loved you since the day I left off reading your palm and disappeared all of a sudden. Now you know the answer to the question you asked me that day, don't you?'

Hearing that man say, 'I love you,' like that, without any hesitation at all, made her lose her footing.

'But I thought that you . . .' she hesitated.

'Love Saulat Apa,' Sajjad completed her sentence. 'Yes, that's what I thought too. And I was in anguish and despair in my love for her, but . . . then, suddenly I realised that my condition was like that of a man who throws himself into reading a book, in order to kill time whilst waiting to meet someone, or to talk to someone.'

'If you love me then what's the meaning of bringing me here?' There was a trace of fear in her voice.

'The purpose was to be able to talk to you more peacefully, and now you should think it over and answer me.'

'What shall I say?'

'Tell me what you think about marrying me?'

'What do I think?' she repeated. Out of the blue she remembered something that she had said years ago. One day she had sat on the ledge of the well in their garden and had unabashedly revealed to Masood her love for him, with the same lack of ceremony, and demanded an answer from him.

'What are you thinking, girl?' He bent towards her and asked her with intense fervour.

She found this responsible senior officer sitting at her feet to be a figure of great interest. All of a sudden, she felt very important. Twice she had been out on the Mall and both times she had seen Masood and Kaamni, either busy shopping, or talking to someone. She herself did not wish to face Masood but, along with that, she could not avoid the fear that he had seen her and had ignored her. That fear had made her feel very contemptible and unimportant even to herself. Although she was the woman to whom Masood had once said, 'Can there be anything more loveable than you?' She looked at Sajjad. His eyes held passion, entreaty and impatience. He looked younger than his years.

'All right, Sajjad Bhai! I'll think about it and give you my answer.'

'Why don't you call me just Sajjad?'

'You're older than me.'

'So?'

'So what? I'll tell you soon.'

'But when?'

'In a day or two.'

But she wavered on the way back home. 'If I want to talk to you tomorrow morning, where will I find you?'

'I'm working tomorrow. Will you do it in the evening?' His voice dulled.

'Where?'

'Meet me at Samson.'

'I won't talk somewhere like that.'

'Then?'

'Then what we'll do is, we'll set off. A suitable place will present itself.'

Night-time is always beautiful. It is not conditional upon there being a moon and stars. A dark night is also beautiful. That is the time when reality assumes a spectral form – and this was a night when there were a few stars in the firmament too.

Sajjad had had dinner at Bakhtiar's house and now both of them had strolled a long way from the house. Where the ascent twisted sharply, the groves of pine trees stood looking like silent spectres.

'Ah! This is my favourite spot.'

Both of them advanced towards a bench which lay under a tree. She was silent now, having talked all the way up to this spot. In the valley below, they could see the lights of the settlements and the bazaars, twinkling like fireflies. Their feet were slipping on the sharp and slithery needles of the conifers.

Sajjad bent down to look, 'Look, how they're shimmering like fireflies.' There was a tremor of joy in his voice.

'You've experienced so much of this world, including something fearful like the war, but you still rejoice over little things!'

'Yes. They say that war and other such horrendous experiences numb a human being. His mind becomes engulfed in an endless ocean of silence which cannot be broken by any worldly bustle. But I feel that every bitter experience regenerates my senses. Whenever you observe this world it seems new and interesting, Gaythi!'

For some reason her eyes became dewy and her heart raced. In the dark Sajjad had not seen the moisture in her eyes or the happiness

327

spreading across her face. The breeze rustling through the branches of the pines turned into perfume which rained on them. Then slowly she began speaking, and gradually she came to the end of her story.

'Is that all you wanted to tell me?'

'Yes, that's what I wanted to tell you. Perhaps you see me as a very sensible and balanced girl, but I am not at all normal.' There was pain in her voice, 'Believe me, this has always caused me anguish. I have always been very aware that I am very different from other girls.'

'People say the same thing about me, that I am not a very sound person. But, Gaythi, I knew about all your shortcomings already.'

'Maybe you think that now I look all right, and may have reformed, but possibly, I will never be all right.'

'Then it can't be helped, Gaythi. Sometimes one has to endure someone who is not very nice too. So, never mind! I shall endure you.'

'You've made up your mind?'

Under the shadows of the pines, in the faint twinkly light of the stars, Sajjad drew her close to him, instead of saying anything in reply.

'So, should I talk to Ammah Begum and Bakhtiar?'

'There's no need for you to talk to them. I have never said anything to do with me through others. I will talk to them myself about this matter, which is personal to me.' There was confidence and conviction in her voice.

He left her at the portico in silence and went away by himself.

'Your mind is burdened by your shortcomings and failings, and you're tortured by them. You tried to warn me of them as if I consider you to be virtuous. Silly girl! It is this burdensome sense of yourself, and this anguish of yours, which is so endearing . . . But, even after I have won you, I shall always have to live with one unfulfilled desire in my heart. I wish you had sat on the ledge of that well in the garden and said those words to me, instead of to Masood. Fine, Engineer Sahib! I shall envy you for the rest of my life. But, Gaythi, as for you, I shall never tell *you* that I have been won by that tortured conscience, those self condemnations of your brain! Some things about love have to be kept secret forever.'

89

'Another mature son-in-law!' the very thought made Ammah Begum miserable. What a good thing it would be if time and events did not repeat themselves. Despite her disapproval she was aware that she could not intervene at all in this matter. She could explain the ups and downs of life to Saulat and persuade her to marry an older man, but she could not talk this girl out of marrying one.

She had stayed absolutely silent. Bakhtiar had been the one to speak up, 'All right! What we'll do is give our consent to Sajjad Bhai and he can put a ring on your finger.' Bakhtiar had suggested the easiest option as far as he was concerned.

'Oh, yes, and this time, at least her Chacha and Phuphi should be able to attend. Maybe they'll be able to come by then if we write now; it might take them four months to get their passports.' Ammah Begum also ventured to express her opinion.

'Oh, no, Ammah! Who's going to bother? It is a different country now,' Bakhtiar tried to explain to her.

'But they'll all say to me that I've become so unconcerned since coming to Pakistan that I've not even invited them to my son's and daughter's wedding.'

'Now, since coming to Pakistan, she has started bothering about all that,' Bakhtiar mused to himself, then said, 'So, which one of them has asked you? Chacha Abba has got Ayaz engaged to Talat. Did anyone inform you? Chacha Abba did not consult you, and Chachi jaan did not let you know. Ismat Apa went over, I heard; they could have sent us sweetmeats to announce the engagement.'

She sat absolutely silent and still. Fate had taken an aversion to her. Just a few days ago, she had found herself thinking, 'I may as well write to Dulhan asking her for Talat's hand. Can't see anyone round here who is suitable. And our Saulat does set her mind against things for nothing. How imposing and fortunate Ismat had looked when she came to visit us!' The very thought of her filled her heart with agony. For when she had met her, her impulse had been to embrace her and howl to her heart's content.

'So Bhai Sahib has got Ayaz engaged? Yes, our girls weren't good enough. Our sister-in-law never let the words escape her breath,' she said softly. If Gaythi had not made such a nonsensical decision, she would not have felt mortified about this.

Then she looked at Bakhtiar. There was a look of hurt on his face, and unbounded patience and tolerance.

'I wish my eldest son, whom I loved the most, had been as sensible and realistic.' Without settling anything further she went in quietly. She had decided on only one thing and that was in her heart, 'Every decision of mine has been wrong, and every plan of mine has failed, therefore I have no right to play with the destinies of my children any more.'

After her departure, Gaythi spoke. 'No, Bakhtiar Bhaiya! All that is useless. Forget it, why do you want to take so much trouble?'

'If you think it's all useless, do you intend to just walk off with him, quietly? The thing about taking the trouble is that if you have a sister, you have to give her a proper send-off.'

'It's all nonsense, as far as I'm concerned. Just arrange a marriage ceremony for tomorrow.'

'What a dry and tasteless disposition she has,' Bakhtiar reflected to himself, and then said sarcastically, 'Could you wait if I arranged it for the day after, or the following day, instead of tomorrow? I have to see what suits my availability as well, or if you can manage without me, then . . .'

'OK, we'll wait till you're free.' Then to appease Bakhtiar she added, 'You should bear in mind that the marriage is with someone who is mature, who has been married before. He'll find it so odd to go through all these little rituals.'

'All these are the inventions of your own mind and sensitivities. If he finds it strange then why is he acting like a young boy?'

'Anyway, *bhai*. I've decided on all this now.' When she came to a decision, her voice would become very final and astringent.

'She's such a strangely uncaring and impetuous girl! And such is she, that she will undo whatever she has done herself before.' She seemed highly disagreeable to Bakhtiar at that moment.

90

'Margaret believes: "Knock, and you shall be answered." And those who follow the stony path of Tao believe: "Do not ask. Access shall be granted to you, without being sought."

'What is the difference between the belief espoused by Margaret or

The Holy Bible and that saying upheld by the followers of Tao? Merely one of words. The desire for access and attainment is common to both. The difference is only in how that desire is achieved.

'Margaret was a believer in the Holy Bible, and she knocked again and again, but she did not gain satisfaction. And I am not a follower of Tao but nevertheless I did not knock, and I did not gain access. But the difference in her strategy and mine is only one of desire.

'Margaret knocked because she desired a union, and she did not gain access. I did not knock, not because I wanted access. I knew my fate. The wall between me and attainment was longer and even more insurmountable than the Great Wall of China.' Safdar Yaaseen, commonly known as Liu Chu, pondered these things, as he packed his bags for a long holiday.

'I'm taking this long holiday with the intention of never returning, because that hand which I had restrained from knocking is no longer under my control. One has no control over anything to do with oneself. To such an extent that even something as hidden and weak as the human heart resists control. So where should the dervish go now? The land of love has shrunk and threatens to become infinitesimal.'

He looked at his packed belongings and desolate room with interest, 'And now I'm beginning to sense what the hearts of those must have suffered who were forced to surrender the brick houses and mansions built by their forbears, stuffed with belongings!'

Then he went to Li Fan and his wife who were going to take him to the station. His suitcase was fairly crammed with the numerous small gifts they had given him to carry.

'Now the only way I can return all their kindness is by sending off parcels of their gifts to various places from there. I came through Karachi and that is the way I am going back, too. The words of the prayer with which we face death are so true,' he recited them in Arabic: ' "We came from God, and unto Him we shall return!" '

Then he held the tiny copy of the Quran which hung round his neck and looked at it carefully. 'How pleased my mother will be to see that her son has returned home well and safe. But is it true that I am whole and safe?'

Wistfully, he looked out of the train chugging along the tracks. That city which had delighted him so, as if it had been his own, was now behind them. He loved this happy and dignified ancient city. Not a single tear fell from his eyes. But he had wept bitterly and his heart had repeated again and again,

'Half way to the mountains
He makes a half-broken vow,
and the worshipper moves ahead.
In the forest
a yellow leaf
rustles
and falls off the branch.'

91

'God forgive me, but whenever you go out you do expect that something should be bought for you.'

'Then so what? You scold my daughter too much, *bhai*.'

'How can I not scold her? All the foreign exchange will get used up on her demands, and then what will we do?'

'You'll get the foreign exchange. You buy my girl a pair of shoes. Come on now, what do you think?'

'What can I think? I'll have to buy them. This is how people ruin the children of their old age by simply spoiling them. Come on – !' She went towards the shoe shop, protesting.

Her body had become plump and her hair was speckled with grey, though it was still short. She had never worn a plait.

'My hair is too thick and straight. I can't be bothered to spend more time dressing and adorning it.' Whenever Sajjad requested that she should grow her hair that was the answer he got.

'And now to wear a plait as the mother of two is a little embarrassing, too.' The day she had said that, Sajjad had given up asking her.

The little girl had thrown a tantrum quite suddenly when they found themselves on that relatively quiet street in Hong Kong.

'I want a pair of shoes.' She looked just like her father, and was as stubborn as her mother. She had seen ten pairs of shoes and not liked any. She would find fault with each.

'So where will I find you a pair of shoes, made in heaven, just for you? The girl can't settle on a single pair of shoes she likes.' She sat down exhausted. After a gap of four years she was carrying the third one and this time she tired very easily.

'Show me some more shoes,' the girl ordered the young salesman.

She tried to reason with her in her usual gentle and precise way, 'How

332

many shoes will you look at, my daughter? There is a limit to these things.' And when the elderly but attractive man who was the girl's father had persuaded the salesman very courteously and gently to fetch some more pairs of shoes, her mother complained, 'Why are you putting ideas in her head? She always makes such a fuss when she needs new shoes.'

The man with lustreless eyes, who sat at the counter with great dignity, smiled. For he understood clearly the meaning of those words uttered in a foreign language. He felt a wild impulse to go over to her and ask, 'Have you forgotten those days when you used to visit Sang's shop and I used to make trips exactly like that?' But all he did instead was lower his grey head, pick up the pair of glasses on the counter and muse, as he looked at the newspaper he had read already, 'My eyes are misting over now. I've seen you today after twelve whole years.'

Her mother was probably very tired so the child came to the counter to pay the bill with her father instead. He put his left hand forward and took the bill from her, then held it down with his right as he read it.

'Oh, Abboo! What happened to this man's hand?'

'Be quiet. You don't talk like that,' her father said in his own language.

'What happened to your hand there?' the child asked him impatiently.

'The machine ate it up.'

'The machine! Why? Are you very careless?'

'Yes. I used to forget sometimes that I was standing near a machine – Do you know what this hand says?' He raised his amputated wrist.

'What?' the child's eyes opened wide with amazement.

'It says, Do not knock.'

The stunned child ran to report this to her mother who stood outside the shop, busy negotiating a purchase from a street vendor.

Glossary

arrey bhai/haan bhai used to express affirmation, familiarity, approbation
bhai literally brother (bonding term)
Bibi Miss
bidis crude, locally-made cigarettes
bitya daughter: term of endearment
charpatta shrub
chooran spicey snack
dholak small drum, used at weddings etc. for folk songs, rhythms
gharara item of women's dress
kalima Muslim prayer, also doctrine of faith
lassi drinking yoghurt
loo south westerly winds: (blisteringly hot and dry)
Mali gardener (used instead of a proper name throughout)
methi herb
paan betel leaf
paan daan container for *paans* and their accompaniments such as lime,
    catechu, tobacco and betel nuts
sehra bridegroom's headdress, made from flowers
sherwani and churidar formal outfit for men: long coat and tight pyjamas
tauba 'Forgive my sins . . .' expressing repentance/jocular disapproval
waah well done (meaning is often ironical, determined by context)